Aeneas MacDonell Dawson

Pius IX. and his time

Aeneas MacDonell Dawson

Pius IX. and his time

ISBN/EAN: 9783742858542

Manufactured in Europe, USA, Canada, Australia, Japa

Cover: Foto ©Raphael Reischuk / pixelio.de

Manufactured and distributed by brebook publishing software
(www.brebook.com)

Aeneas MacDonell Dawson

Pius IX. and his time

PIUS IX.

AND

HIS TIME.

BY

THE REV. ÆNEAS MACDONELL DAWSON.

LONDON:

PRINTED BY THOS. COFFEY, CATHOLIC RECORD PRINTING HOUSE.

1880.

CONTENTS.

PREFACE.

The history of Pius IX. will always be read with interest. His Pontificate was, indeed, eventful. In no preceding age were the annals of the Church so grandly illustrated.

The spiritual sovereignty, "with which," to use the words of a British statesman, "there is nothing on this earth that can at all compare," was crowned with surpassing glory. Doctrines which, hitherto, had been open to theological discussion . were ascertained and pronounced to be in accordance with the belief of all preceding Christian ages. The Church was enabled, through the labors of her Chief and the zeal of her Priesthood, to extend vastly the place of her tent. The life of Pius IX. himself was a marvel and a glory. None of his predecessors, not even Peter, attained to his length of days.

On the other hand, the venerable Pontiff, and, together with him, the Catholic people, were doomed to behold and lament the loss of the time-honored patrimony of St. Peter. The Papacy, however, unlike all temporal sovereignties, was able to sustain so great a loss. More ancient than its temporal power, it still survives; "not a mere antique, but in undiminished vigor."

PIUS IX. AND HIS TIME.

BIRTH OF PIUS IX.

JOHN MARY COUNT MASTAI FERRETI was born at Sinigaglia, on the 13th of May, 1792. At the age of twenty-two he came to Rome. Anxious to serve the Holy Father, and yet not aspiring to the priesthood, he resolved to become a member of the Noble Guard. This the delicate state of his health forbade. Repelled by the Prince Commandant, he sought counsel of the Pope. Pius VII. pronounced that his destiny was the Cross, and advised him to devote himself to the ecclesiastical state. The words of the Holy Father were, to the youthful Mastai, as a voice from on high. He decided for the Church, and, as if in testimony that his decision was ratified in heaven, the falling-sickness left him. His studies were more than ordinarily successful, and he already gave proof of those high qualities which were afterwards so greatly developed. The distinguished Canon Grániare, his professor, little dreaming of the exalted destiny which awaited him, held him up as a pattern of excellence to his fellow-students, saying that he possessed the heart of a Pope.

Whilst yet a student, Mastai interested himself in an orphanage, which was founded by John Bonghi, a charitable mason of Rome. He spent in this institution the first seven years of his priesthood, devoting himself to the care of the orphans, who were, as yet, his only parishioners. The income which he derived from family resources was liberally applied in supplying the wants of these destitute children, and even in ministering to their recreation.

It now became his duty to accompany, as a missionary priest, Monsignore Mazi, who was appointed Vicar-Apostolic for Chili, Peru and Mexico. These countries had thrown off the yoke of Spain and adopted Republican forms of government. The Vicar-Apostolic and his companions suffered much in the course of their voyage to America. They were cast into prison, at the Island of Majorca, by Spanish officials, who took it amiss that Rome should hold direct relations with the rebellious subjects of their government. Their ship was attacked by corsairs, and was afterwards in danger from a storm. A single circumstance only need be mentioned in order to show what the faithful ministers of the Church had to endure when traversing the inhospitable steppes of the Pampas. Once, at night, they had no other shelter than a wretched cabin built with the bones of animals, which still emitted a cadaverous odour.

In those arid deserts, they suffered from thirst as well as from dearth of provisions. Great results can only be attained by equally great labors. If, after a period of privation, the travellers enjoyed no more luxurious refreshment than the waters of the crystal brook, it might well be said, "de torrente in via-bibet propterea exaltabit caput." (They shall be reduced to quench their thirst in the mountain stream, and therefore shall be exalted.) The delegates of the Holy Father were received with enthusiasm by the South American populations. Meanwhile, the narrow governments that were set over those countries raised so many difficulties that the mission was only partially successful.

This mission, however, was not without benefit to the Reverend Count Mastai. It had been the means of developing the admirable qualities which he possessed. It had afforded him the opportunity of seeing many cities, as well as the manners and customs of many people. These lessons of travel were not addressed to an ordinary mind. His views were enlarged, elevated and refined by contact with so many rising or fallen civilizations, so many different nationalities, and by the spectatacle of Nature, that admirable handmaid of the Divinity, with her varied splendors and her manifold wonders, astonishing no less in the immensity of the ocean than in the vast forests of the New World.

The mind appears to grow as the sphere of material life extends. Vast horizons are adapted to great souls, and prepare them for great things. The Abbe Mastai had thus received in his youth two most salutary lessons, which are often wanting to the best-tried virtues of the sacerdotal state—the lesson of the world, which Mastai had received before the time of his vocation to Holy Orders, and the lessons of travel, which disengages the mind from the bondage of local prejudices. Both of these teachers he admirably understood. He had, indeed, drank of the torrent which exalts.

Leo XII. now filled the Apostolic Chair. This Pontiff, highly appreciating the good sense and penetration of which Mastai had given proof in the difficult mission to Chili, appointed him Canon of Sancta Maria, Rome, *in via lata*, and, at the same time, conferred on him the dignity of Prelate. Never was the Roman purple more adorned by the learning and genuine virtue of him on whom it was bestowed.

There is at Rome an institution of charity, the greatest which that city or even the world possesses, the immense hospital of *St. Michael a Ripa Grande*. A whole people dwells within its vast precincts. It is at once a place of retreat for aged and infirm men, a most extensive professional school for poor girls, and a sort of workshop, on a great scale, for children that have been forsaken. The greater number learn trades. Some, who give proof of higher talents, apply, at the expense of the hospital, to the study of the fine arts. This hospital is, in itself, a world, and its government requires almost the qualities of a statesman. Pope Leo XII., anxious to render available the rare abilities of Canon Mastai, named him President of the commission which governs this great establishment. There was need, at the time, so low was the state of the hospital budget, of the nicest management, unremitting care, and the highest financial capacity. These qualities were all speedily at work, and in the course of two years all the resources of the institution were in admirable order. The fear of bankruptcy was removed, deficits of income made up, and receipts abundant.

It had not been the custom to allow to apprentice-workmen any share in the fruits of their labors. Herein Mastai effected a great and certainly not uncalled-for reform. Far from impoverishing the hospital, this liberal measure only showed, by its happy results, that justice is in perfect harmony with economy, and that the best houses are not those which make the most of the labor of their inmates, but those which encourage industry by allowing it what is just. The orphans were thus, in two years, enabled to have a small sum, which secured to them, so far, a mitigation of their lot. Meanwhile, the proceeds of the hospital were doubled. This was remarkable success. Count Mastai's reputation for administrative ability was now of the highest order.

In the Consistory of May 21st, 1827, Canon Count Mastai was named Archbishop of Spoleto. Thus did Pope Leo XII. signalize his solicitude and affection for the city of his birth. The appointment came not too soon. It required all the influence of a great mind to maintain peace at Spoleto. Party spirit ran high. One side clamored against abuses; the other, dreading all change, clung pertinaciously to the past. Wrath was treasured in every bosom. If civil war had not yet broken out, it raged already in the breasts of the people. Spoleto resembled two hostile camps, and vividly recalled the state of those cities of the Middle-Age, where stood in presence, and armed from head to heel, the undying enmities of the Ghibellins and the Guelphs. The slightest occasion would have sufficed to cause the hardly-suppressed embers of deadly strife to burst into a flame. Through the zeal and diplomacy of the Archbishop, such occasion was averted. Spoleto may yet remember, and not without emotion, how earnestly he studied to appease wild passions, with what delicacy and perseverance he labored to reconcile the terrible feuds that prevailed, to calm the dire spirit

of revenge, to bury the sense of wrong in the oblivion of forgiveness. At length, in 1831 and 1832, a hopeless rebellion
unfurled its blood-red banner. It was speedily and pitilessly repressed. Such an occasion only was wanting in order to show
what one man can do when sustained by the power of virtue
and the esteem of mankind. The foreign and Teutonic arm
which conquered the insurrection had been always hateful to the
Italian people; nor did its display and exercise of military
force, in restoring tranquillity to the troubled State, conciliate
their friendship.

Only when vanquished did the rebels appear before the
walls of Spoleto. In their extremity, they came to beg for
shelter and for bread. In the estimation of the benevolent Archbishop, they were as lost sheep whom it was his duty, if possible, to save. He hastened, accordingly, to meet the wolf.
The Austrian General, although a stern warrior, was, at the
same time, the servant of a Christian Power. He listened to
the Archbishop's remonstrances, and resolved to refrain from
further military proceedings, the Prelate undertaking to disarm
the rebels, and thus satisfy the sad requirements of war without any recourse to useless and hateful cruelties. Returning
to the city, he addressed the insurgents, and, to his unspeakable satisfaction, they at once came to lay at his feet those
arms which the Austrian soldiers could only have torn from
their lifeless bodies. Thus did the good pastor, by disarming,
save the rebellious flock.

Mastai was now transferred to Imola. This city is less
considerable than Spoleto. The diocese, however, is richer
and more populous. Its Episcopal chair leads directly to the
Cardinalate. It has also thrice given to the Catholic Church
its Chief Pastor. The people of Spoleto sent a deputation, but
in vain, to beseech the Holy Father to leave the good pastor to
his affectionate flock.

He was destined also to reign in the hearts of the good
people of Imola. The numerous institutions there, which owe
their existence to his Episcopal zeal and Christian charity, are

monuments of his pastoral care. The virtue of which Archbishop Mastai was so bright a pattern had no sourness in it, no outward show of austerity; nor was it forbidding and intolerant, but sweet and gentle. Words of forgiveness were always on his lips, and his hand was ever open to distress. He labored assiduously to reform, wherever reform was needed, but, what rarely happens, without alienating affection from the reformer. It was his constant study to elevate the character of the clergy, and he ceased not to encourage among them learning as well as piety. Into the Diocesan Seminary, which was always the object of his most anxious care, he introduced some new branches of study, such as agriculture, practical as well as theoretical, and a general knowledge of the medical art. There was yet wanting to the clergy of his diocese a common centre where they could meet for mutual edification and instruction. To this purpose he devoted his own palace, and founded there a Biblical Academy. The members of this Academy met once a month in order to discuss together some subjects connected with the Sacred Writings. None can be ignorant how powerfully such meetings contribute to promote the study of the Scriptures, pulpit eloquence, and the great science of theology. In order, moreover, to obviate the dangers to which students were exposed, who, whilst they studied at the Seminary, were not inmates, and enjoyed not the safeguards of its discipline, he founded an institution called the "Convitto," where the poorer alumni were boarded without charge.

Anxious also to provide for the comfort of the lowly poor, and to guard against all wasting of their humble means, the good Prelate reformed the hospital of Imola, and set over it the Sisters of Charity—that incomparable Order which owes its existence to the most benevolent of men, St. Vincent de Paul. Nor, in his higher state, did he forget his first care— the orphan. An orphanage at Imola is due to his munificence. There were no bounds to his liberality. At his own expense alone he repaired the tomb of St. Cassien, and decorated the Chapel of Our Lady of Dolours in the Church of the Servites.

When raised to the dignity of Cardinal, by Pope Gregory XVI., in December, 1840, Archbishop Mastai was already universally popular. The ovations of a later period may have originated in political motives—may even have been promoted by a political party; but the honors now spontaneously heaped upon him were awarded to the man and the Christian pastor. Congratulations in prose and in verse, illuminations, fireworks, demonstrations of every kind, announced the joy with which the new Cardinal was welcomed everywhere.

Gregory XVI. had the reputation of being highly conservative. In the true sense of the term, he really was so. Nevertheless, he was not averse to reform, and he showed that he was not when he elevated Archbishop Mastai, whose tendencies were well known, to the rank and office of Cardinal. More than this, in concurrence with the Great Powers of Europe, with whom he took counsel, he labored to introduce certain salutary reforms in his States. Such reforms, indeed, were needed; and the aged Pontiff resolved on them, not only in order to render unnecessary the intervention of foreign arms in the affairs of his government, but also with a view to bring his rule into harmony with the spirit and civilization of the age. If in this most laudable undertaking he did not succeed, he owed his failure to the Socialist party, those enemies of law and order, of property, and life even, whose fatal action at a later period marred the political career of Pius IX. The Roman people, generally, were capable of appreciating, and surely did appreciate, the enlightened efforts of their Pontiff Sovereign. They were not, as some writers would have us believe, in a semi-barbarous condition. Sylvio Pellico, whose testimony cannot be questioned, speaks of them in the following terms: "The eight months I have spent at Rome in 1845 and 1846 (time of Gregory XVI.) have abounded in delightful impressions. It can never be sufficiently told how well this venerable city deserves to be visited, and not in passing only. How the good and beautiful abound in it!" A little later, Pellico writes: "I continue to be quite delighted with Rome, both as regards men and things. In the small book, *Dei Doveri*, I have shown my inclination to avoid being absolute in my judgments, a too common error, especially with minds that dogmatize passionately. By such Rome is often unjustly judged.

"Several types of social customs must be considered as moderately good; and we cannot condemn, as decidedly bad, anything but barbarism, irreligion and a superabundance of knaves and fools. These odious elements are by no means over-abundant in this country. And in the midst of evils that are unavoidable everywhere, I observe great intellectual power, much goodness, cultivated minds, gracious and sincere generosity. Whoever comes to Rome will be morally well off as regards intelligence. He will be so, likewise, on account of the sociability of the inhabitants. The Romans are a jovial people. But even their joviality is as admirably subject to good order as it is graceful, and does not impair the natural goodness of their disposition. But perhaps I am wrong; and it were better I should assume a frowning aspect, and behold only attempts on life, importunate beggary, useless priests and monks, and reserve my praises for those happy nations where there are no crimes, no inequality of fortune, no misery. Impassioned men declaim, exaggerate, lie. For my part, I am neither an optimist nor a pessimist. It is impossible to speak with certainty of the moral of a country if we speak of it too soon. I know that here at Rome I find amiability, science and good sense. It seems to me that everything is much the same as in other civilized countries."

Such was the people over whom, on the 16th day of June, 1846, Cardinal Mastai was called to exercise authority in the twofold capacity of Pontiff and Prince. On the first day of the Conclave several votes were cast for the liberal-minded Cardinal Gizzi, and some in favor of the highly-conservative Lambruschini. The second day all joined for Mastai. And thus was elected to the Papal Chair, by the unanimous voice of the Sacred College, one of their body, who, in all the positions which he had held, as Priest, as Archbishop, as Cardinal, had shown his determination to promote reform and improvement. No better proof could be required that the Cardinals perfectly understood the state of the country, its urgent wants, its relations with the Church and the rest of the world.

There was much rejoicing in the Papal City. It seemed as if, with the elevation of a great character to high authority, the days of the Millennium had at length dawned on the distracted world. There was now question only of forgiveness for the past. Order and peace only were possible in time to come. The new Pontiff was resolved that there should be no element of sorrow to mar the general joy; and so he amnestied the political offenders who had borne arms against the government of his predecessor. Only one condition was required, viz.: that, in the future, they should fulfil the duties of good and order-loving subjects. Thus were fifteen hundred exiles restored to their families, who had lost all hope of ever seeing them again. The cases only of a small number of the ringleaders of the rebellion were reserved for consideration, and they, too, were cheered with the hope of pardon. The preamble of the decree of amnesty, all in the Pope's own handwriting, bore the following words:

"At the time when the public joy occasioned by our accession to the office of Sovereign Pontiff caused us to experience in our inmost soul the most lively emotion, we could not avoid entertaining a feeling of sorrow when we remembered that a great number of families amongst our people could not take part in the general rejoicing, deprived, as they were, of domestic happiness. * * * On the other hand, we cast a look of compassion on the numerous and inexperienced youth, which, although carried away by deceitful flatterers, in the midst of political troubles, appeared to us guilty rather of allowing itself to be led astray, than of deceiving others. On this account it was that, from that moment, we cherished the thought of extending a friendly hand, and offering peace to such of these dear but misguided children as should come to us, and give proof of their sincere reentance."

Night was drawing on when the decree was posted on the walls of Rome. It was observed, however, amidst the growing darkness; and no sooner was the word *amnesty* read than a cry of enthusiasm was heard. People hastened from their houses in all directions, the passers-by stopped in crowds to read, by torchlight, the cabalistic words. Among the fast-assembling masses there was but one feeling. They embraced and even wept for joy. In the depth of their emotion, and whilst yet, as may be said, intoxicated with delight, they sought how to express their gratitude. The cry was raised, "To the Quirinal!" Arrived there, they hailed, with loud and united voice, the beneficent Pontiff—"Vivat Pius Nonus!" "Long live our Holy Father!" Crowd after crowd thus approached the person of the Pope. It was now late, and Pius IX., much fatigued, overwhelmed by his emotions, had withdrawn to the silence of his Oratory. Meanwhile, fresh crowds of overjoyed citizens were pressing forward. Ten thousand men, at least, were now waiting, with respectful anxiety, under the walls of the Quirinal Palace. The French Ambassador to Rome, Count Rossi, was a witness of these events. He became also their historian. He wrote thus to M. Guizot:

" Suddenly the acclamations are redoubled. I had not yet understood on what account, when some one called my attention to the light which was shining through the window-blinds at the farthest end of the Pontifical Palace. The people had observed that the Holy Father was traversing the apartment in order to reach the balcony. It was speedily thrown open, and the Sovereign Pontiff, in a white robe and scarlet mantle, made his appearance, surrounded by torches. If your Excellency (M. Guizot, at that time Minister of the French King, Louis Philippe) will only figure to yourself a magnificent place, a summer night, the sky of Rome, an immense people moved with gratitude, weeping for joy and receiving with love and reverence the benediction of their Pastor and their Prince, you will not be astonished, if I add that we have shared the general emotion, and have placed this spectacle above every thing that Rome had as yet offered to our contemplation. Just as I had foreseen, as soon as the window was closed the crowd withdrew peacefully and in perfect silence. You would have called them a people of mutes; they were satisfied."

It is not so difficult to grant an amnesty. It is delightful, even, to men of the character of Pius IX. to dispense forgiveness. This is particularly the office and the privilege of the Church. Sterner duties devolve upon the statesman. And, however reconcileable the two courses of conduct in public affairs may really be, it is difficult often to reconcile them.

The amnesty, although far from being everything, was, nevertheless, a beginning, and one of favorable omen. The furrow was opened, to use the language of M. Rossi, and no doubt the ploughing would proceed. Many formidable difficulties must, however, be surmounted. On the one hand, stood the influence of the old feudal Conservative party, which frowned on the slightest change. On the other, were the Socialists, who aimed at the destruction of every existing institution—in whose estimation property even was not sacred, nor life itself. It was necessary, meanwhile, to improve the condition of the people, and, in doing so, to guard against anarchy. By wise and well-considered reforms only could the growth and advance of revolution be discouraged and stayed, whilst a political system, almost entirely new, came to be firmly established. For this purpose, it was necessary that there should prevail in the Pontifical States a sounder state of opinion. This was not the work of a single day. It was necessary, nevertheless, as the people could not be safely led by their ever-changing emotions. Based on such quicksands, the government of the Holy Father could have no stability, and it was his aim so to form it that it should be able to keep its ground without the aid of foreign arms. The state of Italy, the peculiar position of the Pontifical States, the character of modern civilization, the spirit of the age—all conspired to produce new wants, and, at the same time, made it a matter of the greatest difficulty to meet them. "This difficulty," writes the Spanish Sage, Balmes, "it was impossible to surmount by chanting patriotic hymns any more than by having recourse to Austrian bayonets."

By none was this better understood than by Pius IX. The study of State affairs was not new to him. He had considered and lamented the condition of things which so often brought upon his country foreign invasion, the horrors of war, and punishments without end, inflicted on his fellow-citizens. It is related even that he prepared and presented to Gregory XVI. a programme of reforms, which he believed would bring the necessary remedy. Now that he was at the head of the State, he believed that the responsibility devolved on him of introducing such reforms as were called for by the exigency of the time, and by which alone he was persuaded the evils which oppressed the country could be brought to an end. It was not possible, as yet, to inaugurate any general measure of reform. In the meantime, however, the rule of the Pontiff was characterized by wise, just, humane and liberal acts, which could not fail to pave the way for the greater improvements which he meditated. Among these lesser, but by no means unimportant, reforms may be mentioned the abolition of an odious law which had long disgraced the legislation of so many Christian nations. The punishment by imprisonment for petty debts was, in the estimation of Pius IX., as unjust as it was cruel and hateful. It answered no better purpose, for the most part, than the gratification of private spite. By a generous contribution from his own funds, the Pope threw open the prisons of the Capitol. He set a great example, which could not fail to promote the cause of virtue whilst it relieved the indigent, by distributing twelve thousand Roman *ecus*, in the form of dowries, among the young women of poor families, whose poverty rendered an honorable settlement extremely difficult. He also encouraged collections in favor of such of the amnestied parties as were in need. His financial reforms were more important. And by these he won a title to the gratitude of the State. The public revenue was alarmingly deficient. Only by some great change could ruin be averted. First of all, he proposed that his faithful clergy should make a sacrifice; and every convent engaged to pay ten *scudi* yearly, and every parish priest a *scudo* during three consecutive years. He himself set the example of the most rigid economy by reducing the scale of his establishment. He at the same time retrenched those rich sinecures which were, so to say, engrafted on the temporalities of the Papacy. What was well worthy of a great statesman, he showed the most enlightened sympathy for all the sciences which contribute to the material and intellectual well-being of the populations, such as physiology, natural history, political economy and mathematics. Nor was he unwilling that his people should avail themselves of the knowledge of foreigners. He went so far as to intimate his intention to re-establish the celebrated Scientific Academy, *Di Lincei*.

He could not, as yet, by any other than such isolated acts as these, evince the elevated and liberal tendencies of his mind, in which were blended boldness with moderation, and views of reform with all that became his position, and was adapted to the wants of the country and the age.

Pius IX., although not a constitutional sovereign, and unable so to constitute himself, was anxious, neverthless, to give to his people all the benefits of constitutional government. A first step was to choose a popular Minister, and Cardinal Gizzi was called to the counsels of the State. This Cardinal was beloved at Rome, and not undeservedly. When Legate at Forli, he had opposed the establishment of an arbitrary court, and thus won for himself the sympathies of all national reformers. His loyalty, sincerity and patriotism were well known; nor was he wanting in any other quality of the statesman. Of a patient and enquiring mind, he was incapable of coming hastily to a decision; but, when once resolved, he could not be easily diverted from his purpose. The ministry of such a man was full of promise; but in this lay its weakness. It held out hopes which, in the state of parties which at that time prevailed, it was unable to realize. There were two great parties at Rome, with neither of which the Gizzi ministry was in sympathy. There existed no party with which it could act harmoniously. There were no reformers. It would have been most fortunate for Pius IX. if such a party could have been formed, but the elements were wanting. The true idea of constitutional government was as little understood in Italy as in the rest of continental Europe. The only party at Rome who desired change were the Socialists, who identified reform with subversion, who denied every right, and sought the destruction of all existing institutions. No wonder if, in presence of such a faction, the aristocracy, so highly conservative, dreaded and opposed all change. The Socialists, whilst by the fear which they inspired strengthened the hands of the conservative party, opposed and prevented the formation of a body of reformers who, like Gizzi and Pius IX., would have labored intelligently to forward the cause of reform, never losing sight of the great principles of humanity and justice, never sacrificing to Utopian theories inalienable rights, above all the rights of property—the very groundwork of the social fabric. Without the aid and countenance of a body of reformers, the able ministry that now surrounded the Pope found it difficult to proceed. They could not determine for any important constitutional change. They could not even undertake any considerable improvement.

They were, however, not inactive. They studied to educate the people by improving and extending the public schools, and by what was, indeed, an advance in continental Europe—establishing a periodical press.

There were few cities so highly favored as Rome as regards the facilities for educating youth. Nevertheless, there was room for improvement, and Pius IX. accordingly established in the city a central school for the instruction of the youth of the operative classes. This was a school of arts and manufactures, and, at the same time, a military institution, in which the pupils

were qualified to become either tradesmen or subordinate officers in the army. Whilst Cardinal Gizzi was Minister many other useful schemes met the approbation of the Pontiff, and were sanctioned by his signature.

Not a few commissions also were appointed—some for the study of railway communication in the Roman States, others for the improvement of both criminal and civil procedure, and others for the amelioration of the municipal system and the repression of vagrancy.

Rome, so richly endowed in many respects, could scarcely be said, as yet, to possess a periodical press. To establish such a press was, for the reforming ministry, a labor of love. Whilst they were preparing a law by which it should be called into existence and its liberty secured and regulated, Pius IX., in anticipation of their labors, authorized the publication of several journals. First, came the "Contemporaneo," which was followed in due time by the "Bilancia," the "Italico," the "Alba." These publications were in sympathy, at first, with the Pontiff and his reforming ministry. They advocated only rational reform, real improvement, such changes as were both practicable and useful. They had not yet discovered the excellence of the Socialist utopia. Their enthusiasm and their *vivats* were all for the reformer Pope.

It is far from being matter of surprise to Catholic people, at least, that the See of Rome should be the first to practice the virtues—the high morality which it teaches. In regard to their treatment of the Jewish people, the Christian nations generally stood in need of such an example as Papal Rome has always shown in her consideration for the race of Israel. The nations, although professing Christianity, have been anything but Christian in their conduct towards these people. It was their idea, one would say, that they were called of heaven to execute justice on an offending race. The Popes never believed that they or any other Christians were entrusted with such a mission. Accordingly, the Jews, when cruelly persecuted in other countries, always found protection and safety at

Rome under the wing of the Pope. Even such restrictions as they were subject to, contributed to maintain them in security and peace. The Holy Father, although it was his sublime mission to preach the Gospel, could not always cause its precepts to be obeyed. If prejudice was against living on terms of charity with the Jews, was it not kind, as well as wise and politic, to assign to them a quarter of the city where only they should dwell, free from all interference on the part of the rest of the inhabitants? Pius IX. believed that the time had come when a more liberal arrangement might be advantageously adopted. In pursuance of this conviction, he regulated that the Jews should enjoy the privilege of establishing their habitations wherever they should deem it most suitable, that they should be governed by the same laws as the other citizens, and in no way be treated as a foreign people. Such of them as stood in need of assistance Pius IX. admitted to a share in his benefactions, and without occasioning the slightest murmur on the part of his Christian subjects.

The Jews, whilst considered as foreigners in Rome, were subject to the custom of coming yearly to the Capitol to pay tribute. With this custom the Holy Father generously dispensed. All this liberality and kindness were highly appreciated. The Jewish people generally beheld in the wise, and Holy Pontiff the looked-for Messiah. The aged Rabbins, more considerate, affirmed only that the Pope was a great prophet. The chief of the Synagogue, Moses Kassan, composed in his honor a canticle marked by poetic inspiration. It extols and blesses the Holy Father for having gathered together in the same barque all the children whom God had confided to his care . . . . for having snatched from the contempt of nations, and sheltered under his wing, a persecuted people.

There being many Christians of the United Greek rite throughout the dominions of the Sultan, it was necessary that the Holy Father should negotiate, occasionally, with the successor of Mahomet. Pius IX. yielded not to any of his predecessors in zeal for the welfare of all Catholic people. Those who lived and often suffered under the Moslem yoke were, especially, objects of his fatherly solicitude. Policy had not yet brought the Cross into the same field of strife in union with the Crescent, when, on the 20th of February, 1847, the portals of the Quirinal were thrown open to the Ambassador of the Sublime Porte. To the Jews the Rome of Pius IX. was as a new Jerusalem. Islamism, from its tottering throne at Constantinople, looked towards it with hope and rapture.

The armed protection of Christians in the Turkish dominions, by the great European Powers, was, no doubt, galling to the Sultan's court. It was, therefore, ardently desired, we can readily believe, to place the Christians of the Levant under the peaceful guardianship of the Roman Pontiff. The Embassy may also have had other objects in view. Be this as it may, it was new and quite extraordinary to behold the representative of the prophet at the palace of the Sovereign Pontiff. No wonder if all Europe was moved to admiration. The presentation was very solemn—in the high ceremonial of Eastern lands. Chekif Effendi, the Turkish Ambassador, saluted the Holy Father in Oriental style, and addressed to him a magnificent oration, which was richly interspersed with metaphors—the pearls and diamonds of his country's eloquence. The Sublime Porte was compared to the Queen of Sheba, and Pius IX. to King Solomon. Whatever may be thought of the figures, the sentiments expressed in the speech were appropriate and affecting. The Pope replied by assuring the Ambassador that he was anxious to cultivate friendly relations with the Sultan, his master. Three days later Chekif Effendi took his departure from Rome, bearing with him on his breast, as a *nishun* (decoration), the portrait of the Holy Father.

This Embassy was more than mere show—more than an interchange of friendly sentiments. It enabled the Pope to adopt a measure which was calculated to be highly beneficial to the Christians of the East. The Latin Patriarchate of Jerusalem was restored. And thus was accomplished a wonderful revolution in European diplomacy as regarded the Eastern world. At the request of the Porte, the Latin Patriarch became bound to reside in the city of Jersualem. In the confidential position which he held there, he was the natural protector of the Catholic subjects of the Sultan. In addition to the duties of his sacred office, he was, as a consul, appointed by the Holy See to watch over the interests of religion—interests as important, surely, as those of trade and worldly policy. The first whom the Pope named to the dignity of Latin Patriarch was Monsignore Valergo, who had formerly been a missionary at Paris.

There appears to have been something irresistibly attractive in the character of Pius IX. That illustrious champion of Ireland and of liberty, Daniel O'Connell, resolved, towards the close of his days, to visit Rome and pay the homage of a kindred spirit to the Holy Father. Not only was he anxious to be enriched with the choicest heavenly benedictions, whilst kneeling reverently at the shrine of the Apostles, but he desired also, with a fervor which finds place only in the most nobly-moulded souls, whose love of liberty and whose patriotism are unfeigned and pure, to hold communion with one who was, no less than himself, a friend of liberty, and whose exalted station, and whose high duties towards mankind at large, hindered him not from laboring, as did Ireland's patriot, to liberate his country, not, indeed, from such cruel bondage as that under which the land of O'Connell had for so many ages groaned, but from the no less dangerous tyranny of abuses which, like weeds that grow most luxuriantly in the richest soil, it becomes necessary, in due season, to extirpate.

It was not, however, appointed that Ireland's liberator should ever see Rome. His illness continued to increase. No sooner had he reached the shores of Italy than the strength of his once powerful frame declined rapidly, and he was unable to proceed. Arrived at Genoa, O'Connell understood that his last hour on earth was near at hand. He now expressed the wish that his heart should rest in the Holy City.

Thither, accordingly, it was borne by friendly hands to com-
mingle with the consecrated dust of heroes, saints and martyrs.
To Rome it was a relic of incomparable price. Although cold
and inanimate, it was still eloquent in death, and grandly
emblematic of all that he had been to whom it was the centre
of life, and to whose generous impulses it had so long and so
faithfully beat responsive.

That son of O'Connell who bore his name, together with
the Rev. Dr. Miley, of Dublin, who had accompanied him to
Genoa and ministered to him in his last hours, now proceeded
to Rome and sought the presence of the Holy Father. On
their arrival at the Quirinal, the halls and ante-chambers were
already filled with groups of personages in every style of
costume, from the glittering uniform to the cowl. The
travellers, therefore, must wait till all these have had an
audience. But no. The name of O'Connell, as if possessed
of talismanic power, caused them to be at once admitted to the
presence of the Holy Father. The reception was most cordial.
"Since the happiness I had so much longed for," said the
Pontiff, "was not reserved for me, to behold and embrace the
hero of Christianity, let me, at least, have the consolation to
embrace his son." "As he spoke," writes Dr. Miley, "he drew the
son of O'Connell to his bosom and embraced him, not unmoved,
with the tenderness of a father and a friend. Then, with an
emotion which stirred our hearts within us, this great Father
of the faithful poured out his benign and loving soul in words
of comfort, which proved that it was not new to him to pour
the balm of heaven into broken and wounded hearts." "His
death," said the Pontiff, "was blessed. I have read the letter
in which his last moments were described with the greatest
consolation." The Pope then proceeded to eulogize the
liberator, as the great champion of religion and the Church,
as the father of his people and the glory of the whole
Christian world. "How else," observed Monsignore Cullen,
late Cardinal Archbishop of Dublin, who was present, "could
the Pope have spoken of him than he has done, even if he had

been the bosom friend of the liberator, as well as the ardent admirer of his career." Nor must we fail to record the terms in which the venerable Pontiff, on this memorable occasion, referred to Ireland. The thought of O'Connell was one with that of his native Erin. Death, even, could not sever them. Whilst the living image of grief and bereavement stood in his presence, the Holy Father could not refrain from giving expression to his paternal sympathy. But, at the same time, the country of O'Connell was not forgotten. Writes Dr. Miley : "While he spoke of the sufferings of the Irish, of their fidelity, of his solicitude and his hopes regarding them, it was beautiful and impressive beyond my power to describe, to observe that countenance, which, like a mirror, reflects the charity, the compassionate care, the fortitude, with a hundred other sentiments divine, which are never dormant within his breast."

Pius IX., anxious that due honor should be done to the memory of O'Connell, gave orders for the celebration of a solemn funeral service, and intimated his will and command that it should be celebrated in his name. "The achievements also of his wonderful existence I desire to be commemorated and made known to the world—not that this is necessary, 'because," said the Pontiff with a sublime look and gesture, "his grand career was ever in the face of heaven—he always stood up for legality—he had nothing to hide; and it was this, with his unshaken fidelity and reverence for religion, that secured his triumph." It is only justice to the people of Rome to state that they vied with the Sovereign Pontiff, the magnates of their country and the representatives of European nations at the Holy City, in doing honor to the memory of O'Connell. " From the Campus Martius," writes Dr. Miley, "and the Roman Forum, from both sides of the Tiber, and from all the seven hills and their interjacent valleys, this people, who grow up from infancy with the trophies of thirty centuries of greatness around them on every hand, assembled with enthusiasm to supplicate heaven for the eternal happiness of Ireland's liberator, and to exult in the wonders he had achieved, as if he had been their own." The greatest homage paid by Rome on this melancholy occasion, was undoubtedly, the funeral oration, which was spoken by the Bossuet of Italy, the celebrated preacher, Father Ventura, the friend and fellow-student of Pius IX. This most eloquent discourse was listened to with attention and delight by the vast congregation that had gathered round the cenotaph of the immortal patriot. Let a passage or two here suffice to give an idea of the magnificent panegyric:

"It is, then, because these two loves—the love of religion and the love of liberty, common to all good Princes, to all great minds, to all truly learned men, to all elevated souls, to all generous hearts might be said to be personified in Daniel—O'Connell—because in him they manifested themselves in all the perfection of their nature—in all the energy of their deeply-felt conviction—in all the potency of their strength—in all the splendor of their magnificence, and in all the glory of their triumph; it is because of all this that this singular man—who was born and has lived at such a distance from Rome—is now admired, is now wept for by you, as if he had been born in the midst of you. Hence it is that this great character, this sublime nature, has awakened all your sympathies."

O'Connell had studied for some time at the College of St. Omer, in France. What he saw and learned in that country is ably described by the Italian orator:

"He saw with his own eyes monarchy compelled to degrade itself, and to inflict its death-wound with its own hand; he saw the throne that base courtiers had dragged through the mire defiled by the grip of parricidal hands, and buried, fathoms deep, beneath a sea of blood; he saw the best of kings expire upon a scaffold, the victim not less of other men's crimes than of his own weakness; he saw that vice was hailed, as if it were virtue, wickedness uplifted, as if it were morality atheism, proclaimed aloud, as if it were religion; that the "Goddess of Reason" (or rather a vile strumpet) was recognized as the only Deity, and honored with hecatombs of human victims; the people decimated and oppressed by cruel tyrants, in the name of the people; whilst beneath the shade of the tree of liberty was instituted universal slavery; and that the most Christian, as well ss the most civilized of all nations, had fallen down to the lowest limits of impiety and barbarism.

"Now, God having so disposed that the young O'Connell should be witness of these events—the most celebrated and the most instructive to be found in the annals of history—they served to inspire him with the greatest horror for tumults and rebellion; they persuaded him that there is nothing more insane, and, at the same time, more pernicious than to proclaim the rights of man, in trampling upon those of heaven—in establishing liberty on the ruins of religion—in making laws, under the dictation of passion, or through the inspiration of sacrilege—and, finally, they convinced him, that to *regenerate* a people, religion is omnipotent—philosophy of little or no avail."

In alluding to the well-known piety of O'Connell, the preacher said: "What more moving spectacle than to see the greatest man in the United Kingdom—to see him, who was the object of Ireland's devotion, of England's fear, and of the world's admiration, kneeling with the people before the altar, practicing the piety of the people, with that humble simplicity, that recollection, that devoutness, and that modesty, which supercilious science and stolid pride abandon as things fit only to be followed by those whom they disdain as the people?"

It is matter of notoriety that the Tory party, whose death-knell was soon to be tolled, constantly poured on the great Irish Tribune the most scurrilous abuse. One of the mock titles with which they honored him was that of "King of the Beggars." Such pitiful ribaldry awakened the highest powers of the Roman orator. "Poor, miserable, and most pitiful fatuity which, while intending to mock, actually did him honor. For, what sovereignty is more beautiful than that whose tribute is not wrung from unwilling fear, but that is a voluntary, love-inspired offering? What sovereignty is more glorious than that whose sword is the pen, and whose only artillery the tongue; whose only couriers are the poor, and its sole bodyguard the affections of the people? What sovereignty more beneficent than that which, far from causing tears to flow, dries them; which, far from shedding blood, stanches it; which, far from immolating life, preserves it; which, far from pressing down upon the people, elevates them; which, far from forging chains, breaks them; and which always maintains order, harmony and peace, without ever inflicting the slightest aggression on liberty? Where is the monarch who would not esteem himself happy in reigning thus? Of such a sovereignty, we may with truth say what was said of Solomon's, that none can equal its grandeur, its glory and its magnificence."

So favorable an opportunity for instructing the Italians was not thrown away. False liberty was already strewing their path with its meretricious allurements. "As true liberty diffuses around it peace and grace and calm, so does false liberty disseminate, wherever it is implanted, terror, dismay and horror. The brows of one are illuminated with the splendid halo of order, and those of the other are covered with the red cap of anarchy. One holds in her hand the olive-branch of peace; the other waves the torch of discord. One is arrayed in robes white as those of innocence, and the other is enveloped in the dark, blood-stained mantle of guilt. One is the prop of thrones; the other a yawning abyss beneath them. One is the glory and the happiness of nations; the other their disgrace and their punishment. The latter bursts out of hell as if it were a poisonous blast issuing from the jaws of the devil himself; whilst true liberty descends sweetly and gently upon the earth, as if the spirit of God had sent it down to us a holy and blessed thing from heaven. *Ubi spiritus Domini ibi Libertas.*"

None will be surprised to learn that on hearing these singularly eloquent words, the immense auditory could no longer control their emotions. A general murmur of approba-

tion was heard throughout the vast temple and was breaking
out into loud applause, when the preacher, mindful of the
reverence due to the holy place, made haste to repress it.

This great demonstration may well be considered as the
best testimony that could be given as to the real sentiments
of the Italian people. They were not ignorant of the nature
of that liberty for which O'Connell had so long and successfully
contended. Nor were they under any erroneous impression as
to what the gifted preacher meant when he extolled in such
glowing terms that true liberty which is the glory, at once,
and the best security of nations. If, a little later, they
pursued the phantom instead of the reality, it must be considered that, as yet, they had no political education or experience,
and that no high-principled Tribune, like O'Connell, stood
forward to lead them. All who aspired to guide them, and
who won their confidence, were tainted with the doctrines of the
Socialist party, whose ideas of government and liberty were
utterly utopian.

If it could be said that public rejoicings afforded any
assistance to the Pope, in his labors as the head of the Roman
State, he was not left without aid in his great undertakings.
Such things, however, rather hindered than promoted his
endeavors. His people had, so to say, commenced, under his
auspices, a long and laborious journey. There was no time for
mere pleasure and amusement. Nevertheless, whenever a new
scene or landscape opened to their view, they stopped to rejoice,
and gave themselves up, without control, to the intoxication of
delight. In so doing they laid themselves open to the snares
and attacks of many secret enemies, who availed themselves
of their frequent gatherings to sow the seeds of discord and
corrupt their minds with false political doctrines. Far better
would it have been if they had left to the Sovereign in whom,
at first, they placed unbounded confidence, and the wise
Ministers whom he called to his counsels, the care of forward-
ing the cause of reform. It had been most benevolently and
successfully begun, and was proceeding, in the estimation of all

but an impatient people, with rapidity which had no
parallel in the history of nations. The people, by assembling
tumultuously on occasion of every popular measure, no doubt
meant no more at first than to show gratitude and affection to
their pastor and prince. Such meetings, however, were not
without danger to the cause of reform. The political enemies
of the Pope easily foresaw that, by his wise and popular
improvements in the State, he would certainly secure to himself
a peaceful, strong and glorious reign. So, laying hold of the
general enthusiasm, they trained and disciplined to their will a
people who were naturally good and unsuspecting. These
men came at length to give the watchword, and, according to
their wishes and the views which it suited them to insinuate
into the popular mind, the uneducated and fickle multitude
expressed satisfaction or discontent, as they defiled in imposing
masses before the mansion of the Pontiff. Thus was formed a
sort of government out of doors, which, if it did not yet oppose
or appear to oppose at least, powerfully swayed the official
authority. Cardinal Gizzi, whose ministry was so popular,
deemed it necessary to require by proclamation that these
noisy demonstrations should cease. It was too late. The
people, defying the Cardinal's mandate, hastened in crowds to
the Quirinal, saluted, as usual, the Pope with enthusiastic
rivats, expressing, at the same time, their detestation of his
ministry, which they were wont to applaud so loudly, and
which, if it had not by any great activity done much to acquire,
had certainly done nothing to forfeit their favor. "*Viva Pio
Nono! Pio Nono Solo!*" was now their cry. The Pope himself
next came to be considered as intolerably dilatory in preparing
measures of reform. Nor did he escape the accusation, at the
same time, of sacrificing to his zeal, as a temporal ruler, the
higher duties which he owed to religion and the Church.
According to one set of revilers, he was breaking with inviolable
tradition. Others insisted that so enthusiastic a reformer of
the State must be a revolutionist in the Church. Such attacks
were met by anticipation in the Encyclical of 9th November,

1846. This well-known document was received with applause by the civilized world. It leaves no ground for the charges in question. It would only destroy the Church to pretend to reform its dogma and revolutionize its discipline and government. Such an idea could proceed from no other source than the stratagems of unbelief, or from the snares of the wolf, who, in sheep's clothing, seeks to insinuate himself into the fold. It is nothing short of sacrilege to hold that religion is susceptible of progress or improvement, as if it were a philosophical discovery, which could advance with the march of science. The Holy Father enumerates also in this Encyclical the principal grounds of faith, and exhorts all bishops to oppose with all their zeal and learning those who, alleging progress as their motive, perversely endeavor to destroy religion by subjecting it to every man's individual judgment. He condemns indifference as regards religion, eloquently defends ecclesiastical celibacy, and, mindful that the Church is the teacher of the great as well as of the humble, he enforces the obligations of sovereigns towards their subjects, not forgetting the fulfilment of all the duties which the people owe to their rulers. In a former Encyclical, Pius IX. had expressed his predilection for the religious orders. This expression was now renewed. Time may have interfered, more or less, with their discipline. Anxious to preserve them and .promote their prosperity, he was ever willing to correct such abuses as may have existed. To some communities he offered the most admirable suggestions. Others he honored with personal visits, evincing always a truly pastoral zeal for the well-being of institutions so precious to religion.

Pius IX., although deeply occupied with affairs of State that would have commanded all the attention and energy of any ordinary mind, found time, nevertheless, for the discharge of duties of a still higher order. He never forgot that he was the Bishop as well as the Sovereign of Rome. The Romans, although inhabiting the Holy City, like all other people, stood in need of the instructions and warnings of religion. The

Pope was aware, besides, that bad habits prevailed, such as profane swearing, luxurious living, the neglect of parents in the training of their children. The knowledge of such things grieved him exceedingly. He now resolved to have recourse to a measure which was as striking as it was unexpected. In the trying days of the Crusaders, and moved by their zeal for the safety of Christendom, the Popes of an earlieir time had addressed, as the ministers of God, immense public assemblages. No Pope, however, had appeared in the pulpit since Gregory VII. The Church of St. Andrew, where the eloquent Father Ventura was accustomed to preach, was selected, but, lest there should be too great a crowd, no notice of the Pope's intention was published. At half-past three o'clock on a Sunday afternoon, just as the congregation were expecting to see Abbate Ventura enter the church, the Pope himself made his appearance. The sermon was not a long one; but it was memorable, and to be long remembered. "In this city," said the Holy Father, "which is the centre of Catholicity, there are men who insult the holy name of God by profane and blasphemous language. On all those who now hear me I lay this charge: publish everywhere that I have no hope for such men. They cast in the face of Heaven the stone which will, one day, recoil upon them and crush them. I would also most earnestly exhort you as regards the duty, of fasting. Many fathers and mothers come to me in order to impart to me the sorrow which they experience in considering the melancholy fact which cannot escape their observation, that the demon of uncleanness exercises a destructive empire over the youth of Rome. Our Lord Himself in the Holy Gospel assures us that, by no other means than prayer and fasting, is it possible to overcome this demon who poisons the sources of life and works the ruin of immortal souls." The sermon, although comparatively short, spoke of the chief obligations of a Chirstian life. It was delivered with great unction, and the Holy Father concluded with a fervent prayer for Rome and the Roman State. "Look down upon this vine, O Lord, which Thy right hand hath planted ! Look upon it in mercy, and remove from it the hand of iron which weighs so heavily upon it. Pour into the bosoms of the rising generations those two most precious attributes of youth,—modesty and a teachable mind. Listen to my prayer, O Lord, and bestow upon this congregation, on this city and all people, Thy most precious blessings."

Appropriate gesticulations added to the power of words. Another influence, also, came in aid,—an influence peculiar to Pius IX.,—that indescribable expression of goodness which lighted up his countenance as he spoke. The people, whose feelings are naturally fine, were moved even to tears and sighs. The occasion itself was well calculated to move the minds of a Catholic audience. It was an element, no doubt, which, together with the eloquence of the preacher, and the power of apostolic preaching, could not fail to produce a profound impression. And, indeed, the whole congregation were filled with enthusiasm.

Whilst thus finding consolation in the exercise of his sublime ministry, the benevolent Pontiff was destined to encounter formidable attacks on the part of political opponents. On the one hand, the ultra-Conservatives, who held in abomination the mere idea of reform, endeavored by every means to confound in the popular mind the beneficial measures which the Pope was introducing into the economy of the State, with radical changes in the most essential points of religion itself. The Socialists, on the other hand, studied to excite the people and increase their impatience by misrepresenting all the acts of the ministry, and causing it to be believed that, by the delay which was unavoidable in labors of such magnitude and importance, they were only abusing the confidence of the sovereign and betraying the cause of reform. Some remains of chivalry might have been expected in the ranks of the high Conservative party. But, alas ! too truly the age of chivalry was gone, and these sticklers for the usages of a bygone age, only showed by their modes of proceeding that they clung to an empty and inanimate form of things from which life and substance had departed. As was related at the time, they stepped down to the depths of calumny and published a cruel libel, in which the Holy Father was held up to the scorn of all right-thinking men as an "intruder," "an enemy of Religion," "the chief of *Young Italy*." In the estimation of such men discretion is the better part of valor. But whilst they fought with the coward's weapon—slander—they could not wholly escape detection. Their libel was seized in the hands of a *colporteur*. This wretched man offered to disclose the names of the libellers. Pius IX. declined his offer, generously forgave him the offence, and even bestowed upon him a sum of money in order to induce him and enable him to give up his nefarious trade.

Meanwhile, there was at Rome a still more numerous body who sustained the policy of the Holy Father. These friends of order, it is most pleasing to record, made every effort to aid him in carrying out the measures of reform which he contemplated. This influential body of faithful and patriotic citizens, who can never be sufficiently praised, organized a considerable force which kept the populace in check. This party consisted, chiefly, of the burghers of Rome. They were encouraged and headed by the higher nobles, such as the Borghese, the Rospigliosi, the Riguano, the Piombino, and the Aldobrandini. Acting as a noble guard, they were able to preserve order in the city, when, on occasion of celebrating the memorable amnesty, it was seriously threatened by the factions. They were, indeed, a party of reform, order-loving and law-abiding. It can never be sufficiently regretted that, unaccustomed as they were to political turmoil, they knew not how to keep their ground in the face of new dangers which arose so soon.

The health of Cardinal Gizzi had begun to decline. The toils of office were not calculated to improve it, and so he relinquished a post which was, every day, becoming more onerous and difficult. There was another Cardinal whose high character had endeared him to the Romans. Ability and learning were not his only qualities. He was energetic and resolute, faithful, straightforward and self-sacrificing. When the dread scourge of cholera swept over his episcopal city and impoverished his people, Cardinal Ferretti gave up for the relief of the sufferers all that he possessed—money, clothing, plate, furniture, and remained in his empty Palace, as destitute as a pauper. To this eminent Cardinal Pius IX. appealed, offering him the high office which Gizzi could no longer hold. On 26th July, 1847, the new Chief Minister arrived at Rome. He was warmly received. The citizens gave him an ovation.

Shortly before his arrival, news had come to Rome that Austrian troops were marching on Ferrara, a city of the Papal States. They were, indeed, entitled, by the treaty of 1815, to occupy this fortress, as well as that of Camachio. They could urge no better excuse for a display of military power in the Pope's States on occasion of the threatened disturbance of 16th July. This parade was only the prelude to further military operations. On 13th August, General Count Auesperg occupied all the posts of Ferrara. Whatever may be said as to treaty rights, this was, undoubtedly, an insult to the Papal flag. The most energetic remonstrances were immediately addressed to the Cabinet of Vienna. Austria endeavored to justify her proceeding by a wide interpretation of the right of occupation, by alleging the disturbed state of the public mind at Rome, and by insisting on certain precedents. But to no purpose. The diplomacy of Ferretti contended successfully with that of Metternich. And Austria, yielding with the best grace possible to the representations of the Holy Father, evacuated Ferrara.

The Pope, far from allowing himself to be disquieted by the presence in his States of Croat troops, proceeded with the work of reform which he had undertaken, slowly, indeed, but with energy and perseverance. In these labors of the Statesman,

he was ably aided by the Cardinal Minister Ferretti. A promise was given that before the end of the year two great political
and administrative institutions would be called into existence.
Accordingly, so early as the month of October, two State papers
appeared, the one instituting the municipality of Rome, which
was to be called *the Senate*, the other decreeing an assembly
that should be, to a certain extent, representative, under the
name of *Council of State* (consulta). The City of Rome had
not, for a long time, possessed, like the other cities of the Pontifical States, municipal institutions. It was now ordained
that there should be a City Council, consisting of the mayor
(in the language of the country, *Senator*), with eight colleagues
and a hundred other members. This is not unlike our own
municipal magistracy, wherein are the mayor, aldermen and
common councilmen or councillors. With us, however, aldermen could hardly be called the colleagues of the mayor. This
functionary stands alone in his worshipful dignity. The first
nomination of the members of this municipal body was reserved
to the Pope. But it was appointed that, ever after, it should
be chosen by free popular election. None will question the
wisdom and liberality of the language in which the Pope
expressed himself in the preamble to the new law. "When
we were called by Divine Providence to govern the Church and
the State, our paternal solicitude was at once directed to every
portion of the Dominion subjected to our Government, but
especially towards the capital, the chief of all our cities, to
which it is consoling for us to devote our watchings and our
labors. What was, above all, important, and what we think
will be a subject of joy to all, is the restoration to this beloved
city of its ancient glory of communal representation, by granting to it a deliberative council. The study of this project has
been particularly pleasing to us, and we have not allowed ourselves to be discouraged by any difficulty." This important
decree was published on the 2nd day of October, 1847. On
the following day there was a national festival. The people
were in raptures, and loudly demonstrated their gratitude to

the Holy Father for an institution which recalled the glorious associations of ancient Rome, and restored it to its place and rank among modern cities.   The Cardinal-prince Altieri was named president.   He opened the first session of the municipal council by a speech which was marked by the homage paid therein to Pius IX.   "He considered not," said the orator, "whether the work be difficult.   He sees its utility and hesitates not."   The council almost unanimously elected to the post of Senator (Mayor) Prince Corsini, who was, at that time, devoted to the policy of the reforming Pontiff.

A measure of more general importance now occupied the attention of the Sovereign Pontiff and his Ministers.   The Council of State (consulta) was established.   It was a deliberative assembly.   It was not sovereign, but possessed the right to advise the Sovereign.   There were twenty-four councillors. The President was a Cardinal Legate.   Each councillor was chosen by the Pope from a list of three candidates presented by each Province of the Pontifical States.   The Council was divided into four sections, whose office it was to prepare laws relating to the Departments of Finance, Home Affairs, Public Works and Justice.   It was the duty also of these four Committees to hold a general meeting on certain days, in order to take counsel together on the draughts of proposed laws which they had separately prepared.   On the 25th November, 1847, the National Representatives met for the first time.   Their place of meeting was the throne-room of the Quirinal Palace. Cardinal Antonelli was the first President.   The proceedings were commenced, and most appropriately, by a respectful address to the Holy Father.   It was well known to Pius IX. that the creation of this institution had awakened exaggerated and premature hopes in the minds of a portion of the people, and that some of the Deputies were not disinclined to encourage them.   So he considered it necessary, in his reply, to define, in a very decided manner, the true character and functions of the National Representative Body.   "It is chiefly," said he, "in order that I may become better acquainted

with the wants of my people, and that I may better provide
for the exigencies of the State, that I have called you together.
I am prepared, in time, to do everything, without, however,
diminishing the Sovereignty of the Pontificate. That man
would be grievously mistaken who should behold in the functions which devolve on you, or in your institution itself, his own
Utopias, or the commencement of anything incompatible with
the Pontifical Sovereignty." In concluding, he spoke in a still
more determined tone, and reproached his people with the
ingratitude which they had already begun to manifest. "There
are some persons who, having nothing to lose, wish for disorder
and insurrection, and go so far as to make a bad use even of
our concessions."

There was in this Council a commencement of representative government. Deputies from the Provinces assembled—
deliberated. They heard a Speech from the Throne. They
presented an address in reply. In due time this germ of constitutional monarchy would be developed. But the Sovereign
would not proceed rashly. The full measure of reform, he was
well aware, must, like all great works, be the fruit of time, of
much labor and patient consideration.

Count Rossi, the French Ambassador, considered that it
was already time to introduce a lay element into the political
administration of the Papal States. The Holy Father, accordingly, after due consideration, appointed some distinguished
laymen to the Ministry. In so doing, no doubt, he sacrificed
time-honored usage; but not so much to the wishes of his friends
and allies, as to the spirit of the age, which, whether right or
wrong, will have men of the world to deal with the world.

Italy, although divided into several States, looked to Rome
as its centre and its capital. Whatever occurred in the city
of the Popes was at once known throughout the whole peninsula. Such important and unlooked-for measures of reform as
were now carried into effect could not fail, as they were communicated, to affect deeply the Italian mind. Public opinion
was aroused. The most profound sympathy was everywhere

felt and expressed. Liberty had revived under the auspices of Religion. It had emanated as a new blessing from the Cross. The Chief of Religion, the Father of the Faithful, had become its High Priest. His name was held in benediction. His praises were proclaimed not only by the Italian people, but also by every civilized nation. It was no longer violence—no longer insurrection—that contended for liberty. The greatest of all sovereigns had announced its reign. It was not indebted to any secret society. It relied upon society at large. It rested secure, so men believed, on the firm foundation of enlightened public opinion. Philosophy, as represented by M. Cousin, hailed its advent. The statesmanship of France, headed by M. Thiers, extolled its champion. Protestantism, forgetting its illiberal prejudices, re-echoed with enthusiasm the warm *vivats* of reformed Italy. Pius IX., meanwhile, enjoyed his reward,— not in the flattering echo of the thousand voices which sounded his praise, but in the one still voice of approving conscience. He was consoled, moreover, by a profound conviction that the cause which he had taken in hand would, one day, prove triumphant.

With every new concession came the desire for further change. The people generally were satisfied, even grateful, and they frequently expressed their gratitude in the most sincere and enthusiastic manner. They were not, however, all sincere. There were not wanting those who studied only to make available for their own ends the tumultuous gatherings and warm expressions of satisfaction in which the people so often indulged. This was the Socialist faction. It aimed at nothing less than to establish a Republic—a *Republic, one and undivided*, or, as it has been called, because of its cruel and blood-thirsty character, the *Red Republic*.

With a view to the establishment of such a Republic, the men of this party took advantage of the numerous assemblages, which could not now either be regulated or diminished in number, to gain new friends, to increase popular excitement, and so to discipline it as to bring it, through some favorite demagogues, under their control. It will shortly be seen with what a dangerous weapon they were arming themselves. It can scarcely be doubted that but for the machinations of these factionists and their influence with the masses, which was every day increasing, Pius IX. would have succeeded in establishing a system of government as constitutional and as free as was at all compatible with his own rights as sovereign. These rights he was not at liberty to abandon. No greater measure of political freedom could be reasonably desired by any people. From all history it is manifest that liberty is as fully enjoyed, and established on a more secure and permanent basis, under the fostering auspices of a constitutional monarchy, than in the best regulated republics. Such a form of government may indeed be said to be more republican than monarchical. But although possessing many properties, and all the popular advantages of a Republic, it does not cease to be a monarchy. The kingly dignity still remains with all that appertains to it, and is an essential element of its constitution. Such was the monarchy that Pius IX. desired to retain, and which he was bound in conscience, he believed, never to relinquish. That in this he was sincere his high character bears witness. Never was there a less selfish sovereign, or a man of more upright mind and sounder judgment. No prince ever held less to prerogative. Essential rights he was firmly resolved to maintain, whilst he never would have shrunk from any legitimate concession. Whatever was adapted to the time and the circumstances of his country, useful to his people, and conformable to a well-informed and sound public opinion, he was prepared to introduce into the economy of the State. But, the complete secularization of public power in the Pontifical States, in other words, the establishment of a Republic based on anti-Christian principles,—the *Red Republic*,—could never for a moment be contemplated. What may be called the consultative Government had just entered upon the discharge of its duties, when Pius IX. resolved to render it completely representative. This important resolution was the subject of frequent conversations with M. Rossi, at the time ambassador at Rome of the French constitutional monarchy. M. Rossi wrote as follows, to his government, in January, 1848:

"It is a problem which, after much reflection, I consider may be solved. The divisions of sovereignty in the world have been numerous and diverse. And as they lasted for ages, we might even try one more, beginning by separating entirely the temporal from the spiritual—the Pope from the King. Only it would be necessary to leave wholly to the spiritual, and the clergy, matters which with us are mixed." A few days afterwards, the ambassador communicated this more decided intelligence—"The Pope will shortly give the constitution. It is his serious and constant study."

Not many days later, the ambassador imparted to his government this more decided intelligence: "The Pope will shortly grant the constitution. It is his serious and constant study." M. Rossi earnestly recommended that there should be no delay in adopting this important measure. It would, he conceived, put an end to agitation,—a most desirable result, surely, when it is considered how fatal to the cause of liberty and reform might any day become the too frequent tumultuous assemblages which, once constitutional government was established, would necessarily cease.

The Pope held the same idea as the eminent diplomatist. The great idea was as yet, however, far from being realized. A new and most serious difficulty unexpectedly arose. On the 5th of March, 1848, a courier arrived, bearing the startling intelligence that the constitutional monarchy of France had fallen, and that a Republic was established at Paris. No greater misfortune could have befallen Rome. The public excitement was increased beyond measure, and exaggerated hopes were enkindled that could never be fulfilled. The people, at first enthusiastic only, were now turbulent. The events in France exercised a still more fatal influence. They caused anarchy to prevail. The extreme or Socialist Republicans, whom the proclamation of the constitution would have paralyzed, were now in the ascendant. What had been done at Paris, they conceived, might be done at Rome. And they induced the inexperienced multitude to share their conviction. Such belief was only an idle and a culpable dream. For surely it could not be guiltless to resolve on sacrificing thousands on thousands of precious lives for an Utopia,—a system that could never be realized. Events have shown that in France itself, which was entirely free to make whatever political arrangement it pleased, a Republic was not possible, even such a Republic as was established at the downfall of the citizen monarchy, in preference to the Red Republic. How, then, should it be possible to build up at Rome an extreme system in opposition to the views and wishes of the whole Christian world,—in opposition even to the people of Rome themselves, who, when free from undue excitement, were the loyal supporters of the sovereign who had already introduced into the economy of the State so many liberal institutions—institutions that were in perfect harmony with their ideas, and admirably adapted to the exigencies of the times ? There was no need, as yet, that the Catholic nations should come to the aid of their Chief. It was necessary only to appeal, in defence of his sovereignty, *from Rome drunk to Rome sober*,—from Rome intoxicated with unwonted draughts of liberty to Rome in its normal state—to Rome, cool, and calm, and intellectual, even as in the days of her ancient glory, when her sages and grave senators sat by her gates sorrowing but dignified in their defeat. With the like countenance ought modern Rome to have met the tide of Socialist invasion, which every successive endeavor to establish the Red or Communist Republic proves to be more destructive than the war of mighty legions, which can only cast down material walls.

A Socialist Republic was impossible at Rome, the city of the Popes. It never could have held its ground against the

sound principle which universally prevailed throughout the
Pontifical States. Nor would it ever have been able to obtain
the countenance, or even the recognition, of the European
governments. Not France and Austria only; every other
Catholic nation as well would have exerted all their influence
against it. Nor in doing so would they have acted unwisely
or unjustly. Had not Rome been the residence of their Chief
Pastor, that great historic city would have ceased long ago to
exist, or would be known only as an insignificant village,
scarcely perceptible on the map of Europe. How often has
not the celebrated city been rescued from destruction by the
direct agency of the Popes? How long have they not governed it with wisdom and blessed it with prosperity? If there
be any such thing as prescriptive right, undoubtedly it is
theirs. If there be any right better founded and stronger
than that of conquest, such right belongs unquestionably to
the saviors of Rome. They have saved it for the Christian
world, for mankind, for the Church. It is no man's property.
It cannot be let, like a paltry farm, to those who shall bid the
highest, in vain compromises and delusive hopes of liberty.
Should the Roman people, of their own free will, pretend to
give themselves away,—to sell themselves to a faction whose
subversive principles they abhor, their forefathers of all preceding ages would protest against their base degeneracy; the
children of the generations to come would curse their memory;
all reflecting men of the present time would accuse them of
black ingratitude,—ingratitude to the mighty dead among
their Pontiffs, to whom they are indebted for their very name,
their city's fame, its honored State, its very existence in modern times; ingratitude, above all, to that ruler who offered
them, who bestowed upon them, liberty, and who would have
gladly rescued them in his day from tyranny,—the tyranny of
faction,—even as his predecessors, in bygone times, snatched
them from the cruel grasp of barbarism.

Pius IX. had made up his mind to institute thoroughly
representative and constitutional government. And this was
all that the Roman people, as yet, desired. They were

only anxious that the views of the Pontiff should be speedily carried into effect. Accordingly, Prince Corsini, the Senator (Mayor), and the eight principal members of the Municipal Council, were commissioned to make known their wishes to the Pope. His reply was dignified and candid. In declaring his intention to grant the constitution which they asked for, he took care to intimate in the most decided manner that he was not making a concession to the urgency of the moment, but accomplishing his premeditated purpose. "Events," said he, "abundantly justify the request which you address to me in the name of the Council and Magistracy of Rome. All are aware that it is my constant study to give to the Government the form which appears to me to be most in harmony with the times. But, none are ignorant, at the same time, of the difficulties to which he is exposed, who unites in his own person two great dignities, when endeavouring to trace the line of demarcation between these two powers. What, in a secular Government, may be done in one day, in the Pontifical can only be accomplished after mature deliberation. I flatter myself, nevertheless, that the preliminary labours having been completed, I shall be able, in a few days, to impart to you the result of my reflections, and that this result will meet the wishes of all reasonable people."

On the 14th of March, accordingly, was published *the fundamental statute for the temporal government of the Holy See*, and so was inaugurated constitutional rule in the most complete and straightforward manner which it is possible to conceive.

The constitution was framed according to the model of the French Liberal Monarchy of 1830, so modified as to render it capable of being adapted to the Pontifical Government. Under its provisions there were a Ministry which was responsible, and two Houses of Parliament, one of which was elective, and the other composed of members who should hold their appointment during their lifetime. To the Council of State belonged the framing of laws to be afterwards submitted to the votes of the two Chambers.

In all constitutional monarchies, the assent of the sovereign is necessary, in order to give the force of law to measures voted by Parliament. So, under the constitution promulgated at Rome by Pius IX., the College of Cardinals were constituted a permanent council, whose office it was to sanction finally the decisions of the Legislative Chambers. Such, in substance, was the statute by which the Pontifical States became undeniably constitutional. A few days later the Ministry was named. Three-fourths of their number were laymen. Cardinal Antonelli was appointed President or First Minister. And thus the constitution was no sooner framed than it came into operation, so anxious was Pius IX. to advance the interests and meet the wants and wishes of his people.

Now, one would say, gratitude only could await the Pontiff. But no! at the moment when, of all others, he was entitled to rely on the devotedness of his people, a new and great difficulty arose.

By the diplomacy of 1815, at the close of the great European War, certain portions of Italy had been left subject to German rule. By war only, some Italians imagined, could this evil be removed. This was an extravagant idea. War could only raise up new enemies to the cause of Italy and that regeneration which appeared to be so near at hand. Diplomacy would have served them better. What it had done at one time, under pressure of the most trying circumstances, it would have been ready to achieve when circumstances were changed, and imperatively demanded a new order of things.

In the new emergencies that had arisen, the learning and ability of statesmen ought, at least, in the first instance, to have been appealed to. As between individuals, it is reasonable that all peaceful means of adjusting a quarrel should be employed, so, in the greater affairs of nations, all the arts of statesmanship ought to be had recourse to before resort is had to bayonets and blood. How successful such a course would have proved, and how beneficial to the cause of Italian liberty, is more than sufficiently shown by the great result which diplomacy obtained, when Austria, insisting on treaty rights, displayed the flag of war at Ferrara. In that case, no doubt, the Pope was the chief diplomatist. But would he not have been so, likewise, when there was question, not of one city only, but of many of the greatest cities and best provinces of Italy? It is not to be supposed, that in these more momentous circumstances he would have found "the Barbarians" more hard to deal with. Austria, indeed, was so barbarous as to ignore that exquisite refinement of modern times, which despises religion and its ministers; and so she would have shown, as of old, her reverence for the Pontiff, by withdrawing, at his request, her soldiers from Italian soil.

The Italians, however, did not think so. They would have war, cost what it would. The people even of the Papal States, whose august Chief could have conquered without war, were bent on the same fatal purpose. They were wholly under the influence of the Socialist agitation, and no wiser counsel could be made to prevail.

It was decided among the popular leaders that the question of war should be agitated in the greatest assembly which it was possible to gather together. The Coliseum was appointed as the place of meeting, and it was destined to present an unwanted spectacle, a grand but ill-omened scene. All Rome, it may be said, was congregated in the ancient arena, the favorite tribunes at their head. These demagogues were determined that the question of war should be settled by acclamation, hoping thus to influence the Sovereign Pontiff to induce him to abandon his policy of neutrality by this imposing display of opinion and excitement, by so much popular enthusiasm, by such intoxication, so to say, of patriotism. At an early hour the vast arena was already crowded. All orders of the State were there—Nobles, Burghers, Soldiers, Princes—everybody. Priests even came in tolerable numbers to swell the crowd, and monks of every order, ecclesiastics of every college, members of every congregation. Such was the immense open air assemblage in which the question of the new crusade was to be solemnly discussed. It would have been a grand and note-

worthy spectacle, had it not been arranged beforehand by skilful leaders who were adepts in the art of getting up revolutionary displays.   In the great assembly there may have been
sincerity.   In the chief actors there was none.   Such a spontaneous expression of public sentiment, if really such, would,
indeed, have been imposing—grand.   Viewed only as a thea-
trical performance of parts learned to order—and it was nothing
more—it was deserving of nothing but contempt.   There was
in this display, besides, a sinister and melancholy feature—a
set of actors practising on the popular mind to-day, in order
to discover what they might safely attempt to-morrow.

Near the tribune which overlooks the arena were ranged
all those agitators who were destined to become, at a later
period, so notorious in the commotions of the time.   Among
them was observed Padre Gavazzi, a Barnabite monk, whose
puerile vanity made him aspire to distinction, and whose
career was already marked by pretentious eloquence, a bom-
bastic style, confused ideas, and a mind still undecided as to
the limits of orthodoxy, which, a little later, he stepped
beyond.   He was the preacher of *the crusade*.   Next came the
shepherd poet, Rosi;   Prince Canino's Secretary, Masi;   a
young French monk of the order of Conventualists, Dumaine:
Generals Durando and Ferrari;   the journalist, Sterbini, afterwards so fatally popular;   and, of course, the demagogue,
Cicerruacho, who had been, at first, enthusiastic in the cause
of the Pope, but who now burned for war, and, ere long, imparted to the revolution a character of fitful fanaticism and
absurd sympathies.   The day was spent in magniloquent addresses, which affected the style of ancient types, urgent ex-
hortations to war, poetical orations, rounds of applause,
rapturous demonstrations.   The result was, lists for the enrolment of volunteers;   the establishment in the different quarters
of the city of tables for receiving patriotic offerings, and a
threatening demonstration against the Quirinal Palace, where
it was intended to force the Pope to bless the colours for the
expedition against Austria.

The movement was now beyond all control. The orders of the Pope were treated with a sort of respect, but not obeyed. The spirit of rebellion was abroad, although the people still made a show of reverence. They were no sooner from the presence of the Pontiff than they transgressed his most sacred commands. Pius IX. had distinctly specified, when he authorized the enrolment and the departure of volunteers, that it was his intention and his will that the expedition should be exclusively defensive ; that it should protect the territory, but avoid passing the frontier. The leaders, notwithstanding, adding perfidy to rebellion, made use of the Pontiff's name in order to deceive the people. General Durando had no sooner arrived at Bologna than he issued a proclamation, in which, falsifying the Pope's wishes, he adduced his authority in order to encourage the war. "Radetsky," said he, "fights against the cross of Christ. Pius IX. has blessed your swords together with those of Charles Albert. This war of civilization against barbarism is not merely national, it is a Christian war. With the cross and by the cross, we shall be victorious. God wills it."

Nothing could have tended more completely to compromise the character of the Pontiff. It became necessary, accordingly, to publish the Encyclical Letter of 29th April, 1848. "Men are endeavouring," said the Holy Father, in this admirable document, "to disseminate suspicions that are injurious to the temporal administration of our States. It is our duty to prevent the scandal that might thus be given to the simple and unreflecting." He then proceeds to declare that he is resolved to expose clearly and to proclaim loudly the origin of all the facts of his Government. He refers to the memorandum of 1831, which contained the collective counsels of the European Cabinets to the Apostolic See, recommending the necessary reforms. Some of these reforms were adopted by Gregory XVI. Circumstances and the danger of the times caused others to be deferred. Pius IX. considered that it was his duty to complete what his predecessor had begun. He does not disclaim having taken the initiative on certain other points. He had pardoned extensively, and he congratulates himself on this clemency. He repels the calumny which would ascribe to the reforms which he had inaugurated the general movement of Italy towards its enfranchisement. This agitation he attributes to events that occurred elsewhere, and which became facts of overwhelming influence for the whole of Europe. Finally, he protests that he gave no other order to his soldiers than that which required that they should defend the Pontifical territory. He cannot be held responsible for the conduct of those amongst his subjects who allow themselves to be swayed by the example of other Italians. He had given his orders distinctly. They had been transgressed. On the disturbing question of war with Austria, the *Encyclical* bears the following words :

'They would have us declare war against Austria. We have thought it our duty to protest formally against such a resolution, considering that, notwithstanding our unworthiness, we hold on earth the place of Him who is the Author of peace—the Friend of charity ; and that, faithful to the Divine obligations of our Apostolate, we embrace all countries, all peoples, all nations, in a like sentiment of paternal love. Nor can we refrain from repelling, in the face of all nations, the perfidious assertions of those who desire that the Roman Pontiff should be the chief of the government of a new republic, consisting of all the peoples of Italy.

" Moreover, we earnestly exhort, on this occasion, these same Italian peoples to keep particularly on their guard against these treacherous counsels. We conjure them to remain devotedly attached to their princes, whose affection they have experienced. To act otherwise would be not only to fail in their duty, but also to expose Italy to discord and factions. As regards ourselves, we declare once more that all the thoughts and all the efforts of the Roman Pontiff tend only to increase every day the kingdom of Jesus Christ, which is the Church, and not to extend the limits of the temporal sover-

eignty, with which Divine Providence has endowed the Holy
See, for the dignity and the free exercise of the sublime Apostolate."

No better argument could have been offered in reply to
those parties who clamored so unreasonably for war. Nor
could the Pontiff have vindicated more eloquently the pacific
character of that religion of which he is the Chief and Representative on earth. At the same time, he offered wise and
authoritative counsel to the Italian nationalities. It was too
late. The voice of friendly warning remained unheard amidst
the din of strife and revolution. Need it be added—the cause
of liberty perished for a time, victimized by its own excess.

The Socialist party had succeeded in gaining the populace of
Rome, and they now constituted a power which prevailed in
the city, whatever it might have been in the field. Skil-
fully managed by its leaders, it gave law to the Pontifical
government. The Pope was not, however, powerless. A
merely secular sovereign would have been crushed. He would
have had no other resource than to abdicate. The Holy
Father was not reduced to this extremity. He was still able
to repel the unacceptable measures which the Socialists en-
deavoured to thrust upon him. They and their myrmidons
vociferated for war with Austria. The Pope could still say
there should be no war, and his people did not engage in the
contest. A few among the Roman youth took the field. But,
as effeminate as they were ardent, their courage cooled at the
first sight of a *barbarian* camp. They returned to their
hearths, and there talked magniloquently of the tented fields
which they had traversed, the savage hordes which they had
encountered, and the dangers they had escaped. The party
succeeded, however, in forcing a ministry on the reluctant
Pontiff. Such a thing, when done through the representative
body, however unreasonable, does not so much shock our idea
of constitutional government. Neither can we approve the
conduct of a faction which, whilst it was anything but constitutional, imposed a minister who held its principles, on the

prince who had, of his own accord, become a constitutional monarch. Count Mamiani was one of those whom the clemency of Pius IX. had restored to their country, of all the parties thus favored, he alone refused to become bound in honor to the Holy Father never to abuse the favor, but to remain always a good and faithful subject. He was not without ability; was well informed, cool and resolute, but without any fixed principle in politics. He would as readily have set up a Red Republic as a constitutional monarchy. His political conduct was guided more by events and circumstances than by any well-conceived idea of what is right and fitting. He was one of those Italian Liberals who might be compared to the Necker of the French Revolution, whilst Mazzini and his followers were the ultra-radicals—the Robespierres of Roman politics. The Mamiani ministry necessarily arose out of the popular commotions, and was a protest of the excited masses against the Encyclical of 29th April. Its policy was no secret. In the days of popular turmoil they immediately preceded his nomination. Mamiani had declared distinctly in his harangues to the people that no priest should be appointed to any public office; that although Pius IX. should remain at the head of the government, they ought to obtain from him the revocation of his Encyclical of 29th April, and a declaration of war against Austria; that a new expedition should be speedily organized, and that an official bulletin of the war should be published daily. The warlike and revolutionary pronunciamentos, thus pompously made, could not fail to arouse the enthusiasm of the multitude, whose excitement was already so great. In matters of this nature, however, it is more easy to make fine speeches than to act. The popular Tribune was no sooner elevated to the ministry than he came to experience this difficulty. So it was convenient to forget the grand lessons which he had labored so vehemently to impress upon the people. He still, however, insisted, or appeared to insist, on the Austrian war. It may have been necessary for the new minister, in order to maintain his influence over

the masses, to announce a war policy. Such policy, nevertheless, was chimerical. It was decidedly opposed by the
legitimately-constituted powers of the State—the Sovereign on
the one hand, who, by his name, his character, his virtues, his
office, was still powerful; and on the other, the representative
body. Accordingly, when this body came together in the
beginning of June, there was an end to the government of the
streets. But there arose new difficulties, and these difficulties
the government of the Holy Father diligently studied to overcome. Cardinal Altieri delivered, on the part of the Sovereign Pontiff, an energetic and moving exhortation in support
of unity and concord.

At the same time, he expressed his earnest hope that the
newly-elected deputies would show their good will by concurring
with the ministry in rendering the new adaptation of the constitution compatible with the Pontifical government.

This address, however ineffectual, possessed the merit of
being thoroughly constitutional. The same praise cannot be
awarded to Count Mamiani's inaugural oration. Next day,
which was the 9th of June, he ascended the Tribune, and there
enunciated ideas which belonged more to the ministry in their
individual capacity, than as the representatives of their Sovereign. This was supremely unconstitutional, and could only
be the result of inexperience. What knowledge could those
men have had of a free and national constitution? They
ought, at least, to have been guided by the laws of honesty
and honor. Who will say that they were so, when they gave
out that the opinion which they expressed in favor of war
was also that of the Pontiff? They endeavored thus to extend
the sanction of a venerated name to designs that were subversive of Pontifical rule. Neither inexperience nor ignorance
of constitutions presents any valid excuse, or even palliation of
such a proceeding. No doubt they called it policy. It was
the basest trickery.

In the hands of honest and judicious ministers the new
constitution might have proved successful. So thought many

persons who were well informed and competent to form an
opinion in regard to so difficult a question. It had also
many well-wishers. But for the war agitation, it would, to all
appearance, have had a different fate. According to the exaggerated idea of Italian patriotism which prevailed, all true
Italians were bound to fight for their country. On the Mamiani
ministry devolved the very arduous task of reconciling this
warlike spirit with the pacific character of the Pontificate.
The Pope, like any other sovereign, had a right, no doubt, to
defend himself. But both the theology which guided him
and the traditions of his sovereignty forbade him to wage
war on any people. Such was the difficulty which it fell to
the lot of his ministry to solve. The arguments to which they
had recourse, however well meant, were certainly very puerile.
The Pope, as such, they insisted, might decide for peace, and
condemn the shedding of blood, whilst, as temporal sovereign,
he would authorize his ministers to act as should seem to them
proper, and they would declare for war. This miserable
sophistry only showed the weakness of the government which
employed it. The Pontiff could not be expected to act as if he
were two distinct persons. Nor whilst his ministers waged
war, could he, whose representatives they were, be considered
as neutral. For a few months that this ministry remained in
office, the Pope continued to save his States by resisting the
war-cry in opposition to their wishes. They were constantly
at variance with him on this one great topic. His repugnance
to war they could neither comprehend nor overcome. Popular
demonstrations of the most threatening kind were often made,
but to no purpose.

> Justum et tenacem propositi virum,
> Non civium ardor prava jubentum mente quatit solida.

The Pontiff could not be moved from his firm resolve.
The ministry, however, was shaken. With no better stay than
sophistry and inconsistency, its weakness became apparent,
and, as had been for some time clearly inevitable, it fell.

Before considering further the statesman-like efforts of Pius
IX. in the cause of reform, it may not be out of place to

review briefly the political opinion of the time. Although all men cannot be expected to accept, especially in many important matters, all the ideas of those distinguished writers, Gioberti, Balbo, D'Azeglio, it would be unjust, nevertheless, to deny them the credit of having imparted new vigor, if not its first impulse, to the cause of reform in Italy. They were not, like so many others, rash and inconsiderate. They desired not to hurry on recklessly to the wished-for goal. They thought it was unwise to aspire, all at once, to the greatest degree of liberty that might be attained. The end in view could be best reached, they conceived, by judicious and well-timed measures of reform, and by such institutions as might be developed at a later period, when the Italian people, unaccustomed as yet to a constitutional *regime*, should be capable of a greater degree of freedom. Nothing more wise can be supposed than this view of educating the people for liberty before bestowing on them the precious boon. Their idea of commencing the work of reform by waging war on Austria does not appear to be so commendable. It was not, surely,. the part of prudence, when on the eve of a great and arduous undertaking, to stir up enemies on every side. And this was really what they sought to do by provoking Austrian hostility. The government at Vienna was not inclined to be hostile. It had joined with other powers in recommending reform to the late Pope. And now it would rather have been an ally than an enemy. But the "barbarian" Germans were entirely odious to the Italian people. The power of education ought to have been brought to bear on this same people, if only in order to disabuse their minds of this one noxious prejudice. It had become necessary at length to extend to them the benefits of a political education. And surely the eradication of illiberal ideas would have formed a profitable branch of study.

Pius IX., as has been already shown, was a practical reformer, and he had zealously undertaken the work of reform. Austria was not inclined to throw any impediments in the

way of his patriotic labors. Only on one occasion did that
powerful empire show a disposition to interfere. It was when
Rome and the Sovereign Pontiff were threatened by popular
commotions. Then, even on the representation of the Holy
Father, Austria laid down her arms. With these constitutional reformers, if we except their insane idea of waging a
needless war, very little fault can be found as politicians.
So lately as the early part of the year 1848, their opinions
were generally accepted throughout Italy. They were, at that
time, also the most powerful party. Their numbers, authority
and talent, gave them a decided superiority, whilst the Republicans were still a weak minority. In a few months, to all
appearance, everything was completely changed. Talent,
respectability, authority, and influence, were still on the side
of the constitutional reformers. But, in the meantime, the
Red Republic had gained the command of numbers. How this
came to pass it may be well now to enquire.

In every great community there are many people who have
no fixed principles in politics, and others, perhaps, not less
numerous, who have no political principles at all. Both these
classes of people depend entirely on other men for the sentiments and opinions by which, at any given moment, they
shall be guided. Such people were sufficiently numerous
at Rome and the other cities and provinces of Italy.
Demagogues, therefore, who were not without ability and possessed fluency of speech, found it no very difficult task to
fashion as they had a mind, for these classes of citizens, any
amount of political principles and *programmes*. Those even
who were fairly imbued with constitutional ideas, but whose
minds were not wholly decided, the leaders of the Red Republic
endeavored, and not without success, to gain to their side, by
persuading them to compromise, as regarded certain points,
to modify their opinions on others, change their designations,
enter into coalitions, and adopt such ingenious arrangements
as were proposed to them. Thus, by degrees, and as was only
to be expected in such circumstances, the ultra-radicals suc-

ceeded but too well in causing the most extravagant political notions to prevail among the masses. As fate would have it, the revolution in France of February, 1848, which brought to an end the constitutional monarchy, afforded no slight aid and encouragement to the Red Republic of Italy. The men of this party might have understood, on reflection, to what extreme peril France became exposed, when she preferred brute force to constitutional proceeding, and tore down by violence a system which was, in many respects, good; and which, inasmuch as it was a constitution, could in due time have been extended and improved, receiving, as new wants arose, and wisdom and experience warranted, new developments, new adaptations, and daily increasing excellence. The constitutional element once removed, there was no medium between and safeguard against absolutism; on the one hand, and on the other anarchy, or the reign of violence and terror.

The extremists of Italy, however, beheld only in the too successful action of the Parisian populace a new step towards liberty. It became the duty of the Italian people, they declared, to march onward in the wake of enlightened France, and seize the prize that was at length presented for their acceptance. By such counsellors were the people abused and led astray. The moderate reform party were themselves excited by the enthusiasm which events had inspired, and heeded not the snares which the radical chiefs were laying for them. They were thus caught in the toils of those designing men, whilst they imagined that they were only working out their own idea. They supposed even that they were gaining Mazzini, whilst, in reality, Mazzini was making proselytes of them. Gioberti and his more immediate friends, who certainly were not without their faults, were abandoned by the crowd.

Reverting to what has been said already concerning Mazzini and his political doctrines, there need be no hesitation in pronouncing him the evil genius of modern Italy. In his book, "Italy in its Relations with Liberty and Moral Civilization," which was published in France, where he was an exile, in 1847,

he formally declared that "Young Italy" (the extreme Republicans) was the only party that could exercise any decisive
influence on the destiny of Italy. At the same time, he treated
with supreme contempt the ideas and hopes of the Reform
party. In his mystic republic only was to be found, he
affirmed, *the principle of unity, the ideal formula of actual progress.* This theory was the idol at whose shrine he offered
sacrifice. His followers were also his fellow-worshippers, and
he was their high priest. They were fascinated by his brilliant
utopias. He was no longer a legislator, a politician, a philosopher only. He was a man of inspiration, a prophet, the
Mahomet of a new hegira. His sayings were oracles. His
doctrines were enunciated in sententious and poetical language;
and from his place of exile they were disseminated over the
Italian peninsula. It has been shown already how generously
Pius IX. had recalled from banishment many subjects who had
violated the laws of their country. These men were, at
one time, no doubt, sincerely grateful, and showed how
highly they appreciated the clemency of the Pontiff. It
is not, however, surprising, if, as is usual in such circumstances, they began to consider more the severity which
punished than the goodness which forgave them. Mazzini, among others, dissembled for a time. It may be—
it has even been suggested that he was at first sincere, and
had nobly resolved to sacrifice his favorite ideas to the cause
of Italy. This opinion, however, was destined to be soon dispelled. It was not long till the newspaper *Italia del Popolo*,
revealed the fact that he still held to extreme and revolutionary views. The minds of the people were poisoned by the
ravings of this journal, and filled with mistrust. It became
the instrument by which sects and parties were stirred up to
work the ruin of the country. "*Unita e non unione. Assemblea
del Popolo Italiano e non dieta.*" "*Unity; not union. The
assembly of the Italian people; not a federal diet.*" Such was
the watchword of Mazzini's paper. And now the masses in
the streets, under the guidance of the revolutionary leader,

vociferated, "Live the Constituent Assembly!" with as much wild enthusiasm as they had formerly shouted for Pius IX. and reform. They had no distinct idea as to the meaning of the cry, but held it to be something extreme—a boundless measure of liberty. The populace wanted nothing better; and so they continued to shout, as they believed, for unity and Republican Government. Such a system was, from the very nature and position of the States of Italy, impracticable, and without pressure from without, foreign war—which the Mazzinians so much deprecated—could never have been established. How bring under the yoke of a general popular convention so many diverse peoples? They were all Italian, no doubt, but of different races, different nationalities, and each of them had for ages enjoyed its own national laws, customs, manners, prejudices, predilections, and antipathies. Nor had they common interests. What would be good and suitable in one State might, by no means, be adapted to the requirements of another; might even in some cases prove disastrous. The Grand Dukes had, by their mild and liberal rule, endeared themselves to the Tuscan people. Piedmont and Naples were alike devoted to their respective monarchies. The people of the Papal States, with the exception of the populace of Rome, were loyal to their government. That populace was greatly increased in 1848 by the influx of strangers—men holding Republican opinions, who were diligently culled from foreign nationalities. All but these abnormal masses were attached to the wise and clement rule of their Pontiff Sovereigns. Of late years many things had occurred to confirm their devoted loyalty. Above all, proof had been given that the sacred monarchy itself could, without any diminution of its real power and dignity, adopt such political reforms as were adapted to the wants of the time. All these monarchies, already so moderate and popular, were becoming every day more constitutional. Were they now to be overthrown? The Mazzinian idea aimed at nothing less. And yet, what would it not have cost? So many time-honored rights would never have been given up without a struggle—

without bloodshed, if they were at all to be sacrificed. The torch of civil strife would have blazed from end to end of the Italian peninsula. And the ruin of the ancient monarchies—if, indeed, they had been destined at that time to fall—would probably have been succeeded by more despotic forms of kingly rule.

If, at the time in question, the people of the different States of Italy had acted in concert, uniting their influence, they would have assumed an imposing attitude, and might have obtained not only the forbearance but the aid even of their powerful neighbors in developing such of their institutions as already contained germs of liberty, in extending constitutional rights which had long existed in monarchies that were by no means absolute. In the place of political wisdom, however, a universal mania appeared to prevail. In the confusion of popular demonstrations, and the clamor of party cries, the " still small voice of reason " was unheard. The revolutionary chiefs harangued anew for war, and Italy, listening to their ill-omened counsels, took up arms against its sovereigns ; and so gave the death-blow to its political existence.

The moderate Reform party conceived a plan which, if it had been carried into effect, would have been attended, no doubt, with great and happy results. They proposed to unite all the States of Italy by means of a Federal Parliament. They directed their efforts in the first place to promote union between the rulers and the people, recommending to the former moderation, to the latter a wise forbearance. They hoped thus to postpone the idea of absolute unity, and of the popular convention by which it was designed to establish and maintain it. The federal diet, an excellent idea of which was reduced to writing by the reverend and learned Abbate Rosmini, would have held the place of this assembly. According to this plan of confederation, the Pope, the King of Sardinia, the Grand Duke of Tuscany and the other Princes would have been united in an offensive and defensive league. Based on these principles, and provided that nothing were admitted in its

details which could interfere with the sacred character and
office of the Sovereign Pontiff, the proposed political arrangement would have found favor generally with all who held constitutional views. Eminent authors, at least, have written
concerning it approvingly. M. Laboulaye, in his learned work
on Count Balbo, says:

" It was necessary that the Princes should be induced to
take an interest in the independence which concerned them so
much, by forming a confederation like the *Zolverein*, which has
so powerfully contributed to the union and the greatness of
Germany. A confederation is undoubtedly that organization
which is most suited to the character and the history of Italy,
and it is also the best means, of reviving Italian nationality
and of checking Austria."

Need it be added, that when there should have been question of restraining Austria, there would have been at hand an
influence which Austria respected, and to which that mighty
empire and its disciplined armies would have yielded more readily
than to all Italy in arms. Without a confederation, or an
arrangement equally good, there could be no better lot for Italy
than civil war and national ruin.

Events, meanwhile, were hastening on with alarming rapidity. The Red Republic persisted in maintaining its idea.
The danger with which the country was threatened from without did not, in the least, moderate its efforts, and they were
attended by the only results which they were calculated to
produce. Italy remained divided. The sword of Charles
Albert could not cope alone with the formidable arms of Austria.
A united people might have stayed the tide of battle. The
imposing spectacle of their union might even have influenced
the German Cabinet, and the legions of Radetsky might never
have presumed to cross the Mincio. But it was fated to be
otherwise. Excess followed on excess, and the inevitable consequence was speedy chastisement. " *Perish Italy rather than
our idea*," was the watch-cry of the Socialist leaders. And as
if fate had combined with their phrenzy to destroy a people,

Italy was crushed by the invader. What cared they? What imported it to them that their country was brought low, and its Princes humbled in the field of Novara? The downfall of the Sardinian monarch, which at the same time was the defeat of Italy, was to them a victory. One more impediment to their designs was removed. " *The war of Kings*," said Mazzini, "*is at an end; that of the people commences.*" And he declared himself a soldier. But Garibaldi did not long command him. His warlike enthusiasm was soon exhausted. *The war of the people* also ended disastrously; and the revolutionary chief, tired of the sword, resumed his pen and renewed his attacks on the moderate Reformers, who alone had fought, like brave men, in the Austrian war. The strife of words was more congenial to the revolutionist; and he set about editing a new publication. In this journal he raged against the Reformers. They were a set of traitors, ante-chamber Machiavels, who had muzzled the popular lion for the benefit of kings and aristocracies.

These *Machiavels* were such men as Count Balbo, who had given his five sons to the war of independence; Signor D'Azeglio, who had been in the campaign with Durando, and who had a leg broken by a ball at Vicenza, whilst defending Monte Benico with two thousand men against twelve thousand Austrians. D'Azeglio, still smarting from his wounds, as well as from the insults of these reckless politicians, replied in a pamphlet, which appeared under the title of "Fears and Hopes." He took no pains to spare those club soldiers, those tavern heroes and intriguers, who could wage war so cleverly against the men who had stood under the enemy's guns. "For my part," he wrote, "I do not fear your republic, but despotism. Your agitation will end with the Croats." And so it fell out. The prediction was but too speedily and too completely realized. A French author, M. Mignet, comments on this subject at some length, and with remarkable eloquence:

"A party as extreme in its desires as in its doctrines, and which believes that it is possessed of nothing so long as it does not possess everything, and which, when it has everything, knows not how to make anything of it, imagined the establishing of a republic in a country which is scarcely capable of attaining to representative monarchy, and where the only thing to be thought of, as yet, was territorial independence. This party divided the thoughts, weakened the efforts of the country, and caused mutual mistrust to arise between those governments and peoples which were reconciled under constitutional liberty, and had an understanding against the common enemy. They thus compromised the deliverance of the land. The King of Naples, threatened by an insurrection in his capital, retained his troops that were on the point of marching to the theatre of war ; the Pope ceased to give encouragement ; the King of Piedmont, already in full march, hesitated ; and Italy, agitated, without being free, became once more powerless, because she was disunited, and beheld the Austrians reappear as conquerors, and re-establish themselves anew as masters, in the recovered plains of Lombardy."

These eloquent words confirm the view so generally entertained, that the Red Republicans were all along the cause of Italy's disasters. In consequence of the national weakness which their baneful operations produced, Radetski was enabled to reconquer Upper Italy, whilst they themselves directed their steps towards Rome, spreading terror as they approached, even as if they had been an army of Goths and Vandals. Swelling by their presence the numbers of men who held the same opinions, who, like them, were dissatisfied, and whom nothing could satisfy, they occasioned an extraordinary agitation of the people, caused fearful disquietude, and excited inordinate hopes. They imbued the masses with their subversive principles, and there was an end to all transaction with the Papal government. They had already done all that lay in their power in order to destroy monarchy in Piedmont. They now brought into play every scheme that could be devised, in order to advance the sinister work of dispossessing the Holy Father. They succeeded in gaining many Reformers, who, too easily, allowed themselves to become their dupes.

At first, as has been shown, the popular demonstrations in honor of Pius IX. were honestly expressive of gratitude to the beneficent Pontiff. The Socialists now succeeded in gaining possession of this great influence, and they employed it, certainly, with consummate ability. The masses, when once under the spell of agitation, are at the disposal of the boldest demagogues. The Reformers who had allowed themselves to be ensnared, continued to sing their patriotic hymns, the Roman *Marseillaises*, without heeding that Socialist radicalism was imperceptibly taking the crown of the causeway, and that the popular demonstrations had undergone a complete change. At an earlier date "Young Italy" had only used them as a threat. They were now an arm in its hands. And so it governed in the streets, making a tribune of every milestone.

There was only wanting to them at this moment a common centre or general headquarters of insurrection, from which should go forth the word of command, the signal for every rising of the people. This was found in the celebrated *Roman Circle*. This circle was a kind of convention without commission—a travelling cohort of two or three hundred agitators, who carried from town to town the dread and dismal flag of the Red Republic. This mob-power had, in opposition to the wishes of the Holy Father, brought into office the Mamiani ministry. This weak and irresolute minister broke the ranks of his own party, and passed over to "*Young Italy*." This party now dictated to him on all occasions. They urged on him with special earnestness war with Austria, knowing full well that the Pope would never agree to it, and so by his refusal would decline in popularity.

The constitution was now in abeyance, the minister being at the orders of a party out of doors, and no longer the organ of the Sovereign and the representative body. The Pontifical authority, although still venerated by many, was no longer obeyed. It was only a name.

The republic reigned, and only waited for the moment, too surely to come at last, when it should be openly recognized. In such circumstances the Mamiani ministry rapidly lost ground. Now in its death agony, and impotent for good, it persisted, with a degree of perverseness which nothing could moderate, in reiterating its declarations of war against Austria. This only added to the confusion which prevailed. The ministers and their more ardent adherents were ready, as became patriots and heroes, to fight for their country. Nevertheless, with all this boasting, they made no haste to be enrolled. Whilst these men were indulging in such idle and vain-glorious talk, the few who had volunteered and taken the field, returned from Vicenza, which, during two days, had been bravely but fruitlessly defended. The forum warriors had only set out in time to meet their defeated and wounded fellow-countrymen, and give them the honors of an ovation on their return to the city. The war agitation was evidently nothing else than a weapon of offence against the Holy See. In its results it was most unprofitable, every day bringing news of fresh disasters. Circumstances now rendered the war-cry more inopportune than ever. Charles Albert, King of Sardinia, had been driven from the Mincio to the Oglio, thence to the Adda, thence to Milan. He was now recrossing the Piedmontese frontier, vanquished, despairing and heart-broken. Piedmont, nevertheless, in the silence of her humiliation, set about preparing for a final effort.

The various ministers whom Pius IX. had called to his counsels were all alike unsuccessful. Circumstances of greater difficulty than ever had now arisen, and not without a sad foreboding of the greater evils that were yet in store, the Holy Father had recourse to the well-known statesmanship of Count Rossi, who had formerly been French Ambassador to the Holy See.

M. Mignet, the able biographer of this eminent statesman, gives a distinct and interesting account of the difficulties with which, as Chief of the Pope's Council of State, he was called to contend:

"M. Rossi at first hesitated. He knew what formidable problems there were to solve. To conduct, according to consti-

tutional principles, a government that had been heretofore
absolute; to administer by the hands of laymen the affairs of
a country that had been hitherto subject to Ecclesiastics; to
unite in an Italian league a state that had been almost always
opposed to a political union of the Peninsula; in a word, to
establish all at the same time, a Constitutional Government, a
Civil Administration, a National Federation, were not the only
difficulties that he would have to overcome. The minister of
a Prince, whose confidence others would dispute with him, a
stranger in a country, where he would exercise public authority,
he would be liable to be left without support notwithstanding
his devotedness, and without approbation notwithstanding his
services; to be attacked as a revolutionist by the blind advo-
cates of abuses, and disavowed as an enemy of liberty by the
impassioned partisans of chimeras. He continued to decline
for a considerable time. The conditions which he at first proposed to the Sovereign Pontiff not having been accepted, M.
Rossi thought that he had escaped the lot that was in store for
him. But the Pope, after having essayed in vain a new
ministry, pressed him more urgently, in the month of September, 1848, to come to his aid, offering him at the same time
his full confidence and unlimited authority. M. Rossi accepted."

At the time of his accession to office Count Rossi was sixty
years of age. He was no stranger to politics. His life, indeed,
had been spent in the midst of political turmoil. As may be
supposed, he suffered much in the course of his checkered
career. He had, at the same time, learned much at the stern
school of experience. He had been several times an exile, and
had thus become the citizen of more than one country. In
1815 he was banished from the Peninsula, on account of 'the
part which he had borne in the cause of Italian liberty; and
having resided at Geneva and Paris, he had made for himself,
in those cities, a brilliant reputation. He wrote on the
important subjects of political economy and jurisprudence,
displaying intimate knowledge of these sciences, great intel-

lectual power and superior penetration. Although relying on principles and theory, he did not ignore facts, nor refuse to accommodate the lofty forms of science to practical requirements. He was versed in the knowledge of mankind, and was far from being one of those, who, adhering rigidly to theories, would force nature itself to yield to their opinion. At a time when the affairs of Italy were in a most dangerous crisis, and anarchy actually prevailed at Rome, he was the ablest counsellor and auxiliary that Pius IX. could have placed at the head of his ministry. Possessing many rare endowments, Count Rossi was not gifted with those outward graces which tend so much to win favor for public men. His manner was such that he appeared cold and reserved; and his keen, searching lynx-like eye, was calculated to cause embarrassment. Familiarity with the objects of science and habits of diplomacy had imparted to him a gravity of demeanor which was easily mistaken for superciliousness and disdain. Withal he cared not to please, preferring to exercise influence by strength of will and the authority of superior intellect, rather than by attractive and amiable qualities and the charm of the affections. He had the mind of a statesman, but owned not that winning exterior which gains the crowd and disarms hostility. None but his own family knew how good he really was, and how tender-minded, so completely was all this excellence concealed by his cold and repulsive manner.

The new minister was resolved, above all, to preserve the sovereignty of the Holy See. "The Papacy," he wrote at the time, "is the last living glory of Italy." His conduct was in perfect harmony with his language. He applied with no less ardour than ability to the work that lay before him. In less than two months he accomplished more than can be well conceived, and further measures were in course of preparation. Those matters to which he first devoted his chief attention were the Interior Government of Rome, the state of the Pontifical finances and the territorial independence of Italy. He found the public treasury in imminent danger of bankruptcy, and he

E

saved it by obtaining three millions of *ccus* from the Roman clergy. Through this munificent donation the minister was relieved from all disquietude as regarded finance, and so was enabled to direct his energies to the more difficult task of adapting the administration to the new institutions. The constitution was, indeed, legally established. The object now to be aimed at was to bring its wise provisions into practical operation; in other words, to create a constitutional Pontificate.

With a view to this desirable end, M. Rossi prepared such legislative measures as were calculated nicely to determine the sphere of action that should be proper to each of the powers. By such means only could the disorderly force of popular movements be controlled and restrained within fixed limits. The Civil Government of the Roman States required to be entirely reorganized. To this task also the minister diligently applied, impressed with the conviction that good laws are at once the strongest bulwark of liberty, and the most efficient check to arbitrary power. Count Rossi was by birth an Italian. He was so in feeling also, and was naturally led to consider how he should best avail himself in his political arrangements, of the sound and enlightened doctrines of Gioberti and Rosmini. With a view to this end he commenced negotiations at Turin, Naples and Florence, for a confederation of the Italian States. It was his policy that all these States should unite under a general government, whilst each State retained the forms, laws and institutions to which it had been accustomed. Certain relations between them, suitable to the time of peace, should be established, as well as such regulations as would facilitate their common action in case of war. Pius IX. saw the wisdom of this great design, and favored its realization. It redounds to his glory, as a ruler of mankind, that he decided for this salutary measure from which, if it had been carried into effect, might have resulted, in time, the complete emancipation and regeneration of Italy. Time, however, was not granted, and as we shall presently see, anarchy resumed its dismal reign.

Anterior to the accession of Count Rossi's Ministry, the Legislative Chambers had only wasted their time in unprofitable debates. It was appointed that they should meet on the 15th of December, 1848, and the minister prepared a bold and energetic, but conciliatory address. The representatives of the people, it was designed, should now hear no longer the ambiguous and factious harangues of a weak-minded demagogue, but the true and candid utterances of a Constitutional Government. Rossi showed himself on this occasion, to which melancholy circumstances have added extraordinary solemnity, a grave and resolute minister, determined to appear as the counsellor of his Sovereign and the exponent of his views, not as the slave of the people and the organ of their blind passions. This discourse was not destined to be delivered. It commenced as follows :

" Scarcely had his Holiness ascended the Pontifical throne when the Catholic world was filled with admiration at his clemency as a Pontiff and his wisdom as a temporal Sovereign. * The most important facts have shown to mankind the fallacy of the groundless predictions of that pretended philosophy' which had declared the Papacy to be, from the nature of its constitutive principle, the enemy of constitutional liberty. In the course of a few months, the Holy Father, of his own accord, and without aid, accomplished a work which would have sufficed for the glory of a long reign. History, impartially sincere, will repeat—and not without good reason —as it records the acts of this Pontificate, that the Church, immovable on her Divine foundations, and inflexible in the sanctity of her dogmas, always intelligently considers and encourages with admirable prudence, such changes as are suitable in the things of the world."

The oration was, throughout, a bold and luminous exposition of the ideas and policy which M. Rossi was charged to carry into effect. It was, at the same time, an earnest appeal to the representative body in order to obtain the aid, which was so necessary, of their loyal concurrence, and the minister held himself bound in honor to abide strictly by the provisions of the constitution. The constitution, meanwhile, was in presence of very determined enemies. They had sworn its overthrow. They met, however, with a formidable opponent in the ministry, which was resolved to sustain the new order of things, and prepared to defeat all the schemes of the radical faction. The constitution itself was also a serious impediment to their contrivances. Both constitution and ministry accordingly became the objects of violent attacks at street meetings and in the revolutionary journals. The minister was undaunted. "To reach the Holy Father," said he, "they must pass by my lifeless body." This noble determination only rendered him more odious to the revolutionists. The leaders of the Red Republic party, on their return from a scientific Congress at Turin, where the name of science was only used as a cloak the better to conceal their plots, decreed that Rossi should be put to death. Mazzini, in a letter which was published, declared that his assassination was indispensable. In one of the clubs of Rome the Socialists selected by lot the assassins who should bear a hand in the murder of the minister. The wretched man who was appointed to be the principal actor in the deed of blood actually practised on a dead body in one of the hospitals. The day on which Parliament was summoned to meet, 15th November, was to see the full purpose of the faction carried into effect. As almost always occurs in such cases, warnings reached the ears of the intended victim. Some of the conspirators, struck with remorse, had so far revealed the plot. Others boasted cynically that they would soon be rid of the oppressor. The Duchess de Rignano conjured the minister to remain at home. Equally solemn and urgent words of warning came from other quarters, and were alike unheeded. If, indeed, he believed that there was a plot, he relied on disarming the hatred of the conspirators by his courageous bearing, and proceeded from his house to the Quirinal Palace. When there he addressed comforting words to the Pope, who was in a a state of great anxiety. Pius IX., in bestowing a parting benediction, earnestly recommended that he should keep on his guard.

At the door of the Pope's apartments he met an aged priest, who beseeched him to remain. "If you proceed," said he, "you will be murdered." M. Rossi paused a moment and replied: "The cause of the Pope is the cause of God."

A guard of carabiniers, treacherously disobeying the orders which had been given them, were absent from the approach to the house where parliament assembled. The minister had reached the stairs, and was ascending when a group of conspirators came around him. At first they insulted him. Then one of the assassins struck him on the shoulder. As he turned indignantly towards this assassin, his neck was exposed to the poniard of another, who, availing himself of the opportune moment, dealt the fatal blow. The minister fell, bedewing with his blood the steps at the very threshold of the legislative chamber. As the details of the murder were related to the members, they remained ominously silent. Not one of them uttered a word in condemnation of this monstrous crime. They proceeded at once to the business of the day. Although in the open space at the foot of the stairs which led to the assembly hall the civic guard was stationed in arms, nobody arrested, or showed the slightest inclination to arrest, the murderer. On the contrary, the criminal was conducted, not only unpunished but in triumph, through the streets of the city by his accomplices. A new hymn was sung —"Blessed be the hand that slew Rossi." The dagger of the assassin was enwreathed with flowers and exposed for public veneration in the *cafe* of the Fine Arts. The populace, in the excess of their phrenzy, insulted the widow of the murdered minister; and, by an extravagance of irony, they required that she should illuminate her house. The newspapers expressed approval of the crime, as it was, they pretended, the necessary manifestation of the general sentiment. The whole people, by their silence, although not by actual participation in such demon-like rejoicings, declared themselves accomplices in the deed of blood.

Together with the noble Rossi perished, for the time, the cause of Rome, the cause of Italy. What might not have been

the gain to both, if the devoted minister had been allowed to
fulfil his appointed mission? Constitutional government
would have been established on a solid and permanent basis;
the wild agitation of the streets would have been brought to an
end, and the excited passions of the revolution, beholding the
sound, regular and beneficial working of free political institutions, would have been awed into composure. But, sad reflection! by an act which history will never cease to stigmatize,
the only man who, by the authority of his reputation, abilities
and experience, was equal to the stupendous labor of building
up on sure foundations the social fabric was struck down, and
the nations of Europe, which had looked on hitherto in sympathy, recoiled with horror. Liberal men throughout the
civilized world had long been deeply interested in the state of
Italy. Such was their belief in the bright future, which they
were confident awaited her, that they could pardon the ill-
controlled agitation of her children, and even their greatest
excesses, when they first began to enjoy, before they knew how
to use it, the unwonted boon of liberty. With crime and the
evils which followed in its train they had no sympathy. A
system which relied on assassination could not prosper. Inaugurated by violence, it could exist only by violence. The
better feelings of mankind were shocked. The die was cast,
and Rome was doomed. The fated city had rejoiced in the
exercise of unhallowed force, and through that legitimate force
which, in due time, Divine Providence allowed to be brought
against her, she met her punishment.

With the death of Rossi ended all hope of liberty.

The conspirators were resolved that nothing should be
allowed to delay the benefits which they anticipated from their
crime. All sense of propriety was not yet extinguished in the
representative body. There was question of sending a deputation to the Pope, in order to convey to him the condolence of
the Chamber, and express their regret for the sad event.
This step, which good sense and proper feeling so urgently
demanded, was opposed, and only too successfully, by Charles
Bonaparte, Prince of Canino.

The revolutionists now resolved themselves into a kind of permanent club. This club set about making a great demonstration, and required that both the civic guard and the army should join them. When all was ready for this purpose, a mob which had for some time been in course of organization marched to the Quirinal Palace, where the Pope resided, and pointed cannon against the gates. They also caused muskets to be discharged from the neighboring houses. Monsignore Palma fell, mortally wounded, and expired* at the feet of the Holy Father. They next set fire to one of the gates. But the Swiss Guards succeeded in extinguishing the flames. The rebels now threatened to put to death all the inmates of the palace, with the exception of Pius IX. himself, unless he consented to their unreasonable demands. Even he would not have been spared, as was but too well shown by the balls which fell in his apartments. Until this moment the Holy Father had resolutely refused to accept a ministry, to press which upon him was an insult. Now, but only in order to save the lives of the people around him, he submitted to this indignity. Mamiani, with his former programme, supported by the constituent assembly, which consisted of the representatives of all Italy, together with Dr. Sterbini, Garetti, and four other persons equally unacceptable, constituted this Socialist ministry.

They desired also to include in the sinister list the celebrated Abbate Rosmini. But this gifted and eminent divine refused to take part with them, or lend any countenance to

*In 1855 the Bonaparte family were without a name in that Europe where they had possessed so many thrones. One man had compassion on them, and acted generously. Pius VIII. welcomed them to his States. A member of this family, Lucien Bonaparte, Napoleon's brother, having always shown great faithfulness to the Holy See, Pius VIII. conferred upon him the title of a Roman Prince and the principality of Canino. Lucien's son has not been gifted to walk in the footsteps of his honorable father. Balleydier, in his history of the Roman revolution, thus portrays him: "Versed in dissimulation, Charles Bonaparte had, under the preceding Pontificate, acted two very opposite characters. In the morning attending in the ante-chambers of the Cardinals, in the evening at the Conciliabula of the secret Societies, he labored to secure, by a double game, the chances of the present and the probabilities of the future. He had often been seen going piously to the Vatican even, to lay at the feet of Gregory XVI. homage which his heart belied." No doubt, in 1847 and 1848, he thought himself an abler man than his father, as he marched, poignard in hand, at the head of the malcontents of Rome.

their proceedings.   On the 17th November several members of
the representative chamber proposed that a deputation should
be sent to Pius IX., in order to express to him their devotedness and gratitude.   They were not wholly lost to all sense of
propriety.   But the Prince de Canino, true to his antecedents,
succeeded in preventing so laudable a purpose from being
carried into effect.   He declared that such a step would be
imprudent, and that they might have cause to repent it.
" Citizen Bonaparte," such was the appellation he gloried in,
further said that the Italian people were undeniably the masters
now, and that they well understood how to humble all parliaments, ministers and thrones that should oppose their energetic impulses.

The Pope aban-
doned by his people.   Meanwhile the Pope, in such a fearful
crisis, was abandoned by all save a few friends, the officials of
his Palace, his faithful Swiss Guards and the foreign ambassadors.   Among those who remained with him were six Noble
Guards, and the Cardinals Soglia and Antonelli.   This was
all the court and army that was left to the great Pontiff, who
had been so deservedly the idol of his people and the hope of
mankind.   In so desperate a condition he never lost confidence.
Throughout all the trying circumstances he was self-possessed
and serene.   Nothing pained him so much as the ingratitude
of his people.   The new ministry of subversion had extorted
from the Pope his forced and reluctant consent to their forma-

The Pope protests   tion.   He deemed it his duty to protest,
against the Socialist
ministry and its acts.   which he did in the most solemn manner,
against them and all their acts, before all the Christian European nations, as represented by their ambassadors.

These ambassadors and diplomatists were Martizez Della
Rosa, the ambassador of Spain, with the Secretary of the
Embassy, M. Arnao ; the Duke d'Harcourt, ambassador of
France ; the Count de Spaur, ambassador of Bavaria ; the
Baron Venda Cruz, ambassador of Portugal, with the Com-
mandant Huston; the Count Boutenieff, who represented at that
time the Emperor of Russia and King of Poland ; Figuereido,

ambassador of Brazil; Liedekerke of Holland, and several other diplomatists, of whom not one was an Italian. There was at Rome also on the occasion, although not in the apartments of the Pope, a British statesman, who was not an ambassador, inasmuch as, whatever may have been his business at Rome, he had no recognized mission, if any mission at all, to the Sovereign of Rome. He was rather officious than official, and whether he had commission or not, he held, as is well known, serious communications with the enemies of the Pope. Lord Minto was enthusiastically received by the secret societies of Rome. The people, forgetting at the time the way to the Quirinal, went to serenade him. Lord Minto frequented " the popular circle " (a band of three hundred chosen agitators, whose office it was to carry the torch of discord into all the cities of the Papal States and of Italy) and the offices of the Socialist newspaper. He went so far as to receive courteously Cicervacchio, and made verses for his son Cicervacchietto.

The Earl of Minto was not, however, a faithful exponent of the opinions of British statesmen. Few of them, fortunately, held the subversive doctrines that were countenanced by his lordship when representing at Rome the least respectable portion of the Whig party.

The multitude, intoxicated with their delusive success, and the desperate men who led them, were still celebrating their ill-gained victory, the frequent discharge of fire-arms and the impassioned vociferations of the crowd were yet reverberating through the venerable edifices of Rome, when the Holy Father addressed the following words, giving proof of the deepest emotion whilst he spoke, to the ambassadors who remained with him :

" Gentlemen, I am a prisoner here. Now that I am deprived of all support and of all power, my whole conduct will have only one aim—to prevent any, even one drop of fraternal blood from being uselessly shed in my cause. I yield everything to this principle ; but at the same time I am anxious that you, gentlemen, should know, that all Europe should be made aware, that I take no part, even nominally, in this government, and that I am resolved to remain an absolute stranger to it. I have forbidden them to abuse my name; I have ordered that recourse should not be had even to the ordinary formulas."

The representatives of the European Powers received respectfully, and with feelings which found expression in tears, the protestation of Pius IX., who was now a prisoner in his own mansion, and a hostage of the revolutionary faction.

Pius IX. was in imminent danger. A prisoner, and surrounded by implacable enemies, he had no power to protect his own life or that of any faithful citizens. Many who were devoted to his cause had been obliged to leave the city. The Cardinals, indeed, were all true to their illustrious Chief. But several were driven by threats of assassination to go into exile. The children of Saint Ignatius withdrew, at the request of the Holy Father, in order to escape the wrath of the excited multitude. The Pope himself knew not whither to direct his steps.

Unsettled state of the European nations. The revolution was everywhere. It had not yet conquered, but it disturbed all Europe. The representatives of the Powers remained devotedly with the Pope. But the countries which would have sustained them were distracted by political commotions. The King of Naples was threatened on all hands by revolution. Lombardy and Venice were in a state of insurrection. Piedmont was making war on Austria, and all Hungary was in rebellion. The Emperor Ferdinand was compelled twice over by civil commotion to abandon his capital. Unable to face the revolutionary tide, he handed over his tottering throne to a youth of eighteen years. The King of Prussia and other German Sovereigns, who hoped at first to direct the revolutionary movement as to derive from it new strength, were obliged either to fly before it or to struggle against it in the streets. France, who commenced the disturbance which was now so general, was compelled to fight for her existence against her own children. Her chief city, Paris, had become a battle-field, where wicked men and equally wicked women slew the soldiers of the country with poisoned balls. A greater number of the best officers of France fell in a single fight against Parisian anarchy than during the whole time of the war with the wild Bedouins of Africa.

Pius IX. retires to Gaeta. At Rome the revolutionary faction was gaining strength, and the position of the Pope was becoming every day more perilous. It was the opinion of his most devoted friends that he should leave the city. But to what country should he repair? All Europe was agitated by revolutionary troubles. The Holy Father was still undecided, when he received from the Bishop of Valence a letter of wise counsel, together with a precious gift—the Pyx which the venerable Pius VI. had borne on his person when an exile and the captive of an earlier revolution. Pius IX., on receiving a present. which was so suggestive, resolved to remain no longer in the power of his enemies. With the assistance of the Duke d'Harcourt, ambassador of France, and the Bavarian Ambassador, Count de Spaur, he left the Quirinal Palace and the city of Rome. He was safely conducted by the latter personage to Albano, and thence in this ambassador's carriage to Gaeta, in the kingdom of Naples. As soon as his arrival there was intimated to King Ferdinand, who was not yet deprived of his royal power, this monarch, attended by a brilliant suite, embarked for Gaeta, in order to welcome the Holy Father and assure him of protection. During seventeen months that Pius IX. resided as a voluntary exile in the kingdom of Naples, Ferdinand ceased not to afford all the comfort in his power to the Sovereign Pontiff. His conduct towards him in every respect was beyond all praise. As a fellow-man, he consoled him in his sorrows; as a prince, he entertained him with truly royal magnificence, sparing nothing that was calculated to lessen, even to do away with the pain and tedium of exile, whilst, as a faithful Christian, he fulfilled every filial duty towards the Vicar of Christ, expiating, as far as was possible, the crimes committed against him by so many ruthless enemies.

The revolution of another country had for chiefs such men as Robespierre. That of Rome and Italy gloried in Mazzini, who ordered the assassination of Count Rossi. There was at Rome another revolutionary leader, the Advocate Armellini, who pronounced the downfall of the Pope from his temporal sovereignty. This consistorial advocate had, six times over, solemnly sworn fidelity to the Pontiff. He had even composed in honor of the Papacy a sonnet, in which are read these remarkable words: "I spoke with Time, and asked it what had become of so many empires, of those kingdoms of Argos and Thebes and Sidon, and so many others which had preceded or followed them. For only answer, Time strewed its passage with shreds of purple and kingly mantles, fragments of armor, wrecks of crowns, and cast at my feet thousands of broken sceptres. I then enquired what would become of the thrones of to-day. What the first became, was the reply—and Time waved the direful scythe which levels all things under its merciless strokes—these also will be. I asked if a like destiny was in store for the Throne of Peter. Time was silent; Eternity alone could reply."

Not long after the departure of the Holy Father, this traitor, Armellini, gave a banquet to the principal chiefs of the revolution. His wife, who had often charged him with the violation of his oath, remained on this occasion in her apartment, lest she should be contaminated by any, even an apparent association with, such men as Sterbini, Mamiani, Galetti and others.

The guests enquired the cause of her absence, when suddenly the door opened, and Madam Armellini, pale, animated, in a threatening attitude, and with a roll of paper in her hand, exclaimed: "You are all accursed! Fear the judgments of God, you, who in contempt of your oaths, although unable to slay, have banished his minister. Dread the Divine anger. Pius IX., from his place of exile, appeals to God against you. Listen to his words." She unrolled slowly, as she spoke, the paper which she held in her hand, and read in a firm voice, emphasising every word, the decree of the Holy Father, which contained a threat of excommunication. This reading came like a lightning stroke on the startled guests. Madam Armellini, after a moment's silence, resumed: "Sirs, have you understood? The avenging hand which none can escape is suspended over your heads, ready to strike. But there is still time. The voice of God has not yet, through that of his Vicar, fulminated the terrible sentence. For the sake of your happiness in this world and your salvation in the next, throw yourselves on his mercy. The cup of your iniquities is filling fast. Dash it from you before it overflow." Having thus spoken, this courageous woman, whose just indignation was at its height, approached her husband and threw down before him, on the table, the decree of the Holy Father. She then withdrew.

Sentiments and declarations of the Revolutionists. About two months and a half after the assassination of the Pope's minister, Count Rossi, the leading conspirators caused it to be decreed, in their revolutionary assembly, that the Papacy was fallen, *de facto et de jure*, from the government of the Roman States. They made a fashion of providing, at the same time, that the Pontiff should have all necessary guarantees for his independence in the exercise of his spiritual office. Above all, they forgot not to declare that the form of government should be purely democratic, and assume the glorious name of *Roman Republic*. All this was very little in harmony with the sentiments which were expressed at the commencement of the popular movements. With regard to these sentiments, which were so loudly and apparently also so sincerely proclaimed, new light was dispensed. Mazzini arrived at Rome as a deputy to the Revolutionary Convention. He had no sooner taken his place there than he declared that the reiterated *vivats* in honor of the reforming Pope were lies, and were had recourse to in order to conceal designs which it was not yet time to reveal. Is there not reason to believe that the new watchword, "Live

the Roman people!" was equally sincere? It is well known
that they never would admit a fair representation of the people.
And had they not declared that they are incapable of governing
themselves, and must be ruled with a rod of iron?

What the world
thought of the pro-
ceedings at Rome.

Public opinion at the same time gave the
lie to their unwarrantable pretensions. The
revolutionary chiefs gave out in an official proclamation, "that
a republic had arisen at Rome on the ruins of the Papal
Throne, which the unanimous voice of Europe, the malediction
of all civilized people and the spirit of the Gospel, had levelled
in the dust." Not only the nations of Europe, but also the
whole civilized world and people, the most remote, who scarcely
yet enjoyed the blessings of civilization, made haste to deny
an assertion which was as false as it was audacious. All the
nations of Christendom were deeply moved when they heard of
the outrages which the Roman populace had heaped upon the
common Father of the faithful. Compassion was universally
expressed, together with professions of duty and obedience,
whilst there was only indignation at the base conduct of the
faction which persecuted him. There was scarcely a Sovereign
Prince in Europe who did not send to Pius IX. most affectionate
letters, expressive of reverence and devotedness, whilst they
promised assistance and defence. The four Catholic Powers,
and not without the consent of the other State., united in
order to drive the rebels from Rome and the Roman States,
and restore to the Pontiff his temporality. In the representative assemblies of France and Spain, the most eloquent orators
upheld the rights of the Holy See, the utility and necessity of
the complete independence of the Roman Pontiff, both for the
government of his States and the exercise of his spiritual
power. At the same time numerous associations were formed
under the auspices of the civil and ecclesiastical authorities,
for the purpose of collecting offerings in aid of the Sovereign
Pontiff, impoverished as he was by the privation of his
revenues. These associations extended not only throughout
Europe, but were established also in North and South America,

India, China and the Philippine Islands. The poorest even, like the widow of the Gospel, insisted on contributing their mite.

Many touching instances are quoted. Some young persons, who were only humble artisans, managed by great economy to save some thirty-five livres, and sent them, accompanied with a very feeling address, to the association of their locality. "If, at this moment," they said, "we were near the Holy Father, we would say to him, whilst reverently kneeling at his feet: Most Holy Father, this is the happiest of our days. We are a society of young persons who consider it our greatest happiness to give proof of our veneration for your Holiness. We claim to be your most affectionate children; and notwithstanding the efforts of ill-disposed persons to separate us from Catholic unity, we declare that we recognize in your Holiness the successor of St. Peter and the Vicar of Jesus Christ. We are prepared to sacrifice all that we possess, and even our life, in order to prove ourselves worthy children of so good a Father." The testimony of youth and innocence is precious in the sight of heaven. Hence, allusion is made to this case in preference to so many others. *Ex ore infantium et lactantium perfecisti laudem.* On occasion of receiving such genuine marks of filial devotedness Pius IX. was often moved to tears.

The revival of the offering of "Peter's Pence" recalls to mind the piety of the early ages. This practice was in vigor when the world had scarcely yet begun to believe. It is not a little remarkable that it has been renewed in an age when so many have fallen from belief. The more the Church was persecuted in the early days the more were her ministers held in honor. Such, one is compelled to say, is her destiny in all ages. Pius IX., when an exile at Gaeta, was the object of the most respectful and devoted attentions of all classes of Christians in every land. Bishops, ecclesiastical communities, religious congregations, all orders of Christian people, vied with one another in their zeal to do him honor. As many as six, eight, eleven thousand signatures were often appended to the

same dutiful address.   The memory of such faith and devotedness can never perish.   A selection of letters and addresses to
the Holy Father was published at Naples in two large quarto
volumes, under the title : *The Catholic world to Pius IX.,
Sovereign Pontiff, an exile at Gaeta from 1848 to 1850.*

The Catholic Pow-   When Peter himself was in prison the
ers resolve to rein-
state the Pope.   whole Church was moved, and prayed for
his release.   It speedily followed.   Prayer, no less earnest, was
made in behalf of his successor.   With what success a few
words will show.   The deliverers were the Princes and people
of Catholic Europe.   If there was still some delay it was only
that for which diplomacy is proverbial.   Austria, that had
more than once obeyed the voice of the Holy Father, in withdrawing her troops from the Roman States, and against which
he had so often refused to allow war to be declared, was the
first now to propose that measures should be adopted for his
restoration.   In a note addressed by this State to the other
Powers we find the following words : "The Catholic world is
entitled to require for the visible Chief of the Church the plenitude of liberty which is essential for the government of Catholic
society, and the restoration of that ancient monarchy which
has subjects in every part of the world.   The Catholic nations
will never allow the head of their Church to be robbed of his
independence and reduced to be the subject of a foreign Prince.
They will not suffer him to be degraded by a faction which,
under the cloak of his venerable name, is endeavoring to undermine and destroy his power.   In order that the Bishop of
Rome, who is at the same time the Sovereign Pastor of the
Church, may be able to exercise the duties of his exalted office,
it is necessary that he should be also Sovereign of Rome."

Spain came next.   On the 21st December, 1848, the
Spanish ministry addressed to the other Catholic nations the
following circular letter : "The government of her Majesty
has decided on doing whatever shall be necessary in order to
reinstate the Holy Father in a state of independence and
dignity, which will admit of his discharging the duties of his

sacred office. With a view to this end the government of
Spain, having been apprised of the Pope's flight, addressed the
French Government, which declared itself prepared to sustain
the liberty of the Pontiff. These negotiations, nevertheless,
may be considered as insufficient when we glance at the turn
which affairs have taken at Rome. There is no question any
longer of protecting the liberty of the Pope, but of re-establish-
ing his authority on a solid and stable basis, and of securing
him against violence. It is well known to you that the Catholic Powers have always had it at heart to guarantee the
sovereignty of the Pope, and assure to him an independent
position. Such position is so important for the Christian
States that it cannot on any account be subjected to the will
and pleasure of so small a portion of the Catholic world as the
Roman States. It is the belief of Spain that the Catholic
Powers cannot commit the liberty of the Pope to the caprice of
the city of Rome. Nor can they permit that, whilst all the
Catholic nations are warmly offering to the Holy Father proofs
of their profound respect, a single town of Italy shall dare to
outrage his dignity, and restrict the Pope to a state of independence which could be so easily abused at any time as a
religious power. These considerations induce the government
of her Majesty to invite the other Catholic Powers to come to
an understanding on the means to be employed for averting
the evils which would arise, if matters remained in their present
position. In furtherance of this object, her Majesty has ordered
her government to address the governments of France, Austria,
Bavaria, Sardinia, Tuscany and Naples, in order to invite them
to name Plenipotentiaries, and appoint the place where they
shall meet."

The Catholic Powers welcomed cordially this admirable
note, which expressed so clearly the idea which they all entertained. Piedmont alone, as if already casting a covetous eye
on Rome and its territory, refused to concur. Its refusal was
expressed by the pen of the once so highly esteemed Abbate
Gioberti, who was President of the Council. It was not long

F

till Piedmont reaped its reward. The following year, 1849, on the 22d of March, it had to lament the disastrous battle of Novara.

Not long after, Cardinal Antonelli, who remained with the Pope, addressed, on the part of the Holy See, to the governments of France, Austria, Spain and Naples, a highly important paper. It recapitulated, in a clear and forcible manner, all that had occurred at Rome from the time of the Pope's departure till the 18th of February, and then requested, in the most formal and pressing way possible, the intervention of these four Catholic Powers. The governments thus appealed to promptly replied by sending Plenipotentiaries to Gaeta, where the Pope desired that the diplomatic conference should be opened. The Catholic countries had already anticipated the intentions of the Sovereign Pontiff—some by acts, others by energetic resolutions. On the one hand, General Cavaignac, to whom France had for the time committed her sword, had concentrated, as early as the month of September, 1848, a body of troops under the command of General Molliere, whose duty it should be to hold themselves in readiness to embark for Italy at the first signal. Spain, on the other hand, prepared her fleet. The King of the Two Sicilies could scarcely restrain the ardor of his soldiers. Portugal, even, which had not been mentioned in the document addressed to the four Catholic Powers, considered it a duty to cause it to be represented to the government of the Pope through its ambassador, the Baron de Verda Cruz, that the Portuguese people would be most happy to take up arms in the interest of the Papal cause. Portugal was among the first, on occasion of the 16th November, 1848, to offer hospitality to the Sovereign Pontiff, and to invite him to one of the finest residences in Christendom, the magnificent palace of Mafra.

The time of the Holy Father at Gaeta was employed, as it usually is, in prayer, the giving of audiences and the business of the Church. In one point, there was an exception to the rules of the Papal Court. The King of Naples, the Queen and the Princes were admitted every day to the table of the Pope. King Ferdinand, notwithstanding his friendly relations with Pius IX., never availed himself of this privilege without a new daily invitation. In all other respects, likewise, his conduct towards the Holy Father was all that the most devout Catholic could desire.

Dutiful conduct of Ferdinand, of Naples, towards the exiled Pope.

The internal state of the Catholic Powers caused their action to be delayed. The political troubles of the Austrian Empire obliged the Emperor Ferdinand to abdicate in favor of his youthful nephew, Francis Joseph. France was laboring to consolidate her newly-founded Republic. There was question of electing a president. And if, on the occasion, Prince Louis Napoleon Bonaparte secured the greatest number of votes, he owed this success, if not wholly, in great measure, at least, to his repudiation of the undutiful conduct of his cousin, the Prince of Canino, at Rome, and his declaration in favor of the temporal sovereignty of the Pope. On the eve of the election he wrote as follows to the Papal Nuncio: "My Lord, I am anxious that the rumors which tend to make me an accomplice of the conduct of Prince Canino at Rome should not be credited by you. I have not, for a long time, had any relations with the eldest son of Lucien Bonaparte; and I am profoundly grieved that he has not understood that the maintenance of the temporal sovereignty of the venerable Head of the Church is intimately connected with the glory of Catholicism, no less than with the liberty and independence of Italy. Accept, my Lord, the expression of my sentiments of high esteem.

Action of the Powers delayed.

Prince Louis Napoleon repudiates the conduct of the Prince of Canino.—Declares for the temporal sovereignty.

LOUIS NAPOLEON BONAPARTE."

Spain had already despatched a fleet to Gaeta, the Austrians had advanced in the direction of Ferrara, and the King of Naples at Terracina, when, on the 25th of April, 1849, a French army, under the command of General Oudinot, disembarked at Civita Vecchia. This military expedition was, at first, considerably thwarted by diplomacy. The general-in-chief was assured at the outset that he had only to show himself before the walls of Rome, and the gates would be opened immediately in consequence of the reaction which was taking place within. Accordingly, the army advanced, on the 30th April, to the foot of the ramparts, and was received with a discharge of fire-arms. Nevertheless, one of the gates was opened to a French battalion. The Romans came out in crowds, waving white handkerchiefs, and shouting, "Peace is concluded! Peace for ever! Enemies in the morning, we are brothers this evening! Long live the French!" The soldiers, deceived by these demonstrations, were persuaded to enter the city. They were at once disarmed and declared prisoners of war. It was now manifest that a regular siege was necessary. An impediment was, however, thrown in the way of military operations, by a civil or diplomatic agent who entered Rome, and in the course of a few weeks concluded with the revolutionists a treaty which was contrary to his instructions, to those of the commander-in-chief, to the honor of France and the objects of the expedition. Odillon Barrot was, at that time, President of the French Ministry—the same Odillon Barrot who, in 1830, was prefect of police, and allowed the mansion of the Archbishop to be demolished without taking any measures for its protection. Such conduct, as has been well observed, showed that this official loved anarchy more than order. Hence, probably, arose those impediments to the Roman expedition which gave time to

Several Powers undertake to restore the Pope. France sends an army to Rome.

Treachery of the Roman populace.

Determination to besiege Rome. The siege delayed by diplomatic manœuvres.

the revolutionists to organize, under the leadership of a chief of banditti, Garibaldi, of Genoa. They availed themselves, at the same time, of the leisure afforded, to massacre many faithful priests, to enable some renegade monks to profane the solemnities of religion, and to commit, in the hospitals, outrages which were, until that time, unheard of. Unfortunate soldiers, sick and at the point of death, beholding persons dressed like Nuns and Sisters of Charity, expected to hear from them the language of religion, in order to assist them in preparing for a Christian death. It can easily be imagined how greatly they were shocked to hear only lascivious expressions and the most infamous provocations to vice. These pretended Sisters of Charity were nothing else than professed prostitutes. Their president, a revolutionary princess, admits, in her memoirs, this melancholy fact.

Excesses of the Revolutionists.

The King of Naples and General Cordova, commander-in-chief of the Spanish army, offered to General Oudinot the aid of their arms. He thanked them, but declined their offer, desiring, for the honor of the French army, that as it had begun, so it should complete the duty which it had undertaken. The French general represented, and with reason, to the Spanish commander, that he would have entered Rome several weeks sooner but for the diplomatic negotiations already alluded to. The Plenipotentiary, who conducted these negotiations, having been disavowed, the general held himself alone responsible, and it was his duty to simplify matters as much as possible. He urged, moreover, that when an army is besieging a place no foreign troops can approach it, unless their assistance is requested either by the besiegers or the besieged. The latter were far from having any claim to the protection of Spain, and the French army was in a position to meet every contingency.

The King of Naples and the Spaniards offer to assist the French.

On the 30th June, 1849, the city surrendered, uncondition-
Rome surrenders to the French. ally. On 3rd July the French army entered Rome, amidst the joyous acclamations of the native Roman people.

On the same day General Oudinot despatched Colonel Niel Colonel Niel despatched to Gaeta with the keys of the city. to Gaeta, in order to deliver to the Sovereign Pontiff the keys of his capital. Pius IX. was overjoyed at the arrival of the French officer. His people were now free. The war was at an end. Blood no longer flowed. There was nothing wanting to his satisfaction and happiness. " O! speak to me of my children of Rome and France," he exclaimed. " How they must have suffered! How earnestly have I prayed for them!" He then listened with interest, and the feelings of a father, to the recital of the sufferings of the French army and their prolonged labors, which were patiently undergone, in order to save the edifices and monuments of Rome from irreparable destruction. Unable, at length, to contain his emotion, he spoke thus to Colonel Niel: " Colonel, I have often said, on other occasions, and I am happy to be able to repeat the same to-day, after so great a service, that I have always relied on France. That country had promised me nothing, but I understood full well, that when opportunity offered she would give to the Church her treasures, her blood, and what is, perhaps, still more difficult for her valiant children, that bravery which can restrain itself, that patience and perseverance to which is due the preservation of Rome, that treasure of the world, that beloved and sorely-tried city, towards which, during these days of exile, I have always looked in great anxiety of mind. Say to the commander-in-chief, to all the generals and all the officers—would it could also be said to every soldier of France!—that there are no bounds to my gratitude. My prayers for the prosperity of your country will be more fervent than ever. My love for the French people has been increased, if, indeed, anything could make it greater than it was, by the great service which I now acknowledge."

At the same time, Pius IX. addressed an appropriate letter

Letter of Pius IX. to
General Oudinot. to General Oudinot. He recognized the well-known valor of the French armies, which was sustained by the justice of the cause which they came to defend, and which won for them the meed of victory. In congratulating the general on the principal share which he bore in the important event, the Holy Father was careful to say that he rejoiced not over the bloodshed which had necessarily occurred, but in the triumph of order over anarchy, and because liberty was restored to honest and Christian people, for whom it would no longer be a crime to enjoy the property which God had bestowed upon them, and to adore Him, with becoming pomp of worship, without incurring the risk of being deprived of life or liberty. In the difficult circumstances which might arise, the Holy Father would rely on the Divine protection. As it might prove useful to the French army to be acquainted with the events of his Pontificate, he sent, along with his letter, a number of copies of the Allocution, in which these events are related. This paper, he stated, proved abundantly that the army had won a victory over the enemies of human society, and that their triumph, consequently, would awaken sentiments of gratitude in the breasts of all honest men throughout Europe and the whole civilized world.

The President of the French Republic, Louis Napoleon, the

General Oudinot
repairs to Gaeta and
invites the Pope to
return to his Capital. French Minister of War and the National Assembly, all joined in congratulating General Oudinot and his army. Pius IX. had just appointed (31st July) a commission of three Cardinals for the government of the Roman States, when General Oudinot arrived at Gaeta, and urged the Pope to return himself to his capital. Pius IX. had already stated to M. de Corcelles, the Plenipotentiary of France, his objections to an immediate return. He now held the same language to General Oudinot. He could not, he said, so far forget the purely moral nature of his power as to bind himself in a positive way, when there was nothing settled as to matters of detail, and especially when he was called upon to speak in presence of a first-class Power, whose exigencies were no secret. Ought he to condemn himself to appear to act under the impulsion of force? If he did anything good, was it not necessary that his acts should be spontaneous, and should also have the appearance of being so? Were not his inclinations well known? Were they not calculated to inspire confidence? Nevertheless, it was his intention to return, in a few days, to his States, and to remain some time at Castel-Gandolfo, in the midst of the French army. General Oudinot returned to Rome fully assured of the speedy return of the Holy Father.

About this time it became manifest that the French Republic desired to restore the Pope as a mere agent of their newly-instituted government. The French ministry, of which Odillon Barrot was the head, saw, with impatience, that Pontifical affairs were not proceeding to such a conclusion as they wished. Accordingly, General Oudinot was recalled and replaced by General Rostolan, the next in command. Two days later, a letter signed "Louis Napoleon," and addressed to Colonel Edgar Ney, who was also the bearer of it, was despatched to Rome. This letter contained insulting allusions to the Pontifical government; and its requirements would have annihilated, in the estimation of Europe, the independence of the Sovereign Pontiff, whilst personally dishonoring him. "I thus recapitulate," said the president, in this memorable epistle, the temporal power of the Pope, *a general amnesty, secularization of the administration, and liberal government.*" It was appointed that General Rostolan should publish this ill-timed letter, and carry it into effect. He refused to do so, tendered his resignation, and thus firmly replied: "Conscience requires that I should sacrifice my position and my sympathies. My successor, more fortunate than myself, will perhaps enjoy the signal honor to terminate peacefully the work which we have begun at the head of the army. As a soldier and a Christian, I will rejoice on account of the Sovereign Pontiff, who will have been restored to his people, and because of France, which will have accomplished a noble and most worthy mission." To the Odillon Barrot ministry, which at one time disowned the letter, and at another acknowledged it, and ordered its publication, the general declared that he would never identify himself with an act which, besides being unjust, would endanger the peace of all Europe. According to his view, which was the same as that of the French ambassadors, M. de Rayneval and M. de Corcelles, a general war would follow the official publication of the letter of 18th August; and such a war could not but prove fatal to the ideas of order which were beginning to resume their empire. He loved his country too well to bear part in incurring for it such fearful risks. Messrs. de Rayneval and de Corcelles wrote to the same effect, and communicated to the French Government the resolution of the Sovereign Pontiff to seek the protection of Austria, or even to repair to America, rather than submit to the constraint with which he was threatened.

It was not, however, ordained that the conditions of the Pope's restoration should be decided by the President of the French Republic, or the Odillon Barrot ministry. The National

Address of Montalembert to the National Assembly of France.

Assembly of France took the matter in hand, and after a keen debate, which lasted three days—13th, 18th and 19th October—came to a resolution favorable to the Holy See. There can be no doubt that the Chamber was greatly influenced by the powerful eloquence of M. de Montalembert. "It has been said," observed this orator, "that the honor of our flag was compromised by the expedition undertaken against Rome in order to destroy the Roman Republic and restore the authority of the Pope. All in this Assembly must feel insulted by this reproach, and cannot but repel it, as I do at this moment. No! the honor of our flag was never compromised. No! never did this noble flag cover with its folds a more noble enterprise. History will tell. I confidently invoke its testimony and its judgment. History will throw a veil over all the ambiguity, tergiversation and contestation which have been pointed to with so much bitterness and so eager a desire to spread discord amongst us. It will ignore all this, or, rather, it will proclaim it all, in order that the greatness of the undertaking may become apparent from the number and nature of the difficulties that have been surmounted.

"History will say that a thousand years from the time of Charlemagne, and fifty from that of Napoleon—a thousand years after Charlemagne had won for himself imperishable glory by restoring the Pontifical State, and fifty years after Napoleon, in the zenith of power and prestige, had failed in his endeavor to undo the work of his predecessor; history will say that France has remained true to her traditions and deaf to odious counsels. History will say that thirty thousand Frenchmen, under the leadership of the worthy son of one of the giants of our great imperial glories, left the shores of their country, in order to re-establish at Rome, in the person of the Pope, right, equity, European and French interest. History will further say what Pius IX. himself said, in his letter of thanks to General Oudinot: '*The victory of the French arms is won over the enemies of human society.*' Yes! gentlemen, such will be the judgment of impartial history; and it will be one of the brightest glories of France and the nineteenth century. You will not attenuate, tarnish, eclipse this glory by plunging into a mass of contradictions, complications, and inextricable inconsistency. Know you what would dim for ever the lustre of the French flag? It would be to set it in opposition to the Cross, to the Tiara, which it has delivered. It would be to transform the soldiers of France, the protectors of the Pope, into his oppressors. It would be to exchange the *role* and the glory of Charlemagne for a pitiful mimicry of Garibaldi."

A large majority of the legislative assembly agreed with Montalembert. The news of their decision, which was in accordance with the general sentiment of the French nation, was speedily conveyed to the Pontifical Court. It dispelled all the un-

The Municipality of Rome invites the Pope to return.

pleasant apprehensions which had hitherto prevailed, and gave great satisfaction to the Holy Father. The influence which it exercised over his plans for the future may be learned from the reply which he gave to a deputation from the municipality of Rome, which now came to pray that he would return to his States. "It was repugnant to us," said he, "to return to our States, so long as France made it a question whether we should be independent. But now that a happy solution has been reached, which appears to put an end to all doubt on this point, we hope to be able, in a short time, to return to our city of Rome." Accordingly, on 12th April, 1850, Pius IX. made his entrance into Rome amidst the dutiful and joyous acclamations of the French army and the Roman people. On the 18th day of the same month he formally blessed the arms and colors of France in front of St. Peter's Church." Thus ended at Rome a political revolution, which nothing less powerful than Catholic sentiment could have overcome.

The Pope returns to Rome.

Whilst the comparatively small Pontifical State was agitated by revolution, the greater kingdom of the Church was steadily pursuing, under the auspices of its august Chief, its grand career of progress and development. A new era seemed to have dawned over all those great countries which the Photian schism had so seriously affected. About the time of Pius the Ninth's accession, more favorable dispositions had come to prevail among the Greeks of Constantinople, of Syria, of Palestine, of Egypt. Among the Armenians and Chaldeans there were numerous conversions, whilst even the Turks showed a better feeling towards the Catholic people, among whom their lot was cast. We have already seen how well such sentiments were encouraged by the newly-elected Pontiff. His words of kindness were repaid by increased affection for the Catholic people, and the wish, not to say the belief, that when the Turkish Empire fell, the fragments of its once great inheritance would be gathered up by Catholics. "Are

State of religion in countries affected by the Photian schism and the Mahometan imposture.

this belief and friendship," asks the Abbe Etienne, "an indication of the speedy reunion of the children of Mahomet with the great Christian family? We have much reason to think so, when we behold Islamism everywhere dwindling away and giving place to the true faith." Damascus, so sacred in Mussulman estimation, and so intolerant that no Christian could pass within its gates except bareheaded, and on paying a capitation tax, now beholds with pleasure the celebration of Catholic rites. So great was the change that in a short time all the inhabitants of a village in the neighborhood embraced the Catholic faith. The Mahometans who are most capable of appreciating religious questions, study Christianity secretly. Not long ago, a Turk of Damascus caused a Catholic priest to be called to his deathbed, and begged to be baptized. Great was the surprise of the missionary to find him as well acquainted with the truths of religion as he was anxious to receive the sacrament of regeneration. A few moments later the good priest beheld his neophyte expire, expressing the most pious sentiments.

In Russia, the most powerful seat of the great eastern schism, Catholics were long subjected to the most trying persecution. It is well known what influence the venerable Pontiff, Gregory XVI., exercised over the mind of the late Emperor Nicholas, and that he succeeded in causing him to mitigate the evils which weighed so heavily on his Catholic subjects. Pius IX. was still more successful. Having concluded a Concordat with the Czar, which was signed at Rome on the 3rd August, 1847, by Cardinal Lambruschini, on the part of the Holy See, and Counts Bloudoff and Boutenieff, on the part of Russia, Pius IX., in a consistory held on 3rd July of the same year, instituted bishops for the following Sees of the Russian Empire: The Metropolitan Church of Mohilow, the united dioceses of Luceoria and Zitomeritz, in Volhynia, the diocese of Vilna, in Poland, and a coadjutor, with right of succession, for the archbishopric of Mohilow. The Concordat contained 31 articles. Article 1st. Seven Roman Catholic dioceses are established in the Russian Empire—an arch-bishopric and six bishoprics, viz.: the archbishopric of Mohilow, which comprises all those parts of the Empire which are not contained in the undermentioned dioceses. The Grand Duchy of Finland is also included in this archdiocese. The diocese of Vilna, comprising the governments of Vilna and Grodno, according to their present limits; the diocese of Telsca, or Samogitia, comprising the governments of Courland and Kowno; the diocese of Minsk, comprising the government of Minsk, as at present limited; the diocese of Luceoria and Zitomeritz, containing the governments of Kiovia and Volhynia; the diocese of Kaminiec, comprising the government of Podolia; the new diocese of Kherson, containing the Province of Bessarabia, the governments of Khersonesus, Ecatherinaslaw, Taurida, Saratow and Astracan, together with the regions that are subject to the general government of the Caucasus.

In glancing at the articles of the Concordat, the Catholic reader will be agreeably surprised to observe that in so many important things the wishes of the Holy Father were acceded to, whilst it is matter for regret that in regard to others the Plenipotentiaries could not come to an understanding. It is provided by the 2nd and 3rd articles that apostolic letters under the leaden seal shall determine the extent and limits of the dioceses, as indicated in article 1st. The decrees of execution shall express the number and the names of the parishes of each diocese, and shall be submitted for the sanction of the Holy See. The number of suffragan bishoprics, as settled by the apostolic letters of Pius VI. in 1789, is retained in the six ancient dioceses. In the following articles, from 4 to 10, it is agreed that the suffragan of the new diocese of Kherson shall reside in the town of Saratow. The annual allowance to the Bishop of Kherson shall be 4,480 silver roubles. His suffragan shall have the same income as the other bishops of the Empire,. viz.: 2,000 silver roubles. The chapter of the Cathedral Church of Kherson shall consist of nine members, viz.: two prelates or dignitaries, the president and archdeacon; four canons, of whom three shall discharge the duties of theologian, penitentiary and rector; and three resident priests, or beneficiaries. In the new bishopric of Kherson there shall be a diocesan seminary, in which from fifteen to twenty-five students shall be supported at the cost of the government, the same as those who enjoy a pension in other seminaries. Until a Catholic bishop of the Armenian rite is named, the spiritual wants of the Armenian Catholics of the dioceses of Kherson and Kaminiec shall be provided for by applying the ninth chapter of the Council of Lateran, held in 1215. The bishops of Kaminiec and Kherson shall determine the number of Catholic Armenian ecclesiastics who shall be educated in their seminaries at the expense of the government. In each of these seminaries there shall reside a Catholic Armenian priest, in order to instruct the students in the ceremonies of their national rite. As often as the spiritual wants of the Armenian Roman Catholics of the newly-instituted diocese of Kherson shall require it, the bishop, besides the means hitherto employed for this purpose, may send priests as missionaries, and the government will supply the funds that shall be necessary for their journeys and sustenance.

Articles 11 and 12 provide that the number of dioceses in the Kingdom of Poland shall remain the same as ordained by the Apostolical Letters of Pius VII., of date 30th June, 1818. There is no change as to the number and designation of the suffragans of these dioceses. The appointment of bishops for the dioceses and the suffragan bishoprics of the Empire of Russia and the Kingdom of Poland shall only take effect after each nomination shall have been agreed upon between the Emperor and the Holy See. Canonical institution will be given by the Roman Pontiff in the usual form.

In articles 13–20 are contained the following regulations: the bishop is the sole judge and administrator of the ecclesiastical affairs of his diocese, having due regard to the canonical obedience which he owes to the Holy Apostolic See. Certain affairs must be, in the first place, submitted to the delibera-

tions of the diocesan consistory. Such affairs are decided by
the bishop, after having been examined by the consistory,
which, however, is only consultative. The bishop is by no
means bound to give the reasons of his decision, even in case
of his opinion being different from that of the consistory. The
other affairs of the diocese, which are called *administrative*, and
among which are included cases of conscience, and, as has been
said above, cases of discipline which are visited only by light
punishments and pastoral admonitions, depend entirely on the
authority and the spontaneous decision of the bishop. All the
members of the consistory are ecclesiastics. Their nomination
and their revocation belong to the bishop. The nominations
are so made as not to displease the government. The officials
of the consistorial chancery are confirmed by the bishop, on
the presentation of the secretary of the consistory. The secretary of the bishop, who is charged with official and private correspondence, is named directly by the bishop; and an ecclesiastic, as the bishop thinks proper, may be chosen. The duties
of the members of the consistory cease when the bishop dies
or resigns, and also when the administration of a vacant See
comes to an end.

From articles 21–29 we read as follows: The bishop has
the supreme direction of the teaching of doctrine and discipline in the seminaries of his diocese, according to the prescrip-
tions of the Council of Trent. The choice of rectors, inspectors
and professors for the diocesan seminaries is reserved to the
bishop. Before naming them, he must ascertain that, as
regards their civil conduct, they will not give occasion to any
objection on the part of the government. The Archbishop
Metropolitan of Mohilow shall exercise in the ecclesiastical
academy of St. Petersburg the same jurisdiction as does each
bishop in his diocesan seminary. He is the sole chief of this
academy—its supreme director. The council or directory of
this academy is only consultative. The choice of the rector,
the inspector and professors of this academy, shall be made by
the archbishop, after he has received the report of the Academi-

cal Council. The professors and assistant-professors of Theo-logical science shall always be chosen among ecclesiastics. The other masters may be selected among lay persons, professing the Roman Catholic religion. The confessors of the students of each seminary and of the academy shall take no part in the disciplinary government of the establishment. They shall be chosen and nominated by the bishop or archbishop. When the limits of the dioceses shall have been fixed according to the new regulation, the archbishop, with the advice of the ordinaries, shall determine, once for all, the number of students that each diocese may send to the academy. The programme of studies in the seminaries shall be regulated by the bishops. The archbishop shall decide upon that of the academy after having conferred with the Academical Council. When the rule of the ecclesiastical academy of St. Petersburg shall have been modified conformably with the principles agreed upon in the preceding articles, the Archbishop of Mohilow will send to the Holy See a report on the academy like that which was made by Archbishop Koromanski when the academy was restored.

Articles 30 and 31. Wherever the right of patronage does not exist, or has been discontinued for a certain time, parish priests shall be appointed by the bishop. They must not offend the government, and must have undergone examination and competition according to the rules laid down by the Council of Trent. Roman Catholic churches may be freely repaired at the expense of communities or individuals who shall please to take charge of this work. When their own resources are insufficient, they may apply to the Imperial Government in order to obtain assistance. New churches shall be constructed, and the number of parishes augmented, when such measures become necessary from the increase of population, the too great extent of existing parishes, or the difficulty of communications.

Such matters as could not be agreed upon and embodied in the Concordat may be gleaned from the allocution which

Pius IX. addressed, at the time, to the Cardinals. "Many things of the greatest importance still remain, in regard to which the Plenipotentiaries could not come to an agreement, and the omission of which awakens our most lively solicitude, and causes us the utmost pain; for they concern, in the highest degree, the liberty of the church, its rights, its essential principles, and the salvation of the faithful in those Russian countries. We allude to that true and complete liberty, which ought to be secured to the Christian people, of being able, in regard to the things which relate to religion, to communicate, without impediment, with this Apostolic See, the centre of Catholic unity and truth, the Father and Master of all the Faithful. All men may understand how deeply grieved we are, when they call to mind the multiplied appeals which this Apostolic See has never ceased to cause to be heard at divers times, in order to obtain free communication of the faithful, not only in Russia, but also in other countries, where, in certain affairs of religion, it is seriously impeded, to the great loss of souls. We would speak of the property which ought to be restored to the clergy. We would have removed from the Episcopal Consistories the lay person chosen by the government, in order that, in these assemblies, the bishops may be able to act with all liberty. We must advert to the law according to which mixed marriages are not recognized as valid, until they have been blessed by a Russo-Greek Catholic priest; and also to the liberty which Catholics ought to possess of trying and judging their matrimonial causes, in cases of mixed marriages, by a Catholic ecclesiastical tribunal. Finally, we would allude to divers laws prevalent in Russia, which fix the age at which religious professions may be made, which destroy entirely the schools that are held in the houses of religious orders, which prevent the visits of provincial superiors, which forbid and interdict conversion to the Catholic faith."

In this same allocution the Holy Father deplores the miserable state of the illustrious Ruthenian nation, which, dispersed throughout the vast countries of Russia, is, from various causes, exposed to great dangers as regards salvation. Without bishops, they have none to guide them in the paths of righteousness, none to administer to them spiritual succour, or to warn them against the insidious approaches of heresy and schism. The Holy Father is confident that the Latin priests will bestow all their care and employ every available resource in affording spiritual aid to these "most dear children." "From our inmost soul," concludes the venerable Pontiff, "we exhort, earnestly and lovingly in the Lord, and urge the Ruthenians themselves to remain faithful and steadfast in the unity of the Catholic Church, or, if they have been so unfortunate as to abandon it, to return to the bosom of their most loving mother, to have recourse to us, who, with God's assistance, will do whatever is best calculated to secure their salvation."

As regards some of these highly important matters, the wishes of the Holy Father were acceded to by the Russian Emperor. The bishop of Kherson was allowed a second suffragan. It was also regulated that matrimonial and other ecclesiastical causes, whether in Russia proper or in the kingdom of Poland, should, on appeal from a sentence pronounced by the ordinary, be heard before the tribunal of the metropolitan, or before the more neighboring bishop, in case of judgment having been first given by the metropolitan. Such causes, in the event of final appeal, should be referred to Rome—to the tribunal of the Apostolic See.

In considering, at some length, the Concordat with Russia, and the more favorable terms by which it was followed, we learn what hopes may be entertained as regards the spiritual well-being of the more numerous Catholics, Armenians and others, who will now, in all probability, come under the sway of Russia.*

The Society of the Holy Ghost had labored successfully in France, the Indies, Canada, China, Acadia, or Nova Scotia, the islands, Miquelon and St. Peter. In the countries referred to, there were bishops, vicars apostolic, of this society, and several mis-

French colonies and foreign missions.— Africa.

---

* This danger is past.

sionary priests. In Cayenne and French Guiana, they maintained an apostolic prefect and twenty missionaries apostolic.
The troubles of the French revolution all but extinguished this
zealous and influential missionary society. It was revived in
the year 1848, under the auspices of Pius IX., and resumed its
labors under the title of Society of the Holy Ghost and the
Immaculate Heart of Mary. During the negotiations which
led to the restoration of this society, the Vicariate Apostolic of
Madagascar became vacant by the death of Bishop Dalton.
Abbe Monnet, Superior of the Society of the Holy Ghost, was
appointed to succeed him, and Rev. Abbe Liebermann, a distinguished convert from Judaism, was unanimously elected to
the post of superior-general of the two united societies. The
labors of Abbe Liebermann were crowned with complete success. In 1850, the Holy Father, in order to confirm and perpetuate the fruit of so much apostolic labor, erected three
bishoprics—one in the low country of Guadeloupe, another at
Fort Francis, in Martinica, and a third at St. Denis, of Bourbon Island. The eminent convert died in 1852, after having
had the satisfaction to behold such great developments of his
missionary work. The death of the first superior-general did
not, by any means, retard the increase of the new society. On
the contrary, new blessings seemed to descend upon it. Under
the guidance of the second superior, the 'Abbe Schwindenham-
mer, who had been the friend and confidential counsellor of the
first, the society came to be as an order of three choirs—
Fathers, Friars, Sisters. To the Rev. Fathers, who were missionaries apostolic, the Father of the great Christian Family,
Pius IX., assigned a field of labor, a hundred times more
extensive than the land which was promised of old to the children of Israel—a territory from eleven to twelve hundred
leagues in length, and broad in proportion. The friars were
lay missionaries, whose duty it was to assist the Rev. Fathers,
teach the neophytes the arts of Christian civilization, and
change the deserts, the wild forest lands and dismal swamps,
into smiling fields. A brother, who is a printer, has already

departed for those missions, carrying with him a complete set of types. The sisters, in order to draw down the mercy of heaven on the negro lands, devote themselves to prayer, works of charity and self-denial, perpetual adoration of the Blessed Sacrament, and the continual offering of themselves in sacrifice for the salvation of the souls that are most neglected. They would even, if it were the call of heaven, repair to Africa, and found there religious communities, in order to confirm the good work commenced by the missionaries. So early as their first year, 1852, they had established two or three houses in France. This great missionary society came into existence at a singularly opportune moment, and none can tell what an important part it may bear in carrying the light of Christianity into that benighted Africa which modern discovery, the discovery of our age, the age of Pius IX., is now throwing open to the many blessed influences of civilization.

In the early days of the Pontificate of Pius IX., the Guinea missions extended over regions of negro-land nine hundred leagues from east to west, and seven hundred leagues from north to south, with a coast-line of eleven hundred leagues. These African countries are very populous; and there are towns of 20,000, 30,000, and even 60,000 inhabitants. The greatest barbarism prevails. With the exception of a few Mahometans in Sanegambia, the people are idolators. They are also cannibals, and human sacrifices are frequent. Polygamy is one of their vices, and those on the sea coast of Guinea have learned many others from contact with Europeans, such as hard drinking and all kinds of excess. Their women are in a degraded condition, doing all the drudgery, and not being admitted to an equality with their husbands. Notwithstanding all this, the missionaries give them a high character. They bear pain with fortitude, and have a horror of slavery, although so many of them are reduced to servitude by greedy traders. A sea captain once offered a negro any amount of money, on condition that he should become his slave. "All the gold your ship could hold," said the spirited African, "is no price for my

liberty." They are very sensitive, grateful, and even affectionate towards those who befriend them. To the missionaries
they always showed hospitality; and the peaceful explorer,
Livingstone, and his friends generally met with the same
kindness. If it was otherwise with the adventurous discoverer,
Stanley, he owed the hostility with which he was often received
by the African tribes to the armed force by which he was
accompanied, and his determination to traverse their countries,
whether they liked it or not. They listened attentively to the
missionaries, and this circumstance induced these excellent
persons to express the belief that, with proper precautions,
they may be induced to embrace the Christian faith. Many
things have occurred, in the course of this favored age, to
encourage this hope for the future welfare of so many millions
of the human race. Science has thrown its light into the
hitherto dark regions of Central Africa, where no European
had, as yet, been able to penetrate. The petty and corrupting
traffic on the coasts will speedily expand into wide extended
and improving commerce. The slave trade is gradually
diminishing, and must, ere long, disappear under the blessed
influences, more active than ever, which are now at work; the
whole church is moved by the edifying narratives of zealous
missionaries; and the countenance of the Apostolic See is
willingly bestowed on missionary effort. So, it is not too much
to say that, with such auspicious commencements in the age
of Pius IX., the days of some future Pontiff, at no very distant
epoch, will be blessed to behold Africa, so long neglected,
happily, at length, brought within the pale of Christianity and
civilization.

    The missionaries speak of a Prince, whose history, if
related by less trustworthy parties, could not fail to be considered fabulous. His territory is situated on the river Gabon.
He speaks English and French fluently, as well as an African
dialect called *Boulou*. He is a man of gentle and polished
manners, and possesses the self-control of the most accomplished European. In point of sobriety, he is equal to the best of

Europeans. He never drinks intoxicating liquor, and forbids his children to use it. He is beloved by his subjects, and respected by the neighboring tribes, who hold with him commercial and friendly relations. He shows great friendship to the missionaries, and takes great delight in assisting them. A good bishop is also mentioned, whose horror of the slave trade was such that he would not allow a negro to serve him. In addition to the mission-house, which is a solid stone building, there is also a seminary, where some of the native youth are educated for the duties of the Christian priesthood. The aboriginal populations receive the bishop and the heads of the missions with extraordinary honors. The salubrity of the climate is favorably spoken of, being nowise inferior to that of France. Everything appeared to favor the Guinea missions in the early years of the Pontificate of Pius IX. With the aid of continued countenance and encouragement, they cease not to be developed every day more and more throughout the vast countries extending from Senegambia to the Equator. At Joal and St. Mary of Gambia, there were flourishing missions so early as 1852. In 1850 M. L'Abbe Arlabosse founded a mission at Galam, 150 leagues in the interior of Senegal. Another mission was successfully established at Grand Bassam, in 1851. The printing press, already referred to, has contributed powerfully to facilitate missionary work. Seven diverse languages are now taught, viz.: Wolof, Serer, Saracole, Abule, Mpongue, Bingue and Balu, or Boulou.

It is somewhat remarkable that in all the countries connected as colonies with Great Britain, where Protestantism is so persistently adhered to, there should prevail the greatest liberty as regards the exercise of the Catholic religion. Thus, Cape Colony (Cape of Good Hope) was no sooner transferred from the rule of Holland to that of Britain than the Holy Father was enabled to extend his care to the Catholics of that remote land. A bishop was appointed, and missions speedily established. There are now three bishops, vicars apostolic, at Cape Town, Graham's Town, Natal. The islands Mauritius

and Bourbon, each of which has a population of more than
100,000 souls, share the solicitude of the church and its august
Head.   They are not both equally favored by their civil rulers.
The former was annexed to Great Britain in 1810.   The Holy
Father provides for its spiritual welfare, confiding its administration to a bishop and a sufficient number of priests, all of
whom receive salaries from the government.   The bishops
hitherto have been members of the illustrious order of St.
Benedict, and some of them have enjoyed a high reputation in
the church, such as the learned and eloquent Bishop Morris,
and the pious and accomplished Bishop Collier.   Bourbon
Island, until of late, 1850, when a bishop was appointed, had
not been so fortunate.   An eminent French writer rather
satirically remarks, that it would have to wait until France
ceded all her colonies to the British.   There are, however, some
priests who, together with the bishop, minister to the spiritual
wants of the people.   Great efforts have been made to establish
missions in the large and populous Island of Madagascar,
which, according to geographers, is 1,000 miles in length.

The priests of the congregation of St. Vincent of Paul, as
zealous now as in the days of their illustrious founder, have
penetrated into Abyssinia, and are laboring to bring about a
complete reconciliation of that once eminently Christian nation
to the church 'of Pius IX.   The Æthiopian may not, indeed,
change his skin.   But, according to the reports of the missionaries, these people are changing their ideas, and giving
proofs of a disposition to return to the centre of Christian
unity.   Everywhere the missionaries are received with kindness by princes and people, and favored with a respectful hearing.

So great is the reverence of the nations of the Turkish
Empire for the character of the Pope, that one would say that
he had a Concordat with those nations and their chiefs.   The
legate of the Holy See, Archbishop Auvergne,'of Iconium, was
received with the greatest honor by the Sovereign of Ægypt, on
occasion of his legation to that country and Syria.   A Catholic

bishop was established at Alexandria, a city so intimately associated with the memory of Saint Athanasius. His jurisdiction extends over the Æthiopian countries, and this circumstance, considering their relations in bygone ages with the Patriarchs of Alexandria, facilitates their communion with the centre of unity. The Catholic bishop 'of Cairo, assisted by thirty priests, so long ago as 1840, governed a flock of nearly twenty thousand Copts of the ancient race of Ægypt. This body of faithful Christians is daily increasing, by the adherence of other Copts who had fallen into the Eutichyan heresy, more from want of instruction than obstinacy. Nothing could surpass the generosity of the Khedive towards the church. He presented to the Pope several marble columns, for the restoration of the Basilick of St. Paul at Rome, and built for the missionaries and sisters of St. Vincent de Paul a college, schools, and an hospital in the city of Alexandria. At Tunis and Tripoli there are 7,000 Catholics, who are ministered to by nine priests of the order of St. Francis. So early as 1840, Sisters of Charity went from France in order to establish a community at Tunis, with the full concurrence of the Mussulman government.

It is well known that as soon as a French colony was founded at Algiers, a bishop was appointed. That African Christendom, so happily commenced, still prospers, and extends its labors under the auspices of the august Head of the church. It is consoling to observe that there are so many nascent and even flourishing churches around the vast continent of Africa, from Senegambia and Sierra Leone, by the Cape of Good Hope, the islands on the south-east coast, Æthiopia and Ægypt, to the gates of Hercules. They stand there as sentinels, ready to intimate the moment when the army of the Cross may penetrate to the central continent, and conquer new kingdoms to the cause of Christ. This is surely not too much to hope for in an age when science has done so much, and commerce, that great handmaid of civilization, is opening a highway to the darkest recesses of the wide and long-lost heathen land.

Some serious-minded Catholics of Germany, dreading lest
a national or schismatical church should
come to be established in that country, conceived the happy idea of organizing, under
the auspices of Pius IX., associations of
laymen, who made it their duty to assist the clergy in everything that could tend to improve morals and education, relieve
suffering, and restore the liberty and rights of the church,
whilst they studied, at the same time, to impart a spirit of
faith to the pursuits of science, the arts, and even the more
humble occupations of trade. The chief founder of these associations, Mr. Francis Joseph Busz, has written a book, in
which he shows what progress they had already made in
1851, and what it still remained for them to accomplish.
They continued to prosper, and gave birth to associations of a
like nature. Thus, at Cologne, Abbe Kolping, Vicar of the
Cathedral, founded a society of *Catholic Companions*, the object
of whose institute was, that they should spend their leisure
hours together in a Christian manner, and increase the knowledge suited to their state of life, instead of losing their time,
their money and their morals in taverns. By the year 1852,
such associations of workmen had taken root in no fewer than
twenty-five cities in Germany.

German associa-
tions of Pius IX.—
State of religion in
Germany.

Ever since the Thirty Years' War, Germany had been distracted by religious divisions. And yet the sectarian spirit
does not appear to have been so bitter as in some other
countries. There was at least a desire for religious peace and
union. This is sufficiently expressed in the articles of the
treaty of Westphalia, which seems to have been intended as a
temporary arrangement for the pacification of the country,
until peace should be permanently established " by the agreement of all parties on points of religion;" "until all controversies should be terminated by an amicable and universal
understanding." " But if, which God forbid! people cannot
come to such amicable agreement on the controverted points
of religion, that this convention shall, nevertheless, be perpetual,

and this peace always continue." Thus was the great treaty only a preliminary of that lasting peace which can only be finally concluded when all minds and hearts are united in the bonds of a common faith.

Whilst many good men labored to bring about this most desirable end, others, such as Frederic of Prussia, and Joseph II. of Austria, by ill-advised measures, and the countenance which they gave to unsound and even irreligious doctrines, sowed the seeds of anarchy and unbelief, which failed not, in due time, to produce fruit according to their kind, and well-nigh accomplished the overthrow of society as well as that of the Christian Church. The Austrian Emperor appears to have understood the situation, and has generally maintained friendly relations with the Chief Pastor. Germany, besides, has not been without able and pious men, who have nobly sustained the cause of Truth and Union. Among these are particularly deserving of honorable mention the Counts Stolberg, father and son, whose writings have exercised a salutary influence. Whilst many other noble laymen contributed, like them, to the regeneration of their country, others, who were noble only in the ranks of literature and science, vied in their efforts with the learned of noble birth. The elder Gœrres headed the Catholic movement when Prussia so cruelly persecuted the Archbishop of Cologne. So good an example was not lost on the son. The younger Gœrres ceased not to emulate his worthy parent until the day of his death, in 1852. Another distinguished author, who, by his writings, greatly contributed to inform and encourage the Catholics of Germany, was Mr. Francis Joseph Busz, already mentioned in connection with the associations of Pius IX. He was a native of Baden, and an Aulic Counsellor of the Grand Duke. He had also been a member of the great National Parliament, which assembled at Frankfort for the purpose of restoring German unity. The best-known of his works are : *Catholic Association of Germany, and the necessity of reform in the instruction and education of the Catholic secular clergy of Germany.* Some of his remarks

ay be appropriately quoted, as they throw light on the present
877-78) state of Germany, and explain in great measure the
traordinary relations between Church and State in the New
erman Empire : " The year 1848 proved to us Germans that
e could not rely on our governments. Both diplomacy and
reaucracy are, and will remain, incorrigible. Our misery is,
deed, great. Dissension prevails among our good citizens;
e ill-meaning are united. The Revolutionary War of 1848
d 1849 was a war of principles, but without results. It was
pressed, but not exhausted. It keeps alive under the appear-
ces by which it is concealed. The inexhaustible volcano is
work amongst us, not only since 1848, but for three hundred
ars. The abjuration of law, and even of all principle of
ght, is only the form or expression; the essence of our
alady is the denial of God and His Church. The revolution
apostacy, the disunion of the nation is schism, its anarchy
theism. Whoever, like myself, has witnessed the public
gotiations of Germany, knows full well that the political
ruggle was, for a long time, and particularly for the last three
ars, a contest between the religious confessions. Such
olutions of evil possess a certain life, although it be only
at which leads to dissolution. They spring one from
other, and the new growth is always an improvement on
at by which it was preceded. I say it with sorrow. The
rife of political parties comes at last to be civil war, which,
its turn, becomes a religious war, and such war soon grows
a war of unbelief against Faith, of antichrist against
rist. The end is not uncertain. Christ will be victorious ;
r it is appointed that the power of hell shall not prevail."
. such a state of things the first duty of German Catholics is
at they be united. It is necessary that the German church
ould remain in intimate union with the Holy Apostolic See,
linquishing all pretension to be a separate National Church.
ie aspiration of our author, so warmly expressed in 1850,
at the German Episcopate should, in mind and action, be one
dy in the nation, acting and suffering together, appears, in

these later days, to have been realized. It was also his firm
conviction that it behooved them to labor to obtain complete
liberty of action for the church, particularly in forming an
exemplary clergy, both in the lesser and greater seminaries, as
well as in those higher institutions, the German universities.
Neither should the laity fail in the fulfilment of all Christian
and charitable duties.

It is well known that, in ancient times, no countries in the
Degeneracy of Spain world were more Catholic than Spain and
and Portugal, and Portugal. The great wealth and power and
their colonies.—Res-
toration under the glory to which they attained was, one would
auspices of Pius IX. say, a mark of Heaven's approbation.
Wealth, however, is a dangerous possession. In the countries
referred to it induced corruption and degeneracy. Principles
of anarchy came to be disseminated. Revolution on revolution
followed. The authority of the Chief Pastor was resisted.
The ministers of religion and the religious orders were treated
with contempt—were persecuted in lands where they had been
so long cherished and revered. The children of a corrupt
nobility were sent to govern the provinces and churches of the
falling Empire. The result was, it is superfluous to say, the
decline of religion—the overthrow of the once flourishing
churches of Spain and Portugal. And yet were they not
destined to perish wholly. A remnant was left; and it was
appointed that this remnant should take root and fructify in a
soil which trials and persecution had prepared for a new
growth. It was reserved for the age of Pius IX. to behold
Spain and Portugal renew their early fervor. They have
returned to the centre of Catholic unity; and in both countries
arrangements have been entered into for staying the spoliation
of ecclesiastical property, appointing learned and edifying
bishops to the vacant Sees, restoring seminaries and clerical
education. The clergy, who had been infected more or less
by the Jansenist heresy, now purified in the crucible of persecution, have resumed the sound doctrines and the heroic virtues
of the apostolic men who will ever be the brightest glory of

their land—Thomas of Villa-Nova, Francis Xavier, Ignatius of Loyola, Peter of Alcantara, Francis Borgia, St. John of the Cross, and Saint Theresa. The Holy See, with the concurrence of the Spanish Government, has organized anew the churches of Spain. In the consistory of 3rd July, 1848, Pope Pius IX. instituted bishops for the following Sees: Segovia and Calahorra, in Old Castile; Tortosa and Vich, in Catalonia; Porto Rico, in North America; Cuenca and St. Charles de Ancud de Chiloe, in South America. This last-named diocese, at the time of the appointment, was newly erected.

From the epoch of the "Reformation," when the ancient Catholic hierarchy of England, which had been so successfully founded by St. Augustine and the disciples of St. Columba, was swept away, until the year 1850, the church was missionary, and governed, as missions usually are, by prefects, who may be arch-priests, or vicars-apostolic, with episcopal titles. Until the year 1625, the English mission was under the guidance of an arch-priest. In that year Pope Gregory II. appointed a vicar-apostolic for all England. Circumstances appearing favorable to the church after the accession of King James II., Pope Innocent XI. placed the English mission under the spiritual charge of four vicars-apostolic, who were bishops, with titles taken from churches, *in partibus infidelium*. The country was, at the same time, divided into four missionary districts—the London, the Eastern, the Midland and the Western. The numbers of Catholics having greatly increased during the early portion of the present century, the Holy Father, Gregory XVI., took into consideration the new requirements that had arisen, by letters apostolical, of date 3rd July, 1840, made a new ecclesiastical division of the English counties, and doubled the number of vicars-apostolic. There were now eight districts under the spiritual jurisdiction of these vicars-apostolic, who governed and were governed by the wise constitutions given to their predecessors by Pope Benedict XIV. Meanwhile, the state of the Catholics of England was rapidly

State of the Catholic Church in England prior to 1850.

improving. Relieved of so many of their disabilities by the gracious Act of 1829, there were no longer any serious legal impediments to the legitimate development of their church. It grew accordingly, and by the year 1840 had become comparatively flourishing. It possessed many stately churches, eight or ten important colleges, the buildings of which were of a high order of architecture; numerous charitable institutions, each of considerable extent; over six hundred public churches or chapels, and eight hundred clergy. Many of the most ancient families of the land were among its devoted adherents, and it also claimed a not unequal share of the intellect and learning, the literary and scientific distinction of the country. Many of the British colonies had already been favored, and not without the full concurrence of the Imperial government, with that more suitable and normal state of church government, which depends on the institution of bishops in ordinary. Was the Mother Country, the seat of empire, whose church was so much more developed than that of any of the colonies, alone to be deprived of so great an advantage? Were the Catholics of England, who were certainly in no respect behind the rest of their fellow-countrymen, even in an age of light and improvement, to rest satisfied with a primitive state of things, when a broader, a more free, and in every way a more beneficial system of spiritual rule was within their reach? The Chief Pastor was willing to inaugurate such rule, provided that he found, on examination, that it was suited to the spiritual state and religious wants of the Catholic people. There was nothing, besides, in the legislation of the country that could be called an impediment to a new and better condition of ecclesiastical government.

For some time the Catholics of England had desired that their church should enjoy the advantage of Pius IX. restores the being governed by bishops in ordinary. So English Hierarchy. early as the year 1834, they petitioned the Holy See to this effect. At that time, however, nothing was concluded. In 1847 the vicars-apostolic assembled in London, and deputed two of their number to bear a petition to the Holy Father, earnestly praying for the long-desired boon. It was craved, not as a mark of triumphant progress, far less as an act of aggression on the law-established church, but simply in order to afford greater facility for the administration of the affairs of the church, and more effectually to promote the edification of the Catholic people. The existing code of government had been adopted about a hundred years before, when heavy penal laws, together with endless disabilities, were in force, and religious liberty was unknown. Part of this code had been repealed by Pope Gregory XVI. But it still tended to embarrass rather than to aid and guide. Since Emancipation, in 1829, the Catholic church had greatly expanded, and the bishops, vicars-apostolic, were in a situation of great difficulty, as they were most anxious to be guarded against arbitrary decisions by fixed rules, whilst as yet none were provided for them. No doubt the system of church government by vicars-apostolic could have been amended and made more suitable to the altered circumstances of the church. But it would have been necessarily complicated, and at best could only have been a temporary arrangement. It was thought expedient, therefore, that the ordinary mode of church government should be extended to the Catholic church in England, in as far as was compatible with its social position. It was, accordingly, necessary that there should be a hierarchy. The canon law could not be applied under vicars-apostolic, nor could provincial synods be held, however necessary their action might be, without a metropolitan and suffragan bishops. The vicars-apostolic petitioned only with a view to improve the internal organization of the church. They had no idea of attacking any other body, and surely never dreamt of rivalry with the established Anglican church. What they did, besides, was perfectly within the law, and according to the rights of liberty of conscience. The Holy Father kindly listened to the petition, and referred it for further consideration to the congregation of Propaganda. When every point was carefully examined, and objections satis-

factorily replied to, the favor petitioned for was granted. Difficulties having been started in regard to some matter of detail,
the publication of the new code of church administration was
delayed. These difficulties were removed the following year
by Bishop Ullathorne. But the measure was again retarded
by the revolution which broke out at Rome in 1848. The
delay was not without its uses. It gave time to the statesmen
of England to become acquainted with and consider the measure of reform which was proposed for adoption in the internal
organization of the Catholic church in England. It was
officially communicated to them when printed, in 1848. They
made no objection. And yet, when it was promulgated in 1850,
their chief spoke of it, in his ill-timed letter to the Bishop of
Durham, as "insolent and insidious." For many an age to
come, Catholics will read with astonishment 'that so inoffensive
an act of the Holy See, done at the request of the Catholic
bishops of England, and in the interest of the Catholic people,
at the time some seven millions in number, should have
excited the anger of so great a portion of the English nation.
The isle was literally frighted from its propriety. From the
Queen on her throne to the humblest villager, all were seized
with sudden and unaccountable fear, as if the monarchy had
been threatened with immediate overthrow. The Queen, in
terror, called her Council of State around her. But her chief
adviser, a weak-minded old man, had very little comfort to
bestow. He could only help her Majesty's bishops to inflame
the public mind. In all conscience, they had done quite
enough in this direction without his assistance. The spirit of
bigotry was enkindled, and the clergy, with their chiefs, gave
proof of their bitter hostility through every newspaper of the
land. This acrimonious opposition was, however, chiefly confined to the ministers of the church by law established. They
believed, or pretended to believe, that the titles and legal rights
of their bishops were aimed at, whilst, in reality, care had been
taken to avoid offending them, or violating the law, by conferring on the new bishops the titles of the ancient Sees which

were held by the established church. It is impossible to mention anything connected with the establishment of the hierarchy which can at all explain the violence of the bishops and clergy generally of the establishment. The popular commotion arose from misconception and the absurd falsehoods that were industriously disseminated. The masses were still raging, when Dr. Wiseman, who had just been raised to the dignity of Cardinal, published an appeal to the people of England, in which he showed that the measure which had occasioned so much disturbance concerned only the internal organization of the Catholic church, that the Pope had not sought such a measure, but had only acceded to it at the earnest request of the bishops, vicars-apostolic of England ; that there was nothing connected with it contrary to the laws of the country, or that could not be reconciled with liberty of conscience, which was now so completely and generally recognized. It was as ridiculous as it was illiberal to heap torrents of abuse on the Pope, as if he had sought to usurp the rights of the Crown, or seize on the territory and revenues of the established Anglican church. As for himself, he was reviled because he had received the title of Archbishop of Westminster, whilst, in reality, as regarded the church of that name, and any territory or property connected with it, it was only an empty title. He was to be metropolitan. The title of London was inhibited by law. Southwark was to be itself a diocese. To have taken the title of a subordinate portion of the great metropolis, such as Finsbury or Islington, would only have excited ridicule, and caused the new episcopate to be jeered at. Westminster was naturally selected, although not by himself, as giving an honorable and well-known title. He was glad that it was chosen, not because it was the seat of the courts of law, or of parliament, but because it brought the real point of the controversy more clearly and strikingly before the opponents of the hierarchy. "Have we, in anything, acted contrary to law? And if not, why are we to be blamed?" But he rejoiced, also, for another reason. The chapter of Westminster had

H

been the first to protest against the new archiepiscopal title, as though some practical attempt at jurisdiction within the Abbey had been intended. To this more than absurd charge, the Cardinal eloquently replied: " The diocese, indeed, of Westminster, embraces a large district, but Westminster proper consists of two very different parts. One comprises the stately Abbey, with its adjacent palaces and its royal parks. To this portion the duties and occupations of the dean and chapter are mainly confined, and they shall range there undisturbed. To the venerable old church I may repair, as I have been wont to do. But perhaps the dean and chapter are not aware, that were I disposed to claim more than the right to tread the Catholic pavement of that noble building, and breathe its air of ancient consecration, another might step in with a prior claim. For successive generations there has existed ever, in the Benedictine order, an Abbot of Westminster, the representative in religious dignity of those who erected and beautified and governed that church and cloister. Have they ever been disturbed by this titular ? Have they heard of any claim or protest on his part touching their temporalities ? Then let them fear no greater aggression now. Like him, I may visit, as I have said, the old Abbey, and say my prayer by the shrine of good St. Edward, and meditate on the olden times, when the church filled without a coronation and multitudes hourly worshipped without a service. But in their temporal rights, or their quiet possession of any dignity and title, they will not suffer. Whenever I go in I will pay my entrance fee, like other liege subjects, and resign myself meekly to the guidance of the beadle, and listen without rebuke when he points out to my admiration detestable monuments, or shows me a hole in the wall for a confessional. Yet this splendid monument, its treasures of art and its fitting endowments, form not the parts of Westminster which will concern me; for there is another part which stands in frightful contrast, though in immediate contact with this magnificence. In ancient times the existence of an abbey in any spot, with a

large staff of clergy and ample revenues, would have sufficed to create around it a little paradise of comfort, cheer-
fulness and ease. This, however, is not now the case.
Close under the Abbey of Westminster there lie concealed
labyrinths of lanes and courts, and alleys and slums, nests of
ignorance, vice, depravity and crime, as well as of squalor,
wretchedness and disease; whose atmosphere is typhus, whose
ventilation is cholera; in which swarms a huge and almost
countless population, in great measure, nominally, at least,
Catholic; haunts of filth which no sewerage committee can
reach; dark corners which no lighting board can brighten.
This is the part of Westminster which alone I covet, and which
I shall be glad to claim and to visit, as a blessed pasture in
which sheep of Holy Church are to be tended, in which a
bishop's godly work has to be done, of consoling, converting
and preserving. And if, as I humbly trust in God, it shall be
seen that this special culture, arising from the establishment
of our hierarchy, bears fruits of order, peacefulness, decency,
religion and virtue, it may be that the Holy See shall not be
thought to have acted unwisely, when it bound up the very
soul and salvation of a Chief Pastor with those of a city,
whereof the name, indeed, is glorious, but the purlieus infamous
—in which the very grandeur of its public edifices is as a
shadow to screen from the public eye sin and misery the most
appalling. If the wealth of the Abbey be stagnant, and not
diffusive; if it in no way rescue the neighboring population
from the depths in which it is sunk, let there be no jealousy of
any one who, by whatever name, is ready to make the latter
his care, without interfering with the former.''

In the passage which follows, the established clergy are
rather unceremoniously handled; and not undeservedly, for
there can be no doubt that their reckless diatribes in the pulpit,
on the platform, and in the press, were the chief cause of the
unhallowed uproar which attended the publication of the new
and much-needed organization of the Catholic church in England. It certainly was not their fault if the country was not

disgraced by deeds of violence. In one or two places, indeed, such things were attempted. At a town in the north of Eng-. land, where there is a Catholic mission, a mob of excited people threatened the chapel and priest's house. The presence of a counter-mob from a neighboring colliery speedily restored tranquillity. In another town a crowd of the unwashed were proceeding to burn the Pope and Cardinal in effigy, when these august persons were wisely seized by order of the magistrates, and, with some of their unruly escort, secured within the prison walls. Although a few *hired* ruffians could attempt such things (it is known that those last named were hired), the English people were far from contemplating anything like violence. So it is with no small pleasure that is here recorded the high compliment paid to them in the following eloquent passage of Cardinal Wiseman's appeal: "I cannot conclude," he says towards the end, "without one word on the part which the clergy of the Anglican church have acted in the late excitement. Catholics have been their principal theological opponents, and we have carried on our controversies with them temperately, and with every personal consideration. We have had no recourse to popular arts to debase them; we have never attempted, even when the current of public opinion has set against them, to turn it to advantage, by joining in any outcry. They are not our members who yearly call for returns of sinecures or episcopal incomes; they are not our people who form antichurch-and-state associations; it is not our press which sends forth caricatures of ecclesiastical dignitaries, or throws ridicule on clerical avocations. With us the cause of truth and of faith has been held too sacred to be advocated in any but honorable and religious modes. We have avoided the tumult of public assemblies and farthing appeals to the ignorance of the multitude. But no sooner has an opportunity been given for awakening every lurking passion against us than it has been eagerly seized by the ministers of the Establishment. The pulpit and the platform, the church and the town hall, have been equally their field of labor; and speeches have been made and untruths uttered, and calumnies repeated, and flashing words of disdain and anger and hate and contempt, and of every unpriestly and unchristian and unholy sentiment, have been spoken, that could be said against those who almost alone have treated them with respect. And little care was taken at what time or in what circumstances these things were done. If the spark had fallen upon the inflammable materials of a gunpowder-treason mob, and made it explode, or, what was worse, had ignited it, what cared they? If blood had been inflamed and arms uplifted, and the torch in their grasp, and flames had been enkindled, what heeded they? If the persons of those whom consecration makes holy, even according to their own belief, had been seized, like the Austrian general, and ill-treated, and perhaps maimed, or worse, what recked they? These very things were, one and all, pointed at as glorious signs, should they take place, of high and noble Protestant feeling in the land, as proofs of the prevalence of an unpersecuting, a free, inquiring, a tolerant gospel creed!

Thanks to you, brave and generous and noble-hearted people of England! who would not be stirred up by those whose duty it is to teach you, gentlemen, meekness and forbearance, to support what they call a religious cause, by irreligious means; and would not hunt down, when bidden, your unoffending fellow-citizens, to the hollow cry of "No Popery," and on the pretence of a fabled aggression.

The London *Times* might well say, referring to this magnificent appeal, that the Cardinal had at length spoken English. It was easy to mystify the people in regard to theological utterances. They could be no longer deceived now that the Chief of the new hierarchy had addressed them in round Saxon terms, about the meaning of which there could be no mistake. The *appeal* first published in the London *Times* was reproduced in all the newspapers of the country. The public mind was tranquillized, and very little was heard, afterwards, of the "Papal aggression." The Prime Minister, however, was bound, for the sake of consistency, to do something. What he did was highly in favor of the hierarchy. It proved that everything had been done according to law, simply by the fact that parliament was urged to make a new law by which everything that had been done would be illegal. This was the famous Ecclesiastical Titles Bill. It was designed to accomplish a great deal —to extinguish for ever the Cardinal Archbishop, and all the other newly-instituted bishops. It proved utterly futile— *tclum imbelle sine ictu.* The people could not be made to put down the Catholic institution; and religious liberty was so thoroughly recognized that even an act of parliament was powerless against it.

The new Sees constituted by the Letters Apostolical of 29th September, 1850, were thirteen in number— Westminster, the Metropolitan See; Southwark, Hexham, Beverly, Liverpool, Salford, Shrewsbury, Newport, Clifton, Plymouth, Nottingham, Birmingham and Northampton.

Number and names of the new Sees.'

At the time of the restoration of the English hierarchy, Dr. Wiseman was created a Cardinal, not so much in honor of the important act to which it was his charge to give effect, as because the Holy Father having resolved on a creation of Cardinals so eminent a man could not be overlooked. At the accession of Pius IX. there were sixty-one living Cardinals. Of these only nine were not Italians. When, on his return to Rome, after his sojourn in the kingdom of Naples, he determined to add fourteen Cardinals to the Sacred College, only four of the prelates selected were natives of Italy. The rest were, at the time, the most distinguished men of the Catholic world. Of this number Archbishop Geissel of Cologne was one, and the King of Prussia, more liberal than certain magnates of England, thanked the Holy Father, in an autograph letter, for the honor thus done to the Catholic church of his country. Since that time the Prussian monarch appears to have changed his sentiments as well as his ministry.

Dr. Wiseman and thirteen other eminent persons raised by Pius IX.to the dignity of Cardinal.

Notwithstanding the noisy demonstrations in opposition to the Cardinal Archbishop and his brother bishops, they were allowed to pursue in peace their labors of Christian zeal. The English grumbled, as is their wont. But discovering in time that they were neither attacked nor hurt, the rights of liberty of conscience were respected, and no persecution followed what it was at first the fashion to call the "Papal aggression."

Success of the English Hierarchy.

The Emancipation Bill of 1829, by which liberty of conscience, which was so proudly called the birthright of every Englishman, was extended to Catholics, tended powerfully, no doubt, to promote the development of the Catholic church. It grew also by emigration from Catholic Ireland, and there were some conversions occasionally from the Protestant ranks. It was not, however, till the decade immediately preceding the restoration of the hierarchy, that there was a very marked and decided movement of the educated and learned men of England towards the Catholic church. It is not recorded anywhere that Catholic missionaries or envoys of the Pope had penetrated into those sanctuaries of Protestant learning—the celebrated universities of Oxford and Cambridge. There, at least, there was no "Papal aggression," and tract upon tract was issued from the press of those seats of learning, in which it was argued that the doctrines taught by the Fathers of the first five centuries were the real Christian teaching which all men were bound to accept. It appeared to have escaped the learned men of Cambridge and Oxford that these were the very doctrines so perseveringly adhered to by the long-ignored and down-trodden Catholics of England.

Increase of Catholics during the decade—1840-1850.

This fact, however, flashed upon their minds at last, and they who were lights in the Anglican establishment, which had been so long surrounded by a halo of worldly glory, and to be connected with which was a sure title to respectability, hesitated not to place themselves in communion with those whose position as a church had been for so many generations like to that of the early Christians who lurked in the catacombs of Rome. The clergy of the Catholic church in England, although they did not and could not have inaugurated the Cambridge and Oxford movement, recognized its importance, and freely seconded what it was beyond their power to initiate. Foremost amongst those who were ever ready to afford comfort and encouragement to the able and inquiring men who sought the one true fold, was the learned ecclesiastic of worldwide renown who, a little later, bore so conspicuous a part in the re-establishment of the sacred hierarchy in England. This highly-gifted divine was a willing worker in the great Master's field. His labors were beyond even his great powers; and so his career, though brilliant, was comparatively short. The cause which he so well sustained is one which cannot suffer an irreparable loss; and great would be the joy of the pious and devoted Cardinal, so early snatched away, if it were given him to behold the rapid developments of the church which, in his day, he so ably and successfully upheld.

If the increase of Catholics in England was rapid during the decade which preceded, it was much more so immediately after the restoration of the hierarchy. This event appears to have given a new impetus to the growth of the church and her salutary institutions. Religious communities multiplied under the fostering care of the Cardinal Archbishop, and the encouragement which the Holy Father never ceased to afford. From 80, at the accession of Pius IX., they rose to 367; and schools and colleges increased from 500 to 1,800. The number of priests in Great Britain was more than trebled. It grew from 820 to 1,968, whilst churches and chapels rose in proportion—from 626 to 1,268. The number of dignitaries and other ministers of the Church of England, by law established, who, within the same period, embraced the Catholic faith, is estimated at over one thousand. There were, at the same time, numerous conversions among the laity. All this, together with the natural growth of popu-

Wonderful growth of the Catholic Church in England during the Pontificate of Pius IX.

lation and immigration from Ireland, accounts for the increase
of Catholics throughout the British isles in the days of Pius
IX., as well as for the great additions to the number of their
clergy, churches, religious and educational institutions. Monsignore Capel ascribes these extraordinary developments in
great measure to the action of that section of the Church of
England which is known as the High Church or Ritualist
division of the Establishment. This is true, no doubt, as regards any augmentation of the church through conversions
from Protestantism, and the impetus given by the movement
towards Catholic union. "It is scarcely possible," says the
Rev. Monsignore Capel, "to find a family in England that will
not own that one of its members, or, at least, some acquaintance, has relations with the Catholic church, or observes some
of the practices of that church, whether it be adoration of the
Blessed Sacrament, auricular confession, devotion to the Blessed Virgin, or veneration of the saints. This movement is of
such powerful proportions, and possesses such vitality of action,
that no power on earth, no persecution on the part of Protestantism, the government or the press, is able to suppress it.
Catholics would never have been able, themselves alone, to
realize what is now accomplished by a section of the established Anglican church. The members of this party, by their discourses in the pulpit, have familiarized the public mind with
expressions which Catholics never could have spread among
the English people to the same extent, such as altar and sacrifice, priest and priesthood, high mass, sacrament, penance,
confession, &c. The movement has produced this result.
Many persons have become seriously religious, who had been
in the habit of considering that the service of God was only a
fitting employment for Sunday. In fine, the spirit of God
which breathed on the waters at the commencement is now
passing over the British nation and impelling it towards Catholic truth."

Not a few of those who were once distinguished ministers of the Anglican church are now officiating, with great

acceptance, as Catholic priests. Of the 264 priests of the diocese of Westminster, there are 40 who were members of the official or law church. There passed not a week, M. Capel assures us, that he did not receive four or five Ritualists into the communion of the Catholic church. This was no fruit of his labor and ability, he modestly as well as truly declares. They were persons with whom he had no relations whatsoever, until they came to him, their minds made up, and expressed that serious determination which is so characteristic of them.

The publications of the celebrated statesman, Mr. Gladstone, although they have not won for him reputation as a theologian, have, nevertheless, promoted the cause of Catholic theology. The opinions of so eminent a man were naturally subjects of general discussion; and thus, whilst he opposed Pius IX. and his decisions, he caused many, who would never probably have thought seriously of anything a Pope could say, to give their attention to matters spiritual of the highest import. As regards his own theology, it is partly sound, partly the reverse. Whilst entirely misapprehending the doctrine of infallibility, and denying what he conceives it to be, he vigorously maintains the indefectibility of the Catholic church, and acknowledges the claim of her pastors to "descent in an unbroken line from Christ and His apostles." Such is one of the powerful agents in the great movement of the age. The most influential of all, however, was Pope Pius IX. himself. English people and Americans often sought his presence. And who shall tell how many, after having conversed with him or his representatives, have been disabused of their erroneous notions, or have even embraced the Catholic faith?

One chief cause of the remarkable development of the Catholic church in the British isles, is the complete religious liberty which Catholics enjoy. This important fact was thoroughly recognized on occasion of the celebration of the anniversary of O'Connell in August, 1875, when a solemn *Te Deum* was ordered in all the churches by the Cardinal Archbishop, in thanksgiving for the liberty of conscience which was so gloriously won for the United Kingdom as well as Ireland and all the colonies. Pius IX. and the whole Catholic world joined on the same occasion in acts of thanksgiving with the spiritual heirs of Sts. Patrick, Augustine, Columba and St. Thomas of Canterbury. It is a noteworthy fact that the number of archiepiscopal and episcopal sees, together with vicariates-apostolic, &c., created by Pius IX. throughout the British Empire, is not less than one hundred and twenty-five.

For three hundred years the Catholics of Holland were sorely tried by persecution. Until the time of the Concordat of 1827, they were governed by archpriests, whose superior or prefect resided at the Hague. When Holland was separated from Belgium, the king of the former country wisely resolved to act as a constitutional monarch. He was considerate as regarded his Catholic subjects. His successor, William II., to whom in 1840 he resigned the crown, treated them with still greater benevolence. He sought an understanding with the Holy See, and gave effect to the Concordat of 1827. Vicars-apostolic, invested with the episcopal character, were now the chief pastors of the church of Holland. The king also sanctioned the establishment of several religious communities, among the rest the Society of Jesuits and the Liguorians. These arrangements were joyfully accepted by the Catholics of Holland, and paved the way for greater developments. These worthy people were, for a long time, believed to be few in number, and scarcely more than nominally Catholics. Relieved, at length, from the pressure of persecution, they astonished the world, not only by their numbers, but also, and even more, by their zeal in the cause of religion. According to the census of 1840, they were nearly one-half of the entire population of Holland. Total population, 2,860,450; Protestants, 1,700,275; Catholics, 1,100,616. The remainder was made up of Jews and other dissenters. Thus were the Catholics of Holland as eleven to seventeen. Since that time they have not ceased to increase. Nor

State of the Catholic Church in Holland anterior to the restoration of its Hierarchy in 1853.

·have they lost the high character which induced Pius IX., in 1853, to restore, the king concurring, their long-lost hierarchy. An archbishopric, Utrecht, and four episcopal sees were established—Harlem, Herzogenbosch, or Bois le Duc, Breda and Roermonde. This wise and necessary measure was followed by an outburst of wrath on the side of the anti-Catholic party. But in Holland, as in England, it soon subsided, and left only the impression that Protestants and other non-Catholic people claim an exclusive right to religious liberty. Pius IX. never ceased to entertain a high opinion of the good Catholics of Holland. '' Ah !'' said he to visitors from that country, '' could we ever forget that these single-minded, loyal, patient Hollanders formed the majority of our soldiers, who were not native Italians, at Castelfidardo and Mentana.''

Whilst in the old world, wherever really free political institutions existed, the spirit of persecution quailed before the recognized principle of religious liberty, in certain portions of [the new it appeared to gain strength, and to increase in the violence of its opposition to the liberty of the church. This was particularly the case in New Granada, where politicians, without statesmanship or experience, imagined that they had made their people free, when they succeeded in separating them from Spain and establishing a republic, in which the first principles of liberty were ignored. It is not recorded that the clergy of New Granada sought to do violence to any man's conscience, or ever thought of forcing any one to accept the Catholic creed. To say the least, they were too wise to attempt, thus to fill the church with hypocrites and secret enemies. Of such there were already too many in those societies which shun the light, and in the new world as actively as in the old intrigue and manœuvre in order to overthrow every regular and legitimately established government. Even the republic of New Granada, which had been fashioned so much according to their will, was far from perfect in their estimation, so long as the church was not completely subject to the state. So early as 1847, Pius IX. addressed a fatherly remonstrance to the President of the New Republic. It was of no avail. The evil continued. Anti-Catholic legislation was coolly proceeded with. In 1850 the seminary of Bogota was confiscated. The following year bishops were forbidden the visitation of convents. Laws were enacted requiring that lay parishioners should elect their parish priests, and that canons should be appointed by the provincial councils. The clergy were robbed of their proper incomes, and the congress or parliament of the republic arrogated the right to determine what salaries they should enjoy as well as what duties they should fulfil. This surely was nothing less than to reduce the church to be nothing more than a department of the civil government. The church could not so exist. Its principle and organization were from a higher source. The Socialists and secret plotters fully understood that they were so, and that in this lay the secret of the church's power to promote virtue and check the course of evil. It consisted, it appears, with their ideas of justice and liberty, that the church should, if possible, be deprived of this great and salutary moral power. So, whilst neither its members, generally, nor its clergy desired radical and subversive changes in the essential constitution of the church, the republican leaders determined that it should be completely revolutionized. The bishops and priests protested, with one voice, against such fundamental innovations. The republicans, no less resolute, and bent on their wicked purpose, imprisoned and banished the clergy. One dignitary alone showed weakness. He was no other than the Vicar-Caputular of Antioquia. Pius IX. charitably rebuked him, and exhorted him to suffer courageously, like his brethren. The persecution, meanwhile, was very sweeping. The Archbishop of Bogota, Senor Mosquera, and almost all the suffragan bishops, were driven from the country, so that there was scarcely a bishop left in the republic. It was now speedily seen that the godless radicals had overdone their ungracious work. The country was roused. The tide of popular indigna-

tion set in against the short-sighted politicians who persecuted
the church, and they, dreading an insurrection, withdrew, with
the best grace they could command, from the false position
which they had so unwisely assumed.

Whilst the spirit of persecution brooded gloomily over many
countries of the new world, its influence be-
gan to decline in those lands where for
centuries the idea of liberty of conscience
was unknown, where even the slightest toleration existed not.
Those northern lights, those champions in their day of Protestantism and *"religious liberty,"* Gustavus Wasa and Gustavus Adolphus, were not mistaken when they bequeathed to
their country laws which were intended to be as unchangeable
as those of the Medes and Persians, and which forbade all
Scandinavians, whether Swedes, Danes or Norwegians, under
pain of death, to embrace the Catholic faith. Those princes
were wise in their generation. They understood the power of
Truth ; they knew that half measures were of no avail against
it ; and that in order to stifle it, even for a time, all the ter-
rors of worldly tyranny must be brought into play. Their
laws, more terrible than the code of Draco, remained in force
and without mitigation until a great revolution had swept
over Europe, and sent a military adventurer to fill the regal
seat of the formidable Wasas. In the time of Bernadotte (the
Doct Baron), the infamous penal laws were relaxed. To become a Catholic now only led to imprisonment or exile. Six
ladies of Sweden, in defiance of this *milder* law, came to profess the Catholic faith. They were tried, condemned and
sentenced to be banished from the country. The execution of
this barbarous sentence roused all Europe, and caused the
abrogation of the Swedish penal laws against religion. Thus
was a new field laid open to missionary zeal,
and Pius IX., availing himself of so favorable a change of circumstances, appointed a
Catholic pastor missionary apostolic at Stockholm. This
devoted priest labors assiduously and in the midst of diffi-

Persecution ceases at last in the Scandinavian countries.

Pius IX. sends a Catholic pastor to Stockholm.

culties, but not without fruit. He contends, with all the success that can be as yet expected, against prejudices hostile to the religion which brought civilization to the Scandinavian nations, and which have been accumulating for three centuries and a half.

Denmark followed in the wake of Sweden. Within the first two years after the abrogation of the cruel Danish penal code, there were six hundred conversions to the Catholic faith.

Denmark—600 conversions.

The Catholic church in the recently-erected kingdom of Greece was governed by vicars-apostolic. It grieved King Otho, who, as is well known, was of the Catholic royal family of Bavaria, to see his country treated as if it were a heathen land. It was not, however, till the time of his successor, who is a son of the King of Denmark, that Pius the Ninth was able to establish a hierarchy in Greece. There is now an archbishop of Athens as well as an archbishop of Corfu.

Pius IX. establishes a Metropolitan See at Athens.

At a time when crime abounded, the governments of certain petty States of Germany, instead of directing their energies towards its repression, and so fulfilling one of the chief duties incumbent on the State, employed all the authority with which they were invested to disorganize the church and destroy its salutary influence. As is usual, when States, forgetting the great objects for which they are entrusted with the sword of justice, follow such a course, they attacked the ministers of the church, banishing, imprisoning, thwarting and molesting them in every possible way. In the Grand Duchy of Baden the civil authorities arrogated the right to appoint parish priests and other members of the sacred ministry. They went so far as to endeavor to poison religious instruction at its source, and declared that the students in Catholic seminaries must undergo, before ordination, an examination by civil officials. This tyrannical law was courageously opposed by the

Germany — Wars against the Church.

venerable archbishop, Vicary, of Friburg. Although eighty
years of age, he was dragged before the
courts, and placed like a criminal under
charge of the police. The faithful clergy
were banished, imprisoned and fined. The
Holy Father, with his usual zeal, remonstrated. It was to no purpose. At length the Catholics of
Germany were roused. They could no longer be indifferent.
The day was come when the church, in her utmost need, could
not dispense with their assistance. All must now be for her or
against her. The great majority flocked around her standard.
Meanwhile, the public offices in the churches were suspended.
The bells and organs were heard no more. Silence and death-
like gloom overspread the land. Baden gave way. Wurtem-
berg, Hesse Cassel and Nassau, which had done their best to
follow in the wake of Baden, paused in their mad career.
Thus, throughout those lesser States peace reigned once more,
and continued to reign in Germany until a greater State,
Prussia, unwisely disturbed the religious harmony which so
happily prevailed. The chiefs of States, alarmed by the revolutionary spirit which spread, like contagion, throughout Germany as well as the rest of Europe, adopted a more rational
policy. They encouraged the clergy to hold missions everywhere. They invited the Liguorians and Jesuits, as well as the
secular clergy, to assemble the people in the towns and throughout the country, knowing full well that they would preach
peace and concord no less than respect for property and life.
These pastoral labors were attended with extraordinary success. Faith, piety, and every virtue flourished among the
Catholic people. All honest Protestants were filled with admiration. Among the latter there was also a remarkable movement. Some striking conversions took place, especially in the
higher and better educated classes of society. The Countess
de Hahn, so renowned in the literary world for her wit, abilities, and fine writings, joined the Catholic church, and pub-

> *An archbishop and other priests cruelly persecuted. Sustained by Pius IX., and finally by the people.*

lished her reasons for so doing. Not satisfied with this step, she came to the town of Angers, in France, and placed herself as a novice under the direction of the devout sisters of the Good Shepherd. It is on record also, that a Protestant journalist of Mecklenburgh, in view of the commotions which prevailed, and the anti-social doctrines which pervaded society, went so far as to declare that there was no other remedy for Protestant Germany than a return to the Catholic church. His remarks conclude with the following words, extraordinary words, indeed, when it is considered whence they proceed: " Forward, then, to Rome !"

In countries nearer the Holy City, and professing to be Catholic, the venerable Pontiff found not such a source of consolation. Sardinia had banished the archbishop of Turin. It not only refused to recall him, but added to its list of exiles the archbishop of Cagliari. Many more bishops were, at the same time, threatened with banishment. A professor in the Royal University of Turin, encouraged by the government, attacked the doctrine of the church, and was so bold as to deny, in public, that matrimony is a sacrament. Pius IX. issued a condemnation of his anti-Catholic writings. The sentence did not move him. Nor did it stay the hand of the Sardinian government which was raised against the church and her institutions. It continued the preparation of its anti-marriage law. In addition, accusations were laid against the clergy. The king himself, evading the real question at issue, accused them of disloyalty, and declared that they were warring against the monarchy. The Holy Father, in the following letter to the king, distinctly set forth the real state of the case :.

Pius IX. laments the state of religion in Sardinia. — Condemns the Act secularizing marriage.

" If by words provoking insubordination are meant the writings of the clergy against the proposed marriage law, we declare, without indorsing the language which some may have adopted, that in opposing it the clergy simply did their duty. We write to your Majesty that the law is not Catholic. Now, if the law is not Catholic, the clergy are bound to warn the

J

faithful, even though by doing so they incur the greatest dangers. It is in the name of Jesus Christ, whose Vicar, though unworthy, we are, that we speak, and we tell your Majesty, in His sacred name, not to sanction this law, which will be the source of a thousand disorders. We also beg your Majesty to put a check to the press which is constantly vomiting forth blasphemy and immorality. Your Majesty complains of the clergy. But these last years the clergy have been persistently outraged, mocked, calumniated, reviled and derided by almost all the papers published in Piedmont."

That country, unfortunately, appears to have been entirely at the mercy of the party of unbelief. It was ever ready to inflict new wrongs on the church, and occasion anxiety and sorrow to the Holy Father.

There are few readers of ecclesiastical history who are not deeply interested in that portion of India which was the first field of the extraordinary apostolic labors of Saint Francis Xavier.

Pius IX. puts an end to the celebrated Goa Schism in 1851.

The blessing of the Saint appears to have rested on the land of Goa ; for after many years of trial and difficulty and schism, this Portuguese settlement, once so great and important, still remains a province of the church. The Portuguese government, by unjustly claiming right of patronage, originated the schism which, unfortunately, was of such long continuance. It was reserved for Pius IX. to restore harmony to the Colonial church of Goa. Happily, in 1851, the schism was brought to an end.

Pius IX. was still an exile at Gaeta when, observing the increasing piety of the Catholic world towards the Blessed Virgin, and moved by the representations of many bishops that were in harmony with his own conviction, he issued the Encyclical of the 2nd February, 1849, addressed to the Patriarchs, Primates, Archbishops and Bishops of the whole world, in order to obtain from them the universal tradition concerning the Immaculate Conception of the Blessed Mother of God. In this

Encyclical on the Immaculate Conception—1849.

Encyclical the Holy Father recognizes the fact that there was a universal movement among Christians in favor of the belief in question, so that the complete acknowledgment of it appeared to be sufficiently prepared both by the liturgy and the formal requisitions of numerous bishops, no less than by the studies of the most learned theologians. He further states that this general disposition was in full accordance with his own thought, and that it would afford him great consolation, at a time when so many evils assailed the church, to add a flower to the crown of the most holy Virgin, and so acquire a title to her special protection. He declares, moreover, that with this end in view he had appointed a commission of Cardinals in order to study the question. He concludes by inviting all his venerable brethren of the Episcopate to make known to him their sentiments and join their prayers with his in order to obtain light from on high.

As the cross itself was folly in the estimation of the early unbelieving world, so were such theological occupations, at a time when the Sovereign Pontiff had not an inch of ground whereon he could freely tread, a subject for jesting and sarcasm to the worldly-wise of the nineteenth century. It was some time before they came to understand that a Pope is a theologian more than a king, that, as such, he is sure of the future, and that the solemn proceeding in regard to the Immaculate Conception was a triumphant reply to all the errors of modern thought. This dogma brings to naught all the rationalist systems which refuse to acknowledge in human nature either fall or supernatural redemption. The means, besides, which were adopted in order to prepare its promulgation, tended to bring the various churches throughout the world into closer relation with their common Head and Centre. They who had hitherto laughed, now raged when they saw this great result, and attacked with the utmost fury what they called the "new dogma." Both sectarianism and the schools of sophistry descanted loudly, although certainly not learnedly, on the ignorance and ineptitude of the institution which so powerfully opposed them. All this was only idle clamoring. It never hindered the Holy Pontiff from prosecuting calmly the important work which heaven had inspired him to begin.

The Encyclical was warmly responded to by the Episcopate. Six hundred and three replies were duly forwarded to the Holy Father. Five hundred and forty-six urgently insisted on a doctrinal definition. A few only, and among these was Mgr. Sibour, Archbishop of Paris, doubted whether the time were opportune. But there was no doubt as to the sentiments of the Catholic world. Only in our time, when the facilities of communication are so much greater than in any former age, could the plan of consulting so many bishops in all parts of the world have been successfully adopted. Pius IX. was now at Rome, and invited around him all bishops who could travel to the Holy City. No fewer than one hundred and ninety-two from every country except Russia sought the presence of the Chief Pastor. The absence of the Russian bishops was all the more surprising, as the Russo-Greek church vies with Rome in the honor which it pays to the Blessed Mary. The bishops, however, were not to blame. Their good purposes were frustrated by the jealous /policy of the Emperor Nicholas. The bishops assembled at Rome, in obedience to the wishes of Pius IX., did not constitute a formal council. They were, nevertheless, a very complete representation of the universal church. There were of their number some highly distinguished cardinals, archbishops and bishops, such as Cardinals Wiseman and Patrizzi, Archbishops Fransoni of Turin, Reisach of Munich, Sibour of Paris, Bedini of Thebes, Hughes of New York, Kenrick of Baltimore, and Dixon of Armagh, together with Bishops Mazenod of Marseilles, Bouvier of Mans, Malon of Bruges, Dupanloup of Orleans, and Ketteler of Mayence. Who will say that the learning of the Catholic world was not at hand to aid with sound counsel the commission of cardinals and theologians whom the Holy Father had appointed to prepare the Bull of definition? There had never been so many eminent bishops together at Rome, since the

Occumenial Council of 1215. On so great an occasion Pius IX. had requested the prayers of the faithful, and throughout the Catholic world supplication was made to heaven, in order to obtain, through the light of the Holy Ghost, such a decision as could tend only to promote the glory of God, the honor due to the Blessed Virgin Mary and the salvation of mankind. The bishops at one of their sessions gave a very practical utterance as regards the infallible authority of the Pope. The question having arisen whether the bishops were to assist him as judges in coming to a decision, and pronounce simultaneously with him, or leave the final judgment solely to the word of the Sovereign Pontiff, the debate, as if by inspiration from on high, came suddenly to a close. It was the Angelus hour. The prelates had scarcely resumed their places after the short prayer, and exchanged a few words, when they made a unanimous declaration in favor of the supremacy of St. Peter's chair: *Petre, doce nos; confirma fratres tuos*—"Peter, teach us; confirm thy brethren." The teaching which the Reverend Fathers sought from the lips of the Supreme Pastor was the definition of the Immaculate Conception.

The 8th December, 1854, was the great triumphal day which, according to the fine language of Bishop Dupanloup, "crowned the expectation of past ages, blessed the present time, claimed the gratitude of the centuries to come, and left an imperishable memory—the day on which was pronounced the first definition of an article of Faith which no dissentient voice preceded, and which no heresy followed." All Rome rejoiced. An immense multitude of people of all tongues crowded the approaches to the vast Basilica of St. Peter, which was by far too small to contain the imposing host. Then were seen advancing the bishops, in solemn procession, placed according to seniority, and followed by the cardinals. The Sovereign Pontiff, surrounded by a brilliant cortege, closed the procession. Meanwhile was heard the grave chant of the Litanies of the Saints, inviting

Pius IX. solemnly promulgated the Dogma of the Immaculate Conception.

the heavenly court to join with the Church militant in doing
honor to her who was Queen alike of angels and of men. Pius
IX. ascended his throne; and as soon as he had received the
obedience of the cardinals and bishops, the Pontifical Mass
began. When the Gospel had been chanted in Greek and in
Latin, Cardinal Macchi, Dean of the Sacred College, accompanied by the deans of the archbishops and bishops, by an
archbishop of the Greek rite, also, and an Armenian archbishop,
advanced to the foot of the throne, and begged of the Holy
Father, in the name of the whole church, "to raise his apostolic voice and pronounce the dogmatic decree of the *Immaculate
Conception.*" The Pope, bowing his head, gladly welcomed the
petition; but wished once more to invoke the aid of the Holy
Ghost. Then rising from his throne, he intoned in a clear and
firm voice, which rang through the grand Basilica, the *veni
creator spiritus.* All who were present, cardinals, bishops,
priests and people, mingled their voices with that of the Father
of the Faithful, and the sonorous tones of the heavenly hymn
resounded through the spacious edifice. Silence came. All
eyes were rivetted on the venerable Pontiff. His countenance
appeared to be transfigured by the solemnity of the act in which
he was engaged. And now, in that firm and grave, but mild
and majestic, tone of voice, the charm of which was known to
so many millions, he began to read the Bull, which announced the sublime dogma of the Immaculate Conception.
It established, in the first place, the theological reasons for the
belief in the privilege of Mary. It then appealed to the ancient
and universal traditions of both the Eastern and the Western
churches, the testimony of the religious orders, and of the
schools of theology, that of the Holy Fathers and the Councils,
as well as the witness borne by Pontifical acts, both ancient
and more recent. The countenance of the Holy Father showed
that he was deeply moved, as he unfolded these magnificent
documents. He was obliged, several times, so great was his
emotion, to stop. "Consequently," he continued, "after having offered without ceasing, in humility and with fasting, our

own prayers and the public prayers of the church to God the Father through His Son, that He would deign to guide and confirm our mind by the power of the Holy Ghost, after we had implored the aid of the whole host of heaven, to the glory of the Holy and Undivided Trinity, for the honor of the Virgin Mother of God, for the exaltation of the Catholic faith and the increase of the Christian religion; by the authority of our Lord Jesus Christ, of the blessed apostles Peter and Paul, and by our own "—at these words the Holy Father's voice appeared to fail him, and he paused to wipe away his tears. The audience was, at the same time, deeply moved; but, dumb from respect and admiration, they waited in deepest silence. The venerable Pontiff resumed in a strong voice, which shortly rose to a tone of enthusiasm: " We declare, pronounce and define, that the doctrine which affirms that the Blessed Virgin Mary was preserved and exempt from all stain of original sin from the first moment of her conception, in consideration of the merits of Jesus Christ, the Saviour of mankind, is a doctrine revealed by God, and which, for this cause, the faithful must firmly and constantly believe. Wherefore, if any one should be so presumptuous, which, God forbid! as to admit a belief contrary to our definition, let him know that he has suffered shipwreck of his faith, and that he is separated from the unity of the church." As the Pontiff concluded, a glad responsive " Amen " resounded through the crowded temple.

The Cardinal-dean once more reverently approached, and petitioned that order be given for the publication of the apostolic letters containing the definition ; the promoter of the Faith, accompanied by the Apostolic Protonotaries, also came to ask that a formal record of the great act should be drawn up. At the same time the cannon of the castle of Saint Angelo, and all the bells of Rome, proclaimed to the world that the ever-blessed Mary was gloriously declared immaculate. Throughout the evening the holy city echoed and re-echoed to the sounds of joyous music, was ablaze with fire-works, and decorated with innumerable inscriptions and emblematic transparencies.

The example of Rome was immediately followed by thousands of towns and villages over the whole surface of the globe. It would require libraries rather than volumes to reproduce the expressions of pious concurrence which everywhere took place. The replies of the bishops to the Pope before the definition, were printed in nine volumes; the Bull itself, translated into all the tongues and dialects of the universe, by the labors of a learned French sulpician, the Abbe Sire, appeared in ten volumes; the pastoral instructions, publishing and explaining the Bull, together with the articles of religious journals, would certainly make several hundred volumes, especially if to these were added the many books by the most learned men, and the singularly beautiful hymns and poems which flowed from the pens of Catholic poets, no less than the eloquent discourses of the most gifted orators. Descriptions of monuments and celebrations would also immensely swell the list. Sanctuaries, altars, statues, monuments of every kind, as well as pious associations rose everywhere in honor of the Immaculate Conception. The ever-increasing devotion to Mary had become greater than ever. It was to the unbelieving a phenomenon in the moral world of the nineteenth century, which they could neither comprehend nor account for. They could only see that it was as a source of new life to the church.

The education law of France, enacted in 1850, had given rise to differences of opinion among earnest Catholics. These only increased after the celebrated *coup d'etat* of 2nd December. M. de Montalembert, who had become hostile to Prince Louis Napoleon, on occasion of the iniquitous confiscation of the Orleans property, M. de Falloux, and their friends of the *Correspondant* and the *Ami de la Religion,* insisted that they ought not to accept the protection of Cæsar in place of the general guarantees which were so profitable to the liberty of the church. They were right, as was but too well shown in the sequel. M. Louis Veuillot and the writers of the *Univers* opposed their views, and so they accused these gentlemen of servility. But this was too much, as the event also showed.

Dispates concerning the study of the ancient classics happily terminated by Pius IX.

The congregation of the "Index" had condemned several French works, some absolutely, and others only until they should be corrected. Among these last were books generally used, notwithstanding their faults, in the public schools, such as the *Manual of Canon Law*, by M. Lequeux, vicar-general of the Archbishop of Paris, and the theology, so long in use, of Bailly. The authors of these works at once submitted. One of the sentences, however, that which affected the Dictionary of M. Bouillet, greatly offended the Archbishop of Paris—Mgr. Sibour, who had signified his approval of this publication. He blamed the *Univers* and the lay religious press in general. He formulated his complaints in a charge of 15th January, 1851, and by a still more vigorous one in 1853, which was written at the instigation of a Canon of Orleans, M. L' Abbe Gaduel, who had accused Donoso Cortes, in the *Ami de la Religion*, of several heresies, and who complained of having been refuted in the *Univers* with a warmth that was far from respectful. Mgr. Sibour forbade the priests of his diocese to read the *Univers*, and threatened with excommunication the editors of this journal, if they presumed to discuss the sentence which he had pronounced against them. A similar sentence came to be uttered by Mgr. Dupanloup, Bishop of Orleans, against the same writers, condemning the opinions which they held concerning the study of the classics. M. Veuillot, following in the wake of M. L'Abbe Gaume, maintained that one of the principal causes of the weakening of faith since the time of the *renaissance*, was the obligation imposed on youth of studying, almost exclusively, Pagan authors. Mgr. Dupanloup contended rather against exaggerations of this opinion than against the idea itself. But having developed his views in an episcopal letter to the professors of his lesser seminaries, he would not allow them to be opposed; and so, like Mgr. Sibour, interdicted the *Univers* to his clergy. M. Louis Veuillot appealed to the supreme bishop.

The French episcopate was *greatly* divided on the subject of these untoward controversies. The Bishops of Chartres,

Moulins and others, had publicly defended the *Univers* in opposition to the Archbishop of Paris. Cardinal Gousset, Archbishop of Rheims, patronized the opinions of M. Veuillot in
regard to the use of heathen classics. An anonymous paper
on *the right of custom*, addressed to the episcopate, now added
to all these subjects of controversy the recriminations of Galli-
canism, which was almost extinct. The author denying that
the customs of the church of France were abrogated by the
Concordat, maintained that the disciplinary sentences of the
Popes could not be applied in any diocese until they were first
promulgated therein. He disputed the authority of the decrees
of the "Index," blamed the liturgical movement, reproached the
religious journalists with seeking, above all, to please the Court
of Rome, and concluded by advising the bishops to come to an
understanding among themselves, in order to obtain from the
Pope a modification of his decisions. Pius IX. could be silent
no longer. Accordingly, he addressed to all the French bishops
an Encyclical, which is known in history as the Encyclical *inter
multiplices*. He commenced by acknowledging the subjects of
joy and consolation afforded him by the progress of religion in
France, and especially by the zeal and devotedness of the
bishops of that country. He gave special praise to these prelates, because they availed themselves of the liberty which had
been restored to them in order to hold Provincial Councils, and
expressed his satisfaction, "that in a great many dioceses,
where no particular circumstance opposed an impediment, the
Roman Liturgy was re-established." He could not, however,
dissemble the sorrow which was caused him by existing dis-
sensions, and for which he blamed, although indirectly, political
opposition and party spirit. "If ever," said the Holy Father,
"it behooved you to maintain among yourselves agreement of
mind and will, it is, above all, now, when, through the disposition of our very dear son in Christ, Napoleon, Emperor of the
French, the Catholic church amongst you enjoys complete
peace, liberty and protection." In speaking of the good education of youth, which he earnestly recommended as being of the

highest importance, he gave a practical solution of the vexed question of the classics. "It is necessary," he insisted, "that young ecclesiastics should, without being exposed to any danger of error, learn true elegance of language and style, together with real eloquence, whether in the very pious and learned works of the Holy Fathers, or in the most celebrated Pagan authors, when thoroughly expurgated." In this same Encyclical also, the venerable Pontiff, speaking of the Catholic press, declared it to be indispensible. "Encourage, we most anxiously ask of you, with the utmost benevolence, those men who, filled with a truly Catholic spirit, and thoroughly acquainted with literature and science, devote their time in writing books and journals for the propagation and defence of Truth."

Catholic writers, in return, it is added, ought to acknowledge the authority of bishops to guide, admonish and rebuke them. The anonymous paper is then severely censured, and the Pope concludes by a new and pressing appeal in favor of concord. As soon as this Encyclical of 21st March, 1853, was published, M. Louis Veuillot and his fellow-laborers addressed to Mgr. Sibour a letter expressive of respect and deference, in which they promised to avoid everything that could render them unworthy of the encouragement of their archbishop. This prelate immediately withdrew the sentence which he had issued against them, and thus was peace restored, once more, by the authority of the Supreme Pastor.

On the 12th of April, 1855, the fifth anniversary of his return from Gaeta, Pius IX. drove by the via Nomentana, the beautiful Church of St. Agnes and the Porta Pia, to a spot five miles from the city, where, on grounds belonging to the congregation of Propaganda, catacombs had been recently discovered. In these subterranean recesses were found, among other venerated tombs, that which contained the relics of St. Alexander I., Pope and Martyr, and those of the companions who shared his sufferings. The pro-

Accident at St. Agnes. Narrow escape of Pius IX. and many eminent persons.

fessors and students of Propaganda had assembled at the place
in honor of the Pope's visit. They descended with him to the
Crypt, where the Holy Father, as soon as he entered, knelt in
prayer beside the remains of his sainted predecessor, who,
more than seventeen centuries ago, had sealed his faith with
his blood. After examining the long corridors of the catacomb,
the Holy Father took his seat on the ancient throne of the
chapel, which, no doubt, in the dark days of heathen persecution, several of his predecessors had filled. So placed, he
delivered to the pupils of Propaganda a feeling allocution on
the high career which lay before them as preachers of the true
Faith. He then addressed a few words to the eminent persons
who surrounded him, and proceeded back to the Church of St.
Agnes. Having adored the Blessed Sacrament, and venerated
the relics of the Virgin Martyr, he entered the neighboring
convent of canons regular of St. John Lateran, where a suitable repast awaited the august visitor. This was followed by
a conversazione in the parlor, in which the distinguished
parties who had accompanied the Pope took part. Almost
every Catholic country was represented there ; and, among the
rest, were Archbishop Cullen of Dublin (long since a Cardinal),
and Bishop de Goesbriand of Burlington. The Pope was on
the point of departing, when the Superiors of Propaganda
prayed him to grant an audience to the students. Pius IX.
graciously complied, and resumed his seat in the chair of state
which was appropriately canopied. A hundred young ecclesiastics now rapidly entered the room. All of a sudden the floor
gave way with a loud crash, and the whole assembly disappeared in a confused mass of furniture, stones, plaster, and a
blinding cloud of dust. The joists had given way, and the
whole flooring fell to a depth of nearly twenty feet. The voice
of the Pope was first heard, intimating that he was safe and
uninjured. As a few inmates of the convent had remained
outside, assistance speedily came, and the Holy Father was
promptly extricated from the ruins. Solicitous only for the
safety of the company, he urgently ordered that they should

all be withdrawn as rapidly as possible from their perilous position; and he waited in the garden till every one of them was rescued. Not so much as one was dangerously injured.

"It is a miracle," said the Pope, who was greatly rejoiced. "Let us go and thank God." Followed by the whole company, as well as those who had come to rescue them, he entered the church, where, deeply affected, he intoned the *Te Deum*, and concluded with the solemn benediction of the most Holy Sacrament.

The news of the accident spread rapidly through the city. The people flocked to the churches. At St. Agnes the wonderful deliverance was commemorated by a special service. The interior of this church has been since restored at great cost by Pius IX. A fresco in the open space in front represents the scene at the convent. The 12th of April is now a holiday at Rome, and it is observed every year with piety and gratitude. Twenty years later—12th of April, 1875—the Romans held a magnificent celebration of the anniversary of the accident at St. Agnes. It was also the day of the Pope's return from Gaeta, in 1850. In reply to the address, expressive of duty and devotedness, which was presented to him on that occasion, the Holy Father alluded, in the language of an apostle, to the mysterious ways of Providence. "Our fall at St. Agnes," said he, "appeared at first to be a catastrophe. It struck us all with fear. Its only result, however, was to cause the works by which the ancient Basilica was renewed and embellished to be more vigorously prosecuted. The same will be the case in regard to the moral ruins which the powers of darkness are constantly heaping up against us and around us. The church will emerge from the confused mass more vigorous and more beautiful than ever."

Piedmont, surely, had little to do at the Congress of Paris, the object of which was to make the best arrangements possible for the Christians, and especially the Catholics, of the East.

Piedmont seeks a French alliance against the Pope.

Count Cavour, its representative, nevertheless, found a pretext for being present, and introduced as he was by the Minister of France, Count Walewski, and sustained by the British Plenipotentiary, Lord Clarendon, he became more important than the power of his country, or the share it had in the Crimean War, would alone have warranted. He availed himself of his position to attack and undermine two of the minor sovereigns—the Pope and the King of Naples.

"The States of the Holy See," he insisted, "never knew prosperity, except under the rule of Napoleon I., when they formed part of the French empire and the kingdom of Italy. Later, the Emperor Napoleon III., *with that precision and firmness of view by which he is characterized*, understood and clearly pointed out in his letter to Colonel Ney; the solution of the problem: *Secularization and the Code Napoleon;* but it is evident that the Court of Rome will struggle to the last moment, and by every possible means, against the realization of this twofold combination. It is easily understood that it may appear to accept civil and even political reforms, taking care always to render them illusory. But it knows too well that secularization and the code Napoleon, once introduced into the edifice of the temporal power, would undermine it and cause it to fall, simply by removing its principal supports—clerical privileges and canon law. Clerical organization opposes insurmountable impediments to all kinds of innovations."

Cavour urged, in conclusion, that "the legations" must be separated politically, and a viceroy set over those provinces. Walewski and Clarendon supported these views, but cautiously using the enigmatic language of diplomacy. The Plenipotentiaries of the other Powers were silent, or refused to give an opinion, on the ground that they had no instructions. M. de Manteuffel alone, the Prussian representative, sternly observed that such recriminations as M. de Cavour had brought forward were very like an appeal to the revolutionary movements in Italy. Prussia did not, at that time, foresee what advantage it was destined to reap from the alliance of the Italian revolution with Napoleon III. France, however, had reason to dread lest the chief of her choice should return to the dark practices of his youth. Her too well-founded apprehensions were con-

firmed and aggravated when it came to the public ear, through
the newspapers of the time, that the Emperor had held a too
intimate interview with M. de Cavour at the waters of Plombieres. All this, notwithstanding an alliance of France with
Piedmont, for the destruction of the Pope's temporal sovereignty, appeared as yet to be so completely out of the question,
that the French ambassador at Rome refuted publicly the
calumnies which M. de Cavour had so selfishly promulgated.
Count de Rayneval had been a long time at Rome, first as
Secretary of the Embassy of King Louis Philippe, and afterwards as Plenipotentiary of the Republic, before he was appointed to represent the Emperor Napoleon. None could be
better qualified to give a luminous report of the state of matters at Rome. The revolutionary press, however, never noticed
it, and the government refused to publish ¦it in the *Moniteur*,
preferring the wretched pamphlet of M. About on the *Roman*
Question. The French, who wished to be well informed, sought
the words of M. de Rayneval's report in the columns of the
London *Daily News :*

COUNT RAYNEVAL'S REPORT TO THE FRENCH GOVERNMENT.

" Pius IX. shows himself full of ardor for reforms. He
himself puts his hand to the work. From the very day Pius
IX. mounted the throne he has made continuous efforts to
sweep away every legitimate cause of complaint against the
public administration of affairs.

"Already have civil and criminal cases, as well as a code
relating to commerce, all founded on our own, enriched by
lessons derived from experience, been promulgated. I have
studied these carefully—they are above criticism. The Code
des Hypotheques has been examined by French *juris consults,*
and has been cited by them as a model ¦document. Abroad
(says this distinguished and able writer), those essential
changes that are introduced into the order of things, those
incessant efforts of the Pontifical government to ameliorate the
lot of the populations, have passed unnoticed. People have

had ears only for the declamation of the discontented, and for the permanent calumnies of the bad portion of the Piedmontese and Italian press. This is the source from which public opinion has derived its inspiration. And in spite of well established facts, it is believed in most places, but particularly in England, that the Pontifical government has done nothing for its subjects, and has restricted itself to the perpetuation of the errors of another age. I have only yet indicated the ameliorations introduced into the organization of the administration. Above all, let us remember that never has a more exalted spirit of clemency been seen to preside over a restoration. No vengeance has been exercised on those who caused the overthrow of the Pontifical government—no measures of rigor have been adopted against them—the Pope has contented himself with depriving them of the power of doing harm by banishing them from the land."

ECONOMY OF THE PAPAL GOVERNMENT—MODERATE TAXATION.

"In spite of considerable burdens which were occasioned by the revolution, and left as a legacy to the present government—in spite of extraordinary expenses caused by the reorganization of the army—in spite of numerous contributions towards the encouragement of public works, the state budget, which, at the commencement, exhibited a tolerably large *deficit*, has been gradually tending towards equilibrium. I have had the honor recently of pointing out to your Excellency, that the deficit of 1857 has been reduced to an insignificant sum, consisting for the most part of unexpected expenses, and of money reserved for the extinction of the debt. The taxes remain still much below the mean rate of the different European States. A Roman pays the state 22 francs annually, 68,000,000 being levied on a population of 3,000,000. A Frenchman pays the French government 45 francs, 1,600,000,000 being levied on a population of 35,000,000. These figures show, demonstratively, that the Pontifical States, with regard to so important a point, must be reckoned amongst the most favored nations.

The expenses are regulated on principles of the greatest economy. One fact is sufficient. The civil list, the expenses of the cardinals, of the diplomatic corps abroad, the maintenance of Pontifical palaces and the museum, cost the state no more than 600,000 crowns (8,200,000). This small sum is the only share of the public revenue taken by the Papacy for the support of the Pontifical dignity, and for keeping up the principal establishments of the superior ecclesiastical administration. We might ask those persons, so zealous in hunting down abuses, whether the appropriation of 4,000 crowns to the wants of the princes of the church seems to them to bear the impress of a proper economy exercised with respect to the public revenue ?

AGRICULTURE—DRAINING THE CAMPAGNA—PRISON DISCIPLINE—
ADMINISTRATION OF CHARITABLE INSTITUTIONS—
ABUSES—JUDICIAL SYSTEM, ETC.

" Agriculture has been equally the object of encouragement, and also gardening and the raising of stock. Lastly, a commission, composed of the principal landed proprietors, is now studying the hitherto insoluble question of draining the Campagna of Rome, and filling it with inhabitants. There is, in truth, misery here as elsewhere, but it is infinitely less heavy than in less favored climates. Mere necessaries are obtained cheaply. Private charities are numerous and effective. Here also the action of the government is perceptible. Important ameliorations have been introduced into the administration of hospitals and prisons. Some of these prisons should be visited, that the visitor may admire—the term is not too strong—the persevering charity of the Holy Father. I will not extend this enumeration. What I have said ought to be sufficient to prove that all the measures adopted by the Pontifical administration bear marks of wisdom, reason and progress ; that they have already produced happy results ; in short, that there is not a single detail of interest to the well-being, either moral or material, of the population, which has escaped the attention of the government, or which has not

K

been treated in a favorable manner. In truth, when certain persons say to the Pontifical government, 'form an administration which may have for its aim the good of the people,' the government might reply, 'look at our acts, and condemn us if you dare.' The government might ask, 'not only which of its acts is a subject of legitimate blame, but in which of its duties it has failed?' Are we, then, to be told that the Pontifical government is a model—that it has no weakness or imperfections? Certainly not; but its weakness and imperfections are of the same kind as are met with in all governments, and even in all men, with very few exceptions. I am perpetually interrogating those who come to me to denounce what they call the abuses of the Papal government. The expression, it must be remembered, is now consecrated, and is above criticism or objection. It is held as Gospel. Now, in what do the abuses consist? I have never yet been able to discover. At least, the facts which go by that name are such as are elsewhere traceable to the imperfection of human nature, and we need not load the government with the direct responsibility of the irregularities committed by some of its subordinate agents. The imperfections of the judiciary system are often cited. I have examined it closely, and have found it impossible to discover any serious cause of complaint. Those who lose their causes complain more loudly and more 'continuously than is the custom in other places, but without any more reason. Most of the important civil cases are decided in the tribunal of the Rota. Now, in spite of the habitual license of Italian criticism, no one has dared to express a doubt of the profound knowledge and the exalted integrity of the tribunal of the Rota. If the lawyers are incredibly fertile in raising objections and exceptions—if they lengthen out lawsuits—to what is this fault to be attributed if not to the peculiarity of the national genius? Lastly, civil law is well administered. I do not know a single sentence the justice of which would not be recognized by the best tribunal in Europe. Criminal justice is administered in a manner equally unassailable. I have watched some trials throughout their whole details; I was obliged to confess that necessary precautions for the verification of facts—all possible guarantees for the free defence of the accused, including the publication of the proceedings—were taken."

BRIGANDAGE—BANDS OF ROBBERS DISPERSED BY THE GOVERN-MENT.

" Much is said of the brigands who, we are told, lay the country desolate. It has fallen to our lot to pass through the country, in all directions, without seeing even the shadow of a robber. It cannot be denied that, from time to time, we hear of a diligence stopped, of a traveller plundered. Even one accident of this kind is too much, but we must remember that the administration has employed all the means in its power to repress these disorders. Thanks to energetic measures, the brigands have been arrested at all points and punished. When in France a diligence is stopped ; when in going from London to Windsor a lady of the Queen's palace is robbed of her luggage and jewels, such incidents passed unnoticed; but when, on an isolated road in the Roman States, the least fact of this nature takes place, the passenger, for a pretext, prints the news in large characters, and cries for vengeance on the government. On the side of Rome the attacks which have taken place at distant intervals have never assumed an appearance calculated to excite anxiety.

" In the Romagna, organized bands have been formed, which, taking advantage of the Tuscan frontier, easily escaped pursuit, and were for a time to be dreaded. The government declared unceasing war against them, and after several engagements, in which a certain number of *gens d'armes* were either killed or wounded, these bands have been in a great measure dispersed. The Italians always depend for the completion of their projects on foreign support. If this support were to fail, then they would adopt a proper course much more readily than would be necessary. Meanwhile, in England and Sardinia, the organs of the press should cease to excite the passions, and Catholic Powers should continue to give the Holy See evident marks of sympathy. But how can we hope that enemies, animated with such a spirit as influences the opponents of the Holy See, should put a stop to their attacks when they have been made in so remarkable a manner?"

EXTRAORDINARILY SMALL NUMBER OF ECCLESIASTICS EMPLOYED BY THE PAPAL GOVERNMENT.

Those who are generally mentioned as *ecclesiastics*, are not necessarily priests or in holy orders.

"Count Rayneval took occasion to show, with proofs in his hands, that the half of these supposed priests were not in orders.   The Roman prelates are not all bound to enter into holy orders. For the most part they dispense with them. Can we then call by the name of priests those who have nothing of the priest but the uniform? Is Count Spada a more zealous or a more skilful administrator now than when, in the costume of a priest, he officiated as Minister of War? Do Monsignor Matteuci (Minister of Police), Monsignor Mertel (Minister of the Interior), Monsignor Berardi (substitute of the Secretary of State), and so many others, who have liberty to marry to-morrow, constitute a religious caste, sacrificing its own interests to the interests of the country, and would they become, all of a sudden, irreproachable if they were dressed differently? If we examine the share given the prelates, both priests and non-priests, in the Roman administration, we shall arrive at some results which it is important to notice. Out of Rome, that is, throughout the whole extent of the Pontifical States, with the exception of the capital—in the Legations, the Marshes, Umbria, and all the Provinces, to the number of eighteen, how many ecclesiastics do you think are employed? Their number does not exceed fifteen—one for each Province except three, where there is not one at all. They are delegates, or, as we should say, prefects. The councils, the tribunals, and offices of all sorts, are filled with laymen. So that for one ecclesiastic in office, we have in the Roman Provinces one hundred and ninety-five laymen."

The following table, which appeared in the London *Weekly Register*, shows at a glance what a small proportion the clerical bore to the lay element in the government of the Papal States :

MINISTRIES.	PLACES HELD		Annual Salary Recv'd.	
	BY ECCLES.	BY LAYMEN.	BY ECCLES.	BY LAYMEN.
Secretariate of State.........	14	18	$100,500	$8,340
Ministries—Home, Grace, Justice and Police	277	3,271	110,205	637,602
Public Instruction........	3	9	1,320	1,824
Finance...............	7	3,084	10,329	730,268
Commerce, P. Works	1	347	2,400	69,808
Arms ...:...............		125		51,885
Total.........	303	6,854	$224,755	$1,490,747

[*The Weekly Register, June,* 1859.]

M. De Rayneval admits that the people are not enterprising. If they do not show much industrial activity, this is to be ascribed not to the government, but to the climate, the facility with which everything necessary for comfort is obtained, and the long-established habits of the natives of the South of Europe. "The condition of the population, nevertheless," adds the ambassador, "is comparatively good. They readily take part in public amusements, when pleasure may be read on every countenance. Are these the misgoverned people *'whose miseries excite the commiseration of all Europe?'* There is misery, no doubt, as there is everywhere. But it is less than in lands that are not so highly favored. The necessaries of life are so cheap as to be easily procured. Private charity never fails; and there are numerous and efficient public benevolent establishments."

It may be said, by way of supplement to M. De Rayneval's report, that Pius IX. did all in his power to

Pius IX. encourages Science and the Fine Arts—" Vindex antiquitatis."

encourage both science and the fine arts. His many foundations for their promotion are his witness. Among the rest are the College of Sinigaglia, and the *Seminario Pio* at Rome, together with the educational establishments, endowed from his private resources, at Perugia, Civita Vecchia, Ancona and Pesaro. To him also are due the high renown to which rose the studies of the Roman university, the restoration of the Appian way, and the many archæological works which have won for their august promoter the glorious surname of *Vindex Antiquitatis*. His day would be memorable if it had been illustrated only by the names of Vico, Secchi, Rossi and Visconti.

It is impossible to overrate the importance of Count de Rayneval's report, or the influence which it exercised over the public mind of Europe, when, at length, through the agency of the British and Belgian press, it obtained publicity. A refutation of Cavour's interested calumnies, so able, distinct and straightforward, powerfully impressed the minds of British statesmen, and caused them to see the grievous error into which they had been betrayed at the Congress of Paris, by Count Cavour and the Emperor Louis Napoleon, in the interest of their fellow-conspirators against the sovereignty of the Pope.

Lord Clarendon was the first who had knowledge of the now celebrated state paper. He was also the first who, for the sake of truth and justice, made it public, committing it to the English press, whence it found its way to continental Europe. This eminent British statesman promptly communicated with Count Cavour, and took him to task severely for his double dealing at the congress, and for having induced him, as British Plénipotentiary, by false statements, to sanction his views.

Lord Clarendon rebukes Count Cavour.

The calumnies and misrepresentations of the Cavour-Napoleon party had, indeed, been met by anticipation in the decree, known as *motu proprio*, which Pius IX. issued from Portici, shortly before his return to Rome. This decree indicated the reforms which, as we learn from Count de Rayneval's report, were afterwards carried out. It even granted a constitution as complete as was consistent with the existence of the Papal Sovereignty. More could not be looked for. The much-vaunted constitution of England itself does not abrogate or nullify the monarchy. But neither this nor any other measure of reform, however well

" Motu proprio."

adapted to circumstances and the character of the people, could ever have satisfied the *Italianissimi*, whose hatred of every existing institution was boundless as it was incomprehensible. The Holy Father solemnly declared that he decreed the measures in question for the good of his people, and under the eye of heaven. " They are such," he adds, at the conclusion of the document, *motu proprio*, " as to be compatible with our dignity, and, if faithfully carried out, we are convinced that they will produce results which must command the approval of all wise minds. The good sense of all among you who aspire to what is best, with a fervor proportionate to the ills which you have endured, shall be our judge in this matter. Above all, let us place our trust in God, who, even in fulfilling the decrees of His justice, is never unmindful of His mercy." It could not be expected, and it was not expected, that the Pope should resign his sovereignty. The words of Donoso Cortez, spoken in the Spanish parliament, in defence of the temporal sovereignty, were received at the time with universal acceptance.

" Civilized Europe," said this distinguished author and statesman, "will not consent to see enthroned in that mad city of Rome a new and strange dynasty begotten of crime. And let no one here say, that in this matter there are two separate questions—one a temporal question, the other entirely spiritual—that the difficulty lies between the temporal sovereign and his subjects; that the Pontiff has been respected and still subsists." Two words on this point—just two words—shall suffice to make us understand the whole matter.

Donoso Cortez, in the Spanish Parliament, supports the Papal Sovereignty.

" It is perfectly true that the spiritual power of the Papacy is its principal power; the temporal is only an accessory, but that accessory is one that is indispensible. The Catholic world has a right to insist upon it, that the infallible organ of its belief shall be free and independent. The Catholic world cannot know with certainty, as it needs must know, whether that organ is really free and independent, unless it be sovereign. For he alone who is sovereign, depends on no other power. Hence it is that the question of sovereignty, which everywhere else is a political question, is in Rome a religious question."

"Constituent assemblies may exist rightfully elsewhere; at Rome they cannot; at Rome there can be no constituent power outside of and apart from the constituted power. Neither Rome herself nor the Pontifical States belong to Rome or belong to the Pope—they belong to the Catholic world. The Catholic world has recognized, in the Pope, the lawful possessor thereof, in order to his being free and independent; and the Pope may not strip himself of this sovereignty, this independence."

The greatest statesmen of the age, such as Guizot, Thiers, and Montalembert, in France; Normanby, Lansdowne, Disraeli, and even Palmerston, in England; the statesmen of Prussia, and even those of the Russian Empire; the Emperor of Austria and his advisers; Spain, Portugal and Naples, all shared the opinion of the illustrious Spanish statesman, Donoso Cortes. All alike favored the restoration of the Holy Father, and the securing of his government against the accidents of revolution in the future by placing it under the protection of the Great Powers. "The affairs of Rome," wrote the Russian Chancellor in a circular, "cause to the government of his Majesty the Emperor great concern; and it were a serious error to think that we take a less lively interest than the other Catholic governments in the situation to which his Holiness Pope Pius IX. has been brought by the events of the time. There can be no room for doubting that the Holy Father shall receive from the Emperor a loyal support towards the restoration of his temporal and spiritual power, and that the Russian government shall co-operate cheerfully in all the measures necessary to this result; for it cherishes against the court of Rome no sentiment of religious animosity or rivalry."

Sardinia alone held aloof. Its minister did not, like the other European ambassadors, seek the presence of the Pope when he was pressed by the revolutionists. Nor did he repair, as they did, to Gaeta, but remained in Rome, and, to the great surprise and scandal of all the European Courts, transacted business with the governments which reigned there in the absence of the legitimate sovereign. The absorption of all the states of Italy, not excepting that of the Pope, by Piedmont, was the ruling idea of Piedmontese statesmen. They were guided by a selfish view to what they considered their own interest, not by principles that were universally recognized. Such were continental liberals. The English liberals, the party of reform, thought differently. One of their chiefs, Lord Lansdowne, whose high character as a statesman gives weight to his words, declared, in the British House of Peers, when the French expedition to Rome was discussed there, that "the condition of the Pope's sovereignty is especially remarkable in this, that so far as his temporal power is concerned, he is only a sovereign of the fourth or fifth order. In his spiritual power he enjoys a sovereignty without its equal on earth. Every country which has Roman Catholic subjects has an interest in the condition of the Roman States, and should see to it that the Pope be able to exercise his authority independently of any temporal influence that could affect his spiritual power." Thus did all Christendom—all the states which owned the Christian name—true to immemorial tradition, consider that they lay under the obligation to watch over the freedom and independence of the great central power whence proceeded their early civilization.

Lord Lansdowne, together with all the statesmen and States of Christendom, recognize the principles laid down in Pius the Ninth's "motu proprio."

The French government, in restoring Pius IX., only obeyed the will so often and so clearly expressed of the European nations. Now that he was once more firmly seated on the Pontifical throne, it was time, thought the Cavour-Napoleon-Mazzini party, that he should introduce into his states what they called true reform—*the Code Napoleon and the secularization of his government.* This, as has been seen, he could not do.

It was tantamount to the abdication of his sovereignty. That he did reform, however, wisely and efficiently, Count de Rayneval has abundantly shown. His measures of reform were large and liberal, and, in the judgment of eminent statesmen, left little room for improvement. It is necessary to bestow a few words in making this fact still more apparent; for it was long the fashion to say and insist that the policy of Pius IX., after his restoration, was reactionary, and that the once-reforming Pope had, with inconceivable inconsistency, ceased to be a reformer.

In the *motu proprio*, published by the Pope on occasion of reorganizing his states in 1849, '50, there was inaugurated as full a measure of liberty as was compatible with the circumstances of the country and the character of the people. Two political bodies, a council of state and a council of finance were instituted. These were designed as temporary institutions, whose object it should be to remedy the fearful evils caused by the revolution—in plain terms, to bring order out of anarchy and chaos. M. de Rayneval has shown that in this they were successful, and that they also put an end to the disorder and difficulty caused by the issue of forty millions of worthless paper which the *Republic* had bequeathed to them. The *Moniteur*, as well as the ambassador, admitted that by the end of the first seven years the finances had nearly reached an *equilibrium*, the deficit at that time being only half a million of dollars. This temporary state of things was destined, once its objects were accomplished, to give place to a more ample constitution, which certainly would have been granted in due time but for the hostile intrigues of those who blamed the most free and complete constitutional system. It will not be without interest to consider what was thought among distinguished foreigners in regard to the Pope's early measures—measures which, it is well known, were intended as a preparation for more advanced constitutional government. The French Republic appointed a commission, consisting of fifteen of its best statesmen, to examine and report upon the political wisdom and practical value of the institutions which Pius IX. had granted to his states. M. Thiers, to whom none will give credit for being over friendly to the Holy See, drew up, signed and presented this report:

"Your commission," the report states, "has maturely examined this act, *motu proprio*, in order to see whether the counsels which France believed herself authorized to offer had borne such fruits as to prevent her regretting having interfered in Roman affairs. Well, by a large majority, twelve in fifteen, your commission declares that it sees in the *motu proprio* a first boon of such real value, that nothing but unjust pretensions could overlook its importance. We shall discuss this act in its every detail. But limiting ourselves, at present, to consider the principle on which is based the Pontifical concession, we say that it grants all desirable provincial and municipal liberties. As to political liberties, consisting in the power of deciding on the public business of a country in one of the two assemblies, and in union with the executive—as in England, for instance—it is very true that the *motu proprio* does not grant this sort of political liberty, or only grants it in the rudimentary form of a council without deliberative voice. This is a question of immense gravity, which the Holy Father alone can solve, and which he and the Christian world are interested in not leaving to chance. That on this point he should have chosen to be prudent; that after his recent experience he should have preferred not to reopen a career of agitation among a people who have shown themselves so unprepared for parliamentary liberty, is what we do not know that we have either the right or the cause to deem blameworthy."

A well-known British statesman expressed similiar views. "We all know," said Lord Palmerston, "that the Pope, on his restoration to his states in 1849, published an ordinance called *motu proprio*, by which he declared his intention to bestow institutions, not indeed on the large proportions of a constitutional government, but based, nevertheless, on popular election, and which, if they had only been carried out, must have given his subjects such satisfaction as to render unnecessary

the intervention of a foreign army." These words were uttered
in 1856, when Lord Palmerston ought to have known, if indeed
he did not actually know, that the proposed reforms of the
Pope had been faithfully and successfully carried out. The
report of Count de Rayneval was before the world, and so important a state paper could not have been unknown to a statesman who interested himself so much in European affairs generally, and those of Rome in particular. The Rayneval report,
besides, which showed how completely Pius IX. had fulfilled
his promises—how assiduously and effectually he had labored
in the cause of reform—had been specially communicated, as
has been seen, to an eminent member of the British Cabinet,
Lord Clarendon. It is not so clear that the Pope's subjects
were not satisfied. None knew better than Lord Palmerston,
that there was always a foreign influence at Rome which never
ceased to cause discontent, and was ready, on occasion, to raise
disturbance. This alien and sinister influence was only too
powerfully seconded, both by some members of the British
ministry and the intriguing head of the French government.

Baron Sauzet, who was President of the French Chamber
of Deputies in the reign of Louis Philippe, and who was, by
no means, over partial to Rome, wrote in 1860 on the system
of legislation which obtained in the States of the Church, and
gave utterance to the opinion that it was a solid basis on which
Pius IX. was endeavoring to raise such a superstructure of
improvement as was adapted to the wants of modern society.
Criminal law was regulated according to the wise codes of
Gregory XVI., which were a real progress. Civil legislation
had for its groundwork the old Roman law, which the Popes,
at various times, had wisely adapted to their age and the circumstances of their people. There are certain points of great
delicacy, with regard to which, in Christian communities, religious authority only can legislate. These excepted, the
Justinian code, with some necessary modifications, prevailed.
Few changes have been made since Gregory the Sixteenth's
time, and they are codified with such perfect scientific lucidity

as to be available to practitioners. This is one of the special labors of the Council of State, which is aided by a commission consisting of the most eminent and learned jurists of Rome. The distinguished statesman (Baron Sauzet), moreover, repels the idea of thrusting on the Romans the Code Napoleon, as was intended by the Emperor Louis Napoleon.

Galeotti, who was Minister of Justice in the Mazzini ministry, and who cannot be suspected of much favor to the Holy See, declares that, " in the Pontifical government there are many parts deserving of praise; it contains many ancient institutions which are of unquestioned excellence, and there are others of more modern date which the other provinces of Italy might well enjoy. One may confidently say that there is no other government in Italy in which the principle of discussion and deliberation has been so long established and so generally practised."

Galeotti further says, speaking of the Judicature : " The tribunal of the Rota is the best and the most respected of the ancient institutions of Rome. Some slight changes would make it the best in all Europe. The mode of procedure followed in it is excellent, and might serve as a model in every country where people would not have the administration of justice reduced to the art of simply terminating lawsuits."

Another author, whose remarks are deserving of attention, Monsignor Fevre, says that law expenses are very moderate, the proceedings very rapid, and the rules of the Judiciary among the very best of the kind. Besides, the poor are never taxed by the courts, while they are always supplied with counsel. In Rome itself the pious confraternity of St. Yeo (the patron saint af lawyers) takes on itself, gratuitously, the cases of all poor people, when they appear to have right on their side." The arch-confraternity of San Girolamo Della Carita, also undertakes the defence of prisoners and poor persons, especially widows. " It has the administration of a legacy left by Felice Amadori, a noble Florentine, who died in the year 1689. The principal objects of their solicitude are persons confined in prison. These they visit, comfort, clothe, and frequently liberate, either by paying the fine imposed on them as the penalty of their offence, or by arranging matters with their creditors. With a wise charity they endeavor to simplify and shorten causes ; and they employ a solicitor, who assists in settling disputes, and thus putting an end to litigation. This confraternity embraces the flower of the Roman prelacy, the patrician order and the priesthood."

One is naturally inclined to ask how it came to pass that a people, possessing such [wise institutions, such an admirable system of legislation, and a sovereign who constantly studied to enlarge and improve their inherited benefits, were never satisfied ? It would be hard to say that the Romans, the real subjects of the Pope, were not satisfied. But there were not wanting those who succeeded in making it appear that they were not, and who also contrived to induce many of the Romans themselves to believe that they had cause to be discontented. It was the fashion in Piedmont to rail against everything clerical, and to such an extent did this mania proceed, that they began to persecute the clergy. Through the agency of the secret societies, whose chief was Mazzini, this anti-clerical prejudice spread through all Italy, and even extended to Rome, the government of which, as a matter of course, was bad, for no other reason than that, being conducted by the Chief of the clergy, it was reputed to be clerical. Thus did Count Cavour and the Piedmontese government use the Mazzinian faction for the furtherance of their own ambitious ends, whilst the Mazzinians believed that they were using them as they intended to use them, and their king and all kings, as long as there should be kings, for their subversive purposes, in the first instance, and for the establishment, finally, of their Utopian republic on the ruins of all thrones and regular governments whatsoever. As will be seen, most recent history shows the first act of the drama has been played, apparently to the profit of a king. Time will prove to whom, in the end, victory shall belong. One institution at least will remain, for no power, not even that of hell, can prevail against it. As in the early days, when society had fallen to a state of chaos, and orderly government had become impossible, it may, once more, raise the standard of order and reconstitute the broken and scattered elements.

Rome and the Catholic world were yet rejoicing on occasion

Canonizations at Rome.—Two American Saints.

of the happy restoration of Pius IX. to his states, and pilgrims still flocked from every region of the universe to the holy city, when two remarkable events came to add new glory to the flourishing church of America. Hitherto America could reverence and invoke only one native saint. On 16th July, 1850, took place the beatification of the venerable Peter Claver, of the Society of Jesus, the apostle of New Granada ; and in October, Mariana de Paredes, of Flores, "the lily of Quito," was beatified. The latter was first cousin and contemporary of Saint Rose of Lima. This circumstance vividly awakens the idea, that already saints, although there were few as yet who could claim the honors of cononization, were not uncommon in America. Whatever may have been the measure and excellence of her children's sanctity, the church was rapidly extend-

Pius IX. erects four Metropolitan Sees in the United States.

ing. So great was her growth that, in the year 1850, Pius IX. considered it opportune to erect four metropolitan sees in the United States—New York, Cincinnati, St. Louis and New Orleans. Baltimore, the primatial see, was already metropolitan.

The Holy Father showed no less solicitude for the welfare

New See of Laval. —Rennes becomes Metropolitan.—Restoration of the Chapter of St. Denis.

of the church in France, Spain, and other European countries. Napoleon III., anxious to gain the good-will of Catholic France, prayed the Holy See to erect a new diocese at Laval, to raise the see of Rennes to metropolitan dignity, to reorganize the grand chaplaincy, and restore the chapter of St. Denis. All this was done by a brief of 31st March, 1857, and there was now a thoroughly good

understanding between the Pope and the Emperor, between
the latter and the people over whom he
ruled. It was even said that Napoleon III.
desired, like his uncle, to be anointed Emperor by a Pope; that with a view to this end,
he made many advances to Pius IX., and went so far even as
to propose in confidence the abolition of the organic articles,
and a modification of the Code Napoleon, in so far as that
parties who marry before the church should be exempted from
the civil ceremony. A still less doubtful pledge of the continuance of amicable relations between Rome and Paris was
the baptism of the Prince Imperial. The Emperor had asked
the Pope to do him the favor to act as
sponsor for the child that Providence had
deigned to give him, and Pius IX. readily
consented. As he could not be present in
person at the ceremony, he caused himself to be represented
by his legate, *a latere*, Cardinal Patrizzi. This cardinal, at
the same time, presented to the Empress the golden rose,
which is blessed every year on the fourth Sunday of Lent, in
order to be sent to the princes, cities and churches on which
the Pope desires to confer special honor. The blessed rose
was a small rose-tree in gold, covered with rose-flowers. The
vessel which contained it was of massive gold. It stood on a
pedestal of lapis lazzuli, which bore in Mosaic the arms of the
Pope and the Emperor. On the vase itself were sculptured
the birth of the Blessed Virgin, and the Presentation in the
Temple.

It would have been well if all this friendship had been as
sincere as it was warmly expressed. It cannot, however, be
forgotten that the government of the Emperor Napoleon had
suppressed the Rayneval report, and Pius IX. must have
thought, although prudence forbade him to say, that there was
reason to doubt the fidelity of his apparently devoted ally.
"Timeo Danaos et dona ferentes."

Napoleon desires to be crowned by the Pope.

Pius IX. sponsor for Napoleon's son.— Golden rose sent to the Empress.

It may be said that, at this time, the Powers of the world vied with one another in seeking the favor of the Pope. Isabella II., Queen of Spain, like Napoleon of France, was anxious that Pius IX. should, through a representative, stand godfather to her son, who afterwards became Alphonso XII. Other princes sought the like consideration, and among the rest, Victor Emmanuel, whose daughter, the Princess Pia, thus became the godchild of Pius the Pope. This princess is now the Queen of Portugal.

Pius IX. godfather to Alphonso XII. of Spain.

Another bond of friendship with the world's Powers was secured, apparently, by the conclusion of a Concordat with the great Austrian Empire. The negotiations which led to this Concordat had lasted several years. It was abundantly liberal in the true acceptation of this term. Nevertheless, it awakened the hatred and contempt of the professed liberals, who enjoy this appellation, one would say, simply because they are not liberal, just as in Latin a grove is called by a word expressive of light, because it is not light (*lucus a non lucendo*). How can they be called truly liberal, who have no liberality for any but themselves, who know no other liberty than that which enables them to tyrannize over the church, and trample under foot her most sacred and beneficial institutions? The Concordat with Austria provides that the Catholic, Apostolic and Roman religion shall be preserved in its integrity throughout the whole extent of the Austrian monarchy, together with all the rights and prerogatives which it ought to enjoy in virtue of the order which God has established and the canon law.

Concordat with Austria.

The Roman Pontiff having, by divine right, in the whole church the primacy of honor and jurisdiction, mutual communication, as regards all spiritual things, and the ecclesiastical relations of the bishops, the clergy and the people with the Holy See, shall not be subject to the necessity of obtaining the royal *placet*, but shall be wholly free.

L

In a consistorial allocution of 5th November, 1855, Pius IX. gave expression to the joy which it afforded him to have obtained, after so much tedious negotiation, such happy results. The following year, on the 17th of March, he addressed a brief to the bishops of the Austrian Empire, exhorting them to avail themselves of the spiritual independence which they had once more won, in order to guard their dioceses against the ravages of rationalism and indifference.

Meanwhile, new difficulties arose in Spain and Spanish America. The government of Isabella II., regretting the good to which it had so recently been a party, commenced a new war against the church. Notwithstanding the Concordat, it exposed for sale such ecclesiastical property as was not yet sold, forbade religious communities of women to receive novices, and forcibly removed several bishops from their dioceses. The excesses were such that Pius IX. was obliged to recall his representative from Madrid. There were similar persecutions in the South American Republics and in Mexico. The congress of Mexico forbade monastic vows, banished the Archbishop of Mexico, and imprisoned the Bishop of Michoacan. Germany, at the same time, was not without its troubles. A learned theologian of the diocese of Cologne, Dr. Anthony Gunther, had allowed himself to drift from the sure ways of tradition, imperceptibly gliding into rationalism, and confounding reason and faith. His ideas had partisans in several countries of Germany. The vigilant eye of Pius IX. discovered in them germs of heresy, which it was important to check before they attained development. Gunther, on being condemned, accepted humbly the judgment of the Holy See. But there was a long contest with some of his partisans who were less pious than himself.

Difficulties in Spain and Spanish countries.

Errors of Gunther.

The record of Pius the Ninth's progress through his States, in 1857, is alone a sufficient reply to the

Pius IX. makes a progress through his States.—His popularity. calumnies of those enemies who never ceased to assert that ever since his return to Rome he had pursued a retrograde policy. Reform was always an object of his solicitude. It was with a view to improve the condition of his people that he undertook, when almost a septuagenarian, a four months' journey through the States of the Church. He travelled slowly, and sometimes on foot, in order the better to observe and ascertain the state of the provinces. All could approach him and address him freely. He visited churches, hospitals and workshops. He examined the works of the ports and the public ways. Many addresses and petitions were presented. Far, however, from asking the abolition of priestly rule, the petitioners prayed for a return to the former state of things, when cardinals and prelates only were set over the provinces. The progress of the Holy Father was a series of joyous ovations from the time that he left Rome—4th May—till his return on the 5th September. His journey was at first in the direction of Ancona, Ravenna and Bologna. He returned by way of Florence and Modena. His progress would have been crowned with success if it had only served to show the loyalty and devotedness of his people. But it was attended with still greater results. The Holy Father bestowed much time at every place in seeking, personally and through his ministers, information which became the basis of reform and improvement. Thus, as is known by the authentic accounts which have been published, many localities derived very material benefit from the Papal visit. The port of Pesaro was to be almost entirely reconstructed, the Holy Father bestowing $80,000 from his own resources. The port of Sinigaglia was also considerably improved, and a new sanitary office built. The cities of Ancona and Civita Vecchia were to be enlarged. At Bologna the High street was widened and beautified; the fine façade of the cathedral was to be completed, the Pope contributing $5,000 for fifteen years. At

Perugia new prisons were to be constructed, and the condition of the prisoners was to be in every way improved; a liberal annual contribution was given towards preserving the splendid native collections of art. Ravenna, although long neglected and in decay, was not forgotten. Pius IX. wished to revive, as far as possible, the ancient commercial prosperity of this city, and promised $4,000 annually for ten years towards improving the port. At Ferrara many improvements were ordered, and $9,000 contributed for the completing of the Pamfilio canal. The Holy Father also appointed a commission of engineers, in order to devise a plan by which the river Reno should be turned into the Po, and an extensive tract of fertile land thus saved from periodical inundations. Funds were provided for the relief of poor sailors. Liberal grants were allotted for artesian wells, where required, and for bridges and public roads. Especially were large allowances devoted for the improvement of the highways at Pesaro, Macerata, Imola, Camerino, &c. Telegraphic communication was widely established. Prisons, hospitals and schools were special objects of the Holy Father's care. It was the duty of Monsignor de Merode, who accompanied the Pope, on arriving in any city or town, to visit the prison, enquire into everything connected with it, and report accordingly. Monsignor Talbot had commission to look to the state of charitable, industrial and educational institutions, in all of which he aided in promoting valuable reforms.

It is impossible to consider, without emotion, the reception which greeted the Holy Father in his former diocese of Spoleto. At every step proof upon proof was given of reverence and affection, which time had not diminished. Etiquette and state ceremony were laid aside. The youthful and the aged alike would see their good shepherd, and he was anxious to salute his people, and converse with them all. Many a face, familiar to him of old, was recognized with pleasure, and even names were not forgotten.

As has been seen, the days of the Holy Father's journey were not all spent in pleasurable greetings or official receptions. He never forgot or neglected the work of reform and improvement. Nor were such care and labor new to him. It had often been said that the Popes were hostile to all modern improvements. Why did they not favor railways? Why did they not drain the Pontine Marshes, and cause the *Campagna* to be cultivated? Let the labors of Pius IX. reply. A railway through the States of the Church was one of his favorite ideas, and he beheld it realized. It must have afforded him no ordinary satisfaction to see the railway which his princely care had provided now winding along the valley of the Tiber, now climbing the heights and stretching its arms across the Apennines, reaching down to the seaboard at Ancona, now passing beyond the limits of the Papal territory, and extending away to the Tuscan capital.

The uneducated or half-educated traveller, who surveys the uncultivated and malarious plains around the city of the Popes, at once discovers, in this desolation which prevails, an argument against priestly rule. With a little more information, however, he would see the ruins and the vestiges of a mighty empire, the works of which, like its conquests, were the wonder of the world. How such works came to be so successfully executed is easily understood, when it is remembered that heathen Rome commanded the wealth, the intellect, and the strong arms of many subject nations. The Popes, on the other hand, though they often tried, as did Pius IX. among the rest, to cultivate the Campagna and drain the Pontine Marshes, had so little means at their disposal, that they could never accomplish anything important. Among other difficulties that the Roman Pontiffs had to contend with, was that of obtaining an outlet towards the sea, whilst ancient Rome commanded all the seas and lands of the known world. Surely it does not require a Solomon to understand that without access to the Mediterranean, it is physically impossible to drain and cultivate such low-lying lands as the Pontine Marshes.

At Perugia the Holy Father received the kindly visit of the Archduke Charles, who came, on the part of his father

Leopold, to compliment the Sovereign Pontiff. Archduke Maximilian, of Austria, who, at the time, little thought of a Mexican Empire, came to salute the Pope at Pesaro. Neither he nor Pius IX. had been, as yet, betrayed and abandoned by Napoleon III. The Grand Duke of Tuscany and all his family, together with the Dukes of Parma and Modena, came to pay their homage at Bologna. The Holy Father accepted their pressing invitation to visit Tuscany and Modena, the sovereigns showing publicly, in presence of their people, such reverence and devotedness as recalled the faith and loyalty of the Middle Ages. The Pope himself bears witness to the truly noble and chivalrous conduct of these provinces. "He introduced us himself into Florence," says Pius IX., in speaking of the Grand Duke Leopold, "walking by our side, and accompanied us to every Tuscan city which we visited. All the archbishops and bishops of his States, all the clergy, the corporate bodies, the magistrates and the nobles showed their delight by testifying their devotion to us in a thousand ways. Not only at Florence, but wherever we went in Tuscany, the people from town and country, far and near, came forth to greet us, acclaiming the Chief Pontiff of the church with such ardent affection, showing such an intense desire to see him, to do him reverence, to receive his benediction, that our fatherly heart was moved to its inmost depths." On the Holy Father's return to Rome there was high jubilee among all classes of the people a fact which the traducers of Pius IX. would do well to note, as it proves beyond a doubt how idle and ill-founded was all their clamor, to the effect that in the holy city his popularity had departed.

A case in itself comparatively unimportant now became a *cause celebre*, and agitated all Europe. One Mortara, a Jew of Bologna, had, in violation of the laws of the country, taken into his service a Christian maid. Meantime, one of his children, a boy about seven years of age, became dangerously ill. The Christian girl, unadvisedly, and also in opposition to the law, baptized him. Her act could not be undone, and the law required that every

The Mortara case.

baptized person should be educated as a Christian. Pius IX.
refused to interfere with the action of this law. Hence the
torrents of abuse that were poured upon him by the infidel
liberal press of Europe, as well as by the ultra-Protestant
organs of England. He had ignored liberty of conscience,
abused his authority, &c. Now, let us suppose that he had
acted otherwise, and prevented the execution of a well-known
law, what would have been the result? He would have been
denounced as a despot, whose arbitrary decision was the only
law. But might not he, who was so great a reformer, have contrived to cause the law to be altered? Such alteration could not
have affected the Mortara case. A change, besides, would
have been quite unnecessary, as it was not probable that after
such a storm, and the lesson which it taught, either Jews or
Christians would expose themselves to the consequences of a
violation of their country's laws. And were not those laws a
sufficient protection to the Jewish people?

From the first days of his Pontificate, America engaged the
solicitude of Pius IX. So rapid was the
growth of the church on that continent that
it became necessary to give bishops to
several countries where the Catholic faith had been scarcely
known. So early as 1846 Oregon was constituted an Archiepiscopal See. In 1850 Episcopal Sees were erected at
Monterey and Santa Fe, in the Spanish American territory,
which was recently annexed to the United States, and in
Savannah, Wheeling, St. Paul and Nesqualy. The Indian
territory became a Vicariate Apostolic, under the jurisdiction
of a bishop. Three years afterwards six more sees were established—San Francisco, Brooklyn, Burlington, Covington,
Erie and Natchitoches. Later still, 1857, Pius IX. gave
bishops to Illinois; Fort Wayne, in Indiana; and Marquette, in
Michigan. This last city derived its name from the celebrated
missionary who first explored the river Mississippi. It was
now more important than ever, having become a centre of
Catholic life and action.

New Sees erected by Pius IX. in America.

In 1852, Pius IX. beatified John de Britto, a martyr in India, John Grande and the renowned Paul of the Cross, who founded the zealous and austere order of Passionists. In 1853, the like honor was conferred on the pious French shepherdess, Germaine Cousin, and the Jesuit father, Andrew Bobola, who was martyred by the Cossacks. In 1861, John Leonardi was beatified.

Several names added to the number of the Saints.

It is now time to record events of a less pleasing nature. In 1853, several attempts had been made on the life of the Emperor Napoleon III. In 1855, Pianori made a similar attempt. In 1858, Count Felix Orsini almost succeeded in assassinating him. This Orsini was an accomplice of Louis Napoleon in raising an insurrection in Romagna in 1831. He was condemned for conspiracy in 1845, and was amnestied by Pius IX. In 1849, he was a member of the Roman Constituent Assembly. In his political testament, dated at the Mazas prison, and read before the jury by Jules Favre, his counsel, he coolly declared that the object of his crime was to remind the Emperor of his former secret engagements in favor of Italian independence; that he was only one of the conspirators who had charge so to remind him; and that, although he had failed in his aim, others would come after him who would not fail. " Sire," he wrote, "let your Majesty remember—so long as Italy is not independent, the tranquillity of Europe and that of your Majesty are-mere chimeras." French authors remark that it is painful to enquire what measure of influence these threats may have exercised on the subsequent resolutions of the man to whom they were addressed, and still more painful to be compelled to recognize the unworthy motive of fear at the first link of the fatal chain which inevitably led to Sedan, where this same man had not the courage to seek a manly death. God only could see his secret mind. But it is impossible not to observe very sad coincidences. Immediately after Orsini had penned his memorable testament, the imperial policy was

Count Orsini attempts to murder the Emperor Napoleon III.

completely changed. The declaration of Orsini is as the dividing point between the two portions of the Emperor's reign, the former openly, reasonably conservative and glorious, the latter sometimes decidedly revolutionary, sometimes vacillating, contradictory, or unwillingly conservative, and finally terminated by a catastrophe unexampled in the annals of France.

All who take an interest in public affairs cannot fail to remember the startling words which the Emperor Napoleon III. addressed to the representative of Austria, on occasion of the diplomatic reception at the Tuileries, on New Year's day, 1859: "I regret that my relations with your government are not so good as in the past." This language of Napoleon astonished all Europe. It was as a sudden clap of thunder on the calmest summer day. Ten days later, Victor Emmanuel gave the interpretation of this mysterious speech, at the opening of the Piedmontese parliament, when he declared that "he was not unmoved by the cries of pain which reached him from so many parts of Italy." Finally, the marriage of Prince Napoleon, the Emperor's cousin, with a daughter of the Sardinian King, removed all doubt. France was made to adopt, without being consulted, the enmities and the ambition of the Cabinet of Turin.

The war of 1859.—The legations severed from the States of the Church.

On the 4th of February appeared a pamphlet which increased the alarm of the friends of peace and order. It may not have been written by Napoleon, but it was according to his ideas and dictation. Its title was, "*Napoleon III. and Italy;*" and it set forth a programme of the political reconstituting of Italy. It exonerated Pius IX. of all the things laid to his charge by the revolution, but only in order to lay them at the door of the Papacy itself. "The Pope," it alleged, "being placed between two classes of duty, is constrained to sacrifice the one to the other. He necessarily makes political give way to spiritual duty. This is condemnation, not of Pius IX. but of the system; not of the man, but of the situation; since the latter imposes on the former the formidable alternative of im-

molating the Prince to the Pontiff, or the Pontiff to the Prince.'"
The pamphlet further taught : " The absolutely clerical character of the Roman government is opposed to common sense,.
and is a fertile source of discontent. The canon law does not·
suffice for the protection and development of modern society."
The document concluded by proposing the secularization of the·
Roman government, and the establishment of an Italian confederation, of which the Pope should have the honorary presidency, whilst Piedmont should have the real control. The
pamphlet urged, in support of its arguments, the " abnormal
position " of the Papacy, which was obliged, in order to sustain
itself, to rely on foreign armies of occupation. Such a reproach on the part of one of those who lent succor to the Pope
was anything but generous. Pius IX. hastened to remove this
cause·of complaint. On the 27th of February Cardinal Antonelli notified France and Austria that the Holy Father was
grateful to them for their good services, but that he thought he
could himself maintain order in his States, and so would beg of
them to withdraw their troops. This would not have suited
Piedmont, which was interested in maintaining the grievance,
as well as in rendering it possible to involve the Roman States
in the war which was so rapidly approaching. `The troops
were not removed. Pius IX. was too clear-sighted not to foresee what was so soon to happen. In an Encyclical of 27th
April, he asked prayers for peace of all the patriarchs, primates, archbishops and bishops. *"Pax vobis! pax vobis!"* he
painfully repeated. But it was already too late. The young
and rash Emperor of Austria, driven to extremity, thought himself sufficiently strong to contend at once against France and
the revolution. He summoned Piedmont to disband such of
her regiments as were composed of Lombards and Venetians,
who were Austrian subjects. As this was refused, he declared
war. He fell into a second error. He assumed the offensive·
tardily, and did not push forward rapidly to the point where
the French army must concentrate, before its concentration
could be accomplished. He made a third and more serious

mistake, which proved ruinous. He withdrew from the war after his first defeats when his army was beat, indeed, but neither broken nor disorganized, when he still held the unconquered quadrilateral, and when Prussia and Germany were arming to support him. In 1866 he was equally imprudent in the war against Prussia, when a continuation of the contest would have obliged France, whether willingly or otherwise, to intervene, and would probably have saved both Austria and France.

Meanwhile, Napoleon felt that it was necessary to reassure the Catholics of France. "We do not go to Italy," said he, boldly, but untruly, in his proclamation of 3rd May, "in order to encourage disorder, nor to shake the power of the Holy Father, whom we have replaced on his throne, but in order to liberate him from the foreign pressure which weighs upon the whole peninsula, and assist in founding order on legitimate interests that will be satisfied." M. Rouland, the Minister of Public Worship, wrote to the bishops, in order to inspire them with confidence as to the consequences of the contest. "The Emperor," he said, hypocritically, "has weighed the matter in the presence of God, and his well-known wisdom, energy and loyalty will not be wanting, either to religion or the country. The prince who has given to religion so many proofs of deference and attachment, who, after the evil days of 1848, brought back the Holy Father to the Vatican, is the firmest support of Catholic unity, and he desires that the Chief of the Church shall be respected in all his rights as a temporal sovereign. The prince, who saved France from the invasion of the democracy, cannot accept either its doctrines or its domination in Italy." These declarations, which promised so much, were joyfully accepted by the Catholics. Events, however, soon made it appear how hollow they were. The grand conspiracy, whilst it amused the friends of order and legality with fine words and lying protestations, acted in such a way as to favor the revolution and meet all its wishes. On the 27th of April, the Grand Duke of Tuscany, uncle of Victor Emmanuel, was overthrown in consequence of intrigues and plots at the house of Signor Buoncompagni, ambassador of the Piedmontese King, a fact to which Mr. Scarlett, the British representative, bears witness in an official despatch. The same blow was struck, and with the like success, against the excellent and popular Duchess of Parma. But this princess was immediately recalled by the people, who had been taken by surprise, and remained until Piedmont took military possession of the Duchies, which it never gave up. Prince Napoleon, who commanded the 5th French Army Corps, looking out for the enemy by a devious route, in the direction of Romagna, reached the battle-field of Solferino too late to take part in the fight, but quite in time to make it available to the revolution. The Austrian troops who occupied Bologna, being threatened by the movement, made haste to recross the Po, without waiting to be replaced by a Pontifical garrison, and without even advising the Holy See. M. de Cavour's emissaries immediately availed themselves of so good an opportunity, took possession of the city, where there was not a soldier left, and offered its government to Victor Emmanuel.

They were preparing at Rome to celebrate the thirteenth anniversary of the coronation of Pius IX., when the news of these sad events reached the city. The addresses of the Pope, on this occasion, therefore, were necessarily full of melancholy feeling. " In whatever direction I look," said he, in his reply to the cardinals, " I behold only subjects of sorrow ; but, ' væ homini illi per quem scandalum venit !' Woe to that man by whom scandal cometh ! For my part, personally, I am not shaken ; I place my trust in God." Three days later, the 18th June, he announced, in a consistorial allocution, that Cardinal Antonelli had been commissioned to protest at the courts of all the Powers against the events in Romagna. But his position as sovereign required of him something more than words, and he did not shrink from any of his duties. Perugia had followed the example of Bologna, and to the former city he despatched troops, who retook it without any difficulty. In the contest some twelve men were either killed or wounded, and the clamors of the revolutionary press rung throughout Europe, denouncing the massacres and the "sack of Perugia."

Letter of the Honorable Mrs. Ross from Perugia, *vide Weekly Rigester*, February 11th, 1860.

THE TRUTH ABOUT PERUGIA.—We have received from Rome an original English copy of the letter of Mrs. Ross of Bladensburgh, written from Perugia on the 23rd of June last, and an Italian version of which we announced last week to our readers as having appeared in the *Giornale di Roma* of 23rd ult., and which is referred to in our special correspondence from Rome this week. We really never expected that our former Perugino antagonist, Mr. Perkins, of Boston, should have turned out to be such a very *unfortunate* man. We have now a fair sample of the authorities consulted by travellers of his class to procure evidence against the Pontifical government.

Extract from a letter written by the Hon. Mrs. Ross of Bladensburgh, to her husband, from Villa Monti, at Perugia, dated Perugia, June 21st, 1859.]

"To David Ross, of Bladensburgh, Hautes Pyrenees, France.

"I wrote to you last Wednesday, 15th inst., to announce a revolution which occurred here on the previous day; now I write to relieve your mind of anxiety in case an exaggerated account of what has occurred here be given in the public papers. I have to tell you of the re-entrance of the Papal troops, which took place yesterday after a stubborn resistance of four hours on the part of the revolutionists.

"When the revolt at Perugia was known at Rome, orders were given to a body of Swiss troops to replace the little garrison which had been driven out. The revolutionary junta was well informed of what had been decided on at Rome, and immediately prepared to oppose the re-establishment of social order in the town. Victor Emmanuel, to whom they had offered the town, returned no official answer, but, instead, reports were industriously circulated among the citizens of sympathy and support from Piedmont. An honest refusal on the part of Victor Emmanuel, or an open acceptance, would have prevented subsequent events, which his calculated silence brought about. On Saturday last, the 18th inst., we heard that the Pope's troops were close to * * * and on Sunday that they had actually arrived there. In the * * * Buoncompagni sent from Tuscany, I am told, 300 muskets in aid and wagons were despatched to Arezzo for arms and ammunition; barricades were commenced. The monks were turned out of their convent at St. Peter's Gate (one of them came down to us); and 500 armed men instead were put in to defend the gate and first barricade. After two o'clock p.m., the gates were closed, and no one could go in or out of the town without an order. It was then I wrote a note to Mr. Perkins, warning and requesting him and his family to accept a shake-down with us; and with difficulty I got the note conveyed up to town by a woman who happened to have a pass. Nothing could induce any of the peasants about us to go near the town, as the revolutionary party were making forced levies of the youth of the place, and arming them to resist the coming troops. Next morning (Monday the 20th) a body of shepherds coming up from the place, told us that they had just seen the Swiss troops at Santa Maria degli Angioli, where they stopped and had mass,* having heard that the citizens contemplated resistance. About ten o'clock that same morning I got Mr. Perkins' answer to my note; it was to this effect—that he had gone to the president (of the Junta), who assured him that the Swiss had not yet even reached * * * and that certainly they would not arrive before the next day at sunset. And the inn-keeper (the notorious Storti), he added, said that they were not coming here at all, but going to Ancona! I cannot imagine how he could trust such people, who were all implicated in the

---

* Mr. Perkins, in his letter to the *Times*, makes out that they forced open the houses of the inhabitants to make them give up their wine, and that they got drunk.

business. His messenger, who was one of the servants of the hotel, said, as he gave the note, 'Don't delay me, or I shall not be in time to kill my three or four Swiss,' showing how well informed and prepared the hotel was. I should have written again to the poor Perkins' to undeceive them; but it was too late, for almost immediately the columns of the Swiss appeared in the plain below, which you know we see from our villa, and the president (revolutionary Junta) and other heads of the rebellion had their carriages and horses ready waiting. They fled at the first gun, leaving the people to act for themselves after having inflamed, deceived and armed them, and gathered into the town all the *canaille* they could get from the neighboring country. From the moment the troops appeared, all the peasants belonging to the villa flocked around us. Anxiety was depicted on every face. The countenance of one old man in particular was very striking—'bad times,' he murmured. 'We have fallen on evil days—respect and awe are gone, and the people are blinded.' The parish priest was also with us, and the monk I mentioned before. We watched with great anxiety the slow ascent of the troops up the long five miles to the city gate. There the colonel and his men halted, and he parleyed with the people. We could see him stop and address them, and then we saw a volley fired down on them by the armed men in the convent windows. The first fire was from the people on the troops. We could see all from our villa windows like a scene on the stage; while the distance was sufficient to veil the horrors of war. Then we saw some troops separate from the main body and advance to the foot of the wall, and in the twinkling of an eye they scaled it, amid a hot fire from the insurgents, whom we heard shouting out, 'Coraggio! coraggio!' from behind the walls. Then we saw one soldier rush up and tear down the revolutionary flag, and carry it in triumph back to the main body of the troops, and then we saw the Pontifical flag float where the revolutionary one had been. In the meantime the rest of the troops had planted their cannon opposite to the city gate. Boom! boom! they went at the barricades, and in an hour after the firing of the first gun, they had driven out the 500 armed men from the convent of St. Peter's, and entered the first enclosure of the town. We then saw no more, but sat all that afternoon in the window, listening to the incessant firing in deep anxiety. As the soldiers fought their way up to their barracks, and as the report of the arms became more and more distant, we could judge pretty well of the advance of the troops, knowing as we did the chief points of resistance within. The first gun fired was at three o'clock p.m. precisely, and at seven p.m. all was silent again; the soldiers had reached their barracks. I hear that * * * have fled out towards Arezzo; all the *canaille* of the villages of the place were enlisted to defend the city, and it was the talk of the country that had the Swiss been beaten, the city was to have been pillaged by that armed mob. They say that had they not had promises of succor from Victor Emmanuel (the 'Re Galantuomo'), and of encouragement from Princess Valentini (nee Buonaparte, who resides here), they would not have resisted as they did: thus were they deceived! There is more in it all than one sees at first; and clearly it was an affair got up to make out a case against the Pope. Piedmontese money was circulated there just before the revolution. N—— got it in change in the shops.

"June 22.—P.S.—Our servant has been to town to-day; he brings me a letter from the Perkins', and such news as is the general talk of the *cafés*. Our poor friends in the Hotel de France (Locanda Storti) suffered much. Deceived to the last, they had not even been told of the actual arrival of the troops, and had just sat quietly to dinner when the roar of the guns startled them, They strove to go to another hotel, but alas! the gates of their inn were fastened; they could not stir. The letter I got from them said that the troops were *irritated on account of the firing from the roof*. We knew beforehand how it would be *there;* and in fact they did shoot an officer and two men while passing the door. It was on this that the soldiers, infuriated, rushed and assailed the house.   *   *   I hear every one blames the imprudence of these people. They could not afford to be hostile; for the hotel, if you remember, commands the street from the base up the hill. No troops, therefore, could risk going up that hill with a hostile house in that position ready to take them in the rear. The escape of the poor Perkins' is a perfect miracle; they, I hear, lost everything. The innkeeper, waiter and stableman, they say, were killed in the fray. The number of deaths among the Swiss were 10, and 33 of the Perugians. Several prisoners were made. I went up on this same afternoon (June 22) with the two little boys to see the colonel of the regiment. The town is wonderfully little injured, only broken windows   *   after a mob riot, with the exception of a few] houses [in the suburbs, between the outer and inner gates. One was burned by the accident of the [falling of a bomb-shell. The other was cannonaded as being a resort of the rebels. There is great talk of how the heads of the revolution scampered off, betraying thus the tools and dupes of their faction."

[Extract from another letter to David Ross of Bladensburgh: "There is great terror here among all the country people, who dread, sooner or later, vengeance being taken upon them by the revolutionary party, because they would have nothing to say to the movement."]

It is well known how rapidly events succcceeded one another, when Napoleon's friendly relations with Austria came to an end. On May 3rd he declared war. On the 12th he arrived at Genoa, commanded in person, on the 4th of June, at the battle of Magenta, where, but for the superior generalship of Marshal McMahon, he would have lost his life, together with his army, and on the 24th of the same month won the great victory of Solferino. He now gave out that he had enough of glory and would fight no more, whilst in reality he was constrained to yield to powerful pressure from without. Prussia, foreseeing that, if Austria experienced a few more defeats, she herself would suffer, deemed it wise to interfere. Prussia had,

The peace of Villafranca.

M

indeed, concerted matters beforehand with the Emperor of the French, and had undertaken to isolate Austria, her hereditary rival in Germany.

But at the first rumor of the Franco-Piedmontese aggression, the German States were moved. The Diet of Francfort insisted that the confederate nations should proceed to assist the Emperor, who was President of the German Confederation. It fell to Prussia to head the movement. But, as may be conceived, she was not hearty in the cause. Her statesmen hesitated, argued, equivocated, and made a show of preparing, but slowly, for war. Meanwhile, the news of the successive defeats of Austria roused still more the patriotism of the Germans. The Prussian monarch, finding that he was on the point of being overwhelmed, addressed to his Imperial accomplice, the day after the battle of Solferino, a most pressing telegram, informing him that he must make peace, cost what it would. Napoleon, it need hardly be said, obeyed, and so *the peace of Villafranca was concluded.* By this treaty was established an Italian Confederation, under the honorary presidency of the Pope, Lombardy given to Piedmont, Venice left to Austria, the rights of the Grand Duke of Tuscany and the other sovereigns, who were for the moment dispossessed, expressly reserved. Thus appeared to end the intrigues of the revolution. Pius IX. promptly invited the faithful of Rome to join with him in offering thanksgiving to God. His letter thus concludes: "What do we pray for? That all the enemies of Christ, of His Church and of the Holy See, may be converted and live."

So clear, apparently, was now the political atmosphere, that men could not avoid accusing them-

How the treaty was observed.

selves of having judged rashly the mighty conqueror, who, by a word, could restore serenity as easily as he had disturbed it. It was not yet known by what power he was restrained. In compliance with the requirements of the treaty of Villafranca, Piedmont, indeed, withdrew her commissioners from Central Italy. The public, however, soon learned, to its great astonishment, what, at first, it could not believe, that provisional governments took the place of the Piedmontese Commissioners, and that Baron Ricasoli, at Florence, Signor Farini, at Modena and Parma, and Cipriani, at Bologna, all agents of Count de Cavour and the revolution, dismissed everywhere such officials as were suspected of looking seriously to the return of the legitimate sovereigns, and had recourse to popular suffrage. This, it is no exaggeration to say, was a mere mockery. The voting directed, expurgated by these parties, never extended to the landward districts, but, confined entirely to the towns, was necessarily calculated to produce the result at which they aimed—a *plebiscitum* in favor of annexation to Piedmont. In Romagna, for instance, where there were about two hundred thousand electors, only 18,000 were registered, and of these only one-third presented their votes. By such means was a national assembly constituted. This assembly met at Bologna on the 6th of September, and at its first sitting voted the abolition of the Pontifical government, and invited Victor Emmanuel. This potentate dared not, at first, to accept, but appointed Signor Buoncompagni, governor-general of the league of Central Italy. It did not appear from the state of the polls, if, indeed, the polling of votes was even made a fashion of, that the people of the Papal States were at all anxious to do away with the government under which they and their fore-fathers had enjoyed so many blessings, together with the sur-passing honor of possessing, as their capital, the metropolis of the Christian world. They were too happy in being ruled over by the elective monarch whom they themselves had chosen, to desire, in preference to him, the mere shadow of a king—the satrap of an Imperial despot. It was not they who, in a pre-tended *patriotic* endeavor to shake off the Pontifical yoke, raised the standard of rebellion in so many cities and provinces of the Papal States. This was wholly the work of foreigners. A Bonaparte, attended by a numerous and well-disciplined army, invaded Italy. His arms were, to a certain extent, successful; and so rebellion was encouraged. Another Bonaparte excited to revolt the city of Perugia. The disturbance was speedily settled by a handful of troops whom the sovereign had despatched from Rome, to the great satisfaction of the citizens of Perugia. In other cities, by the like instrumentalities, were like movements occasioned. They were invariably suppressed by the loyal and devoted people. So much was this the case that the Pontifical government warmly thanked the mayors and municipalities of no fewer than seven or eight cities for their good services in putting down the nascent revolution. At Bologna, the capital of the Romagnol or Æmilian provinces, a cousin of the Bonapartes, the Marquis Pepoli, whom the benevolence of Pius IX. had restored to his country, stirred up rebellion, and caused the Pontifical government to give place to revolutionary misrule. The abettors of Pepoli, in this most base and ungrateful proceeding, were his associates of the secret societies; others who were foreigners at Bologna, and a few malcontents of that city itself. But all these were far from being the citizens of Bologna, far from being the people of the Bolognese provinces. Whilst such things were done, where was the peace of Villafranca? It had become, or rather, never was anything better than, waste paper. The head of the Bonapartes was the offender, and he contrived to make France the partner of his guilt.

"It is France," the illustrious M. de Montalembert affirms, "that has allowed the temporal power of the Pope to be shaken. This is the fact, which blind men only can deny. France is not engaged alone in this path, but her overwhelming ascendancy places her at the head of the movement, and throws the great and supreme responsibility of it upon her. We know all the legitimate and crushing reproaches that are due to England and Piedmont; but if France had so willed it, Piedmont would not have dared to undertake anything against the Holy See, and England would have been condemned to her impotent hatred. * * The Congress of Paris, in 1856—having solemnly declared, 'that none of the contracting powers had the right of interfering, either collectively or individually, between a sovereign and his subjects '*—after having proclaimed the principle of the absolute independence of sovereigns in favor of the Turkish Sultan against his Christian subjects, thought itself justified by its protocol of April 8th, and in the absence of any representative of the august accused, in proclaiming that the situation of the Papal States was *abnormal* and *irregular*. This accusation, developed, aggravated and exaggerated in parliament and elsewhere, by Lord Palmerston and Count Cavour, was, nevertheless, formally put forward under the presidency and on the *initiative* of the French minister for foreign affairs. Consequently, France must be held accountable for it to the Church, and to the rest of Europe." The war which "the skilful but guilty perseverance of Piedmontese policy" succeeded in occasioning between France and Austria facilitated not a little the work of revolution in the States of the Church. In order to dispel the fears that prevailed, the following words were addressed to the Bishops of France by the minister of the Emperor: "The prince who restored the Holy Father to his throne in the Vatican wills that the Head of the Church should be respected in all his rights as a temporal sovereign." A little later, the Emperor of the French, elated with his military success, issued a proclamation which renewed the apprehensions that had been so happily allayed. "Italians!—Providence sometimes favors nations and individuals by giving them the opportunity of suddenly springing into their full growth. Avail yourselves, then, of the fortune that is offered you! Your desire of independence, so long expressed, so often deceived, will be realized, if you show yourselves worthy of it. Unite then for one sole object, the liberation of your country. Fly to the standards of King Victor Emmanuel, who has already so nobly shown you the way to honor. Remember that without discipline there can be no army, and animated with the sacred fire of patriotism, be soldiers only to-day, and you will be to-morrow free citizens of a great country."

* Protocol, March 18th.

"The Romagnese," continues Montalembert, "took the speaker at his word. Four days after the appearance of this proclamation, they rose against the Papal authority, created a provisional government, convoked a sovereign assembly, voted the deposition of the Pope, and the annexation to Piedmont. Finally, seeing their audacity remained unpunished, they organized an armed league, officered by Piedmontese, and commanded by Garibaldi—that Garibaldi, who, having been vanquished by French troops ten years ago, now avails himself of our recent hard-won victories, to boast that he will ' soon make an end of clerical despotism.' "

Three months after the revolution had been established in the Romagna, M. de Montalembert wrote : " The revolution, triumphant, is still asking Europe to sanction its work. France has to impute to herself all the scandals and all the calamities that will follow. Great nations are responsible not only for what they do, but for what they permit to be done under the shadow of their flag, and by the incitement of their influence. The war which France waged in Italy has cost the Pope the loss of the third part of his dominions, and the irreparable weakening of his hold on what remains. The eldest daughter of the church will remain accountable for it before contemporaries, before history, before Europe, and before God. She will not be allowed to wipe her mouth like the adultress in Scripture, *quæ tergens os suum dicit, non sum operata malum*."

Another power which was, in the full sense of the term, *foreign* in the Roman States, still more directly aided the revolution. This power was the army of Garibaldi. It will be seen, when it is considered what troops this army was composed of, that it was wholly alien in the States of the Church. In this motley corps there were :

6,750 Piedmontese volunteers.
3,240 Lombards   "
1,200 Venetians.
2,150 Neapolitans and Sicilians.
  500 Romans.

1,200 Hungarians.
  200 French.
   30 English.
  150 Maltese and Ionians.
  260 Greeks.
  450 Poles.
  370 Swiss.
  160 Spaniards, Belgians and Americans.
  800 Austrian deserters and liberated convicts.

Could such an army as this be held to be a representation of the people of the Papal States? One-third of it was supplied by two hostile nations, one of which, Piedmont, had actually, by the intrigues of its government and in pursuance of a policy which an able statesman, a most candid writer and an honorable man, Count Montalembert, has stigmatized as *criminal*, caused the rebellion in Romagna, and has since earnestly labored to avail itself of the state of things, by annexing Central Italy to the territories of the Piedmontese King. It were superfluous to direct attention to the numbers of foreigners from various states. It is, however, deserving of remark that the whole population of the Papal States, amounting to 3,000,000, should have shown its alleged sympathy with the "cause of Italy," by sending only 500 men to fight its battles. They did not want courage, as was shown in 1848, when neither the considerate advice and paternal remonstrances of the Holy Father, nor the wise counsel of grave statesmen and learned cardinals, could moderate the ardor of the Roman youth, believing, as they had been persuaded, that patriotism and duty called them to follow the standard of King Charles Albert. Then they took up arms, as they conceived, in the cause of Italian liberty. But now that honorable cause was manifestly in abeyance; and they would not leave their homes and endanger their lives for the phantom of national independence offered them by the revolution.

The French were equally wary. They sympathized with Italy. They fought for their Emperor. But they had no

admiration for Piedmontese ambition, or that of Murats, and
Pepolis, and Bonapartes.

England was more cautious still. However much her
demagogues may have exerted their oratorical powers at home,
they carefully avoided perilling either life or limb in the cause
of the revolution. A more numerous band of fighting men of
English origin, in Garibaldi's ranks, would have shown more
sympathy with rebellion in some Italian States than the pro-
posal made by a right honorable member of the richest peerage in the world to raise a penny subscription in order to
supply the rebels with bayonets and fire-arms. When we call
to mind that this suggestion was made by that very lordly
peer who was once Governor-General of India, we have little
difficulty in understanding why his superiors, the members of
the East India Company, dismissed him from the high and
responsible office with which he had been entrusted.

It cannot be pretended that the army of Garibaldi was, in
any degree, a national representation. No nation or community can be fairly represented by a number of its people, insig-
nificantly small, unless, indeed, these few individuals hold
commission from their fellow-countrymen. We have not read
anywhere that the Garibaldian army was thus honored. Social
status, character and respectability, may, on occasions, give to
individuals the privilege of representing their country. But
on these grounds the motley troop of the revolutionary leader
possessed no claim. They were men for whom peace and
order have no charms. The powerful corrective of military discipline was applied to them in vain. Their insubordination
was notorious. To Garibaldi even it was intolerable. And
this man, daring as he was, withdrew from the command in
disgust. He had scarcely retired when many of his men
deserted. These the people refused to recognize, and would
not afford them assistance on their journey. Some fifty of
them arrived at Placentia, after having been reduced to mendicancy before they could reach their homes. The revolutionary governor, Doctor Fanti, issued an order of the day,

requiring that these men, on account of their insubordination and bad conduct, should not be admitted anew into the army of the League. The general-in-chief also published an order, under date of 26th November, 1859, absolutely forbidding to accept any person who had belonged to Garibaldi's force. An army so composed could, by no means, claim to represent the highly refined, intellectual, and moral populations of Italy. Far less did it afford any proof that the people of the Papal States were anxious to forward the work of the revolution.

The inhabitants of Rome and the Roman States, far from showing any inclination to side with the revolutionary party, were wont never to let pass an opportunity of manifesting their satisfaction with the government of the Pope. His Holiness walked abroad without guards. And although he sought the most retired places, for the enjoyment of that pedestrian exercise which his health required, numbers of the people often contrived to throw themselves in his way, in order to testify to him their reverence and affection, as well as to receive his paternal benediction. When taking his walk, one day, on Monte Pincio, many thousands came around him, declaring loudly their unfeigned loyalty. The following day, still greater crowds repaired to the same place. But the Holy Father, with a view to be more retired, had gone in another direction. It ought not to be forgotten, that when returning, in the autumn of 1859, from his villa at Castel Gandolpho, the road was thronged on both sides to the distance of four miles from Rome with citizens who had no other object in view than to give a cordial and loyal welcome to their Bishop and Prince. This was an ovation—a triumph which the greatest conqueror might well have envied. It has already been recorded that, on occasion of the progress which the Holy Father made through his States, he was everywhere received with the most lively demonstrations of enthusiastic loyalty, reverence and affection. On the 18th of January, 1860, the municipal body, or, as it is called, "the Senate," of Rome, presented to the Sovereign Pontiff, as well in their own name as on behalf of all the

people, an address expressive of their filial duty and loyal
sentiments.   On the following day, January 19th, one hundred
and thirty-four of the nobility of Rome, who are, in all, one
hundred and sixty, approached the person of the Pontiff in
order to present an equally loyal and dutiful address.   The
sentiments of this address will be best conveyed in its own
plain and energetic language—language which does honor to
the patricians of mod rn Rome :

"We, the undersigned, deeply grieved by the publication
of various libels which, emanating from the revolutionary
press, tend to make the world believe that the people subject
to the authority of your Holiness are wishing to shake off the
yoke which, as it is reported, |has become insufferable, feel
necessitated to show fidelity and loyalty to your Holiness, and
to make known to the rest of Europe, which, at the present
moment, doubts the sincerity of our words, the fidelity of our
persons towards your Holiness, by a manifestation of attachment and fidelity towards your person, proceeding from our
duty as Catholics, and from our lawful submission as your
subjects.

"It is not, however, our intention to vie with the miserable cunning of your enemies—enemies of the faith—of that
very faith which they profess to venerate.   But placed, as it is
our fortune, by your side, and seeing the malignity of those
who attack you, and the disloyal character of their attacks, we
feel bound to gather ourselves at the foot of your twofold
throne, with vows for the integrity of your independent sovereignty; and once more offering you our whole selves, too
happy if this manifestation of our fidelity may sweeten the bitterness with which your Holiness is afflicted, and if you are
pleased to accept our offerings.   Thus may Europe, deceived
by so many perverse writings, be thoroughly convinced that if
the nobility have hitherto been restrained from the expression
of their desires by respect and the fear of throwing any obstacle
in the way of a happy solution, so anxiously desired, they have
not the less retained them, and expressed them as individuals;

and that they, this day, unite to declare them, heartily and
sincerely pledging to them before all the world their honor
and their faith.

"Accept, Holy Father, Pontiff and King, this energetic
protest and the unlimited devotedness which the nobles of
Rome offer in reverence to your Sceptre, no less than to your
Pastoral staff."—(*In the Weekly Register of January 28, 1860,
from the Giornale di Roma.*)

The like loyal and patriotic feeling was manifested throughout all the cities and provinces of the Papal States. One of
the most eminent of liberal British statesmen, the Marquis of
Normanby, bears witness to the fact that very few of the citizens
of Bologna could be compelled, even at the point of the sword,
to express adherence to the revolution. A portion of the periodical press labored to keep such facts as these out of view.
But they would have required better evidence than they were
ever able to produce in order to convince reasonable and reflecting men that people, blessed with so great a degree of material
prosperity as the subjects of the Pope and the other Princes
of Italy, were anxious to see radical changes introduced into
the governments under which they were so favored. That
they were highly prosperous and but slightly taxed, many distinguished travellers, members of both houses of the British
parliament, and others bear witness. None will question the
evidence of these facts which are known on the authority of
such men as the Marquis of Normanby and his Excellency the
Earl of Carlisle. The Hon. Mr. Pope Hennessey stated in the
House of Commons: "That the national prosperity of the
States of the Church and of Austria had become greater, year
after year, than that of Sardinia (where a sort of revolutionary
constitution had been established), and that documents existed
in the Foreign Office, in the shape of reports from our own
consuls, which proved it, with respect to commercial interests
in Sardinia. Mr. Erskine, our minister at Turin, in a despatch of January 7, 1856, gave a very unfavorable view of the
manufacturing, mining and agricultural progress of Sardinia.

But from Venetia, Mr. Elliott gave a perfectly opposite view, showing that great progress was being made there. The shipping trade of Sardinia with England had declined 2,000 tons. But the British trade with Ancona had increased 21,000 tons, and with Venice 25,000 tons, in the course of the last two years. He attributed these results to the increase of taxation in Sardinia, through the introduction of the constitutional (the *Sardinian* constitutional) system of government, and to the comparatively easy taxation of Venetia. The increased taxation of Sardinia from 1847 to 1857 was no less than 50,000,000 francs. With respect to education in the Papal States, he contended that it was more diffused than it was in this country— Great Britain."

In countries that were so prosperous, every man literally "sitting under his own vine and his own fig-tree," it is difficult to believe that there was wide-spread discontent and a general desire for radical changes. To prove that there was, it would have required evidence of no ordinary weight. All testimony that can be relied on shows a very different state of feeling. Lord John Russell, in his too memorable Aberdeen speech, gave expression to an opinion which, through the labors of the newspaper press, had become very prevalent in England, that "under their provisonal revolutionary governments the people of Central Italy had conducted themselves with perfect order, just as if they had been the citizens of a country that had long enjoyed free institutions."

* The Marquis of Normanby, in his place in the British House of Peers, made reply to this allegation:

* "If we were to sift the pretensions of all our public men, to discover that one person who is necessarily best informed of the past and present state of Italy, and the causes and means that have produced the anarchy which now prevails over the greater part of that unfortunate peninsula, Lord Normanby would inevitably be the man for our purpose. His long residence in Italy, his intimate acquaintance with all that is there distinguished for literature, science, art and statesmanship, and his unquestionable liberality of sentiment, as a politician, give him a paramount claim to our respectful attention, and even to our confidence, when he comes forward to enlighten his countrymen, with respect to Italian affairs—a claim to which no other

"I should like to know where the noble Lord found that information. There is not in Central Italy a single government that has resulted from popular election. They were all named by Piedmont—which had, as it were, packed the cards. Liberty of speech there was none, nor liberty of the press, nor personal liberty. *   *   The Grand Duchess of Parma was expelled by a Piedmontese army, and restored by the spontaneous call of her people. She left the country, declaring that she would suffer everything sooner than expose her subjects to the horrors of civil war. *   *   Numberless atrocities have been committed under the rule of these governments which, according to my noble friend, are so wise and orderly. I read to you the first day of this session the letter of a Tuscan, whose character is irreproachable. Since that time I have received from him another letter, in which he says: 'You will not be surprised to learn that my letter to you has been the occasion of the coarsest invectives. For what reason I cannot tell, if it was not because it spoke the truth.'

"Here is a second letter, which I received a few days ago from an English merchant of the highest standing at Leghorn: 'No intervention is allowed in Tuscany; and nevertheless, my Lord, intervention appears everywhere; even armed and foreign intervention. The governor-general is a Piedmontese; the minister of war is a Piedmontese; the commander of the armed police is a Piedmontese; the military governor of Leghorn is a Piedmontese; the captain of the port is a Piedmontese; without reckoning a great number of other functionaries of the same nation. This is what I call armed and foreign intervention. Let us be disembarrassed of all this; let

---

member of the legislature can have the slightest pretensions. He has, too, throughout a long public career, always maintained such an independence of character, and so nobly and generously subordinated his personal interests to his sense of public duty, as to entitle him as a right to our confidence, when he unbosoms himself either in print or in speech, of that knowledge which he has acquired by long study and experience in official and non-official life, and tells us important truths which it is necessary for us to know, in order to be able to form a correct judgment upon momentous passing events."—*Weekly Register, February* 11, 1860.

us be free from the despotic pressure of this government, and
the great majority of the country would vote the restoration of
the House of Lorraine. Almost all the army would be for the
Grand Duke, and on this account it is kept at a distance from
Tuscany. I can say the same of two-thirds of the national
guard. All the Great Powers have observed strict neutrality
here, inasmuch as they have not been present at any ceremony
which could be looked upon as a recognition of the existing
government. But since the peace of Villafranca, the English
agents have taken part in all the ceremonies, in all the balls.
Assuredly, thus to recognize such a government is far from
being faithful to the assurance given last session by the noble
Lord at the head of the foreign department (cheers)."

Lord Normanby's trustworthy correspondent says, moreover, in the letter referred to, that the Tuscan troops being
kept at a distance from Tuscany, the people dreaded making
any demonstration, being well aware that an imprudent word
would be punished with imprisonment. "At Leghorn, however, some private meetings were held, at which influential
persons were present. Public meetings are impossible. Twenty-three members of the assembly asked that it should be convened. This was refused them. At the private meetings,
however, it was decided that Ferdinand IV. should be recalled,
on condition of granting a constitution and an amnesty. The
people have been dreadfully deceived. All promises have been
violated, the price of provisions has risen, the national debt
has been enormously increased."

Lord Normanby also laid before the House of Peers the testimony of a distinguished Italian writer, Signor Amperi, whom
he described as a man of high character. This gentleman
addressed the governments of Central Italy in the following
terms :

"The false position in which you have placed yourselves
has reduced you to the necessity, in times of liberty, as you
pretend, but of false liberty, as I conceive, to make falsehood
a system of government. Of the promises of Victor Emmanuel

that he would sustain before the Great Powers the vote of the Tuscan Assembly, you have made a formal accepting for himself of this vote, and, in order to deceive the ignorant multitude, you ordered public rejoicings in honor of a fact which you knew to be false. You declared yourselves the ministers of a king who had not appointed you. You administer the government in his name; you give judgments in his name: you pledge the public faith of a sovereign who has given you no commission to do any such thing; and although you forced the Tuscans to acknowledge him for king, you despise his authority to such an extent as to impose upon him the choice of a regent. What right have you to do this, if he be really king, and if he be not, is your right any better founded?"

The Marquis of Normanby laughs to scorn the various attempts that were made to establish a government in Central Italy against the will of the people. First of all, a certain Signor Buoncompagni was appointed governor-general by the King of Sardinia. The Emperor of the French judged that the ambitious satrap had exceeded his powers, and Buoncompagni was immediately recalled. The Prince de Carignan was then offered the regency of Central Italy. He thought it prudent to decline: but, unwilling wholly to relinquish a cherished object of ambition, he named in his place the above-mentioned Signor Buoncompagni. It would be hard to say in virtue of what right he so acted. The appointment, it is well known, caused the greatest indignation at Florence, and elicited a protest from the liberal representatives themselves. Will it be believed, in after times, that the British ministry, at that time in power, actually recognized this spurious government, ordering the Queen's representative to pay an official visit to Signor Buoncompagni? Whilst all Europe held aloof, anxious to avoid wrong and insult to the Italian people, whence this zeal and haste on the part of the British cabinet? At first they had resolved to be neutral. But there occurred to them the chimerical idea of a great kingdom of Central Italy; and, as Lord Normanby stated, they hastened in their ignorance to carry this idea into effect. "Yes," continued the illustrious Peer, when assailed by the laughter of the more ignorant portion of his hearers, "yes, in complete ignorance of the aspirations and the prejudices of the Italian people."

"It is a painful duty," said the illustrious statesman, in concluding his eloquent appeal to the common sense and honorable feeling of the British peerage, " to have to dispel the illusions of public opinion in regard to Italy. I have endeavored to fulfil this duty by laying before you information that can be relied on ; and I have the pleasure to observe that light is now beginning to penetrate the darkness which has hitherto enveloped this question. There is already a greater chance that Italian independence will be established on a more legitimate basis, free from all foreign intervention, and in such a way as to favor the cause of fidelity, of truth, of honor and general order (cheers)."

If there were no foreign intervention, it was long the fashion with certain parties to say, we should soon see the end of Papal rule, as well as that of all the other sovereignties of Italy. Such, however, were not the views of the great majority of the Italian people. It has been satisfactorily proved, those people themselves being the witnesses, that such of them as were subjects of the Pope, far from being discontented and anxious to do away with the government which was set over them, and substitute for it either a republic or a foreign monarchy, highly appreciated and were steadfastly devoted to the wise and paternal rule of their Pontiff Sovereign. The subjects of the other Italian Princes, as well as the inhabitants of the revolutionized portion of the Papal States, were only prevented by the armed intervention of foreign Powers from declaring in favor of their rightful sovereigns. There is no pretension to deny that there were reformers and constitutionalists in those States. Of their number the Pope himself was one. But the well-informed and intellectual Italians were not ignorant that all reforms must be the fruit of time and of opinion, and that under the sway of enlightened and benevolent sovereigns, aided by the learning and wise counsel of able and conscientious statesmen, such changes, in matters of civil polity, as were adapted to the wants of the people would not have been delayed beyond the time when circumstances called for and justified their adoption.

All eyes were turned towards the victor of Solferino, who was the absolute master of the situation.

The French Emperor connives at the violation of the Treaty.

What would he do? Would he allow to be violated the definitive treaty which his Plenipotentiaries were actually completing at Zurich? Napoleon III. did positively nothing. He repeated in the treaty the stipulations in favor of the dispossessed sovereigns, just as if the pretended plebiscitums were null, and he had no knowledge of them. He quietly permitted these plebiscitums to take effect with all their consequences, quite the same as if the treaty had never existed. Austria saw the treaty executed, as regarded every sacrifice to which she had consented, and not without pain, that it was set aside in all the points which set a limit to those sacrifices. But Austria was not the strongest Power. Piedmont, meanwhile, adhibited her signature without wincing under those of France and Austria. Thus, as Mgr. Pie of Poitiers declared, the church was deprived of all human stay. Such a state of things was not witnessed without emotion. Even in the frivolous society of France a change had taken place since the days of the great revolution. Catholic sentiment had gained among the lettered classes. The dethronement of Pius VI. had passed unnoticed, like that of an ordinary sovereign. That of Pius VII. had excited only some isolated animadversions. That of Pius IX. raised storms of protestation on the one hand, and on the other thunders of applause. One party so hated the Papacy as to become traitors to their country, and bind themselves with a sort of wild enthusiasm, first to the car of Italian unity, afterwards to that of Germany. They who thought otherwise carried their love of the imperilled institution to such an extent as to forget all their calculations, all their political alliances, and to incur freely the displeasure of men in power, even to sacrifice the favor of the multitude, favor which was not less valuable in times of universal suffrage than that of power. The Roman question became the inexhaustible subject of public discussions and private conversations. It sometimes even occasioned family quarrels, and was a trying ordeal for long-established friendships. Such extraordinary emotion on account of an idea— an abstraction, as it was called by the indifferent, who took part with neither one side nor the other—showed that society was not yet corroded to the core by selfishness and purely material interests. It was sick, indeed, but far from dead. The French government ought, surely, at the outset, to have taken warning. It ought to have learned something from the unanimity with which all the enemies of order, who were also its enemies, supported its new policy, and the unanimity, not less remarkable, with which religious people who, generally, had been its friends, combated that policy. Both liberal and ultramontane Catholics, Protestants even, such, at least, as were earnest Christians, and practised what they believed, forgot their divisions. The bishops were the first who spoke out. Mgr. de Parisis, who had so nobly contended for the liberties of the church in the reign of Louis Philippe, gave the keynote, and all took part with him and their venerable colleagues of Italy and Germany, of Ireland and Spain, of England and America. To say all in a word, the note of alarm was sounded throughout the whole extent of Christendom.

In this magnificent concert was heard the courageous language of Mgr. Dupanloup, the learned and illustrious Bishop of Orleans. On the 30th of September, 1859, this prelate wrote, no less boldly than eloquently:

"People say that to touch the sovereign is not to touch the Pontiff. Certainly his temporal power is not a divine institution ; who does not know this ? But it is a providential institution, and who is ignorant of the fact ? Doubtless, during three centuries, the Popes only possessed independence enough to die martyrs ; but they assuredly had a right to another sort

of independence; and providence, which does not always use
miracles for its purpose, ended by founding on the most lawful
sovereignty in Europe the freedom and the independence
necessary to the church. History proves it beyond the possibility of doubt; all eminent intellects have confessed it; all
true statesmen know it. Yes, that the church may be free,
the Pope must be free and independent. That independence
must be sovereign. The Pope must be free, and he must be
evidently so. The Pope must be free in his own interior as
well as in his exterior government. This must be so, for the
sake of his own dignity in the government of the church as
well as for the security of our own consciences. This must be
so, in order to secure to the common parent of all the faithful
that neutrality which is indispensable to him amid the frequent
wars between Christian Powers. The Pope must not only be
free in his own conscience, in his own interior, but it must be
evident to all that he is so; he must show himself to be so, in
order that all may know and believe it, and that no doubt or
suspicion be possible on this subject. But, say the Italian
revolutionists, we do not propose to do away with the Papal
sovereignty; we merely wish to limit and restrain it. And
why so, I ask you in my turn, if thereby you also diminish
and debase the honor of the Catholic religion, its dignity and
independence? Why do so, if thereby you lower and degrade
the most Italian sovereignty of the whole peninsula? Why,
more especially, do so now, in presence of all these unchained
evil passions, and thereby give against the Holy See a sentence
of incapacity, and thus, in the eyes of Christendom, insult that
unarmed and oppressed Majesty? You say he will only lose
the Romagna and the Legations. But allow me to ask you
by what right you take them? And why not take all the rest,
if you please? Why, in your dreams of Italian unity, should
other Italian cities fare otherwise than Bologna and Ferrara?
Why have you not made up your minds to take everything
outside of Rome, with the garden of the Vatican? You have
said this, you know. But why leave him, even in Rome?

Why should not Dioclesian and the catacombs be the best of all governments for the church? Where are you going? How far will your detestable principles lead you? At least, tell us clearly? Is this a clever calculation of yours? and, not daring to do more at present, or unable to do more, are you waiting for time and the violence of events to accomplish the rest? But who, think you, is to be deceived by you? Must we say, with the highest organ of the English press, that in the present business France is aggressive and insidious? I do not admit that our country is willing to play the part designed for her. Such calculations are not suited to French generosity. For my part, I protest, with my whole soul, against the perfidious intentions that we are supposed to entertain. But, in concluding, I must protest, still more solemnly, as a devoted son of the Holy Roman Church, the mother and teacher of all others—I protest against the revolutionary impiety which ignores her rights and would fain steal her patrimony. I protest, in the name of good sense and honor, indignant at beholding an Italian Sovereign Power become the accomplice of insurrection and revolt, and at the conspiracy of so many blind and unreasoning passions against the principles proclaimed and professed throughout the world by all great statesmen and politicians. I protest, in the name of common decency and European law, against this profanation of all that is most august, against the brutal passions which have inspired acts of inconceivable cowardice. And if I must speak out, I protest, in the name of good faith, against this restless and ill-disguised ambition, those evasive answers, that disloyal policy, of which we have the saddening spectacle before our eyes."

These burning words of the eminent and patriotic French bishop must have pierced the soul of Napoleon III. To any other man, at least, an Orsini shell would have been less terrible. But, "*Perversi difficillime corriguntur.*" No reproaches, however severe and well deserved, no remonstrance, however well founded, could move the French Emperor. A greater power than that of words had impelled him towards the evil courses which the great majority of the French nation, together with the whole Catholic world, condemned. The bishops, meanwhile, continued to protest. The Archbishop of Sens, Mellon-Jolly, dared to say, in accents of sorrow: "Events, alas! are far beyond all that we feared." De Prilly, Bishop of Chalons, Dean of the French Episcopate, thus wrote a few days before his death: "Ah! who deserved less than Pius IX. to be attacked by so many enemies! If the tears which he sheds are so bitter for himself, they are terrible to those who cause them! A poor bishop, at the point of death, so assures him and craves his benediction." The expiring prelate, one would say, had foreseen the humiliation of Sedan. The courageous language of the bishops was so much feared that it was thought necessary to silence them. Napoleon, having endeavored in vain to remove their disquietude by renewing his hollow protestations, denounced them as violent agitators, abandoned them to the jeers of the infidel press, for which alone there was liberty in those days, and finally forbade all journals whatsoever to publish episcopal writings that bore any relation to the Roman question. Thus did he think to escape the danger with which he was threatened by silencing the tongues which warned him.

The learned Cardinal Donnet, so celebrated as a theologian, now showed the abilities of a diplomatist. When Napoleon III. was at Bordeaux, on the 11th October, 1859, the cardinal, whose duty it was to compliment the Emperor as his sovereign, failed not at the same time to remonstrate against his tortuous policy. "We pray," said the pious cardinal, "we pray confidently, persistently, and with hope which neither deplorable events nor sacrilegious acts of violence extinguished. Our hopes, the realization of which appears to be so remote, are founded on yourself, sire, next to God. You were and you still desire to be the oldest son of the church, and it cannot be forgotten that you spoke the memorable words: 'The temporal sovereignty of the venerable head of the church is intimately connected with the lustre of Catholicism, as also with the

liberty and independence of Italy. Grand idea! perfectly in
harmony with that of the august Chief of your dynasty, who
said in regard to the temporal power of the Popes: '*The
centuries made it, and they did well.*'" The only reply of the
all-powerful Emperor was a refusal to reply. "I cannot here,"
he said, "discuss all the weighty matters, the development of
which would be required by the serious question to which you
have alluded. So I confine myself to reminding you that the
government which restored the Holy Father to his throne can
only give him counsel inspired by sincere and respectful
devotedness to his interests. But he is anxious, and not without cause, as to the time, which cannot be far distant, when
our troops must evacuate Rome. For Europe cannot allow
the occupation, which has already lasted ten years, to be prolonged for an indefinite period. But when our army shall be
withdrawn, what will be left behind? These are questions of
the importance of which none are ignorant. But, believe me,
in order to solve them, we must, considering the age in which
we live, avoid appealing to ardent passions, calmly seek truth,
and pray Divine Providence to enlighten both peoples and
kings, in order that they may wisely use their rights and fully
discharge their duties." From these last words the Emperor
appeared to have forgot that when there are duties to be fulfilled prayer alone will not suffice. His speech at the opening
of the legislative session, 7th March, 1860, showed that either
irresistible illusion or a foregone conclusion of complicity
guided his Italian policy. He accused the Catholics of becoming excited without grounds, and of ingratitude towards him.
The logic of events, so plain to all besides, was a dead letter to
the imperial mind, blinded as it was by the habit of dark
manœuvres.

"I cannot pass unnoticed," said he, "the excitement of a
portion of the Catholic world. It has accepted, without reflection, erroneous impressions, allowed itself to become passionately alarmed. The past which ought to have been a guarantee for the future has been so ignored, and services rendered

so forgotten, that profound conviction, absolute confidence in the public good sense, was necessary for me, in order to preserve, amid the agitation which was industriously occasioned, that serenity of mind which alone maintains us in the way of truth."

Meanwhile, a Congress for settling the difficulties of Italy was announced. This Congress was to be composed of all the great European Powers —of France, whose government had no good will; of Austria, which had not the power to cause the treaty of Zurich to be put in execution; of schismatical Russia; of Protestant Prussia, and of Protestant England, which favored revolution so long as it kept at a distance from its own doors. Pius IX. beheld in it many causes of disquietude. Nevertheless, he accepted the congress. The public were discussing, and not without impatience, the names of the presumed negotiators, when there appeared on the 22d of December, 1859, a new pamphlet which, like the former, was anonymous, and was ascribed as it also had been, to an author who was in too high a position to append his signature. Its title was, "*The Pope and the Congress.*" It abounded in high sounding words, and was full of contradictions from beginning to end. It demonstrated, indeed, that the temporal power of the Pope was an essential guarantee of his spiritual independence, but that this power could only be exercised within territorial limits of very small extent, which could not enable him to sustain himself, whilst, nevertheless, his dignity and the general interest forbade him to seek foreign intervention. The pamphlet concluded by insisting that the Pope ought to begin by giving up all claim to Romagna, and so prepare for ceding, a little later, the rest of his states, when he would be satisfied to hold the Vatican with a garden around it, and receive a magnificent salary provided by all the Catholic Powers. Hundreds of pamphlets and articles in the Catholic journals appeared in reply to this anonymous writing. They proved that the proposed arrangement would subject the Head

A European Congress proposed for settling the affairs of Italy.

of the Church to the caprice of the Powers, and then enquired what security he would have against those who were his securities, especially at a time like the present, when the ancient law of nations, which was founded on respect for the weak and sworn faith, is suppressed by the revolution, and the reason of the strongest is the only one attended to ; when the most solemn treaties are violated with impunity by those who have signed them, and as soon as they have signed them. The bishops raised their voice anew. They stated with sorrow that the pamphlet decided in favor of the revolution. But the boldest condemnation proceeded from Rome itself. The Popes, it is well known, hesitate not to use the proper terms when there is question of stigmatizing iniquity. No matter though they be at the mercy of those whom they brand, they define each error and each act of injustice with the same precision as in writing a theological thesis. Pius IX., who was mildness itself, more than once startles the delicate ear by the liberty of his language, so different from the minced and often ambiguous style of diplomacy. On the 30th of December, the official journal of Rome published the following note : " There appeared lately at Paris an anonymous pamphlet, entitled, ' *The Pope and the Congress.*' This pamphlet is nothing else than homage paid to the revolution—an insidious thesis addressed to those weak minds who have no sure *criterium* by which they can detect the poison which it holds concealed, and a subject of sorrow to all good Catholics. The arguments contained in this writing are only a reproduction of the errors and outrages so often hurled against the Holy See, and so often victoriously refuted. If it was the object of the author, perchance, to intimidate him whom he threatens with such great disasters, he can rest assured that he who has right on his side, who seeks no other support than the solid and immovable foundations of justice, and who is sustained especially by the protection of the King of kings, has certainly nothing to fear from the snares of men."

On 1st January, 1860, Pius IX., in his reply to the complimentary address of General Goyon, who commanded the French military at Rome, characterized the pamphlet as " a signal monument of hypocrisy, and an unworthy tissue of contradictions." The Holy Father further observed, before expressing his good wishes for the Emperor, the Empress, the Prince Imperial, and all France, that the principles enunciated in the pamphlet were condemned by several papers which his Imperial Majesty had some time before been so good as to send to him. A few days later the *Moniteur* published a letter of the Emperor to the Pope, dated 31st December, 1859, in which the former renews his hypocritical expressions of devotedness, but admits, at the same time, that " notwithstanding the presence of his troops at Rome, and his dutiful affection to the Holy See, he could not avoid a certain partnership in the effects of the national movement provoked in Italy by the war against Austria." In this same letter Napoleon III. reminds the Pontiff, that at the conclusion of the war he had recommended, as the best means of maintaining tranquillity, the secularization of his government, and he still believes that, " if, at that time, his Holiness had consented to an administrative separation of the Romagna, and the nomination of a lay governor, the provinces would have come, once more, under his authority." What, then, could the people have meant when they petitioned, on occasion of the Pope's progress, to have a cardinal for governor, as formerly, and not lay prefects, as was then the case, under the regime inaugurated by Pius IX. ? The Pope having neglected his advice, Napoleon, of course, was powerless to stay the tide of revolution. " My efforts were only successful in preventing the insurrection from spreading, and the resignation of Garibaldi preserved the marches of Ancona from certain invasion." No doubt it did. But, as will soon be seen, this modern crusader was let loose in order that he might follow his calling more vigorously, *i.e.*, rob and slay on a more extensive scale. The Emperor now approaches the subjects of the Congress. In his letter he recognizes the indisputable right of the Holy See to the legations. But he does not think it probable that the Powers would think it proper to have recourse to force, in order to restore them. If the restoration were effected by means of foreign troops, it would be necessary, for a long time, to hold military occupation of these provinces ; and this would only feed the enmities and hatred of the Italian people. This state of uncertainty cannot always last. What then is to be done ? The Imperial revolutionist concludes, expressing the most sincere regret, and the pain which such a solution gives him, that the way most in harmony with the interests of the Holy See is that it should sacrifice the revolted provinces. For the last fifty years they have only caused embarrassment to the government of the Holy Father. If he asked of the Powers to guarantee to him, in exchange for them, the possession of what remained, order, he had no doubt, would be immediately restored. This letter left no room to doubt that the policy of the pamphlet, " *The Pope and the Congress*," was that of Napoleon III. As soon as this was known the Congress became impossible. The Pope could not agree to deliberations based upon the principle of his dispossession. Austria could not be a party to combinations which removed the bases of the treaty of Zurich. This opinion was expressed by Count de Rechberg, first Minister of Austria, in a note of 17th February, 1860, and by Lord John Russell, in a despatch to Lord Cowley, the British Ambassador at Paris. " The pamphlets are important," said the latter statesman ; " the result of the one entitled, ' *The Pope and the Congress*,' is to prevent a Congress, and to cause the Pope to be deprived of one-half of his dominions."

It was not without significance that M. Thouvenel was French Minister of Foreign Affairs from the 4th of January. Piedmont understood this fact. It caused its troops to cross the Romagnese frontier, whilst M. de Cavour, triumphant, affirmed, in the Piedmontese Senate, that the letter of Napoleon III., declaring that the temporal sovereignty was not sacred, was a fact as important in the Italian question as the battle of Solferino.

The Pope's reply to Napoleon's letter of 31st December is of some length. Elegant in expression, forcible in reasoning, it can only be briefly reviewed. "I am under the necessity of declaring to your majesty that I cannot cede the legations without violating the oaths by which I am bound, without causing misfortune and disturbance in the other provinces, without doing wrong and giving scandal to all Catholics, without weakening the rights of the sovereigns of Italy, unjustly despoiled of their dominions, but also the sovereigns of the whole Christian world, who could not see with indifference great principles trampled under foot." The Emperor had insisted that the cession of the legations by the Pope was necessary, in order to put an end to the disturbances, which, according to him, although he knew that such disturbances proceeded wholly from foreigners, had, for the last fifty years, caused embarrassment to the Pontifical government. "Who," said the Pope, "could count the revolutions that have occurred in France during the last seventy years? And yet, who would dare maintain that the great French nation is under the necessity, in order to secure the peace of Europe, to narrow the limits of the Empire? Your argument proves too much. So I must discard it. Your majesty is not ignorant by what parties, with what money, and with what support, were committed the spoliations of Bologna, Ravenna, and other cities."

The Imperial letter was communicated to all the newspapers. The reply of the Pope was carefully withheld from them. It only became known in France, some time later, through a German translation in the Austrian *Gazette*. Pius IX. was anxious, meantime, that the public should hear both sides of the question. He therefore brought to the knowledge of the Catholic world the principal points of his answer to Napoleon in the Encyclical, *nullis certe verbis*, of date 19th January, in which he declared that he was prepared to suffer the last extremities rather than betray the cause of the church and of justice. He also invited all the bishops to join with him in praying *that God would arise and vindicate his cause.*

The government having information that there was a copy of this document in the hands of the distinguished Catholic journalist, M. Louis Veuillot, the Minister of the Interior, M. Billaut, sent for this courageous writer, and gave him to understand that if he published the Encyclical it would be the death-warrant of his journal. But M. Veuillot was not to be intimidated. Next morning, 29th January, there appeared in his paper, *l'Univers*, the Latin text of the Pontifical document, together with a French translation. The same day, without trial or sentence, was signed a decree suppressing *l'Univers*. Yet was not this paper destined wholly to perish. Ten years later it reappeared, when the tyranny of Napoleon III. was crushed for ever at Sedan. Several other Catholic journals shared the fate of *l'Univers*, such as the *Bretagne*, of Saint Brieue, and the *Gazette*, of Lyons. The government of the Emperor thus showed by what spirit its counsels were guided. All the Catholic journals of France were already under the ban of two warnings, so that they had only a precarious existence, a third warning, according to the legislation of the time constituting their death-warrant.

So early as 3rd December, 1859, whilst yet a Congress was believed to be possible, Pius IX. had written with his own hand to Victor Emmanuel, in order to remind him of his duties, and induce him to defend at the meeting of the Powers the rights of the Holy See. The latter had answered, 6th February, 1860, "that he certainly would not have failed in this duty if the Congress had met." For, "devoted son as he was of the church, and the descendant of a most pious family, it never was his intention to neglect his duties as a Catholic Prince." He protested, therefore, that he had done nothing to provoke the insurrection, and that when the war was ended he had renounced all interference in the legations." But he added, "it is an acknowledged fact, and which I have personally verified, that in those provinces which, lately, were so unmanageable and dissatisfied with the court of Rome, the ministers of worship are actually respected and protected, and the temples of God more frequented than ever." Victor Emmanuel surely now thought that the Pope would never think of disturbing this happiness and self-satisfaction. "The interests of religion required it not." He even hoped that the Holy Father, not satisfied with refraining from a renewal of his claim on Romagna, would also hand over to him the marches and Umbria, in order that they might enjoy the same prosperity. And so he discoursed anew to Pius IX., about his "frank and loyal concurrence, his sincere and devoted heart," and ended by craving the Holy Father's apostolic blessing.

The King of Piedmont must have been sadly blinded by revolutionary teachings not to see—if, indeed, he did not see—that such professions of loyalty and devotedness were positively derisive. Pius IX. so viewed them, and gave the intriguing monarch to understand that he did so. The moderation of his language is but slightly indicative of the sorrow and indignation which he must have experienced. "The idea which your majesty has thought fit to lay before me is highly imprudent, unworthy, most assuredly, of a king who is a Catholic and a member of the house of Savoy. You may read my reply in an Encyclical which will soon appear. I am deeply affected, not on my own account, but by the deplorable state of your majesty's soul. You are already under the ban of censures, which, alas! will be aggravated when the sacrilegious act which you and your accomplices are meditating shall have been consummated. May the Lord enlighten you and give you grace to understand and to bewail the scandals which have occurred, and the fearful evils with which unfortunate Italy has been visited through your co-operation."

About this time diplomatists discovered the convenient political doctrine of non-intervention. It was, like most diplomatic devices, a fallacy. But it served its purpose. The Catholic Powers, however friendly to the Holy See, were unable to intervene. The greatest of them all, Austria, was put *hors de combat* at Solferino. Prussia had intervened, as far as its

Diplomatic doctrine of non-intervention.

policy required, when it forbade further hostilities after the great battle which made France the mistress of the destinies of Italy. England, which, as a Protestant Power, had no great friendship for the Holy See, found it suitable to preach non-intervention, as an excuse for not being able or for not daring to aid her ancient and faithful ally, the Pope, in opposition to her new friend, the Emperor of the French. England, at least, was consistent, for, while she proclaimed and practised non-intervention in favor of the French Emperor's subversive intervention in Italy, she adhered most devoutly to the doctrine when there was question, a little later, of aiding France against the crushing power of Prussia.

Whilst the European Powers lay dormant under the spell of the new doctrine of non-intervention, the King of Piedmont vigorously pursued his career of spoliation. Having accepted a sham plebiscitum, he annexed, by a formal decree of 18th March, the Grand Duchy of Tuscany, the Duchies of Parma and Modena, and that portion of the Papal States known as the Legations, to his ancient kingdom of Sardinia and Piedmont. This was done with the full consent of his Imperial patron, Napoleon III. For, at this time, Victor Emmanuel ceded to France, as compensation for Central Italy, Nice and Savoy. This boded ill for France. Some French writers consider that this transaction would have been less disgraceful if these provinces had been exchanged for Lombardy, which had been won from Austria with French blood and treasure. But, as evil destiny, which was hastening to its accomplishment, would have it, they were given as payment for the spoils of the widow and orphan of Parma and the aged man of the Vatican. Thus for once was non-intervention dearly purchased.

Tuscany, Parma, Modena and the Legations finally annexed to Piedmont.

Price of the spoil.

The usurping monarch having now accomplished a long-cherished purpose, ought, one would suppose, to have obeyed the dictates of prudence, and held his peace. But no. He must write to the Pope, in order to justify his nefarious proceeding. Piedmontese bayonets and four millions of Piedmontese gold had won for him the plebiscitum of which he was so proud. Nevertheless, he declared, addressing the Holy Father, that, "as a Catholic Prince, he believed he was not wanting to the unchangeable principles of the religion which it was his glory to profess with unalterable devotedness and fidelity." Notwithstanding, "for the sake of peace, he offered to acknowledge the Pope as his Suzerain, would always diminish his charges and contribute towards his independence and security." He ended his letter by most humbly soliciting, once more, the apostolic benediction. There is more plain speaking in the reply of Pius IX. than could have been to the liking of the *Re galantuomo*. "I could say that the pretended universal suffrage was imposed, not voluntary. I could say that the Pontifical troops were hindered by other troops, and you know well what troops, from restoring the legitimate government in the provinces." The Holy Father then bewails the increasing immorality occasioned by the usurping government and the insults constantly offered to the ministers of religion. Even if he were not bound by solemn oaths to preserve intact the patrimony of the church, he would, nevertheless, be obliged to repel everything that tended in this direction, lest his conscience should be stained by even an indirect sanctioning of, and participating in, such disorders, and justifying, by concurrence, unjust and violent spoliation. The Pope concludes by saying, emphatically, that he cannot extend a friendly welcome to the projects of his majesty, but that, on the contrary, he protests against the usurpation, and leaves on the conscience of his majesty and all who co-operate with him in such iniquity the fatal consequences which flow therefrom. Finally, he hopes that the king, in reperusing his own letter, will find grounds for repentance. The Pope, far from being actuated by feelings of resentment, prays God to give his majesty the grace he stands so much in need of in such difficult circumstances. The letter is dated at the Vatican, 2nd April, 1860.

It is related that Victor Emmanuel bedewed with tears this letter, which so gently and tenderly rebuked him. It must have reached him at one of those moments of remorse which, more than once, interrupted his scandalous career. It hindered him not, however, from fulfilling the promise which he had given to the revolution, when, at the beginning of the war of 1859, placing his hand on his sword and looking towards Rome, he said: "*Andremo al fondo*" (" we shall go on to the end").

On the 26th of March of the same year, Pius IX. issued a Bull, excommunicating all who took part in wrenching from him so great a portion of the patrimony of the church. Some parties received the intimation of this sentence with such noisy demonstrations 'of delight as to cause their sincerity to be doubted. Others, and of the number was ' King Victor Emmanuel, were struck with indescribable fear. Napoleon III. insisted that the organic article of the Concordat, forbidding the publication in France of Bulls, Briefs, &c., should be enforced. But he could not, any more than his uncle, forbid the excommunication to take effect. The first Napoleon was at the height of his greatness when struck with excommunication. He received the sentence with jeers. Would it make the arms fall from the hands of his soldiers? How literally this question was answered, let the snows of Russia tell. There are other ministers of the wrath of heaven besides the frosts of a Northern winter. Napoleon III. was in the zenith of his power when he heard the sentence which he vainly tried to stifle. His great political wisdom, and the wonderful success of all he undertook had hitherto astonished the world. There was now a manifest change. But it need not here be said with what unspeakable humiliation his star went down.

The revolutionary party could not have more effectually shown their dread of the Papal sentence, than by their endeavors to suppress it. They went so far as to publish in its place a forged document, as odious as it was extravagant, appended there to the signature of Pius IX., and exposed it to the jeers of the ignorant multitude. The bishops did their best in order to make known the truth; with what difficulty it will be easily understood, when it is remembered that an Imperial decree forbade the newspapers to publish a word in their interest.

Had there been question only of forming a united Italy, and of introducing such reforms as the time demanded into the States of the Church, and those of the Italian grand dukes, such a cause would have had no better friends and supporters than the Pope and the native princes. But the revolutionary party aimed at more than this, and they hastened to show their hand as soon as they obtained any power. As has been seen, the Holy Father himself complained bitterly of the increase of irreligion and immorality under their ill-omened auspices in Romagna. It was not their policy to reconstitute, but to subvert. No existing institution, however excellent, was sacred in their eyes. Thus speak the archbishops and bishops of the Marches in a remonstrance addressed to the Piedmontese Governor on 21st November, 1860: "We scarcely believe our own eyes, or the testimony of our own ears, when we see and hear the excesses, the abominations, the disorders witnessed in the chief cities of our respective dioceses, to the shame and horror of the beholders, to the great detriment of religion, of decency and public morality, since the ordinances against which we protest deprive us of all power to protect religion and morality, or to repress the prevailing crimes and licentiousness. The public sale, at nominal prices, of mutilated translations of the Bible, of pamphlets of every description, saturated with poisonous errors or infamous obscenities, is permitted in the cities which, a few months ago, had never heard the names of these scandalous productions; the impunity with which the most horrible blasphemies are uttered in public, and the worse utterance of expressions and sentiments that breathe a hellish wickedness; the exposition, the public sale and the diffusion of statuettes, pictures and engravings, which brutally outrage

Results of Revolutionary Government.

P

piety, purity, the commonest decency; the representation in our theatres of pieces and scenes in which are turned into ridicule the Church—Christ's immaculate spouse—the Vicar of Christ, the ministers of religion, and everything held dear to piety and faith ; in fine, the fearful licentiousness of public manners, the odious devices resorted to for perverting the innocent and the young, the evident wish and aim to make immorality, obscenity, uncleanness triumph among all classes ; such are, your Excellency, the rapid and faint outlines of the scandalous state of things created in the Marches by the legislation and discipline so precipitately introduced by the Piedmontese government. We appeal to your Excellency. Could we remain silent and indifferent spectators of this immense calamity without violating our most sacred duty?" If anything under the government of subversion has saved Italy from utter ruin, it is nothing less than the zeal and devotedness of its pastors. In the remonstrance referred to, they declare that notwithstanding all the contradictions, the trials, the obstacles they have had to encounter, "not one spark of charity, of zeal, of pastoral and fatherly solicitude has been quenched in our souls. We solemnly affirm it, with our anointed hands on our hearts, and with the help of God's grace, these sentiments shall never depart from us through fault of ours.''

This mode of reforming, so dear to the revolutionists, is further illustrated by the proceedings of Garibaldi in Sicily and at Naples. It will be remembered that this hero of the revolution was eclipsed for a time by the splendors of Solferino. Immediately after that battle he retired into private life, and the motley troop which he commanded disappeared. Whilst, however, there remained any revolutionary work to be done, such a man could not be idle. The kingdom of the Two Sicilies was, as yet, unshaken. This was too much for Count de Cavour, and so he encouraged the ever-willing Garibaldi to fit out an armament against that kingdom. The hero sailed for Sicily, and there,

Garibaldi reappears.

assured of *non-intervention* by the presence of the flags of France, England and Sardinia, he made an easy conquest of the defenceless island. As soon as he got possession of Palermo, and had assumed the title and powers of dictator, he commenced, like a true revolutionist, the work of subversion. Garibaldi, no doubt, was a man of the age, and the great diplomatic discovery which the age had fallen upon was never wanting to him. It served him at Naples as it had done in Sicily; and so, a mere diplomatic idea—*non-intervention*—drove the king to Gaeta, and established the power of the revolutionist.

As soon as Garibaldi was master in Sicily, the work of revolutionary reform commenced. It was always the first aim of the revolutionists to strike at civilization and civilizing influences. Churches were desecrated, the ministers of religion insulted, religious orders suppressed.

Revolutionary reforms in Sicily, Naples, Lombardy, Modena, the Pontifical States, &c.

"The Society of Jesus alone," said the venerable superior, Father Beckx, in his solemn protestation of 24th October, 1860, to the King of Sardinia, "was robbed of three residences and colleges in Lombardy; of six in the Duchy of Modena; of eleven in the Pontifical States; nineteen in the kingdom of Naples; and fifteen in Sicily." "Everywhere," adds Father Beckx, "the Society has been literally stripped of all its property, movable and immovable. Its members, to the number of 1,500, were driven forth from their houses and the cities. They were led by an armed force, like so many malefactors, from province to province, cast into the public prisons, ill-treated and outraged in the most horrible manner. They were even prevented from finding a refuge in pious families, while in several places no consideration was had for the extreme old age of many among them, nor for the infirmity and weakness of others.

"All these acts were perpetrated against men who were not accused of one illegal or criminal act, without any judicial process, without allowing any justification to be recorded. In one word, all this was consummated in the most despotic and savage manner. If such acts had been accomplished in a popular riot, by men blinded by passion, we might perhaps bear them in silence. But, as all such acts have been done in the name of the Sardinian laws; as the provisional governments established in Modena and the Pontifical States, as well as the dictator of Sicily himself, have claimed to be supported by the Sardinian government; and as your majesty's name is still invoked to sanction these iniquitous measures, I can no longer remain a silent spectator of such enormous injustice, but in my quality of supreme head of the order, I feel myself strictly bound to ask for justice and satisfaction, and to protest before God and man, lest the resignation inspired by religious meekness and forbearance should appear to be a weakness which might be construed into an acknowledgment of guilt, or a relinquishment of our rights. I protest solemnly, and in the best form I can think of, against the suppression of our houses and colleges, against the proscriptions, banishments and imprisonments, against the acts of violence and outrage committed against the brethren bound to me by religious ties. I protest before all Catholics, in the name of the rights of the church sacrilegiously violated. I protest, in the name of the benefactors and founders of our houses and colleges, whose will and expressed intentions in founding these good works, for the interest alike of the living and the dead, are thus nullified. I protest, in the name of the sacred rights of property, contemned and trampled under foot by brutal force. I protest, in the name of citizenship and the inviolability of individual persons, of whose rights no man may be deprived without being accused in form, arraigned and judged. I protest, in the name of humanity, whose rights have been so shamefully outraged in the persons of so many aged men, sick, infirm and helpless, driven from their peaceful seclusion, left without any assistance, cast on the highways without any means of subsistence." Such was the revolution which Victor Emmanuel and Napoleon III. were driven by fear, or even worse motives, to patronize and foster. It had, in the days of its power, made France a desolation. It was now sweeping like devouring flames over Italy, and fast approach-ing the city of the Popes.

Pius IX., although not unaware of the fearful calamities with which he was threatened, was far from allowing his mind to be shaken. He trusted in that Providence which watches over the church. "We are as yet," said he on 16th February, 1860, to the lenten preachers of the time, "at the beginning of the evils which must soon overtake us. At the same time, we are consoled by the cheering prospect that, as calamity succeeds calamity, the spirit of faith and of sacrifice will be proportion-ately developed."

Revival of Peter's pence.

There was nothing now to be hoped for from the powers which nominally ruled the world, but which were, in reality, under the control of the revolution. Deprived of so great a portion of his states, and the revenue which accrued to him therefrom, the Holy Father resolved to sustain his failing finances by relying on the spontaneous offerings of the faithful throughout the world. His appeal was not made in vain. The piety and zeal of the early ages appeared to have revived. The word of the common Father was received with reverence in the remotest lands. Offerings of "*Peter's pence*," as in days of apostolic fervor, were poured into the Papal treasury. In Europe, especially, the movement was so general as to show that the people everywhere were resolved to act independently of their governments, which had so shamefully become sub-servient to the will of the revolution. It was scarcely neces-sary that the bishops should speak a word of encouragement. In France, indeed, under a jealous and revolutionary govern-ment, there could be no associations for the collection of Peter's pence. But the government could not, so far, place itself in opposition to the religion of the country as to forbid collections in the churches; nor could it reach such subscriptions as were offered in private dwellings. In Belgium, although the party of unbelief, of Freemasonry and revolution, held the reins of power, the constitution protected all citizens alike, and so the new work which the circumstances of the church required was accomplished by association, pretty much in the same way as the work of the propagation of the faith. By the end of three months, there were in Flanders no fewer than four hundred thousand associates for the collection of Peter's pence. In Italy, a Catholic journal, *Armonia*, collected considerable sums of money, and caskets filled with jewels and other precious objects. Poland, in her sorrow, was magnificently generous. And Ireland, renewing her strength after centuries of misgovernment, persecution and poverty, emulated the richest countries, America, Germany, Holland and England. One of the collections at Dublin amounted to £10,000. All these rich donations, together with thousands of addresses which bore millions of signatures, were humbly laid at the feet of the Holy Father.

Now that it is well known that France was not less hostile than Sardinia and the revolution, to the

The Pope forms an army. — Lamoriciere commands.

cause of the Pope, it appears more a loss of labor than a wise precaution, that the Holy Father should have assembled an army for maintaining order in his states, and repelling any attack on the part of the revolutionary faction. This was all that he contemplated. Deceived by the professions of his French ally, he was far from suspecting that the small force which he was collecting for the maintenance of order would be no sooner organized than it would be attacked by the military power of Piedmont, supported by the Emperor of the French. On the contrary, Pius IX. had every reason to believe that the formation of a Pontifical army, destined for the duties which devolved on the French soldiers, then at Rome, would be acceptable to Napoleon III. The latter had, more than once, said to his Holiness : " Place yourself in a position to be independent of my army of occupation." This recommendation is repeated in a despatch of Messrs. Thouvenel and Gramont, so late as the 14th of April, 1860. As soon as it was known that the Pope desired to have an army

for maintaining internal peace, and finally, in order to replace
the foreign troops which occupied Rome, the youth of many
countries freely offered their services. France, Belgium, Ireland, Spain, Holland, and even distant Canada sent numerous
volunteers. The noble youth of France, whose education, for
the most part, was eminently Christian, were only too happy
to tear themselves from the luxurious life of Paris. Their joy
was equal to their ardor, when they found that they could bear
arms without serving a Bonaparte. Gontants and Larochefou-
cauld Doudeauvilles, Noes and Pimodans, Tournons and Bourbon Chalus, came to range themselves, as private soldiers,
when necessary, under the banner of the Pope. Nor were
they attracted by any hope of gain. A goodly number, on the
contrary, sustained by their ample means the government to
which they offered their lives. The revolution signified its
displeasure by branding these devoted youths with the ignomin-
ious title of "Mercenaries of the Pope." This ungracious
word proceeded from the palace of Jerome Napoleon, on whom
merciless history bestows a more opprobrious epithet. As a
matter of course, it was repeated in all the revolutionary
journals.

The command of the new force was offered to the brave
and experienced General Lamoriciere. At first he hesitated,
the cause of the Pope, as regarded his temporal power, was
already so much compromised. Finally, on the representation
of the Reverend Count de Merode, he gave his consent. It was
pure sacrifice. No success could add to his military renown.
And success was impossible. The general distributed his soldiers, from 20,000 to 25,000 in number, in small bodies, throughout the towns of that portion of the Papal States which still
remained. This was a judicious arrangement, as far as
internal peace and order were concerned. Neither Lamoriciere
nor the Pope had any idea, so firmly did they rely on the hollow professions of France, that a foreign army would have to
be met. The general spoke words of encouragement to his
willing soldiers. "The revolution," said he, in an order of the

day, "like Islamism of old, threatens Europe. To-day, as in
ancient times, the cause of the Papacy is the cause of civilization and of the liberty of mankind." The infidel press was
excited to fury, and showed, by the violence of its writing, that
the comparison of the revolution to Islamism was but too
well founded. Were not both alike ferocious? Did not both
spread terror and desolation in their track? Weigh them
together—Islamism has the advantage. In addition to all its
other barbarities, the revolution violated the temples of God
and the abodes of prayer. The followers of the prophet were
commanded to respect every place where God was worshipped,
and every house where dwelt the ministers of His worship.

The organization of Lamoriciere's army was now so complete that a friendly convention was entered into with the
Cabinet of the Tuilleries, and that the evacuation of Rome by
the French garrison should commence on the 11th of May.

This was not at all to the liking of the revolutionists. M.
de Cavour, who had complained so loudly at the Congress of
Paris that the Pope had not an army sufficiently strong to
render unnecessary the protection of France and Austria, protested against the formation of such an army as soon as he
saw that it was seriously contemplated. He denounced it to
all Europe as a gathering of adventurers from every country,
and feigned the greatest disquietude for the new frontiers of
Piedmont.

On the 4th September, 1860, Napoleon III. was at Chambery, receiving the homage and congratulations of his Savoyard
subjects. A public banquet was held in his honor, and whilst
the guests were yet at table, two Piedmontese envoys, Messrs.
Farini and Cialdini, sought a private interview with the Emperor. Napoleon left the festive board and remained closeted
with the envoys the remainder of the evening. The result of
this conference was the immediate invasion of the Papal States
by Sardinian troops, under the command of General Cialdini.
This officer reports that he was fully authorized by Napoleon.
It is even related that the Emperor, strongly encouraging him

used the words of our blessed Lord to Judas : " *Quod facis, fac citius.*" Napoleon, indeed, denied having uttered these words. It matters not. All his acts, at the time, expressed their meaning. Whilst conferring with the envoys at Chambery, there lay on a table a map of Central Italy, on which he traced in pencil and effaced several lines. The map having been left on the table, was afterwards found to contain one line in crayon, which was not effaced. It showed exactly the route which Cialdini followed in marching to the destruction of the Papal army. Between the conference of Chambery and the arrival of Cialdini on the Pontifical territory, there elapsed precisely the time necessary for the journey by post-carriage and railway. Seventy thousand men were waiting for him on the frontier, ready to march as soon as he brought them the required authorization. General Fanti, who also had an army corps concentrated on the borders of the Marches, had already intimated to General Lamoriciere, that if the Papal troops had recourse to force, " in order to suppress any insurrection in the Papal State," he would, at once, occupy the Marches and Umbria, " in order to secure to the inhabitants full liberty to express their wishes." The Sardinian generals evidently wished to raise an insurrection, but as no insurrection occurred, they managed to do without one. In the meantime, it was thought expedient to perform a piece of mock diplomacy. Count Della Minerva was despatched from Turin to Rome, charged with an *ultimatum* to the Pope. Without diplomatic negotiations or shadow of pretext, purely by virtue of the right of the strongest and most audacious, the Holy Father was suddenly summoned to dismiss his volunteers as foreigners, and was allowed four-and-twenty hours to give his answer. But the party did not wait so long. The *ultimatum*, of a piece with their other proceedings, was a mockery. On 10th September, before the reply of the Pope could have been known, even before Della Minerva had reached Rome, Generals Cialdini and Fanti, without any previous declaration of war, passed the Pontifical frontier. It was the barbarians once more at the gates of Rome.   The orders of the day, which the Piedmontese commanders addressed to their troops, were inexpressibly savage.   Pitiless history fails not to record them.   " Soldiers," said Cialdini, "I lead you against a band of adventurers, whom the thirst for gold and pillage has brought to our country. Fight, disperse without mercy, these wretched cut-throats. Let them feel, by the weight of our arm, the power and the anger of a people who strive to be independent soldiers. Perugia seeks vengeance.   And, although late, it shall have it."   The language of King Victor Emmanuel, although some-what more politely diplomatic, was not less false and savage. His proclamation is a master-piece of Count de Cavour's hypocritical style.   " Soldiers, you are entering the Marches and Umbria, in order to restore civil order in the desolated cities and to secure to the inhabitants the liberty to express their wishes.   You have not to meet powerful armies, but only to deliver the unfortunate Italian provinces from companies of foreign adventurers.   You are not going to avenge the injuries done to Italy or to me, but to hinder the popular hatred from wreaking vengeance on the oppressor.   You will teach by your example pardon of offences and Christian toleration to those who compare Italian patriotism to Islamism.   At peace with all the Great Powers, and without provocation, I mean to banish from Central Italy a constant cause of trouble and discord. I wish to respect the seat of the Chief of the Church, &c." Whatever this king may have wished to do, he was compelled to obey the will of the revolution, and to justify by his acts the comparison of the party which he patronized with Islamism,— a comparison disparaging only to the followers of the prophet. The ferocious sentiments to which Cialdini gave utterance were not mere bravado.   When Colonel Zappi, of the Pontifical service, dared to hold out with 800 men at Pesaro, and check for two-and-twenty hours the whole Piedmontese army before this village, Cialdini, instead of admiring such bravery, refused to cease firing, when Zappi, crushed by numbers, was at last obliged to capitulate.   For two hours longer he took pleasure in discharging grape shot at the little town which had ceased, to reply otherwise than by exhibiting a white flag and sending messengers of peace. Nor did this vandalic soldier show any consideration for the wishes of the people whom he professed to have come to protect. This contempt for the popular will was sufficiently well shown the following month, in his despatch to the Garibaldian Commander of Molise: "Publish that I cause to be shot all peasants taken with arms in their hands. I have this day commenced such executions."

Lamoriciere was far from expecting to be attacked by the armies of Piedmont. The most he could contemplate was an attack by the Garibaldians, and the probability of some partial insurrections in the interior. He distributed his troops accordingly in the towns and along the Neapolitan frontier. The insolent message of General Fanti contributed to confirm him in this idea. He had only 1,500 men with him when the message reached him. He held himself in readiness, but without concentrating his force, which appeared to him dangerous and premature. He learned, unexpectedly, that the frontier on the side of Piedmont was violated at every point of attack at the same time; that an army corps, commanded by General de Sonnaz, was marching on Perugia; another, led by Brignone, on Spoleto; another, under the Garibaldian Mazi, on Orvieto; finally, that Cialdini was advancing on Sinigaglia, thence on Torrede Jesi, Castelfidardo [and Loretto, and that his object was Ancona, the only city except Rome which was capable of making any resistance. Lamoriciere, unable to face so many

Duplicity of the French Government. —The Emperor of Austria restrained by his Council.—Lamoriciere's force cut to pieces by the Piedmontese at Castelfidardo.

enemies at once, saw, with pain, that his scattered garrisons were lost. He was far, however, from being discouraged. Recalling, hastily, all that were within reach, and unfortunately they were not the most considerable, he changed all the arrangements which he had made for another kind of contest; he gave up all idea of opposing Brignone, De Sonnaz and Fanti, who, nevertheless, were in a position to cut off his retreat towards Rome, and rushed boldly to the point of greatest danger between these generals and Cialdini, with the design of piercing the lines of the latter and reaching Ancona before him. There he thought he would be able to hold out a week or two more than sufficient time for France and the other civilized nations to come to his assistance. He, a French general, relied on France, so completely were Frenchmen deceived. He also trusted, and with better grounds, to Austria. This confidence emboldened him to reply defiantly to the insolent message of General Fanti: "We are only a handful of men. But a Frenchman counts not his enemies, and France will support us."

Before the invasion took place, the Ambassador of France, the Duke of Gramont, whose word was corroborated by the presence of a French army at Rome and in the neighborhood, had, several times, reassured Cardinal Antonelli, who was much disquieted, affirming that the concentration of Piedmontese troops was intended to check the banditti, and protect the Pontifical frontier, but would not attack it. Lamoriciere testifies to this fact in the report of his operations. When there was no longer any doubt as regarded the violation of Papal territory, the Ambassador, Gramont, communicated to Cardinal Antonelli, and telegraphed, in clear and distinct language, to the Vice-Consul of France, at Ancona, the following despatch: "The Emperor has written from Marseilles to the King of Sardinia, that if the Piedmontese troops advance on the Pontifical territory he will be compelled to oppose them. Orders are already given for the embarkation of troops at Toulon; and these re-inforcements will forthwith arrive. The government of the Emperor will not tolerate the criminal attack of the Sardinians. As Vice-Consul of France, you will govern yourself accordingly." M. de Courcy, the Vice-Consul, to whom the despatch was addressed, took it immediately to M. de Quatrebarbes, the civil governor of Ancona. His great age would not admit of his carrying it in person to Cialdini, but he lost no time in sending it by an employee of the Consulate, making no doubt that a despatch which bore the signature of France would prevent bloodshed. He was mistaken. Cialdini read the paper, and coolly put it in his pocket, saying: "I know more about these matters than you. I have just had an interview with the Emperor." When the clerk asked for a receipt, he signed one, remarking that "it would make a good addition to other diplomatic papers." He then continued to advance. The general was no less explicit, a few days later, at Loretto, when conversing with Count Bourbon Busset and other prisoners taken at Castelfidardo. "You astonish me, gentlemen," said he; "how could you for a moment entertain the idea that we would have occupied the Pontifical State without the full consent of the government of your country!" As one of the bystanders, in reply to Cialdini, alluded to the fact which was announced, of the disembarkation of a new French division at Civita Vecchia, "And to what purpose?" answered one of the higher officers of Cialdini's staff. "France has no need to re-inforce her army of occupation. See these wires, gentlemen (pointing to the telegraph), if they chose to speak they would suffice to stop us at once." It would have been impossible to express more plainly the omnipotence at that moment of the conqueror of Solferino, and the fearful stigma which he was preparing for his memory. Not only did he disorganize the defence, the responsibility, &c., of which he was understood to have assumed, not only did he deceive the Court of Rome, and inspire it with a false security, as if it had been his purpose more surely to throw Lamoriciere into the snares of Cialdini; but, at the same time, he paralyzed the good intention of the Powers that were sincerely devoted to the Holy See.

Francis Joseph, Emperor of Austria, had dreaded, a month before it occurred, an invasion of the Pontifical State. His army divisions of the Mincio were on a war footing. It was only necessary that they should pass the river and march against Piedmont. An order to this effect was signed. But before despatching the order, and taking on himself such great responsibility, the youthful Emperor, who had been none the better for giving way to his chivalrous impulses in 1859, resolved to call a meeting of his ministers and chief generals. Addressing this grave assembly, he stated distinctly the new situation in which Austria was placed by the violation of recent treaties, and the obligation under which he lay of opposing such proceedings by arms. His duty as a Catholic was concerned as well as his honor and interest as a sovereign. It appeared, besides, that God had blinded the revolution, and the invasion was so odious that Piedmont would not find a single ally. "I have signed," he added, "an order to pass to-morrow into Lombardy. Together with this, I have addressed a manifesto to Europe, in which I declare that I will respect and cause to be respected the treaty of Zurich. Lombardy does not now belong to me. I have ceded it, and I do not recall my word; but I require that the clauses which are burdensome to Austria shall not alone be executed. I claim, at the same time, the incontestible rights of my cousins of Florence, Parma and Modena, so unworthily robbed by one of those who signed and guaranteed the treaty. Finally, I require that the neutrality of the Pope and the integrity of his territory be respected; for the Pope is my ally, as a sovereign, and as the Chief of the Church, my Father. The fleet of Trieste will, at the same time, cruise before Ancona." This noble address was followed by profound silence. The attitude of several of the bystanders was expressive of doubt when the Emperor affirmed that the brutality of the Piedmontese aggression would alone suffice to prevent any one from making common cause with it. The Count de Thun at length rose. He acknowledged the manifestly just grievances of Austria, and admired the manly resolution of the Emperor. He then set forth the dangers of every kind which this resolution would cause to arise. The army had not yet repaired its losses; the wounds of Magenta and Solferino were still bleeding. The French would, once more, pass the Alps, and the revolution, far from being stifled, would be more threatening than ever.

"If my crown must be broken," interposed the Emperor, "I prefer losing it at the gates of the Vatican, in defence of justice and religion, than under the walls of Vienna or Presburgh by the hands of the revolutionists." "Sire," replied Count de Thun, whether at Presburgh or the Vatican, you will always find us by your side, ready to conquer or perish honorably with you. But allow me to repeat that there is not question only of commencing a struggle against the two-fold revolution of the King of Sardinia. If France once more comes to his support, who will be our auxiliaries? What alliances have we, so necessary in case of reverse? Our cruel experience of last year only shows too plainly that we have none; and that Prussia has an understanding with France. And if the war continues any time, if the revolution throws into the arms of Russia Hungary, and our Sclav provinces, and gives to Prussia our German countries, what will become of the great Catholic Empire of Germany? Will not your majesty have hastened, without intending it, the satisfaction of that cupidity which is everywhere aiming at our ruin, and the triumph either of Protestantism or the Greek schism?" Francis Joseph replied by describing the not less serious dangers which the triumph of the Italian revolution would occasion to the tranquillity and integrity of the Empire. He could not but foresee how precarious Austrian rule would become at Venice, and how impossible it would be to preserve, for any length of time, the last remains of the Pontifical State, once the King of Piedmont was master of the rest of the peninsula. The struggle, by being delayed, could not be avoided. We should only have to undertake it later against a usurper consolidated by time, and with less manifest evidence of right on our side. But the embarrassments of the moment engaged the thoughts of his ministers more than those of the future. All the ministers dissenting from his opinion, the Emperor made up his mind, after two hours' discussion, to recall the order which he had signed. The Austrian fleet continued at anchor in the harbor of Trieste, and the army of the Mincio remained inactive, although, as may be supposed, indignant, in its quadrilateral, until Italian unity became a reality, and coalesced with Prussia in order to expel it.

There must now be recorded another proof of the Emperor Napoleon's double dealing. On 13th September, M. Thouvenel wrote to Baron de Talleyrand, the Ambassador of France at Turin: "The Emperor has decided that you must leave Turin immediately, in order to show his firm determination to decline all partnership in acts which his counsels, that were given in the interests of Italy, have not been able to prevent." Vain pretence! inexorable history accepts not such apologies.

With the exception of the Piedmontese, and perhaps also the Austrian ministers, there were none in Europe having knowledge of this document, and the despatch of M. de Gramont to the Consul of Ancona, who did not believe that a rupture was imminent, if it had not already taken place, between the Emperor Napoleon and King Victor Emmanuel. General Lamoriciere was too upright and loyal-minded not to fall into the snare. He wrote promptly to Mgr. de Merode, asking him to send provisions to Ancona, where he purposed establishing his quarters, not having had time to prepare for battle in the open country. He had no disquietude as regarded Umbria. He left it to be defended by France. He hoped also that General de Goyon would not confine himself to guarding the walls of Rome, and that he would, at least, prevent invasion from the direction of Naples, and by way of the valley of Orvieto. He was confident that France would finally intervene. And it would be highly advantageous if, in the meantime, French troops garrisoned Viterbo, Velletri and Orvieto.

The declarations of Napoleon were like the despatches of Messrs. Thouvenel and Gramont, nothing better than empty words—"diplomatic papers," as Cialdini contemptuously called them. His only object was to lull public opinion, and let the Piedmontese have the advantage of a *fait accompli*. Of this there was no room to doubt, when, a little later, he took officially under his protection the fruit of that criminal aggression against which he had so loudly protested. Either from weakness or treachery he was an accomplice, and played a preconcerted game. At first he may have been sincere in threatening, in the hope of intimidating the revolution. But when there was question of acting, and he knew that it defied him, he recoiled. French historians remark, with pain, that this was a sad alternative, as regards the memory of a man who had the honor to govern France—the nation, more than all others, renowned for chivalry. It was also a rebuke to that nation which was so weak as to submit, for twenty years, to his rule. His friends are brought to the extremity of demonstrating that he was a coward, if they wish to hinder mankind from believing that he was a traitor.

Meanwhile, Lamoriciere, by forced marches, on the 16th September, reached Loretto, from which the enemy withdrew at his approach. His inconsiderable force counted scarcely 3,000 combatants, viz.: 2,000 infantry, 800 troopers, and 200 artillerymen. But he had given rendezvous at the spot to the general, Marquis of Pimodan, who brought to him from Terni 2,000 infantry, and arrived a little before night, on the 17th. Thus did it fall to his lot, with 5,000 men at most, and some old artillery which had not been sufficiently exercised, to face Cialdini, who had, at the moment, 45,000 men, and was provided with rifled cannon. An engagement on the 18th was inevitable. The Piedmontese were echeloned along the hills which fill the declivity from Castelfidardo towards the plain, and extend to within 500 metres of the small river Musone. Their artillery swept the declivities in all directions. They occupied, in strength, two farms which were situated, the one 600 metres behind the other, towards the principal hill. By delaying longer, Lamoriciere would only have exposed himself to be surrounded and compelled to lay down his arms. At four o'clock in the morning, the soldiers of the Pope, with the two generals at their head, prepared for death, by devoutly participating in the most holy sacrament of the Eucharist. At eight, Pimodan rushed upon the two farms already mentioned.

His watchword was to carry them and hold them as long as possible, as they commanded the pass of Musone, where the bulk of the army, with the baggage, must defile, and there was no other way than this pass by which the route of Ancona could be gained. The first farm, although warmly defended, was carried, and a hundred prisoners were taken. Six six-pounders were immediately brought up, in order to protect the position against a fresh attack of the enemy. Captain Richter, who commanded them, under the orders of Colonel Blumenstihl, was pierced in the thigh by a ball; he would not, however, leave the field, but remained in the midst of the fire. Two howitzers, commanded by Lieutenant Daudier, with the aid of a hundred Irishmen, who had arrived the night before from Spoleto, were placed in the open space in front of the farm, exposed to the grape shot of the Piedmontese, to which they replied as if they had been in force. Unfortunately, all parties did not do their duty so well. Pimodan was obliged to dismiss, on the battle-field, the commander of the First Battalion of *Chasseurs.* "The moment had come," says Lamoriciere in his report, "to attack the second farm. General Pimodan formed a small column, under the orders of Commandant Becdelievre, composed of the Battalion of Belgian Fusiliers, of a detachment of Carabiniers, and of the First Battalion of *Chasseurs.* This column boldly advanced, notwithstanding a most active fusilade from the farm and the wood. There were 500 metres to march over thus exposed. But when about a hundred and fifty feet from the summit of the hill it was received by the fire of two ranks of a strong line of battle, which put so great a number of the men *hors de combat* that it was obliged to fall back. The enemy pursued. But when he had nearly reached our troops, the column faced round, waited for him at fifteen paces distance, received him with a well-directed fire, and rushed on him with the bayonet. Astonished at so much daring and coolness, the enemy, although superior in number, fell back in his turn, and thus allowed our soldiers to regain the position which they had left. The fire of our artillery, which was well supplied and well directed, protected these movements. The enemy had lost more men; but, relatively, our losses were more felt than his. Pimodan had been wounded in the face; but, nevertheless, he retained his command. I observed that his two battalions and a half were not sufficiently strong to carry the second position; so I sent for the two reserve battalions, and ordered the cavalry to pass the river, and follow on our right flank the march of our columns. During this time the enemy had endeavored to overwhelm us on both sides. Major Becdelievre brought together what remained of his battalion, rushed upon the fusileers and forced them back into the wood whence they had come." These were splendid feats of arms. But the excessive inferiority of Lamoriciere's artillery and numbers made victory impossible. The revolution had its emissaries enrolled as soldiers in the Pontifical army. One of these, by a traitorous blow from behind, slew the brave Pimodan in the height of the battle. These traitors also caused a panic at the decisive moment by spreading false alarms. The youthful soldiers of the reserve, who had never seen fire, became demoralized, and fled in confusion, without hearing the sound of a single ball. Others followed. The artillery, now no longer supported, and, fearing to be taken, sought safety in flight. But instead of gaining the road to Ancona, it fell back on Loretto, where it could not fail to fall into the hands of the enemy. Lamoriciere, always calm in such terrible discomfiture, made unheard-of exertions, as did also his aids-de-camp, Messrs. de Maistre, de Lorgeril, de Robiano, de France and Montmarin, in endeavoring to guide the precipitate retreat. His orders either were not conveyed or were not executed. Then, as was his custom in Africa, he hurried alone on horseback to within a hundred feet of the lines, in order to ascertain the situation, rejoined his staff, labored to stay the flight, and when all was lost, he executed, with five-and-forty horse and a hundred infantry, a movement which with the army was impossible. He took the route of Ancona, which a Piedmontese squadron was preparing to bombard, and reached that place by five o'clock in the evening. The brave Franco-Belgians sacrificed themselves in order to save the rest of the army. They held out in the farm which they had occupied as long as their ammunition lasted. The neighboring fields and hedges were covered with dead and wounded Piedmontese; but they themselves were all either killed or taken. Among the slain and wounded were many of the best nobility of Europe—Paul de Percevaux, Edme de Montagnac, Arthur de Chalus, Hyacinth de Lanascol, Alfege du Bandier, Joseph Guerin, Georges de Haliand, Felix de Montravel, Alfred de la Barre de Nanteuil, Thierry du Fougeray, Leopold de Lippe, Gaston du Plessis de Grenedan, Raoul Dumanoir, Lanfranc de Beccary, Alphonse Menard, Guelton, Rogatien Picou, Anseline de Puisage, George Myonnet. Such are a few of those noble youths who fell victims to their zeal and bravery when engaged with General Lamoriciere in his hopeless attempt to stem the overwhelming tide of revolution which, at the time, successfully defied all the Powers of Europe, to move an arm in opposition to it.

Lamoriciere succeeded in reaching Ancona, but only to prolong, for a few days more, a desperate contest. The available force in the place amounted only to 4,200 effective men, a number quite insufficient to man all the posts of such extensive fortifications. The general did not yet despair of aid from the French at Rome, and he flattered himself with the idea that if he only held out a few days, Austria and the other Catholic States would be shamed into activity. They, however, knew too well the intentions of France, and France had won the battle of Solferino. The brave Lamoriciere was assailed in his last retreat, both by sea and land. The bombardment lasted ten days, and was heard at Venice, the islands of Dalmatia, and even at Trieste. But not a friendly sail appeared in support of the besieged. The prolonged struggle did not even attract such vessels of neutral Powers as are commonly sent for the protection of their consuls and others of their respective nations, as well as to offer their good services to women, children and other non-combatants. Such disgraceful conduct was condemned alike by the Protestant and Catholic press of Europe. The London *Times* reproached M. de Cavour with not having understood that "candid and honorable conduct is not incompatible with patriotism." The same paper quoted, in this connection, the words of Manin, which are a condemnation of the whole conduct of the Piedmontese under Victor Emmanuel: "Means which the moral sense repels, even when they are materially profitable, deal a mortal blow to a cause. No victory can be put in comparison with the absence of self-respect. Ancona was yet undergoing bombardment, when the three sovereigns of the North, who alone could have undertaken efficaciously the defence of the violated law of nations, met at Warsaw; and Napoleon III. presented to them a memorandum by which he engaged to abandon Piedmont in the event of her attacking Venice. But "he presupposed that the German Powers would also confine themselves to an attitude of abstention, and would avoid furnishing a pretext for an Italian attack of Austria." At length, the Piedmontese fleet, under Admiral Persano, succeeded in demolishing the more important portion of the fortifications of Ancona. A white flag was now displayed on the citadel and all the lesser forts; and Major Mauri was sent on board the admiral's ship to negotiate a capitulation. The firing ceased on both sides. But now occurred a circumstance which stigmatizes to all time the character of the Piedmontese generals, Fanti and Cialdini. M. de Quatrebarbes relates, "that whilst the conditions of capitulation were under discussion, the land army, furious at having been repelled, and at having done nothing that could contribute towards the taking of the city, recommenced firing along the whole line. The bombardment and cannonade continued from nine o'clock in the evening of the 28th until nine in the morning of the 29th, and that, although negotiations had been sent, and bells had been rung, announcing the cessation of hostilities, in defiance even of a very pressing letter of the admiral, who would not participate

in such an infamous proceeding. He also recalled on board
his ships the marine who served a land battery. All this
time not a single cannon was fired from the city. Thus the
Piedmontese army bombarded incessantly for twelve hours a
defenceless town, in violation of the law of nations, and all
sentiments of honor and humanity. Admiral Persano himself
reported at Turin the refusal of the land army to cease firing.
Such a fact must excite the indignation of all right-thinking
people." The revolution was highly offended when compared
to Islamism. Are the regular troops of Islam accused of such
barbarities? The Bashi-Bazouks could not have done worse.

When the capitulation was signed at two o'clock in the
afternoon of the 29th, the small Pontifical army had ceased to
exist, and the Piedmontese, now free to follow out their plans,
could go to join the bands of Garibaldi, under the walls of
Gaeta, and, together with him, complete " the extirpation of the
Papal cancer," or, as one of their school, Pinelli, said, " Crush
the sacerdotal vampire." But although right had been
trampled down, it knew how to do battle and to die. "For
the first time," observed a Protestant journal, the new Gazette
of Prussia, " a general of the party of legality has dared to lead
his troops against the enemy. For the first time the revolution has been met in the field of battle. The effort has not
been successful. We know it. And as we repeatedly said
beforehand, we had no hope that it would. But the defeat of
Lamoriciere raises the mind by contrast, For a long time we
had been accustomed to the triumphs of cowardice, treachery
and corruption, of all which the victories of Garibaldi presented such a disgusting spectacle. We are assured that the
Pontifical troops did their duty unto death. This is enough.
It is easily understood how the adversaries of the revolution
had become humble. For years they could only record the
victories of their enemies. But if, at Castelfidardo, a few
individuals were defeated, the principle of legality was at last
asserted. Now, if men contend in battle for a principle its
final triumph is assured."

It was to be expected that Pius the Ninth would avenge the memory of the brave men who had been branded by the name of *Mercenaries*, the greater number of whom served without pay. No wonder if he did justice on the pretended moral order which Piedmont said it had come to restore in the States of the Church. Not only did he honor their noble efforts, he also founded at his own cost, and for their benefit, the chaplaincy of Castelfidardo in the sanctuary of the Scala Santa. He ordered the funeral obsequies of General Pimodan to be celebrated with becoming magnificence, and composed himself an inscription for his tomb in the French Church of St. Louis. He wished to confer on Lamoriciere the title of Roman Count. But the defeated hero declined the honor, saying that he desired always to be called Leon de la Moriciere. Pius IX. then addressed him a few words, which recall the piety of early times : " I send you what, at least, you cannot refuse, the order of Christ, for whom you have combated, and who will, I trust, be your reward as well as mine."

In France the government showed its revolutionary leaning by forbidding a subscription which was undertaken for the purpose of presenting a sword of honor to Lamoriciere. It did even worse than this. It meanly persecuted the vanquished soldiers of the Holy See, as well as those who had hastened to fill their places. This was pure revenge. And now that the success of Piedmont was no longer doubtful, it could serve no other purpose than to establish the fact of the Emperor's complicity. Such of the soldiers of the Pope as were natives of France were deprived of their rights of citizenship. Thus were noble youths, the flower of France, on their return from Castelfidardo and Ancona, deprived of the electoral franchise, and stripped of their right to serve on juries and in the army. Some even were interdicted from inheriting property on the pretext that, as strangers, their signatures required to be legalized. These men were, nevertheless, the actual defenders of a sovereign whom the government pretended to defend officially. The revolutionary papers audaciously said that the same law was not applicable to such French subjects as joined the bands of Garibaldi, on the ground that these bands were neither a government nor a military corporation. This odd interpretation completely met the views of ministerial juris-prudence; and so was presented the extraordinary spectacle of a country out lawing such of her children as served the same cause as her army, and in nowise molesting those who supported the opposite side. All political allusions in the pulpit were now repressed with increased severity. The bishops, however, could not be intimidated. Besides, as they could not be displaced, they were not so easily reached. Mgr. Pie, the eminent Bishop of Poitiers, ascended the pulpit the Sunday after the battle. " My brethren," said he, " you all expected of me that I would speak to-day in my cathedral. It is according to the customs of the church to know how to honor her defenders, and to mourn for them when dead. And because, having taken upon myself a responsibility which I decline not, and having encouraged and blessed the departure of several of those youthful volunteers, I would be ashamed of myself if now, restrained by the fears arising from a pusillanimous prudence, I did not offer them the homage of my admiration together with that of my prayers. Your sympathies are already with my words. If they gave offence to any hearers, I would, indeed, be afflicted. But, by the grace of God, the country which we inhabit is called France, which warrants, or rather commands, that I should be candid." In the absence of that fame which victory confers, the vanquished were consoled by that immortality which eloquence bestows on those whom it celebrates. So long as the great art of oratory shall be appreciated in the countries of Fenelon and Bossuet, the funeral orations on Lamoriciere, by Bishops Pie and Dupanloup, together with the fine pages on the heroes of Castelfidardo, by Bishop Gerbet of Perpignan, Mgr. Plantier of Nismes, and other writers, will not cease to be read.

"They died in order to defend us," said, as if prophetically, Archbishop Manning, who succeeded Cardinal Wiseman in the new See of Westminster, already so illustrious; "the cause for which they fell is our cause. They are blind, indeed, who cannot see that what has been begun by the head will soon be undertaken against all the members; that the attacks will extend rapidly from the centre to the extremities; that revolutionary tyranny and the despotism of civil power will strive to establish everywhere, in detail, the domination which they are endeavoring to exercise over the will and the person of the Holy Father. We are at the commencement of a new era of penal laws against the liberty of the church. It is for us, therefore, that they have given their life. They died whilst the profane world loaded them with its curses, as died the martyrs in the Flavian amphitheatre, whilst the cry resounded, "The Christians to the lions!" (*Christianos ad leones*), and in presence of thousands of spectators of the Imperial and Patrician families of Rome, and for the gratification of the multitude which thirsted for blood, and such blood as was most noble and innocent. Thus died He who is greater than the martyrs, assailed by the insults of the Pharisees and the jeers of the ignorant masses. It is, therefore, glorious to die for a cause which the world will not and cannot understand. If they had died to defend commercial establishments against the indigenous inhabitants of some distant country, or to repel the attacks of a neighbor, or to maintain the integrity of the Ottoman Empire, the world would have understood and honored them, as it did in regard to the combatants of Alma and Inkerman. But, to fall in battle for the independence of the Sovereign Pontificate, to sacrifice themselves for the liberty of Christian consciences, and that of the generations to come —this the world understands not, and for this we proclaim them great and glorious among departed heroes."

Four months later, Mgr. Pie was obliged to refute a new pamphlet, entitled, "*France, Rome and Italy*," and so endeavor to prevent new iniquities. He feared not to formulate the following terrible rebuke, which was denounced as seditious, but which history has already confirmed as a sentence:

"Pilate had it in his power to save Christ, and without Pilate He could not be put to death. The death-warrant could only come from him; *nobis non licet interficere*, said the Jews. Wash thy hands, O Pilate! declare thyself guiltless of the death of Christ. Our only answer every day will be, and the latest posterity will repeat the same : I believe in Jesus Christ, the only Son of the Father, who was conceived of the Holy Ghost, who was born of the Virgin Mary, who suffered death and passion under Pontius Pilate; *Quipassus est sub Pontio Pilato.*"

It was no secret when these words were spoken, as it was to Lamoriciere and his brave army, that the government of the French Emperor encouraged and patronized the iniquitous aggressions of Piedmont, whilst it pretended, in the face of Europe, to support the Holy See.

"It was not Garibaldi and his volunteers," said the Reue des deux Mondes, "that General Lamoriciere had to fight; the odds in that case would not have been so unequal. But he had the regular army of Piedmont before him—an army six times more numerous than his own. Nor was it the attack merely of a revolutionary party which was now directed against the temporal power of the Papacy. It was a government incomparably more powerful than the Pope's, which decreed arbitrarily itself alone, and in the face of the other nations of the world, the suppression of this power, and which accomplished that suppression by the irresistible force of its arms, and under the eyes of our garrison in Rome." Whilst Austria, not from any want of sympathy with the Holy See, but from the dread her cautious ministry, who had penetrated the designs of France, entertained of a new French invasion, looked tamely on from the heights of her quadrilateral, the French Emperor secretly expressed his approval of the Piedmontese attack on the Papal States, and at the same time publicly withdrew his ambassador at Turin, as a protest in the face of mankind against this unprovoked and unjustifiable attack. Eng-

Further expression of opinion.—The Great Powers.

land, which could not be supposed to have much sympathy with the Holy See, notwithstanding the declarations of her best statesmen in support of the temporal sovereignty, openly pronounced in favor of the Piedmontese aggression on the Pope, who, in trying times, had been her most faithful ally. But the days of the elder Bonaparte were forgotten, and too much could not be done to conciliate the new ally whom the English had found in the second Bonaparte. So their representative, Sir John Hudson, remained at Turin, and was the confidential adviser there of Count de Cavour, while Sir Henry Elliot continued to reside at Naples after that city had become the headquarters of Garibaldi. The great Northern Powers, Russia and Prussia, acted a more honorable part. Even before the fall of Ancona was known, they both withdrew their ambassadors from Turin. Von Schleinitz, the Prussian Prime Minister, protested energetically against the unwarrantable aggression of Piedmont. M. de Cavour, who understood the tendencies of the time, replied to Von Schleinitz, as if uttering a prophecy: "I regret that the Court of Berlin should judge so severely the conduct of the king and his government. I am conscious of acting in the interests of my sovereign and my country. I might reply successfully to what M. Von Schleinitz says. But, be that as it may, I console myself with the thought that, on the present occasion, I am setting an example which Prussia, within a short time probably, will be happy to follow."

The cannonade had scarcely ceased to be heard at Ancona, when the Holy Father raised his voice in a consistorial allocution of 28th September, which, although addressed to the cardinals, is intended for the whole civilized world. The allocution briefly enumerates the several acts of aggression successively committed by the Piedmontese. It then alludes to Cavour's audacious letter, which was intended as a justification beforehand of the violation of territory, and the fearful bloodshed which followed. It expresses the false accusations, the repeated calumnies and insults which were put forward as a pretext for the invasion. It also rebukes "the singular malignity with which the Piedmontese government dared to call the Pontifical soldiers *mercenaries*, when so many of them, both Italians and foreigners, were of noble lineage, bearing illustrious names, and had resolved to serve in our troops without pay, and for the sole love of our holy religion." The fact is established, to the disgrace of Piedmont, that the Papal government "could have had no intimation of the enemy's purpose. The general-in-chief commanding our forces could not have entertained the thought of having to contend with the soldiers of Piedmont." The meed of praise is awarded to the fallen warriors, together with the expression of unfeigned sorrow for their loss: "Whilst we must bestow merited praise on the general, his officers and his men, we can scarcely restrain our tears as we remember all those brave soldiers, those noble young men especially, who had been impelled by faith and their own generous hearts to fly to the defence of the temporal power of the Roman Church, and who have met with their death in this cruel and unjust invasion. We are deeply moved by the grief of their families; and would to God it were in our power, by any word of ours, to dry up the source of their tears !" If anything could be worse than the savage and murderous attack of Piedmont, it was the hypocritical pretence under which it was undertaken. The invaders came as "the restorers of moral order and as the preachers of tolerance and charity." The allocution concludes by denouncing this hypocrisy, together with the diplomatic principle of non-intervention, of which France and Piedmont set such brilliant examples.

The King of Sardinia having violently seized Umbria and the Marches of Ancona, must also have a

A Plebiscitum.—
Umbria and the
Marches of Ancona
annexed to Sardinia.

mock plebiscitum, in order, no doubt, to make it appear that these provinces were spontaneously annexed to his kingdom. The fall of Gaeta and the conquest of Naples by Garibaldi encouraged the ambitious monarch in these unjustifiable annexations, and although generally condemned by the European press, he most audaciously issued a proclamation in reply to the Papal allocution. All these nefarious acts, together with the outrages everywhere perpetrated against all who remained loyal to the Holy See and faithful to the sacred laws of the church, induced the Holy Father to publish the now celebrated allocution of March 18th, 1861. This allocution is perhaps the greatest doctrinal utterance of the Pontificate of Pius IX. But it must be considered in connection with the *syllabus*, which will now shortly be noticed.

The Emperor Napoleon had, indeed, suspended public diplomatic relations with the court of Turin. This was intended merely as a blind, for he continued to negotiate secretly, through Prince Jerome Napoleon, concerning Rome, and what yet remained to the Pope of his states. He appeared to bind Piedmont to respect the sovereignty and independence of the Holy See, and had no objections that the Pope should raise an army designed only for defensive purposes. On such conditions the Emperor would acknowledge the new kingdom of Italy. In all this there was a want of sincerity. Count Cavour, Prince Napoleon and the Emperor, were perfectly agreed that the Holy Father was, in due course of time, to be given up to his enemies.

In order to prepare the world for this consummation of Franco-Sardinian policy, there appeared a new pamphlet, entitled *La France, Rome et l'Italie*. It was signed by M. de la Gueronniere, and published on the 7th day of March. It was suggested, if not actually written, by the Emperor himself. The allocution already alluded to, dealt by anticipation with the chief points of this publication. It was, however, directly replied to in a letter of the eminent Cardinal Antonelli, to the Papal Minister at Paris. The cardinal begins by stating that the chief object of the pamphlet was "to throw on the Holy Father and his government the responsibility of the condition to which Italy and the Pontifical States in particular were reduced." He then proceeds lucidly,

The pamphlet La France, Rome et l'Italie.—Cardinal Antonelli's reply.

logically, and not without eloquence, to attack all the positions assumed by the writer, and exposes the treachery, baseness and duplicity of the principal adversaries of the Holy See in its long struggle with revolutionary Piedmont, supported as it was by the Emperor Napoleon III.   It will be recollected that it had been proposed, indeed it was one of the articles of the treaty of Zurich, that there should be a confederation of the States of Italy. The writer of the pamphlet audaciously accused the Pope of having rejected the plan of an Italian confederacy, just as if he and not the Emperor and his ally, the King of Piedmont, had violated the treaty which succeeded the battle of Solferino. "The official proposition of such a confederacy," the cardinal states, "and of its presidency came only after the preliminaries of Villafranca and the treaty of Zurich; and the Holy Father showed himself disposed to accept it as soon as its basis should be defined. The author, nevertheless, says that it was then too late. He does not, in saying so, seem to perceive that he seriously insults his own sovereign, as if he and the other Powers had proposed as the basis of a solemn treaty and the great means of conciliation, a thing which was at that moment neither possible nor opportune. Be that as it may, it was only then that the proposition was made by the person authorized to make it; and it is unjust to pretend that his Holiness had taken any action thereon before it was laid before him. Since, therefore, the plan fell through independently of his refusal, how can he, without a positive act of calumny, be accused of obstinacy on this point?"

The cardinal's letter is of great length. In one place he recapitulates the heads of accusation contained in the pamphlet. "Putting aside," says he, "the unfounded assertions, the matters foreign to the case, which helped to fill up the pamphlet, the obstinacy which it imputes to the Holy Father amounts to his having declined an abdication which his conscience condemned, to his having deferred some reforms that were promised till the revolted provinces had returned to their allegiance;

to his having proposed to recruit an army for himself instead
of accepting the troops offered to him; to his having preferred
the voluntary offerings of the faithful to subsidies furnished by
governments which are not all nor always equally disposed to
be friendly.   And these acts of firmness, of noble disinterested-
ness, which must appear most praiseworthy to the unprejudiced
mind, which have appeared and do still appear worthy of the
admiration of Protestants, seem, on the other hand, to the
Catholic author of the pamphlet, to be so blameworthy that
he could not find more bitter words of censure were he to write
against those who are alone responsible for the sad disorders
of the present time.   But this is precisely what is of a nature
to surprise us.   The Imperial government of France had given
advice to his Holiness; it had also given advice to the Piedmontese government.   Now, if the Holy Father must be
accused of not having followed such advice, the Piedmontese
government does not seem to have been more docile.   His
Holiness did not deem it expedient to do some things desired
by the French government.   But Piedmont did a great many
things which the French government had publicly declared it
was opposed to.   The Imperial government forbade the violation of the neutrality of the Papal States; and to this the
Piedmontese government responded by occupying the Romagna.
The Imperial government disapproved annexation; and the
Piedmontese government only answered by accomplishing
annexation.   The Imperial government forbade, in threatening
language, the invasion of the Marches and Umbria; and the
Piedmontese government responded by pouring grape shot into
the small Pontifical army, by bombarding Ancona from sea
and land, and by refusing to observe any of the laws of war
acknowledged by all civilized nations.   The author of the
pamphlet allows his pen the most cruel license against the
Holy See, but has not one single word of blame for the Piedmontese government.   Who can explain such an attitude?   The
explanation is a very natural one, and is given on the last page
of the pamphlet, where the author tells us that the Emperor

of the French *cannot sacrifice Italy to the Court of Rome, nor give up the Papacy to the revolution;* which means that the Court of Rome must be sacrificed to the exigencies of the peninsula, that the temporal dominion of the Holy See must be done away with, because it is in the way of the unification of Italy, and that this suppression is to prevent the Papacy or the spiritual power from falling beneath the blows of the revolution." It cannot fail to be remarked that in all the French Emperor's manifestos appears the pretext of protecting the Papacy from the revolution, whilst, but for his interference, it needed not such protection. Pius IX. was quite able to contend successfully against whatever revolutionary element there was in the Pontifical States. With the aid of his allies, he could also have repelled the attacks of Piedmont, if unsupported by the French. But against a Power so great that it could command the non-intervention of all other Powers, he was powerless. It may have afforded a momentary pleasure to the Carbonaro Prince, Napoleon III., to annihilate, for the sake of his way of promoting Italian unification, the time, honored sovereignty of the Pope. It afforded him no lasting benefit. Germany caught the idea, and becoming unified, hurled her legions against the common European enemy, who, in his day of sorest need, found not an ally, not so much as one powerful friend even in that Italy for which he had done and sacrificed so much.

It now only remained for young Italy, revolutionized as it was, to assume and wear its blushing honors. Piedmont having seized Umbria and the Marches of Ancona, and having also, through her agent, Garibaldi, taken possession of Sicily and Naples, was mistress not only of the greater portion of the Pontifical States, but also of almost all Italy at the same time. It became such greatness to have a parliament. Accordingly, the first Italian parliament assembled at Turin in February, 1861; and on the 14th of March, Victor Emmanuel was proclaimed King of Italy. It was not, however, till the

24th of June that the French Emperor found it convenient to recognize this extended sovereignty. In doing so, no doubt, he was consistent with himself, although quite at variance with the professions of him who had so lately withdrawn his ambassador from the Court of Turin.

Count de Cavour lived not to enjoy this recognition. He died on the 6th of June. This minister was a politician to the end; and he had no wish ever to be anything else. He was anxious, however, at the close, to have the merit of reconciliation with the church which he had so cruelly persecuted, both in the ancient State of Sardinia and in the newly-annexed territories of the "Kingdom of Italy." Finding that his latter end was approaching, he desired the presence of Friar Giacomo, Rector of the Madonna degli Angeli. This Friar, with whom, as is related, the Count had had a previous understanding, faithfully came. M. de Cavour remained alone with him for half an hour; and when the priest was gone he called Farini, and said to him: "My niece has had Fra Giacomo to come to me; I must prepare for the dread passage to eternity; I have made my confession and received absolution. I wish all to know, and the good people of Turin particularly, that I die like a good Christian. I am at peace with myself. I have never wronged any one." It is a trite saying that the ruling passion of a man's life asserts its power at the hour of death; and the last recorded words of Count de Cavour would seem to show that to the end he was more bent on politics than prayer. As Friar Giacomo was reciting solemnly by his bedside the prayers for the departing soul, "Frate! Frate!" he exclaimed, whilst he pressed the Friar's hand, "*libera chiesa in libera stato!*" (a free church in a free state). Admirable, no doubt. But how was the great idea to be realized, since the church could only be free when her ministers were dictated to, imprisoned, banished, and otherwise tormented? And what freedom for the state, unless it were free to tyrannize over and persecute the church? Judging Cavour and his party by their

Death of Count de Cavour.

R

acts rather than their fine speeches, such was their idea of *a free church in a free state*. If it be true that, as men live so they die, it is not true that Count de Cavour died like a good Christian. None will be inclined to dispute with him the comfort which he claimed of being at peace with himself. But they who are aware of the violence, the spoliation, the rapine, bloodshed, and unspeakable suffering, in all which he was, at least, an accomplice, if not the direct cause, throughout the States of the Italian Grand Dukes, the Pontifical territories and the kingdom of Naples, will not easily acknowledge that he spoke truth when he said that "he had never wronged anyone." But let us now be silent. There is *One*, and only *One*, who judgeth.

Considering the assistance so recently afforded to Turkey by the Christian Powers, her Christian subjects were surely entitled to her protection. But gratitude, it would appear, is not one of the virtues of Islamism. In June, 1860, the Pachas disarmed and delivered up to their deadly enemies the Christian Maronites of Lebanon and Damascus. Over a hundred villages inhabited by these people were completely destroyed. Neither the aged nor the young that fell into the hands of the enemy were spared; and, worse than all, seven thousand young women were carried captive into the desert. In these melancholy circumstances, Napoleon III. acted honorably and independently. He sent an armed expedition to chastise the guilty, and that in defiance of all opposition on the part of his allies, the English, who, from national jealousy, resisted a French protectorate in the East, and so assumed the disgraceful *role* of patronizing hordes of assassins. Incomprehensible conduct! since, a few years later, the same people were so moved by Turkish atrocities in Bulgaria that no British government could have dared to raise an arm in defence of the crumbling Empire of the Sultan. Pius IX. was deeply moved by the sufferings of his fellow-Christians. In a letter of 29th July, to the Patriarch of Antioch and the Bishops of his Patriarchate,

The Lebanon Massacres. — Generosity of Pius IX.

he expressed his sorrow and indignation at the fearful crimes that were committed. "It is particularly afflicting," said he, as he condemned certain speeches that were delivered in the British Parliament in favor of the guilty parties, "that more sympathy is accorded, and even more assistance extended, in our age to the fomenters of troubles and revolutions than to their victims." He commended France, that had remembered in the circumstances her Catholic traditions, and intimated that he would encourage with all his power the liberal offerings of the Christians of the West in support of their brethren of Syria. He himself, although he was deprived of his accustomed revenue, together with the greater portion of his states, contrived to bestow considerable assistance.

A little later in the same year, the Holy Father met with unlooked-for consolation in the conversion of the Bulgarian nation. On the 20th December, bishops, priests, and a great many lay persons of that country, abjured the Photian schism, and addressed to Rome a solemn act of union in the name of the majority of their fellow-countrymen. Pius IX. replied on the 29th of January, 1861. He was pleased himself to consecrate in the Sistine chapel their new archbishop, Sokolski. The latter, as he renewed the profession of faith, which had been already formulated in writing at Constantinople, said to the Holy Father: "It is your work that, although dead, we are come to life, and that, being lost, we are found again." Pius IX. referred all the glory to God. "Such works," he said, "are wholly divine. To Thee praise, benediction, everlasting thanks! O, Jesus Christ! source of mercy and of all consolation!" The Bulgarians were unfortunately situated. Jealousies of race prevailed among them, and did much to shake religious principle. Add to this that the schismatical Patriarch of Constantinople agreed to grant ecclesiastical autonomy, as it might be called, to Bulgaria. This was a deadly blow to the noble impulse which led them towards the centre of Christian unity. At first they were three millions of Catholics. The

number speedily diminished to some tens of thousands. Archbishop Sokolski suddenly disappeared. It is not known whether
he abandoned his post or was carried away by force. The
latter supposition is, as yet, the more probable. He is thought
to have been recognized, several times, in a Russian monastery,
whither he is supposed to have been taken by surprise, and
obliged to remain against his will. Pius IX., understanding
how necessary it was that the new flock should have a resident pastor, appointed a provisional successor to Sokolski, with
the title of Administrator of the United Bulgarians, and
labored assiduously to found for him churches and schools.
Three schismatical Greek bishops, who had sought protection
at Rome from the violent proceedings of their patriarch, did
not persevere any more than the majority of the Bulgarians.
A fourth, however, Melethios, Archbishop of Drama, happily
remained steadfast, together with the Protestant bishop of
Malta, another Protestant bishop, who was an American of the
United States, and several prelates of the Greek schism,
Armenians, Chaldeans or Copts. All these, about this time,
placed themselves under the crook of the Supreme Pastor.

Shortly before the death of Count de Cavour, the Emperor
Napoleon was pleased to define the new
limits of the Papal domain. In doing so,
he left the recently alienated provinces to
Piedmont, and confined the Pontiff to a
comparatively small territory around the
city of Rome. He could not have sanctioned more decidedly
or more publicly the unjustifiable spoliation of the Sardinian
king. Such a proceeding cannot but appear inconsistent to
such as are aware only of his apparent quarrel with this monarch, and the withdrawal of his ambassador from Turin. To
those, on the contrary, who have knowledge of, and consider
his secret conference with, the Piedmontese Envoys at Chambery, and the violent attack on the Papal States, which, notwithstanding the public and official protest of the French government through their consul at Ancona, immediately followed,

*The annexation to Piedmont of Umbria and the Marches pub-
licly sanctioned by Napoleon III.*

it will appear that Louis Napoleon Bonaparte, Emperor of the French, was only acting up to his policy and character. Soon after this new distribution of territory, the "Kingdom of Italy" was officially recognized by the government of the French Emperor; and this recognition paved the way for that of the other Powers, by most of whom, after some time, it was reluctantly given.

Cavour was dead. But Sardinian ambition died not with him. Baron Ricasoli, who succeeded him **Piedmont seeks to reign at Rome.** as Prime Minister, encouraged by the support of France, which was no longer disguised, actually wrote, in the name of his king, both to the Pope and Cardinal Antonelli, urging them to give up the sovereignty of Rome. This was done, not, of course, from any ambitious motive, but with a view to carrying out their great designs, such as the regeneration of society, and, above all, their conception of a "free church in a free state." The minister concludes magniloquently: "It is in your power, Holy Father, to renew, once more, the face of the earth. You can raise the Apostolic See to a height unknown for ages. If you wish to be greater than earthly sovereigns, cast away from you the wretched kingship which brings you down to their level. Italy will bestow upon you a firm seat, entire liberty, and new greatness. She reveres in you the Pontiff; but she will not stop in her progress for the Prince. She intends to remain Catholic; but she purposes to be a free and independent nation. If you will only hearken to the prayers of that daughter whom you love so dearly, you will gain over souls more power than you can lose as a prince, and from the Vatican, as you lift your hand to bless Rome and the world, you will behold the nations, restored to their rights, bow down before you, their defender and protector." The new minister, less wary than his predecessor, immediately set about realizing his grand idea. With what success will soon be seen.

The Piedmontese conquests had not been made without cost. Enormous sums had been spent in corrupting the Neapolitan people. Large amounts were still scattered throughout the annexed provinces, in order to maintain their loyalty to the new power; and the press was liberally subsidized, both in Italy and abroad. For such heavy expenditure money must be had. *Rem! quomodocunque modo rem!* An expedient which occurs so readily to revolutions was had recourse to. The properties of the convents and the treasures of the churches were seized. Members of religious communities were expelled from their monasteries and reduced to mendicity. The laws of the church were trampled under foot, together with the rights of citizens. The Jesuits were banished and cruelly maltreated like so many felons. Religious corporations were suppressed, the faithful clergy were thrown into prison, and many dioceses and parishes deprived of their pastors. Pius IX. deplored these calamities in his Allocution of 30th November, 1861. In that of 18th March of the same year, he had replied to those who conjured him to be reconciled with modern civilization: "The Holy See," the Pontiff insisted, "is always consistent. It has never ceased to promote and sustain civilization. History bears witness to this fact. It shows most eloquently that, in every age, the Popes carried civilization into barbarous nations, and even to the remotest lands. But is that true civilization which enslaves the church, makes no account of treaties, and recognizes not the rights of weaker parties? It is quite certain that the church can never come to an understanding with such civilization. What is there in common, says the apostle, between Christ and Belial? As to making friendship with the usurpers of our provinces, before they have shown repentance, let no such thing be hoped for. To make such a proposition to us, is to ask this see, which has always been the rampart of justice and truth, to sanction the principle that a stolen object can be possessed in peace by the thief, and that injustice which succeeds is justi-

The Piedmontese Government fills its coffers by plundering the church.

fied by success. We loudly declare, therefore, before God and men, that there is no reason why we should be reconciled with any one. Our only duty, in this connection, is to forgive our enemies, and to pray for them, in order that they may be converted. This we do in all sincerity. But when we are asked to do what is unjust, we cannot give our consent: *Præstare non possumus.*"

A little later, January, 1862, Cardinal Antonelli replied in the name of Pius IX. to the Marquis de Lavallette, the French Ambassador at Rome, showing that it was by no means true to say that the Pope was at variance with Italy. "An Italian himself, and the chief Italian, he suffers when Italy suffers, and he beholds with pain the severe trials to which the Italian church is subjected. As to arranging with those who have robbed us, we never will do any such thing. All transaction on this ground is impossible. By whatever reservations it might be accompanied, with whatever ingenuity of language it might be disguised, we could not accept, without appearing to consecrate the wrong. The Sovereign Pontiff, before his exaltation, as well as the cardinals before their nomination, bind themselves by oath to cede no portion of the territory of the church. The Holy Father, therefore, will not make any concession of this kind. Neither a Conclave, nor a new Pontiff, nor his successors in any age, would be entitled to make such concession."

The revolutionists, however, could help themselves. It would not be difficult to imagine the people of Italy, a few generations hence, if, indeed, the kingdom of Italy be destined to last so long, looking back to their founders with that same kind of pride which animated the great Romans when they thought of Romulus and Remus, and the band of brigands who helped them to found the city.

About this time the French parliamentary chambers began to enjoy, to a certain extent, liberty of speech.

The Emperor Napoleon induced to modify his Italian policy. They could now discuss an address to the sovereign, and give full publicity to their debates. Inquiry could now be made to some purpose, whether the Italian policy of Napoleon III. was sanctioned by France, whether that aberration were national which impelled to the violation of all right and law, in order to unify Italy, and pave the way, at the same time, for the unification of Germany. The revolutionary left of the French parliament, as a matter of course, favored the Emperor's revolutionary foreign policy. But the liberty of debate showed that there was a powerful minority opposed to them, and this minority enjoyed the sanction of the greatest statesmen of the age. In the Senate, notwithstanding the absence of every member of the Legitimist party, as well as that of Messrs. de Montalembert and de Fallou, whom a coalition of the despotism of the day with radicalism had caused to lose their seats, a tolerable number of the most devoted partisans of the empire showed a boldness of language, together with well-defined statesmanlike views, to which the Imperial *regime* was not accustomed. Several of the ablest orators concurred in presenting an amendment to the address to the throne in favor of the Pope's temporal sovereignty. It was, of course, opposed by the government, but was supported, nevertheless, by sixty votes to seventy-nine. In the legislative assembly, notwithstanding all the ability displayed by the representatives of the government, the Emperor's Italian policy could obtain the support of only 161 votes, whilst it was condemned by the powerful minority of ninety-one. The radical leaders of the majority now thought the time opportune for demanding the recall of the French troops from Rome. The government went dead against it, and invited the deputies to join with it in condemning the inordinate and persistent ambition of the revolution. This the assembly did by a solid vote of the whole house to five. Of this precious quintet, Jules Favre and Emile Olivier, the leaders of the government, were two.

Such national demonstrations in favor of the sovereignty which he had done his best to crush were very irritating to the Emperor Napoleon ; and although he endeavored to appear wholly absorbed by his life of Cæsar, he could not avoid showing by his acts how profoundly he was disturbed by being thwarted. Everywhere throughout France the Catholics were made to suffer. The clergy were persecuted as far as the laws of the country would allow, and the Imperial anger went so far as to wreak its vengeance on the poor by suppressing that benevolent and non-political institution, the Association of St. Vincent de Paul. Needless to say that, at the same time, the Catholic press was held in fetters. There was no relaxation in its favor till the year 1867, when the law extending the liberty of the press became available to Catholic as well as all other writers. The Emperor even sacrificed the best supporters of the Imperial system on account of their dislike to his anti-Roman policy. Not only from such men did warnings come, but also from eminent statesmen of former *regimes*, such as Messrs. Sauzet, de Broglie, Vitet, and even M. Guizot, who was a Protestant, together with Messrs. Thiers, Cousin and Dufaure, who were only nominal Catholics. " Madame," said M. Thiers, one day, to the Empress, with more truth than *politesse*, " history lays down the law that *quicouque mange du Pape en creve*."*

So many and such decided manifestations of public opinion were not without their effects. No less a personage than Garibaldi, relying, as he thought he could do, on Piedmontese support, now undertook to realize to the full the revolutionary programme—the Kingdom of Italy, with Rome for its capital. The King of Piedmont, whilst he publicly disowned the fili-buster, as he had affected to disown him in Sicily, held an army in reserve for his support. He expected himself to be officially condemned, whilst in reality, as usual, privately sustained.

---

* Whoever thinks to devour the Pope will die of indigestion. These words, though not very polite, proved to be prophetic.

In the meantime, however, the policy of his Imperial patron was considerably modified; and orders were despatched. to his Sardinian Majesty, which he could neither take as a blind nor dare to disregard. So the Piedmontese army, which was intended to aid the filibusters in the sack of Rome, was obliged to fight them. It came up with the bands of Garibaldi, at a place called Aspromonte, on the 29th of August, 1862. The irregular force was defeated, its leader wounded in the heel and taken prisoner. Garibaldi being so renowned a warrior— Achilles was nothing to him—was immediately released. Napoleon had spoken sincerely at last. If he had always done so there would have been less disorder, less violation of all right and less bloodshed, in bringing together the provinces and states of Italy. If it had been his policy to concur with the Pope and the party of true reform, instead of patronizing a filibustering prince, he might have lived to see a less objectionable and more lasting unification of Italy than that which he so powerfully aided in achieving.

Garibaldi defeated at Aspromonte.

The intriguing Cabinet of Turin took great credit to itself for having so vigorously acted, although against its will, in preventing Garibaldi from seizing Rome. As a reward for this signal service, it boldly proposed to go there itself. But the time had not yet come. The fall of Rome was destined to occur simultaneously with another event, in which the Emperor Napoleon was directly and personally interested. To do him justice, he was from this time anxious that matters should be settled advantageously to the Holy See, but without prejudice to the revolution. The idea was chimerical. But that is no reason for supposing that it was not sincerely entertained.

The venerable Pontiff derived some comfort from the resolve of the French nation, in which all

Canonization of the Martyrs of Japan. parties, as has been seen, concurred, and the determination of its Imperial head to check the career of revolution, and leave Rome to its legitimate sovereign. But meanwhile more abundant consolations in the spiritual order were showered upon him. In the course of the great struggle in which there was now, at length, a pause, he was practically abandoned, even by the most friendly nations. It now fell to his lot to fulfil a high duty incident to the Pontifical office, and the nations, through their numerous representatives, flocked around him. No earthly prince was ever so sustained by the sympathies of mankind. The time had now arrived, all research and investigation having come to a close, when those heroes of the Christian faith who, in the year 1597, had suffered martyrdom at the hands of the Japanese, should be solemnly canonized. They were twenty-six in number. One of these was an American, and suffered at Nagasaki in the year just mentioned. Another process of canonization had also been concluded—that of the blessed Michael de Sanctis, a Trinitarian, and member of the order for the Redemption of Captives. Pius IX. had invited the bishops to attend the important ceremony. The Sardinian government, which took credit to itself for having established a "free church in a free state," forbade the Italian bishops to visit Rome on this occasion. No fewer than ninety bishops protested against this mockery of liberty, and declared that nothing but the strong hand of power could have prevented them from repairing to the holy city.

Notwithstanding the forced absence of so many bishops, there were at Rome three hundred and twenty-three cardinals, patriarchs, archbishops and bishops, more than four thousand priests, and one hundred thousand strangers of various nations and classes. Humble curates of the Alpine regions, who were too poor to undertake the journey, subscribed in order to send a few of their number in the name of the rest.

Numerous ships which were, for the time, as floating convents, sailed from the ports of France, Spain and Italy, invoking Mary the Star of the Sea—*Ave Maris Stella*—whilst masses of people responded from the shore; the hearts of all were with them. There was high festival at Rome from Ascension Day to Whitsuntide. All thoughts of politics were dismissed; the grand religious celebration absorbing all attention. As often as Pius IX. appeared in public, he was honored with an ovation. On one occasion, in particular, there was a great demonstration by the clergy and the artillerymen of the French army, on the day before Pentecost Sunday. The Bishop of Tulle, Mgr. Berteaud, Mgr. Dupanloup of Orleans, and other bishops, addressed immense crowds, and produced religious emotion in which unbelievers could not help participating. It is not recorded that Pius IX. had preached in public since the beginning of his Pontificate. He now, on the 6th of June, delivered the word of God in the Sistine Chapel, speaking first in Latin and afterwards in French. His audience consisted of four thousand priests, as many as could be assembled within the spacious edifice. All were deeply moved, and only refrained through reverence from giving vent to their feelings. As soon as the Holy Father had announced the apostolic benediction, one of the priests happily intoned the liturgical prayer: "*Oremus pro Pontifice nostro Pio.*" "Let us pray for our Pontiff Pius." All present, as if with one voice, responded: "The Lord preserve him and give him life, and make him blessed upon earth, and deliver him not to the will of his enemies." One may have some idea how the Catholic mind was impressed, from the words of M. Louis Veuillot: "We traversed our beloved Rome with filial affection. And if the thought occurred to us that there existed a design to rob us of it, our feeling was one of anger rather than of fear. We passed from sanctuary to sanctuary, inquiring as to the places where Pius IX. would appear, in order to pay profoundest reverence to the Holy Pontiff. 'No, no,' exclaimed a bishop, as he came from the presence of the Holy Father, "it is not true, it is not possible! Do not believe that there are Victor Emmanuels, Garibaldis, Ratazzis! Such a man cannot have enemies!'"

On Pentecost Sunday, June 8th, 1862, it was known that the Basilica of St. Peter would be open at five o'clock in the morning. All night the neighboring streets were crowded, and when the gates were thrown open that greatest of earth's temples was filled in a few minutes. The Pontifical troops were on guard inside. The foreign ambassadors, the royal family of Naples, and other distinguished persons filled the tribunes; and the French infantry was massed on St. Peter's place. The church was appropriately decorated with paintings representing scenes in the lives of the martyrs and illustrious confessors. The thousands of lights which shone around added splendor to the scene. At seven o'clock the great procession began to move. First came a troop of orphans, then appeared the students of the ecclesiastical seminaries. These were followed by religious communities and the secular clergy. Bishops came next, and archbishops, patriarchs and cardinals. Then appeared the Supreme Pastor, preceded by the banners of the saints that were to be canonized. All besides was now forgot, as the Holy Father was borne slowly along, seated on the *sedia gestatoria*, which was carried by twelve attendants in scarlet cloaks. The Tiara added dignity to the noble figure of the Pontiff. In his left hand, which was veiled with white silk, embroidered with gold, he held a lighted wax taper, while his right was left free to bless the people as he passed along. The correspondent of the London *Times*, who was a Protestant, says: "Looking over the sea of heads placed between me and the procession, I observed that all knelt before Pius IX., the meek and the good, for it is only justice so to speak of him. The chanters of the Vatican chanted in angelic tones: *Tu es Petrus*, and these tones, softened rather than weakened by distance, pervaded the whole edifice like spirits. At intervals, another group chanted: *Ave Maris Stella*, and thus the Pope was borne, through the thousands of Christians who had come from every country on which the sun shines, to the high altar behind the tomb of the apostles."

In the midst of so much pomp and glory, Pius IX. was humble and collected, referring all to Him of whom he was only the representative on earth. At the same time, his soul overflowed with happiness when he saw that there was still so much faith in Israel. The Sovereign Pontiff now took his seat upon the Papal throne, and having received the obedience of the cardinals and bishops, he was approached by the consistorial advocate, who thrice petitioned him to permit the names of the glorious martyrs and confessors to be inscribed on the diptychs of the saints, which the church recognizes and holds sacred. After the request had been made the third time, the Holy Father read in a clear and audible voice the decree of canonization. He then intoned the *Te Deum*, which was chanted by the immense congregation. The ceremonies concluded with a solemn High Mass, which was celebrated by the Pope himself, surrounded by the cardinals and bishops. The people spent the remainder of the day in pious rejoicing. They were gay and expansive, but calm and brotherly; thus exhibiting, without being conscious of it, a spectacle unknown to the inhabitants of other capitals.

The demonstrations which took place at Rome on the following day were not less important, and perhaps had greater significance, although not accompanied by so much pomp and ceremony. There was held in the Palace of the Vatican a semi-public consistory, at which all the bishops who were at Rome attended. The venerable Pontiff denounced, in his allocution to the attentive audience, those errors which are too ancient to have even the merit of originality, but which are the more dangerous that, at the present time more than ever, they are loudly preached and widely disseminated. He alluded in particular to that German criticism, which views our sacred books as nothing better than a system of mythology, and to that too well-known romance of a French writer, M. Renan, entitled: "The Life of Jesus." He condemned materialism, pantheism,

The Pope's consistorial allocution to the assembled bishops. He denounces the errors of the time.

naturalism, and all those more or less degrading systems
which deny human liberty, proclaim a morality independent
of the laws of God; which derive from material force and
superior numbers all law and authority; and which in philosophy make reason their God, the state in politics, and passion
in the daily conduct of life.   The Holy Father then thanked
the bishops who were present, regretting the absence of those
of Portugal and Italy, the latter of whom were restrained by
the Piedmontese government, and exhorted them all to continue to combat error, and to turn away the eyes and hands of
the faithful from bad books and bad journals, and to promote,
without ever wearying, the instruction of the clergy and the
good education of youth.   He concluded, in a voice which was
impeded by his tears, and with his eyes raised to heaven, by
joining with all present in beseeching the Father of mercies,
through the merits of Jesus Christ, His only Son, to extend a
helping hand to Christian and civil society, and to restore
peace to the church.

Cardinal Mattei, dean of the Sacred College, replied in the
name of all the bishops.   Three points chiefly, among others,
were affirmed in his declaration.   First of all, the supreme
doctrinal authority and infallibility of the Roman Pontiff.
"You are in our regard the master of sound doctrine. You
are the centre of unity.   You are the foundation of the church
itself, against which the gates of hell shall not prevail.   When
you speak, we hear Peter.   When you decree, we obey Jesus
Christ.   We admire you in the midst of so many trials and
tempests, with a serene brow and unshaken mind, invincibly
fulfilling your sacred ministry."   Next, the temporal sovereignty of the Holy See.   "We acknowledge that your
temporal sovereignty is necessary, and that it was established in fulfilment of a manifest design of Divine Providence.   We hesitate not to declare that this temporal
sovereignty is required for the good of the church and
the free government of souls.   It was necessary that the
Supreme Pontiff should be neither the subject nor even the

guest of any prince. There was required in the centre of
Europe a sacred bond, placed between the three continents of
the ancient world, an august seat, whence arises in turns, for
peoples and for princes, a great and powerful voice, the voice
of justice and of truth, impartial and without preference, free
from all arbitrary influence, and which can neither be repressed
by fear nor circumvented by artifice. How could it have been
that at this very moment the prelates of the church, arriving
from all points of the universe, should have come here in order
to represent all peoples, and confer in security on the gravest
interests, if they had found any prince whomsoever ruling in
this land who had suspicions of their princes, or who was suspected by them on account of his hostility? In such case their
duties as citizens might have conflicted with their duties as
bishops." Finally, the intimate union of the Catholic world
with the Pope. "We condemn the errors which you have condemned. We reprove the sacrilegious acts, the violations of
ecclesiastical immunity, and the other crimes committed against
the chair of Peter. We give utterance to this protest, which
we claim shall be inserted in the annals of the church, in all
sincerity, in the name of our brethren who are absent, in the
name of those who, detained at home by force, lament and are
silent, in the name of those whom the state of their health or
important affairs have prevented from joining us in this place.
To our number we add the clergy and the faithful people who
give you proof of their love and veneration by their assiduous
prayers, as well as by the offering of Peter's pence. Would to
God that all kings and powerful men in the world understood
that the cause of the Pontiff is the cause of all states. Would
to God that they came to an understanding in order to place
in security the sacred cause of the Christian world and of social
order."

Pius IX. made reply: "United as we are, venerable brethren, we cannot doubt that the God of peace and charity is with
us. And if God be with us, who shall be against us? Praise,
honor, glory to God! To you, peace, salvation and joy!

Peace to your minds; salvation to the faithful committed to your care; joy to you and to them, in order that you may all rejoice, chaunting a new canticle in the House of God for evermore!"

The address which Cardinal Mattei read bore the signatures of all the bishops who were in Rome. The bishops of Italy hastened to express their concurrence, with one exception, Ariano, who had participated in the revolutionary movement, and who came to an unhappy death within the year. There came, in due course, numerous adhesions from all parts of the world, together with countless addresses from the clergy of the second order. The laity, on their part, received the bishops on their return home with triumphal honors. They came around them and escorted them to the pulpits of their cathedrals, in order to hear from their lips all that had taken place at Rome. The Bishop of Moulins, Mgr. de Droux Breze, admirably expressed in a few words the impressions of the venerable pilgrims: "Rome is a city of wonders; but the wonder of Rome is Pius IX."

The moral result of all these manifestations was incalculable. At a time when universal suffrage had come into vogue, it was impossible not to see in all this, from a merely wordly point of view, indirect, indeed, but strikingly universal suffrage. The vote of the whole Catholic world was shown, united with that of the Romans, in affirming the rights of the Catholic world over Rome, whilst appeared, at the same time, the determination of the Romans to retain their cherished autonomy, and to remain the capital of the Catholic world. The parliament of Turin was greatly agitated. There was indescribable confusion, so that discussion was impossible. They voted, in opposition to the Episcopal and Pontifical allocutions, an address to Victor Emmanuel, the character of which may be gathered from the following few words : " Sire, bishops, almost all strangers in Italy, have proclaimed the strange doctrine that Rome is the slave of the Catholic world. We reply to them by declaring that we are resolved, to maintain inviolable

s

the right of the nation and that of the Italian metropolis,
which is, at present, retained by force under a detested yoke."
It was of a piece with many other assertions of the revolutionary party that the Romans detested the rule of the Holy Father.
It was particularly audacious to make such an assertion in face
of the enthusiastic demonstrations which had just been made
in the city of the Popes. They had forbidden the presence of
the Italian bishops at Rome, and nevertheless they dared to
complain that almost all the bishops who gathered around the
Sovereign Pontiff were strangers in Italy. But what did this
avail them? Did not the Italian bishops decidedly express
complete concurrence with their brethren?

It is still more surprising that the Emperor Napoleon took
no warning from the words of the Turin parliament, and went
so far as to conclude an agreement with them for the preservation to the Pope of the Holy City.

It is difficult to understand how a people numerically so
weak as the inhabitants of that portion of
the once great kingdom of Poland, which
fell to the Russian Empire at the time of
the unfortunate partition, could have undertaken a rebellion against so great a Power as Russia. But
provocation, patriotism, the sense of nationality, together with
the ardent love of liberty, set the laws of prudence at defiance.
That provocation must have been of no ordinary kind which
could excite, in Russian Poland, a third rebellion, which had
no better prospect of success than the two former, which
resulted so disastrously for the unhappy Poles. And, indeed,
what could be worse or more calculated to cause insurrection
than the cruelties, crimes and sacrilegious acts which the
Russian government was guilty of throughout Poland in the
years 1861 and 1862? The churches of that ill-fated country
were seized and profaned, divine service interdicted, and the
bishops arraigned before courts-martial and cast into prison.
Such atrocities, instead of crushing, only increased the patriotism of the people. Russian policy, baffled as was to be expected,

*The Church in Po-
land persecuted. Pius
IX. raises his voice
in its behalf.*

in its design of establishing tranquillity by such barbarous proceedings, had recourse to a rigid conscription intended
to have the effect of forcing all the patriotic youth of the country into the ranks of the Russian army. This violent recruiting was first attempted at Warsaw, at dead of night, on the
15th of January, 1863. When the news of this violence
spread throughout the country, all the young men capable
of bearing arms fled to the steppes and forests, and, in eight
days, all Poland was in rebellion for the third time, in order to
break the yoke of the foreigner. A word from the great Powers,
or any one of them, would have restored peace. But they all
alike refused to speak this word. The British, after having
encouraged the Poles to resistance in public speeches, were
on the point of intervening in their behalf, when a hint from
M. de Bismark suddenly cooled their zeal, and determined
Lord John Russell to recall by telegraph threatening despatches which were already on their way to St. Petersburgh.
It need scarcely be said that Prussia, which was an accomplice of Russia in the iniquitous partition, made common cause
with Russia in the work of repression. Austria was at the
time paralyzed, as Italy was threatening Venice. Italy simply
expressed to Prince Gortschakoff, the Russian Chancellor, "its
confidence that the Emperor Alexander would persevere in the
reforms so unfortunately interrupted by the rebellion." Innocent Italians! They, of course, were not guilty of causing
rebellion, which was now, in their estimation, so deplorable in
Sicily, Naples, the Grand Duchies, &c. Napoleon remained,
as was his wont, undecided. He would neither assist the
Poles nor give them to understand that he would not assist
them. A word from him would have shortened, by eighteen
months, a hopeless struggle of two years, which ended by
exhausting them.

There was one, however, who protested. Pius IX. denounced
the oppressor as fearlessly as if he had been the least of the
princes of the earth. He wrote to him, at first, in a tone of
mild remonstrance, on the 22d of April, 1863. But finding

that his representations were not heeded, he renewed them
more pressingly. He did not confine himself to merely official
acts. He sent Cardinal Reisach on a confidential mission to
Vienna, and addressed a warm and feeling letter to the Emperor Francis Joseph, in order to induce him to take action
energetically in common with France. He invited the whole
Christian world to join with him in praying for the suffering
nation which he nobly declared to be "the soldier of civilization and of faith." Such as were at Rome, at the time of these
prayers, will never forget how enthusiastically the Roman
people responded to the call of Pius IX. In praying for the
defenders of a distant country, they seemed to pray, at the
same time, for their own, which was now, more than ever,
threatened. But the time of mercy had not yet come, and
persecution was redoubled. Ecclesiastics were deported or put
to death, simply for not having refused the aid of religion to
the dying on the field of battle. Families and whole populations were doomed to choose between exile and apostacy. All
the bishops, without exception, were driven from their dioceses,
and some of them perished on the way to Siberia. Pius IX.
could no longer contain his grief and indignation. On the 27th
of April, 1864, in replying to the postulators in the cause of
blessed Francis of the five wounds, he said: "The blood of
the helpless and the innocent cries for vengeance to the throne
of the Almighty against those by whom it is shed. Unhappy
Poland! It was my desire not to speak before the approaching consistory. But I fear lest, by being silent any longer,
I should draw down upon myself the punishment denounced
by the prophets against those who tolerate iniquity. No, I
would not that I were forced to cry out, one day, in presence
of the Sovereign Judge: "Woe to me because I have held my
peace!" (*Væ mihi quia tacui.*) I feel inspired at this moment
to condemn a sovereign whose vast Empire reaches to the
Pole. This potentate, who falsely calls himself the Catholic of
the East, but who is only a schismatic cast forth from the
bosom of the true church, persecutes and slays his Catholic

subjects, and by his ferocious cruelty has driven them to insurrection. Under the pretext of suppressing this insurrection, he extirpates the Catholic religion. He deports whole populations to inhospitable climes, where they are deprived of all religious assistance, and replaces them by schismatical adventurers. He tears the pastors from their flocks, and drives them into exile, or condemns them to forced labors and other degrading punishments. Happy they who have been able to escape, and who now wander in strange lands! This potentate, all heterodox and schismatical as he is, arrogates to himself a power which the Vicar of Christ possesses not. He pretends to deprive a bishop whom we have rightfully instituted. Can he be ignorant that a Catholic bishop is always the same, whether in his see or in the catacombs, and that his character is ineffaceable? Let it not be said that in raising our voice against such misdeeds we encourage the European revolution. We can distinguish between the socialist revolution and the legitimate rights of a nation struggling for independence and its religion. In stigmatizing the persecutors of the Catholic religion, we fulfil a duty laid on us by our conscience. It behooves us to pray, with renewed earnestness, for that unfortunate country. In consequence, we impart our apostolic benediction to all who shall, this day, pray for Poland. Let us all pray for Poland!" It was as if the breath of God's anger were on the lips of the Holy Pontiff. Pius IX., remarks M. de St. Albin, swayed by his deep emotion, had risen from his throne, his voice was like thunder, and his arm appeared to threaten as if possessed of omnipotence.

Such apostolic courage commanded the admiration of the enemies of the Papacy. The deputy, Brofferio, said in the parliament of Turin, whilst his colleagues, revolutionists like himself, applauded: "An old man, exhausted, sickly, without resources, without an army, on the brink of the grave, curses a potentate who slaughters a people; I feel moved in my inmost soul; I imagine myself borne back to the days of Gregory VII.; I reverence and applaud."

The revolutionists admire the courage of Pius IX.

M. Meyendorf, the *charge d'affaires* of Russia, having been admitted to a private audience on occasion of the Christmas festivities of 1866, Pius IX. naturally directed the conversation to the painful state of ecclesiastical affairs in Poland. The Russian minister denied everything, even the most notorious facts, and ended by casting all the blame on the Catholics, who, he affirmed, had openly transacted with the Polish insurrection, whilst the Protestants generally sided with the government. "Nor was this astonishing," he added, "considering that Catholicism and revolution are the same thing." Pius IX. could not tolerate this false assertion, which was so absurd that it could have no other object than to insult him and the whole body of the faithful of whom he was .the Chief. "Depart," said he to the minister, as he dismissed him, "I cannot but believe that your Emperor is ignorant of the greater part of the injustice under which Poland suffers. I, therefore, honor and esteem your Emperor ; but I cannot say as much of his representative who comes to insult me in my own house." Pius IX. vainly hoped that the Envoy would be disowned, and diplomatic relations between Rome and St. Petersburgh continued. When Alexander II. suppressed, by his own authority, in 1867, the Catholic diocese of Kaminieck, Pius IX. was obliged to have recourse to the newspaper press, in order to make known to the Catholics of that unfortunate country that he appointed the Bishop of Zitomir provisional administrator. "I have no other means of communicating with them," said he "I act like the captain of a vessel who encloses in a bottle his last words to his family, and confides them to the storm, hoping that the waves will deposit them on some shore where they will be gathered up."

The Russian Envoy insults the Pope.

Pius IX. showed himself as generous to princes as to peoples, acting always as the champion of justice in the cause of the former, as well as in supporting the undoubted rights of the latter. Francis II., of Naples, dethroned by his ambitious cousin, King Victor Emmanuel, was, as the Bonapartes had once been, an exile at Rome, and

Pius IX. insists on protecting the ex-King of Naples, and takes Napoleon severely to task.

enjoyed the same princely hospitality which his predecessor, in 1848, had extended to the Holy Father in the Kingdom of Naples. Victor Emmanuel remonstrated against this kindness to a fallen enemy. But in vain! He was powerless. His ally and patron, however, the French Emperor, was not so easily resisted. This potentate gave it to be understood, although not in express terms, that the stay of the French troops at Rome was dependent on the departure of the exiled monarch. The Pope, alluding to the family of Napoleon I., whom Pius VII. had kindly received at Rome, replied, satirically, that the Roman Pontiffs had traditions of hospitality, as regarded their persecutors, and much more in favor of their benefactors. Napoleon was ashamed to persist; and Francis II. remained at Rome as long as Pius IX. was master there.

It was quite natural that Napoleon III. should entertain the idea that he was born to found empires. He had succeeded in establishing one on the ruins of a republic in the Old World. He now sought to build up Imperial power side by side with a republic in the New. Mexico was designed to be the seat of this empire; and, as that country greatly needed government of some kind, the time was deemed opportune for carrying into effect Napoleon's idea. The Imperial dignity was offered to the Archduke Maximilian of Austria; and this prince, relying on the support of France, consented to ascend the throne of the Montezumas. Before crossing the seas, Prince Maximilian came, together with his wife, the Princess Charlotte of Belgium, to Rome, in order to beg the prayers, the wise counsel and the apostolic benediction of the venerable Pontiff. So desired the new Emperor to inaugurate a reign which, it was hoped, would be great and prosperous. The Holy Father, at the solemn moment of communion, spoke to the Prince of Him by whom kings reign and the framers of laws decree just things. In the name of this King of kings, he recommended to him the Catholic nation of Mexico, reminding him, at the same time, that he was, under God, the constituted protector of the rights of the people as well as those of the church. The Emperor and his youthful spouse were moved to tears; and Maximilian, on leaving Rome, declared that he depar—ted under the protection of God, and with the benediction of the Holy Pontiff. "I am confident, therefore," he added, "that I shall be able to fulfil my great mission to Mexico."

Unfortunately for him, however, liberalism, or, rather, ill-disguised socialism, was enthroned, for the moment, in what was destined to be, for a little while longer, the chief seat of European Power. It is not difficult to imagine whence counsel proceeded, and the inexperienced Emperor came to believe that Mexico might be governed as France was, whilst its ruler thwarted the will of the great majority of her people. He may not, indeed, have been free to reject the advice which swayed him. Be this as it may, he most unwisely cast himself into the arms of the party to whom monarchy and religion were alike hateful. He now framed a Concordat which, whilst it could not be acceptable to his new friends, was far from being such as the Pope could ratify. The revolutionary party had gained the new Emperor.

The Holy Father, ever anxious to promote the well-being of the church, sent a nuncio to Maximilian,

A Papal Nuncio sent to remind Maximilian of his promises made at Rome.

in order to remind him of his promises, and induce him to abolish the laws that had been enacted for the purpose of oppressing the church, and completely to reorganize ecclesiastical affairs with the full concurrence of the Holy See. The letter borne by the nuncio required that the Catholic religion should continue to be the stay and glory of the Mexican nation; that the bishops should be entirely free in the exercise of their pastoral ministry; that the religious orders should be restored and organized according to the instructions and faculties imparted by the Sovereign Pontiff; that the patrimony of the church and the rights connected therewith should be guaranteed and protected; that none be allowed to disseminate false and subversive doctrines; that public as well as private education be directed and superintended by ecclesiastical authority; and, finally, that those fetters be broken which had hitherto for some time held the church dependent on the arbitrary will of the civil power. "If," continued the Holy Father, "the religious edifice be re-established, as we doubt not it will, on such foundations, your Majesty will satisfy one of the greatest wants and realize the most ardent aspirations of the religious people of Mexico; you will dispel our disquietude and that of the illustrious Mexican Episcopate; you will pave the way for the education of a learned and zealous clergy, as well as the moral reformation of the people. You will thus, also, consolidate your throne, and promote the prosperity and glory of your Imperial family." In all this the Emperor would have been sustained by the great majority of the Mexican people. And there was nothing impossible required of him. It is not shown anywhere that the restoration of church properties, which had been long alienated and had often changed proprietors, would have been exacted, any more than in England, when religion was restored under the reign of Mary. The policy indicated by Pius IX. would have won for Maximilian a host of friends and supporters. The line of conduct which he pursued was most unacceptable to the Catholic nation of Mexico, whilst it was not in the least calculated to satisfy the revolutionary party. Refusing to concede everything that the church required, he wished to retain for himself the ancient regal privileges of the Crown of Spain—the investiture of bishops, the regulating of ecclesiastical tariffs, the limitation of the number of monastic orders and religious associations, &c. So far the revolution was pleased. It was loud in its applause. With what sincerity events failed not to show. Pius IX. insisted on the Emperor's solemn pledges so recently given at Rome. Maximilian was deaf to the counsels, the complaints, the earnest prayers of the Holy Father. So it remained only for the Papal Nuncio, Monsignor Meglia, to take his departure from Vera Cruz (1st June, 1865). Meanwhile, Maximilian's chief support, the French Emperor, dreading the formidable hostility of the United States of America, which could not tolerate an empire on the borders of their great republic, was obliged to withdraw from Mexico the army which, from the first, was necessary to sustain the new empire. Napoleon, one would say, was pledged to Maximilian, having induced him to assume the Imperial Crown, and having also promised all necessary support. He could not, however, command success; and chivalry, even if it had still existed, would have availed but little, when power alone could win.

Maximilian was now all alone, face to face with anarchy and the Mexican nation which he had slighted. Faction ruled in his place. The revolutionary party which he had favored proved untrue; and falling into the hands of his enemies, he was solemnly murdered by the ruling brigand of the day. The officers of Napoleon's army sincerely believed that no better fate could be anticipated; for they earnestly advised him to accompany them on their return to Europe. This he could have done without dishonor. The idea of a Mexican empire was Napoleon's, and he alone was answerable for its success. On the part of Maximilian it was more than chivalry to remain in Mexico when his guard was gone. But the idea of the youthful Prince in regard to honor appears to have been, like his policy, unsound. The policy may not have been, most probably was not, his. But the sentiment of honor was all his own. And although, in an age of chivalry even, it would have appeared exaggerated, it redounds to his credit. It is not surprising that a man animated by such noble sentiments should have died as became a hero and a Christian.

The potentate, on whom, as far as worldly power was concerned, depended the Pope's temporal sovereignty, was throwing himself every day more and more into the hands of the enemies of the church. His ministers, more audacious than himself, carried their blind hatred of "Clericalism" to such an extent as to sacrifice many of the best supporters of the empire. This was singularly apparent at the general

A further step towards the abolition of the Papal sovereignty.

election of 1863. M. de Persigny hesitated not to employ all
the influence of the government against such Imperialists as
had voted for or shown themselves favorable to the Pope's
temporal power, He succeeded in causing such friends of
Napoleon as De Caverville, Cochin and Lemercier to be replaced
by the most bitter enemies of the Imperial *regime*. He also
managed to exclude from parliament Messrs. de Montalembert,
de Falloux and Keller. But Messrs. Plichou, Berryer and
Thiers, notwithstanding his hostile efforts, were elected. This
last-named statesman was himself a host, and his eloquent
speeches in support of the temporal sovereignty made all the
more impression that they were known to be dictated by far-
seeing policy, rather than any leaning towards religion. They
deeply impressed the parliament and the country; but availed
not with Napoleon III., whom an unprincipled ministry were
leading blindfolded to destruction. Meanwhile, the question
of Rome entered on a new phase. The Cabinets of Turin and
Paris concluded an agreement in regard to the Roman State
on 15th September, 1864. The text of this notorious agreement was known to Europe, whilst its meaning remained a
mystery. The ministry of Napoleon III. made it appear in
France as a guarantee for the safety of the Pope. The Piedmontese government flattered the revolutionary element of
Italy, by representing that it did not in the least change their
programme, the keynote of which was "Rome the Capital."
They were right. This proved to be the true solution of the
mystery. The first article provided that the King of Piedmont
should not attack, and he bound himself by oath not to attack,
the remaining territory of the Holy Father, to prevent by force,
if necessary, all aggression from any other quarter, and to pay
the debts of the former States of the Church. By the second
clause France became bound to withdraw her troops in two
years. A protocol was added, by which Victor Emmanuel
engaged to transfer his capital from Turin to Florence in six
months. It was more than disrespectful to the Pope; it was
of evil omen, of sinister import, that the sovereign whose state

was concerned was not a party to the treaty—was not even consulted. The minds of all Catholics were greatly disquieted, and their anxiety was only increased by the Italian interpretation of the agreement. Pius IX., who understood well by what men and by what principles the Cabinet of the Tuileries was governed, made a remark which indicated more his fears for the great French nation than for the fragment which remained to him of his territory. He would have nothing to do with the pecuniary compensation that was offered to him. He could only say that "he pitied France." The crime of that country was that her government made any agreement at all with the monarch who had so unscrupulously violated the treaty of Zurich, and who was, besides, the chief hero of Gaeta, Naples, Castelfidardo and Ancona. One of the most eloquent of Bishop Dupanloup's publications, the one which, perhaps, has been the most generally read, exposes the hollowness of this arrangement, which is known in history as the September agreement.

The 8th of December, 1864, the tenth anniversary of the **The Syllabus.** proclamation of the dogma of the Immaculate Conception, was marked by the publication of the Encyclical, "quanta cura," and, together with it, the "Syllabus." This great doctrinal act was a crushing reply to the erroneous assertions of the time, as well as to the vain ideas of those politicians who boasted that, through their efforts, the spiritual office no less than the temporal sovereignty of the Pope was drawing to a close. The Encyclical letter is addressed to all bishops in communion with the Holy See, and through them to all the faithful throughout the world. It contains the teachings of Pius IX., and the Popes, his predecessors, in opposition to the errors of the present age—the mistaken ideas of natural religion; religious indifference which, falsely assuming the name of liberty of conscience and of worship, establishes the reign of physical force in the place of law and justice; communism and socialism; the subjection of the church to the state; and the independence of Christians in regard to the Holy See.

The "Syllabus" consists of eighty propositions, which are a summary of the false teachings of the enemies of the Catholic church, as found in the periodical press, as well as in their writings of a more permanent character. The first seven propositions briefly express the errors on pantheism, naturalism, and absolute rationalism. All who have any Christian belief, to whatever denomination they may adhere, must surely acknowledge the justice of denouncing philosophers of the school of Strauss, who insist that Christ is a myth, and His religion a system of mythology.

From the eighth to the fourteenth proposition inclusively, are pointed out and condemned the errors of modern rationalism. From the fourteenth to the eighteenth, indifferentism and latitudinarianism are exposed. Throughout the rest of the catalogue, secret societies and communism are condemned; erroneous views, as regards church and state, natural and Christian ethics, and Christian marriage are expressed and denounced. Finally, are pointed out the errors that have been uttered in regard to the temporal power of the Pope, together with such as have reference to modern liberalism.

These important documents, the Encyclical, "quanta cura," and the "Syllabus," are not so much the work of Pius IX. as of all the Popes of a century back, from the Council of Pistoia, Febronianism and Josephism. Whilst the "Syllabus" was yet in embryo, it was, with the exception of a few propositions which were not yet formulated, confidentially communicated to the bishops on occasion of the canonization of the Japanese martyrs. Each bishop was at that time invited to select two theologians in order to examine the propositions, and give their opinion in six months. The church, therefore, was not taken by surprise, when the "Syllabus" appeared, however much its publication may have struck with astonishment and alarm the party of revolution and unbelief. Catholics, at least, could not fail to be swayed by such a masterly exposition of Catholic theology on so many subjects, all intimately connected with human conduct in private life as well as in affairs of public import. And there were Catholics everywhere—among the rulers of the world and its leading statesmen, no less than in all classes and grades of society. Such now could have no excuse for favoring opinions which were so distinctly condemned by that authority which they all recognized as the highest upon earth. Nevertheless, whatever impression the clear teaching of the "Syllabus," in regard to the church and her rights, civil society, and both natural and Christian morality, was destined, in time, to produce, but little disposition was shown to be guided by it at the outset. There was all but a universal clamor that the church had pronounced a divorce between modern society and the spiritual order. Nor could it be otherwise, so long as the former held principles which were essentially incompatible with the latter. Neither could reconciliation be easily or speedily brought about. The principles which religion condemned were in the ascendant. The existing civil law of all European nations was founded on them. There was no government that had not adopted them and shown itself inclined to be entirely guided by them. The formal condemnation of the cherished ideas of the age was as a thunderbolt hurled against the social elements of the day. But why disturb their peace? They had no peace. They were already discordant. "*Non est pax impiis.*" Peace could not be born of unbelief. It could come only through the truth, even as health conquers disease by the most trying curative process. Napoleon III. was the first who openly resisted the "encroachments" of Rome, just as if they had constituted the only danger to his throne. By a decree dated 1st January, 1865, he forbade the publication of the Encyclical and the Syllabus, whilst he caused to be tried and condemned, as guilty of abuse, the Archbishop of Besançon and the Bishop of Moulins, because they had read the Encyclical in their pulpits. The other prelates of France so far submitted as to avoid printing the obnoxious documents, lest their printers should be uselessly compromised. Several bishops declared that the ¦Encyclical was already sufficiently published in their dioceses by the voice of the press. They thus expressed the idea of the whole episcopate. Pius IX. highly commended their zeal. "We must go back," he said, "to the early ages of Christianity, in order to find an episcopal body that could show such courage."

To persons accustomed to theological studies, it is sufficiently apparent why each proposition of the "Syllabus" stands condemned. To others, cause is shown in the consistorial allocutions, Encyclical and other letters apostolical of the Holy Father, in relation to each proposition. Some things must be interpreted by the conduct of the Pope himself. For instance, what is said in regard to the liberty of public worship and of the press must be read in the light of that reasonable tolerance which the Popes were accustomed to exercise when they ruled at Rome as sovereign Princes. There is no liberty without some restraint. The press, in this respect, is in the same position as individuals. According to the laws of all civilized lands, when it abuses its liberty and commits crime, it is visited with severe punishment. The greater liberty which the press enjoys, and must enjoy, in the present circumstances of the world, by no means clashes with the condemnation of proposition 79 of the "Syllabus." The press can no more be free to publish anything whatsoever, however offensive it may be, than persons are free to perform such acts as necessarily subject them, even in states where there is the greatest attainable degree of liberty, to condemnation and punishment. If every organized community possesses, as it certainly does possess, the right so to stigmatize an offending citizen, and that without any violation of liberty, it is equally entitled to judge and punish an offending press.

. Not satisfied with the blow which so greatly weakened Austria in the Italian campaign, Napoleon III. plotted with Prussia for a further humbling of the great Catholic Power. To this end he held dark consultations with Count Bismark, at Biarritz, as he had formerly done with Count de Cavour at Plombieres. The former, however, proved to be more than a match

Successful efforts of Napoleon III. to humble Austria.

for him. Hence the great victory of Sadowa which paved the way for Sedan. Prussia, without a rival in Germany, could freely pursue her ambitious schemes. Napoleon, apparently suspecting nothing, left the Rhine frontier comparatively unprotected; and Prussia, victorious in the struggle with Austria, refused to France all compensation for her complicity and encouragement, This hindered not Napoleon from taking part in the treaty of Prague, as president, and sanctioning by his signature the expulsion of Austria from Germany, and the confiscation of Hanover, Nassau, the two Hesses and other small independent sovereignties, in the interest of Prussia. This Power, besides, assumed the military direction of Southern Germany, and so was, literally, doubled in extent and population. Thus was swept away in the course of seven years, through the agency of Napoleon III., the barrier of small states which the wisdom of ages had placed along the continental frontier of France, from the Mediterranean to the ocean, and which moderated the shocks of the greater Powers. France, accordingly, by her own act, was confined between unified Italy on the one hand, and on the other, the formidable German Empire.

In exchange for combinations which proved so disastrous, Venice was ceded to Napoleon, and immediately made over by him to Italy. Defeated both by sea and land in his struggle with Austria, Victor Emmanuel, nevertheless, accepted the present, as if it had come to him by conquest, and Italy was free to the Adriatic, and the celebrated Milan programme of 1859 completely carried out. This result, whilst it flattered the vanity of Napoleon III., crowned the wishes of the secret societies. Protestants, Jews, Freemasons, and people of all shades of unbelief, deputies of the French left, and the revolutionary journals, all zealous in the service of Prussia, enthusiastically applauded. The French Emperor's ministers, even, M. Rouher, in the Legislative Chamber, and M. de Lavalette, in a diplomatic circular, were not ashamed to congratulate themselves publicly on the stipulations of the treaty of Prague.

In their mania for Italian unity, these wise statesmen became blind to the interests of their own country—condign punishment, surely, of their disloyal and unprincipled policy.

Whilst the political world was extraordinarily agitated, and a great potentate was endeavoring to destroy the last remnant of Papal sovereignty, and was himself, at the same time, hastening blindly but surely to ignominy and ruin, the Pontiff against whom he warred calmly and successfully continued to accomplish the sublime work of his spiritual mission.

Pius IX. devoted to the duties of his spiritual office.

Nothing tends more to the instruction and edification of the Catholic people than the canonization of saints and martyrs. But for the care which the church bestows in bringing to light the acts and sufferings of those heroes of the Christian faith, many of them, remaining unknown, would be lost as examples to the rest of mankind. It is also due to the saints themselves that the church should honor them, although, indeed, earthly celebrity and true fame which lasts throughout all time is as nothing compared to the glory which they enjoy.

Canonization, 1859.

John Baptist de Rossi (de Rubæs) was a canon of the Collegiate Basilica of Saint Mary, *in cosmedin*. The venerable John Baptist de Rossi was in every respect a worthy minister of God. He labored last century at Rome, in the vineyard of the Lord, with so much patience, longanimity and meekness, and was so filled with the Holy Ghost and sincere charity, that he spent his whole life in evangelizing the poor, to the great gain of souls. He instructed others unto righteousness, and God willed that he should shine for evermore as a star in the firmament. And not only was he crowned with light in heaven, in order that, transformed to the Divine image, he should appear in God's presence environed with heavenly splendor; but God, through His unspeakable bounty, appointed that His servant, enriched by an abundant harvest of merits, illustrated by triumphal honors, and glorified by miracles, should also enjoy upon

John Baptist de Rossi.

T

earth a name glorious in the estimation of mankind, and should thus be a new ornament to the church militant. The process of canonization was commenced in the time of Gregory XVI., and completed by Pius IX., when in March, 1859, the name of John Baptist de Rossi was inscribed on the sacred diptychs.

John Sarcander was born at Skoczovia, in Upper Silesia, in the year 1577. He obeyed the call of God and joined the ranks of the priesthood.

John Sarcander.

When ordained priest, he showed himself in every way a pattern of excellence—by his good works, his science, the integrity and gravity of his character. He was appointed, accordingly, to the charge and guidance of souls. He fulfilled so well all the duties of a good pastor that the four parishes to which he was successively called by episcopal authority received him as an angel sent to them from heaven, and bore witness by their tears to their regret when they were deprived of his presence. Meanwhile, the ministers of the sect of Pikardites were driven from the parish of Holleschow, where the scourge of heresy, like the wild boar of the forests, had spread devastation during eight years. John Sarcander was selected in order to repair the incalculable evil that had been done to that unfortunate vineyard. He shrunk not from the struggle which it behooved him to maintain in the cause of the true faith. He was in every sense an example to his flock. He exhorted, beseeched, reprimanded with patience and wisdom, neglecting nothing that was calculated to strengthen whatever was weak and heal what was sick, to reunite those who were separated, to raise up the fallen and seek such as were astray. Such exemplary conduct only excited the extreme hatred of the heretical party, and he was obliged to leave Holleschow and retire to Poland. But moved by the dangers to which were exposed the people whom he loved so dearly in Christ, he returned to his parish, after having venerated the Holy Virgin at her shrine of Crenstochow, in fulfilment of a vow which he had made. Soon after his return the heretics cast him into prison as a traitor to his country, but, in reality, on account of his zeal in preaching the Catholic faith. He was subjected to vigorous interrogatories, and in order to induce him to reveal what the supreme head of the administration in Moravia had confided to him in confession, he was made to undergo the most exquisite torture. Preferring a glorious death to a miserable life, he combated to his last breath for the work of Christ, and gave up his soul to God, leaving to all the people the remembrance of his death as an example of fortitude and courage. Fearfully tortured on the rack for three hours, burned slowly in almost every part of his body, by torches and bundles of feathers steeped in rosin, oil, pitch and sulphur, he was carried back almost lifeless to his prison. There he lingered a whole month, suffering more than the pain of death, whilst his mind and heart were so fixed on God that he ceased not to sing His praises as long as life remained. He fell asleep in the Lord, the sixteenth of the calends of April, 1620. It was not appointed that such heroic suffering should be doomed to oblivion. Public report, the witness of contemporary writers, the monuments of the time, and the splendor of miracles caused them to be so celebrated that, notwithstanding the wars, losses and other impediments which had prevented the Archbishops of Olmutz from considering this grand and beautiful cause, and reporting it to the Holy See sooner than the 18th century, the sanctity and martyrdom of the venerable John Sarcander were not only known to the populations of Moravia and the neighboring countries, but were also remembered with the most profound veneration. From 1754 till the time of Pius IX., this celebrated cause was before the church, and subjected to the usual searching investigation. Finally, in February, 1859, it was concluded, and the blessed John Sarcander recognized, as a saint and martyr, by the universal church.

This same year, 1859, was canonized the venerable servant of God, Benedict Joseph Labre, of the diocese of Boulogne. Voluntary poverty was the lot in life of this saint of modern times.

Benedict Joseph Labre.

Worldly wisdom condemns as folly, the choice of this devoted Christian who preferred to all earthly advantages the most abject poverty. God is, indeed, wonderful in His saints; and as He often chooses what is folly in the estimation of the world, in order to confound what it holds to be wise, so He appointed that the humble Labre who, for the love of Christ, led a life of poverty, and taught mankind the excellence of self-denial in an unbelieving and selfish age, should be exalted, even upon earth, and ranked among the princes of God's people. In June, 1842, Gregory XVI. declared, by a solemn decree, that Benedict Joseph Labre had practised, in a heroic degree, all the Christian virtues. The necessary investigations and formalities were continued, and in September, 1859, Pius IX. ordained that apostolic letters should be issued, ordering the celebration of the solemn rite of his beatification in the Patriarchal Basilica of the Vatican.

The year 1859 was also marked by the solicitude of Pius IX. for the Church of Ireland. In a letter to the archbishops and bishops of that country, he commends their zeal in promoting

Mixed schools—Ireland.

Catholic education, and concurs with them in pointing out the dangers of mixed schools. In the same letter the Holy Father earnestly entreats the venerable pastors of the Irish Church to pray that the designs of the wicked may not succeed, that it would please God to bring to naught the machinations of those misguided men who, by their false teachings, endeavor to corrupt the people everywhere, and to overthrow, if that were possible, the Catholic religion. At the same time, it was appointed that the feast of Saint Patrick, the Patron Saint of Ireland, should be celebrated according to a higher rite.

The anti-President Juarez had succeeded in establishing himself at Vera Cruz, whilst Miramon was

Troubles of the Church in Mexico. recognized by Mexico, after General Zuloago, as the successor of Santa Anna. Juárez was a revolutionist and persecutor of the church; Miramon, a conservative and friend of religion. As proof of the tyranny of the former, may be cited a decree which he published in July of this year (1859). This decree, which aimed at nothing less than the destruction of religion, and was, at the same time, a cruel outrage on the Catholic nation of Mexico, accounts for the earnestness and determination with which Pius IX., a little later, as has already been shown, insisted that the Emperor Maximilian should adopt a policy friendly to the church, and in harmony with the wishes of the great majority of the Mexican people. Such policy, if only followed in time, would have so strengthened the hands of Maximilian that, in all probability, he would have been able to hold his ground when most unchivalrously abandoned by his faint-hearted ally. No doubt the anti-president claimed that he was a reformer of the church. And surely, indeed, he was, if it was reform to suppress all religious societies whatsoever, to rob the clergy of their property, and that so completely as to reduce them to mendicancy. But let the decree speak for itself:

Art. 1. All property administered under divers titles, by the regular or secular clergy, whether real or personal, whatever its name or object, is henceforth the property of the nation.

Art. 3. There shall be complete independence between affairs of state and such as are purely ecclesiastical. The government will confine itself to protecting the public worship of the Catholic religion the same as any other religion.

Art. 4. The ministers of religion can accept such offerings as may be made on account of the administration of the sacraments and the other duties of their office. They may also, by an agreement with those who employ them, stipulate for remuneration for their services. But in no case can these offerings or this remuneration be converted into permanent property.

Art. 5. All religious orders, whatever their name or their object, are suppressed throughout the whole republic, as well as confraternities or associations connected with a religious community or any church whatsoever.

The 6th article, whilst it prohibits the erection of new convents and new confraternities, forbids also the use of the religious habit.

THE EIGHTEENTH CENTENARY OF THE MARTYRDOM OF SS. PETER AND PAUL.

A new joy awaited the Holy Father. The year 1867 will be ever memorable in sacred annals, as the year of the great centennial celebration of the glorious martyrdom of SS. Peter and Paul. "Peter went to Rome," St. Jerome writes, "in the second year of the Emperor Claudius, and occupied there the priestly chair for twenty-five years." On the same venerable authority it is known that Peter suffered two years after the death of the great Roman philosopher, Seneca, who was executed by order of Nero in the sixty-fifth year of the Christian era. In the same work (*de viris illustribus*), St. Jerome says that SS. Peter and Paul were put to death in the fourteenth year of Nero's reign, which corresponds with the sixty-seventh year of our era, when reckoned from the first of January, and not from the 13th October, the date of Nero's accession.

The French troops had scarcely been withdrawn from Rome in fulfilment of the September agreement, when Pius IX. invited all the clergy and people of the Catholic world to visit the city in order to participate in the celebration of the centenary, and witness the canonization of several holy persons long since deceased. Their names were Josaphat, the martyr Archbishop of Solotsk; Pedro de Arbues, an Augustinian friar; the martyrs of Gorcum; Paul of the Cross, founder of the Passionists; Leonardo di Porto Maurizio; Maria Francesca, a Neapolitan of the third order of St. Peter of Alcantara, and Germaine Cousin, of the diocese of Toulouse. Shortly before, in the preceding December, the Holy Father enjoyed the great happiness of celebrating, with even more than ordinary solemnity, the beatification of the Franciscan Monk, Benedict of Urbino, who died in odor of sanctity, at Fossombrone, in 1625, within a few miles of Sinigaglia, the birthplace of the Pope, leaving the whole country bordering on the Adriatic and the province of Umbria in a manner embalmed by a life of sanctity and extraordinary self-denial. Pius IX., from early youth, was familiar with the history of this saint, whose noble birth and distinguished abilities opened to him the way to worldly fame and prosperity, but who, nevertheless, chose the cross, becoming a Capuchin, and having no other ambition in the seclusion of the cloister than to be a worthy disciple of his crucified Saviour.

It was by no means to indulge his own pious feelings, or to gratify the clergy and Catholic people, that the venerable Pontiff invited so many from Italy and all parts of the Christian world to take part with him in celebrating these canonizations, and, at the same time, the eighteen hundredth anniversary of the martyrdom of the blessed Apostles, the founders of the Church. His object was to edify, to place in contrast with, and in opposition to, the worldly and unbelieving spirit of the time the teachings and the solemn offices of religion, together with the power of holiness, so admirably shown forth in the lives and glory of the saints. The revolution aimed at nothing less than the destruction of everything spiritual. It was good for it to be taught that true spirituality is beyond its reach.

It would hardly be fair to contrast as purely worldly the grand exposition at Paris, the World's Fair, with the religious celebrations at Rome. The rich and varied display of the objects of art and industry, in the beautiful capital of France, was the result of an advanced Christian civilization. It was recognized as such by the greatest statesmen, the ablest men of science, and the wisest rulers of the age. No doubt it savored more of the world and of things worldly than the festivals at Rome. But the holy city bore it no grudge. It was other powers and other arts than those which furnished out so grandly the Parisian exposition against which Rome waged perpetual war. A Roman, let it not be forgotten, and not the least pious among the Romans, the illustrious scientist, Father Secchi, whose recent decease the world laments, took the highest honors at the great industrial and artistic fair.

Paris, indeed, was in contrast with Rome, but more by its materialist philosophy than by its magnificent exhibition of material improvements. This philosophy availed itself of the exposition in order to show to what extent it prevailed; and Paris extolled mere worldly power, luxury, comfort and voluptuousness, whilst Rome had no praise but for humility, poverty, self-denial, chastity. Paris applauded Alexander II., who massacred the Poles; Rome, on the other hand, did honor to a Polish bishop, Joseph Kunicieviez, who was cruelly murdered by Russian fanaticism. Paris celebrated the apotheosis of free-thinking and religious indifference; Rome, on the contrary, heaped honors on an Inquisitor, Peter d'Arbues, who suffered martyrdom. Paris was loud in her acclamations to the potentates and conquerors of the day, whilst Rome exalted an humble shepherdess, Germaine Cousin, and some poor and obscure monks who were hanged by heretics three hundred years ago, in a small town of Holland. Yet was not Paris distinguished only by material glories, nor was Rome altogether free from the taint of modern worldliness. There were those in the latter city who, in the midst of an atmosphere of pious thought, plotted deeds of diabolic wickedness, whilst Paris, which honored the arts, was not without sympathy at Rome, and her prelates, the bishops of France, were far from being the least among those five hundred high dignitaries, twenty thousand priests of God's Church, and more than one hundred and fifty thousand Christian people from all quarters of the known world, who took part in celebrating the glorious centenary and the no less glorious victory of more than two hundred martyrs. The display of art, industry and modern improvements of every kind presented, indeed, in the midst of the beautiful

French capital, a magnificent and cheering sight. It was nothing, however, to the moral spectacle afforded by the presence of ten or twelve mighty sovereigns around the now Imperial author of the *coup d'etat*. It was supremely worldly. Who would then have said that William of Prussia, and Napoleon III., the Czar of Russia, and the successor of the caliphs, who, at the exhibition *fetes*, joined hands in apparent friendship, were so soon to be engaged in deadly strife? and that that capital, where so many great potentates came to honor Napoleon, should, in a year or two, know him no more, and even struggle with all the energy of desperation to obliterate every vestige of the improvements with which he had so enriched and beautified the city? This was the world; for the world is insincere. This was the world; for the figure thereof passeth quickly away.

In Rome it was not so. There art and religion walked hand in hand. Religion fostered art. Art was dutiful, and repaid the boon. It became the handmaid of religion. Everywhere within the walls of her temples were seen the products of art's filial labor, in sculpture, painting, poetry and music, her inexhaustible treasury of thought and history ever presenting new sources of artistic power to the hand of genius. Those temples themselves being, indeed, the finest monuments of architecture, bear glorious witness to the excellent union of art and religion. Worldliness, on the other hand, when at the height of its passion against religion, seeks to destroy all the creations of art and genius. It aims at nothing less than to reduce mankind to the condition of the savage, and is not ashamed to acknowledge that such is its aim.

Let us hear the testimony of the Roman artists. This body, on the one hand, rejoiced in the coming celebration of the centenary; on the other, they were filled with sad forebodings as to the approaching downfall of the Papal sovereignty by the threats of Garibaldi and the predictions of Mazzini. They resolved, therefore, whilst yet the Pope, who, like his predecessors, had shown them much kindness, and munificiently rewarded their labors, reigned at Rome, to present to him a dutiful and affectionate address, which should remain, in time to come, as a testimony of their gratitude to that beneficent sovereignty which they had but too much reason to fear would soon come to an end. This address is so important and tells so much truth, that it is deserving of a place in all histories. It is as follows: "Most Holy Father, religion, policy and mere human wisdom have protested in favor of the temporal power of the Papacy. The arts come, in their turn, to lay their homage at the feet of your Holiness, and to proclaim to the world that this power is to them indispensable. Their voice must be heard and listened to. For when the tide of generations recedes, the arts remain as the irrefutable witnesses of the power and splendor of the civilization amid which these generations lived. The sovereigns who encourage and develop them acquire immortal renown; those who neglect or oppress them meet only with the contempt of posterity. What royal dynasty has in this respect deserved so well of civilization and humanity as that of the Sovereign Pontiffs? They have been the watchful guardians of the master-pieces bequeathed to us by antiquity. They have given these a home in their own palaces to show that religion adopts and ennobles all that is truly beautiful. It is the Sovereign Pontiffs who, by opening new avenues for modern art, have brought it to the point of perfection, embodied in the master-pieces of Raphael and Michael Angelo. They alone support in Rome that unique assemblage of all that is beautiful in every order, that splendid intellectual galaxy in whose light the artists of every land are formed. Holy Father, the little spot of earth which the revolution has not yet taken from you is the only place in which the arts find the inspiration that is for them the breath of life, and the quiet without which that life cannot expand. The soul of the true artist is filled with unspeakable apprehension by the possibility of seeing these master-pieces destroyed or scattered abroad, these treasures plundered, all this wealth annihilated; and especially by the danger of seeing the ungraceful and

meagre forms of modern utilitarianism usurp the place held by
the manners, the habits, the face of all things in this privileged
land of beauty, all consecrated by the admiration of ages.
Alas! Holy Father, what is happening in the rest of Italy
affords but too firm a ground for such apprehensions. The
genius of destruction is abroad there, and proceeds to sweep
away pitilessly what was the glory of ancient Italy. The
spoliation and suppression of the religious orders are one of
the most deadly blows ever aimed at the existence of the fine
arts. Saddened by those forebodings, fearful of what the
future may bring forth, the artists resident in Rome come to
the feet of your Holiness to give utterance to their deep conviction that the splendor, the greatness, the very existence of
the fine arts in Europe are inseparably connected with the
maintenance of the beneficent power of the Sovereign Pontiffs.
Were it not that the rival passions which divide Europe are
of themselves fatally blind to consequences, the reign of your
Holiness would suffice to render this truth evident to all. For
while elsewhere national wealth is wasted in frivolous undertakings, or in preparing instruments of destruction, the modest
revenues inherited by your Holiness are ever employed in continuing gloriously the noble labor of your predecessors. On
the one hand, you have drawn from obscurity the beginnings
of Christian art, thereby affording it new and precious data;
on the other, you have adorned Rome and the Vatican with
works which furnish a new and brilliant page to the grand
history of art embodied in the Vatican itself. While elsewhere
reigned trouble and agitation, here artists were able, beneath
the blessed sway of your Holiness, to enjoy a kindly welcome,
an unrestrained liberty, and the peaceful contemplation of
those venerable structures and sites preserved so happily by
the Pontifical government from the sad alterations blindly
wrought in other cities by the troublous life of modern communities. May the Almighty One hear our prayer, and persuade
both sovereigns and nations that their honor and glory will be
measured, in coming ages, on the degree of protection they

shall have afforded to the temporal power of the Papacy, which
has ever been the unwearied promoter of the development of
all the noblest faculties in man, and which alone can continue
to be the custodian of the works of art originated by itself,
and by it so faithfully treasured for the benefit of all peoples!"
This eloquent address will ever remain carefully guarded by
history, a noble monument of gratitude, and not only this, but
also as a testimony, all the more valuable as it is the spontaneous utterance of men of the most cultivated intellect, in
favor of that sovereignty the destruction of which was sought,
and has been accomplished, by a party in whose ranks could
be counted only rude soldiers, bands of filibusters and politicians, if such they could be called, whose counsels were inspired,
not by the wisdom which distinguishes statesmen, but by blind
passion, and the most unworthy of all passions, the passion of
hatred—hatred of everything connected with the Christian
faith.

The great centennial celebration proceeded. Who would
have dared to say, whilst Nero reigned at Rome, and Christians were as pariahs, tolerated only in order to afford the
spectacle of their tortures to a heathen multitude, that eighteen
hundred years from Nero's time, Christianity would flourish
and celebrate in that city, which was the scene of its greatest
trials, as well as all over the world, its victory and the glorious
martyrdom of its apostolic founders! The month of June,
1867, will ever be memorable in the annals of the church.
Never had so many bishops assembled in the holy city. Nor
were there ever there, at one time, so many priests and pilgrims
of all ranks and classes. The duties of the time were commenced early in the month. On the 11th and 12th of June,
consistories were held in presence of the bishops, in order to
make preparation for the canonization of two hundred and five
Japanese Christians—priests, catechists, laymen, women and
children—put to death in hatred of the Christian faith, from
1617 to 1632. On the 26th of February, 1867, the decree of
canonization had already been solemnly read in presence of

Pius IX., who, on the occasion, went in state to the Roman College. On the 22nd February of the same year, the Holy Father signed decrees bearing on the beatification of several holy persons, among whom was Clement Maria Hofbauer, a Redemptorist. In an age of unbelief, it was only to be expected that the enquiry should be made why the Pope made so many saints?

In February, 1867, his Holiness replied, on occasion of a visit to the Convent of the Capuchin Friars: "I have been shown," said he, "a pamphlet, entitled 'Why so many Saints? Had we ever so much need of intercessors in heaven and patterns in this world?" A little later he also said, alluding to the festivals at Paris : "Man has not been placed on the earth solely in order to amass wealth; still less in order to lead a life of pleasure. The world is ignorant of this. It forgets mind, and devotes itself to matter. Neither you nor I are this world of which I speak. You are come here in the good disposition to seek the edification of your souls. I hope, therefore, that you will bear away with you a salutary impression. Never forget, my children, that you have a soul, a soul created in the image of God, and which God will judge. Bestow on it more thought and care than on industrial speculations, railways, and all those lesser objects which constitute the good things of this world. I forbid you not to interest yourselves in such transient matters. Do so reasonably and moderately. But let me once more beg of you to remember that you have a soul."

None of the ten or twelve potentates who visited Paris came to Rome. But their absence was amply made up for by the immense concourse of clergy and people from every quarter of the civilized world. The reverence shown to Pius IX. by so many prelates was truly admirable. A Chinese bishop, Mgr. Languillat, Vicar-apostolic of Nankin, coming for the first time into the presence of the Supreme Pastor, fell prostrate on the threshold, and with his arms extended towards the Pontiff, began to exclaim: "*Tu es Petrus!*" ("Thou art Peter!")

"Come to me, my brother," said the Holy Father. "*Tu es Petrus!*" replied the Chinese bishop, "*Tu es Petrus!*" Needless to say that when he approached the venerable Pontiff affectionately embraced him, whilst both gave vent to their feelings in tears. The laity of all ranks and classes were no less devoted. A very moving scene which was witnessed this same year (1867) is beautifully described by the Protestant correspondent of the London *Morning Post:* "It is truly delightful to meet Pius IX. in the country on foot, walking faster than one would suppose his age could allow, his majestic person arrayed in a white soutane, and protected by a large broad-brimmed purple hat. The other day, when I was at Aricia, he was proceeding towards Genzano, followed by his guards and his carriage. The ex-Queen of Naples and the Infanta, lately Regent, were walking in the opposite direction, followed by their equipages and domestics. At a turn of the road, exactly below the Villa Chigi, the two groups met. In a moment their Royal Majesties were on their knees. His Holiness quickened his pace in order to raise them up. The peasants of the neighborhood, who were returning from their vineyards and orchards, together with their wives and daughters, were struck with admiration. They also advanced and knelt on each side of the central group formed by the illustrious personages, calling out with all their might: ' *Santo Padre, la benedizione.*' 'Holy Father, your benediction!' It was a splendid tableau."

On occasion of the centennial, substantial proofs of devotedness abounded. The numerous pilgrims not only gave the homage of their faith, but also brought magnificent offerings, as Peter's pence, and presented addresses with millions of signatures. One day fifteen hundred Italians were received at an audience of the Holy Father, and made the offering of a monumental album, together with one hundred purses filled with gold, as the homage of one hundred Italian cities. Cardinal Manning laid at the feet of Pius IX. £30,000—a generous testimony of English piety. The Cardinal Archbishop of Mechlin brought to the centenary celebration £16;000, the Archbishop of Posen £20,000, and the Mexican archbishop £12,000, whilst Cuba offered 100,000 douros. "We are reversing the order of nature," smilingly observed the Holy Father; "here are the children supporting the Father." Nor was it too much for the wants of such a Father. He received with one hand and generously dispensed with the other. He took charge himself to lodge and entertain eighty-five of the poorer bishops from Italy, the East, and remote missions. None of these were allowed to depart without receiving abundant aid for their diocesan good works.

Festival followed festival at Rome, from the 20th June till the 7th of July. On the former day was celebrated the grand solemnity of Corpus Christi. The Pope himself bore the holy sacrament, kneeling and surrounded by the greater half of the whole Christian episcopate. It was remarked that he was as calm and collected in the midst of such a great and imposing multitude as if he had been in his private oratory. The vast assemblage was also rapt in silent contemplation. Not a sound was heard save the murmur of the fountains. An eye-witness has observed that if one closed his eyes he could imagine himself in a desert. Next day was celebrated the 21st anniversary of the coronation of Pius IX. He had already said, in reply to an address read by Cardinal Patrizi, when all the visitors to Rome were assembled on occasion of the commemoration of his election—16th June—"Modern society is ardent in the pursuit of two things, progress, and unity. It fails to reach either, because its motive principles are selfishness and pride. Pride is the worst enemy of progress, and selfishness, by destroying charity, the bond of souls, thereby rendering union impossible. Now God Himself has established the Sovereign Pontiff in order to direct and enlighten society, to point out evil and indicate the proper remedy. This induced me, some years ago, to publish the 'Syllabus.' I now confirm that solemn act in your presence. It is to be, henceforth, the rule of your teaching. We have to contend, unceasingly, with the enemies who beset us. Placed on the mountain-top like Moses, I lift up my hands to God in prayer for the triumph of the church. I ask of you, my brother bishops, to support my arms, for they grow weary. Take courage! The church must triumph. I leave this hope in your hearts, not as a hope merely, but as a prophecy."

On the 23rd was consecrated the Church of St. Mary of the Angels, an admirable architectural monument, built originally according to the plans of Michael Angelo, and rebuilt by Pius IX. The 24th, on leaving the Basilica of St. John Lateran, the Pope was the object of a more splendid ovation than any, perhaps, that he had as yet received. Kneeling on the vast place, and completely filling it, the multitude which had not been able to enter the Basilica waited for the Pontifical benediction. After the Holy Father had raised his hand and pronounced the words of blessing, the whole people rose, and, by a simultaneous movement and with one voice, replied: "Live Pius IX.! Live the Pope-King!" Arms and handkerchiefs waved amidst a rain of beautiful flowers. The Pope's carriage was detained a considerable time, and he himself, accustomed as he was to the demonstrations of a devoted people, was moved to tears. His hood was almost taken to pieces, thread by thread, by French ecclesiastics who were close behind his Holiness, and who deposited the fragments, as precious relics, in their breviaries. The crowd thronged around the Holy Father and continued their acclamations as far as the Vatican, a distance of three miles. Every new day gave proof of a like enthusiasm.

Pius IX. was anxious to address words of encouragement to the twenty thousand priests of the church who had come to Rome. The greatness of their number was a serious hindrance to this laudable purpose. The spacious consistorial hall was by far too small to contain so many. On the 25th of June, however, they came to the hall, crowding its approaches, the passages, the great staircase and the outer court. The Holy Father, desiring to show his respect and affection for so many pilgrims of the sacred order of the priesthood, came to the assembly in more than usual state. The throne was raised a few steps, in order to afford an opportunity of seeing and hearing the Supreme Pastor. The Pontiff was preceded by the noble guard and the household prelates. As he entered the hall, loud and joyous acclamations burst from the assembled priesthood, for whom it was impossible to restrain their feelings of love and veneration. The Holy Father himself was deeply moved, and, gathering enthusiasm from the unusual scene around him, spoke so as to be heard even in the remotest corridors, whilst those at a still greater distance were visibly moved by the thrilling tones of his sonorous voice. There are no readers who will not be interested in the words which fell from the lips of the Sovereign Pontiff on this unique and solemn occasion. He began by thanking the assembled clergy for their attendance in such imposing numbers. They were the tribe in Israel, he continued, whose special inheritance was the Lord. They stood between him and his people evermore, offering with prayer and supplication the spotless victim of the new law. Let them look well to the ministry entrusted to them, shining in the presence of all men by the dignity of their bearing, the innocence of their life, by integrity and charity, and the golden ornaments of every virtue. "You," he said, "who are the interpreters of the word of God, you must preach it unweariedly to the wise and the unwise. Preach to them Christ and Him crucified, not in loftiness of speech, but in the knowledge of the spirit, never ceasing to call into the right road all who stray, and confirm them in sound doctrine. Dispensers of the divine mysteries and of the manifold grace of God, deal it out to the faithful people, to the sick especially, in order that no help may fail them in their last struggle with the evil one. Do not refuse to the little ones of the flock the milk which they need. Let it be your dearest care to teach them, to train them, to form them. Be the faithful and devoted helpmates of your respective bishops; obeying them in all things, zealous to heal in your parishes whatever is ailing, to bind up what is broken, to raise up what is fallen, to

U

seek what is lost, in order that in all things God may be honored through our Lord Jesus Christ. Lift up your souls and contemplate the immeasurable height of glory prepared by him for all true and faithful laborers."

On the 26th a great public consistory was held. The five hundred bishops then at Rome were invited to attend. So great a number had never before assembled in Italy or any part of Western Christendom. Nor indeed was there ever, or could there ever have been, so great an occasion for their assembling. There was question of celebrating the eighteen hundredth anniversary of the glorious martyrdom of Rome's first great bishop, so many prelates had come together, also, in order to venerate Peter in the person of his venerable successor, who had now so long and so gloriously borne witness to the Truth—the Truth in its plenitude, as first committed to Peter and his fellow-apostles. The world was no longer heathen, and no Nero reigned, but the spirit of unbelief was abroad, and its champions were even then seeking to drive the Sovereign Pontiff from the holy city, and were waging war with 'as determined wickedness as that of the early persecutors against whom the apostles had so successfully contended.

The number of pilgrims from all parts of the Christian world, who had come to Rome on occasion of the centennial celebration, is said by some writers to have been not less than half a million. The presence of so great a number of devoted Christian people on such an occasion was the noblest protest that could be imagined against the vain boasts and prophecies of the enemies of the Church which Peter founded. That church was not yet forsaken, or destined soon to perish, which, in the nineteenth century of her uninterrupted existence, could speak through so many witnesses—the representatives of every civilized nation of the world.

The great consistorial hall in the Vatican Palace being too small to contain so great a crowd of dignified listeners, the assembly was held in the more spacious room which is situated above the vestibule of St. Peter's Church. At the opening of the consistory the cardinal's hat was conferred on the Arch-bishop of Seville, Luis de la Lastray Cuesta. A formal peti-tion for the beatification of Marie Rivier, the foundress of the presentation Nuns of France, was then presented. After this ceremony, the Holy Father, as was expected, delivered an allo-cution to the bishops. He was full of admiration for their zeal in coming in such numbers on his invitation, and he could not do less than express to them his gratitude. Their presence was a striking proof of the unity of the Catholic Church. "Yes, everything here proclaims that admirable unity by which, as through a mysterious channel, all the gifts and graces of the Holy Spirit flow into the mystic body of Christ, calling forth in every one of its members those acts of faith and charity which excite the wonder of all mankind. What has brought you here? Are you not come to decree the honors of sanctity to those heroes of the church, the greater number of whom bore away the palm of victory in their glorious witness for Christ? Of these some died in defending the primacy of this apostolic see, which is the centre of truth and unity; others gave their lives in defence of the unity and integrity of the faith; others again shed their blood in the endeavor to bring back schismatics to the one fold. Is it not providential that such heroism should be commemorated and honored at the very moment when the Catholic faith and the authority of the Holy See are the objects of such furious and implacable conspiracies? We are also here to celebrate with solemn rites the memory of that auspicious day, eighteen hundred years ago, when Peter and Paul consecrated by their heroic witnessing and their precious blood this impregnable stronghold of Catho-lic unity. What can be more reasonable than that our joyous commemoration of this triumphant death of the prince of the apostles should be graced by your presence? For he belongs to the entire Catholic world. It is also most important that the enemies of religion should conclude from what they witness here how mighty is the energy, how unfailing the life, of that Catholic Church which they so bitterly hate; how little wisdom they display in matching their strength and their temporary triumphs over her against that incomparable union of living forces which the creative power of Christ has bound around this central rock. More than ever is it needful in our age, that all men should see and understand that the only strong and lasting tie between men's souls depends on the reign over all of the same Spirit of God. Besides, what can make a more abiding impression on Catholic nations ; what can draw them more powerfully and bind them more closely in obedience to this apostolic chair and to us, than to see how much their pastors cherish the rights and duties of Catholic unity, than to behold them journeying from the farthest lands, notwithstanding every inconvenience and impediment, in order to visit Rome and the apostolic chair, as well as to revere in our humble person the successor of Peter and the Vicar of Christ ? We have been always convinced, from the moment we beheld you approaching Peter in the person of his successor, or even entering this city, which is impregnated with his blood, that from thence to each one of you should go forth a special virtue. Yes, from this tomb, where Peter's ashes repose amid the veneration of the Christian world, a hidden power, a salutary energy, emanates which instils into the souls of the Chief Pastors the desire of great undertakings and of vast designs, inspiring that fearlessness and magnanimity which enable them to put down the impudent boldness of their assailants. There cannot be offered to the eyes of men and angels a more magnificent spectacle than what one beholds in such a concourse of pilgrims as this. You who come from the ends of the earth to this home of your Father remind us not only of that pilgrimage which leads us all to the eternal home, you also call to mind the journey of the chosen people from Ægypt to the promised land, the twelve tribes marching together, each under its chief, bearing its own name, having its own appropriate place in the camp. Every family there was obedient to its parents, every company of warriors hearkened to the voice of its captain, and the entire multitude to the divinely-appointed leader. All these tribes, nevertheless, were but one people, adoring the same God, worshipping at the same altar, obeying the same laws, having one Pontiff, Aaron, and one leader, Moses—one people, enjoying common rights in the perils and labors of warfare as well as in'the results of victory, dwelling in the same tents, and fed by the same miraculous bread, whilst all yearned for the same end of their pilgrimage. Nothing is to us the subject of such ardent longing as to see both ourselves and the whole church deriving from this precious union the most salutary blessings. It has long been a serious matter of thought for us, and which, indeed, we communicated to several of the episcopal body, to hold an Œcumenical Council, in which, with the Divine assistance, our united counsels and solicitude should devise such efficient remedies as are necessary for the evils that afflict the church."

Pius IX. had for a long time entertained the idea of holding an Œcumenical Council. And no doubt his mind found relief when he communicated his purpose to the assembled bishops. Two years later, as is well known, the proposed council was convened at the Vatican, and from this circumstance is known in history as the Vatican Council. Bishops, priests and laity heard the intimation with delight. Their fervor and enthusiasm increased as the day of the grand centennial celebration approached. The vigil, 28th June, was enlivened by illuminations. By early dawn on the 29th, the feast of SS. Peter and Paul, people poured into Rome from the surrounding territory. They were welcome visitors. The Romans, far from being jealous of so great a concourse of strangers, hailed them as brothers, engaged, as they also were, in the great object of doing honor to the memory of Rome's apostles. The first grand public ceremony of the day was the solemn canonization, of which no description need be given in this place, as everything was conducted in the same way as in 1852 and 1868. The Holy Father himself then celebrated High Mass, and, what is still more noteworthy, delivered the sermon of the day.

Until the time of Pius IX., no Pope had preached in public since the epoch of the Crusades and the Pontificate of Gregory VII. The Holy Father set an example to all who preach on great and solemn public occasions. His sermon was short, but replete with instruction, and marked by that earnestness which commands attention and moves the soul. The music, as was fitting at so great a celebration, was given by three choirs, in all four hundred voices, which completely filled the immense Basilica, conveying, by the exquisite music which they gave forth, an idea of that more than earthly harmony which ever ascends to the throne of heaven from the angelic choirs. There was also a solemn service in the afternoon, which was alike highly interesting and calculated to inspire devotion. The general illumination which took place at night rivalled the splendor of the bright Italian day. On June 30th was celebrated the special feast of St. Paul in the fine church dedicated to this great apostle, and with scarcely less magnificence than that of St. Peter had been honored.

The bishops now desired, before leaving Rome, to present an address to the Holy Father, as well in reply to his allocution of 26th June as to express their gratitude for the great kindness which he had shown them. The 1st July was the day chosen for the presentation of this address. It is a model of elegant Latinity, and completely refutes the modern assertion that churchmen are unacquainted with the Latin of the classics. The reply of the assembled bishops to the fatherly allocution of Pius IX. affords, moreover, an admirable proof of the sympathy of the united episcopate with the Supreme Bishop. It shows the excellent union of the bishops with one another, and their no less perfect union with their Head. What more could there have been in the brightest days of the church's history?

The French garrison had departed before the commencement of the memorable celebrations that have been just described. Although the population of Rome was literally doubled by the presence of pious strangers, not the slightest breach of order was ever observed. The exercise of filial duty required not to be watched over by any outside power. It was now seven months since Napoleon III. had withdrawn his troops.

Revolutionary aggression.—Treachery of the Italian Government.

On the 6th December, 1866, Pius IX. had taken leave of them in the following words :

" Your flag, which left France eighteen years ago with commission to defend the rights of the Holy See, was at that time attended by the prayers and acclamations of all Christendom. To-day it returns to France. I desire, my dear children, that it may be welcomed by the same acclamations. But I doubt it. It is only too manifest, indeed, that because it will appear to have ceased to protect me my enemies will not on that account cease to attack me. Quite the contrary. We must not delude ourselves. The revolution will come here. It has declared and still declares that it will. An Italian personage in high position lately said that Italy is made but not completed. Italy would be undone if there were here one spot of earth where order, justice and tranquillity prevail ! Formerly, six years ago, I conversed with a representative of France. He asked me if there were anything I wished to transmit to the Emperor. I replied: St. Augustine, Bishop of Hippo, which is now a French city, beholding the barbarians at the gates of the town, prayed the Lord that he might die before they entered, because his mind was horror-struck by the thought of the evils which they would cause. I added : Say this to the Emperor: he will understand it. The ambassador made answer: Most Holy Father, have confidence; the barbarians will not enter. The ambassador was no prophet. Depart, my children, depart with my blessing and my love. If you see the Emperor, tell him that I pray for him every day. It is said that his health is not very good; I pray that he may have health. It is said that his mind is not at ease. I pray for his soul. The French nation is Christian; its Chief ought also to be Christian. Let there be prayer with confidence and perseverance, and this great and powerful nation may obtain what it desires. Depart, my children; I impart to you my benediction, and with it my wish that it may attend you throughout the journey of life. Think not that you leave me here alone and deprived of all resource. God remains with me; in Him I place my trust!"

Pius IX.. in a more private communication, said : " Yes, God sustains His vicar and aids his weakness. He may permit him to be driven away, but only in order to show, once more, that he can bring him back. I have been exiled; I returned from exile. If banished anew, I will again return. And if I die—well! if I die, Peter will rise again!"

Thus did Pius IX. clearly foresee the danger but was not on that account less confident. Nor did his confidence lessen his foresight. What, indeed, he said publicly, " The revolution will come here," everyone capable of reasoning said in secret. The September convention left the small Pontifical sovereignty surrounded on all sides by its enemies, just as the government of Napoleon III. would have been if isolated in Paris and the two neighboring departments, all the rest of the French territory being in the power of a republic, or a Bourbon Monarchy. In vain did M. Rouher endeavor to demonstrate to the Chambers that a stable equilibrium was established, and which was of such a character as to remain by itself for an indefinite period. Nobody was convinced by his reasoning. But the Imperial majorities, recruited as they were by the system of official candidatures, asked not of the complaisant minister reasons which he had not to give. They sought only pretexts which should allow them to vote, with a show of decency, according to the wishes of the master.

The Holy Father was destined to enjoy a period of success before his prophecy came to be fulfilled. Immediately after the disastrous but glorious events of 1860, the courageous Belgian, Mgr. de Merode, as Minister of War, and afterwards General Kanzler, in this same capacity, greatly renewed the small Pontifical army. As their labors deserved, they were attended with success. Lamoriciere died towards the end of 1865; but on the new alarm of danger, many of his veterans of Castelfidardo and Ancona, returned to Rome in 1866. The flower of the French, Dutch, Belgian, English, Swiss and Roman youth made it a point of honor to swell the ranks of the Papal Zouaves. The high tone, the illustrious names of several of these new crusaders, and the admirable discipline which prevailed among them all, soon won for them the respect even of the few revolutionists who were at Rome. These brave and self-sacrificing youths, many of whom served at their own cost, were addressed as " Signor Soldato " (Signor Soldier) by the passers-by, whilst the venal scribes of the outside revolutionary press did their best to stigmatize them as " the mercenaries of the Pope." Whilst some of these warriors devoted their life, others bestowed their gold. It is honorable to the Catholic people that, in the circumstances, they added the good work of supporting the Pontifical army to their collections of Peter's pence. In order to furnish the sum of 500 francs (£20 sterling) yearly, which was required for each soldier, artisans and even domestic servants freely subscribed. In 1867, the Catholics of the diocese of Cambrai, sent two hundred Zouaves; those of Rodez and Arras, one hundred for each diocese ; whilst Cologne, Nantes, Rennes and Toulouse did almost as much.

Meanwhile, having its eyes somewhat opened by the light from Sadowa, the French government appeared to have abandoned, as regarded the protection of the Holy See, its secret maxim of 1860 : " Neither do anything nor allow anything to be done." In withdrawing from Rome, it had authorized the creation, under a chief whom it was pleased itself to designate, a body of volunteers, selected chiefly from the French army, whose duty it should be to guard the Pope. This corps was called the Legion of Antibes, from the name of the city where it was formed. Pius IX., besides, could rely on the fidelity of the Roman army, properly so called. Thus was he more than sufficiently provided against any possible internal disturbance. It was not to be expected that he should be prepared to meet a formidable foreign invasion of his state.

The notorious Garibaldi had already made preparations for invading the Roman territory. Whilst he neglected not to strengthen the *International* at the Geneva Congress of Demagogues, the indefatigable brigand availed himself of the crowding of pilgrims to Rome in order to deceive the Pontifical police, and to introduce into the city bands of cutthroats, munitions of war, and arms of every kind, not excepting Orsini bombs. After the departure of the bishops, he opened publicly, in Italy, subscription lists, and enrolled soldiers. The Piedmontese government stores were at his service as they were in 1860, in order to aid him in clothing and arming his volunteers. These were joined by numerous functionaries and officers of the regular army, who took no pains to conceal their Piedmontese arms and uniforms. Municipalities, at public deliberative meetings, voted subsidies to the Garibaldians, and railway managers provided them with special trains. Whilst so many things that clearly showed the complicity of Piedmont were done, Victor Emmanuel sent protestation after protestation to Paris. He did not, by any means, intend, he said, to disembarrass himself of the obligations which were imposed on him by the first article of the convention of the 15th September, 1865. It might be relied upon, besides, that he would check the agitators and repress by force, even, if necessary, all violation of the Pontifical frontier. Nor did the wily monarch confine himself to words. He acted as he could act so well. Garibaldi was sent to his island, Caprera; but only in order to escape from it at the opportune moment, through the seven vessels by which he was guarded. An order for his arrest was then issued. Active search was made for him at Genoa, at Turin, everywhere except at Florence, where he harangued the people in the most public places, even under the windows of the King's palace. Later, when it was undertaken to arrest him at Florence, it so happened that he had started by a special train for the Roman frontier, together with a complete staff. The telegraph was put in requisition in order to turn back the train. But, possibly through the fault of a disobedient employee, the telegraph failed to accomplish its purpose. The Italian government neglected not to hold an investigation in regard to this matter, and swore that the guilty party, if found out, would be punished. What more could be desired? Was not France satisfied with much less than this in 1860? Whilst diplomacy was thus playing its *role*, Garibaldi and his myrmidons were penetrating on all sides at once the Pontifical territory. Twenty-seven gensd'armes, who guarded the small town of Aquapendente, were surprised by two hundred and fifty Garibaldians, who, on being re-inforced by another band, marched thence on Ischia, Valentano and Canino, pillaging the public chests, sacking the convents and churches, prudently retiring as often as they met Pontifical forces in any considerable numbers. Eighty-five Zouaves, or soldiers of the line, having rashly pursued them at Bagnorea, and [attacked them with the bayonet, were repulsed with loss. It could not well have been otherwise, considering the great disparity of numbers. Garibaldi shouted victory, in his usual emphatic style : "Hail to the victors of Aquapendente and Bagnorea! The foreign mercenaries have fled before the valiant champions of Italian liberty. Those braggarts who thirsted for blood have experienced the noble generosity of their brave conquerors. As to you, priests, who know so well how to burn, torture and imprison; you who drink, with hyena-like delight, in the cup of your deceit, the blood of the liberators; we pardon you, and, together with you, that butcher soldiery, the pestilent scum of a faithless faction."

The conquerors, however, were driven from their easy conquests before they received this proclamation which spoke of mercy in terms that expressed it so poorly. Events which

Garibaldi invades the Papal States.

were a cruel satire on Garibaldi's words, and which he had not
foreseen, caused his bands to fall into the power of the Pontifical troops, so that it was they who sued for pardon and obtained it.   It can even be said that on this occasion the generosity of the soldiers of the Pope was excessive, for the
vanquished enemy had been guilty of many other crimes
besides that of rising in arms against the legitimate government.   They had pillaged the Cathedral of Bagnorea, broken
the tabernacle, stolen the sacred vessels, defiled the image of
the Madonna, pierced the crucifix with their bayonets, decapi-
tated the statues of the saints, and enacting an infernal parody,
shot an inoffensive man, in order that human blood might be
shed on the altar of sacrifice.

At Subiaco, the governor, who was a priest, fell, together
with the town, into the hands of the banditti.   They were
preparing to sack the place and put the governor to death,
when a Pontifical troop appeared.   The struggle was short.
The Garibaldian chief was slain, and the rest fled.   They who
guarded the prisoner threw themselves at his knees, imploring
mercy.   "Have pity on us, my Lord; do not give us up to the
Zouaves; they would kill us."   The governor made them go
into his oratory and closed the door.   Meanwhile the commandant of the Zouaves arrived, gave him the details of the
battle, and spoke of the prisoners he had taken.   "Everybody
makes prisoners," said the governor, smiling.   "I have some
also, although not, like you, a man of the sword."   "Where
are they?"   "Ah! they are mine and not yours.   Promise
that you will respect my absolute right of conqueror; if not, I
will not show them."   The commandant made the desired
promise, and the governor opened the door of his oratory and
made the Garibaldians come out.   These prisoners were greatly
amazed.   Having asked and obtained the governor's priestly
blessing, they freely recrossed the Italian frontier.

The action at Monte-Libretti, which took place on the 14th
October, was of a more serious character.   Eighty Zouaves
contended from half-past five in the evening till eight o'clock

against twelve hundred Garibaldians. Arthur Guillemin, their captain, and Urbain de Quelen, their second lieutenant, fell gloriously. When night came, the Zouaves being unable to fight any longer, and not venturing to establish themselves in the first houses which they had taken, whilst all the rest of the town still swarmed with the enemy, retired in good order, bearing away their dead, and also twelve prisoners. They returned next morning, in order to renew the attack, but found the place evacuated.

The violation of the Pontifical territory was now too flagrant to be denied any longer, and the more so, as the Cabinet of the Tuileries was not ignorant of anything that was taking place. It was, by a fortunate accident, represented at Rome by a diplomatist of a different school from that of Thouvenel and Lavalette. The ambassador, M. de Sartiges, was absent on leave, and was replaced by his first secretary, M. Arman. The latter understood his duty, and, at the risk of being importunate, ceased not to make known, every day, to France, the events which were so rapidly occurring. Thus did a comparatively humble secretary save the honor of his country. Compelled by the terms of the September convention to stay the invasion, the Government of Florence stationed a corps of forty thousand men, under the command of Cialdini, around the Pontifical frontier, and intimated to the Tuileries that it was for its protection. It soon became evident that it was in order to fall upon it, in the wake of Garibaldi, as they had fallen upon the Kingdom of Naples in 1860. Meanwhile, the invaders passed without any difficulty between the different posts, and when beaten and pursued by the Pontifical troops, they retired and reformed behind the ranks of the Piedmontese.

Hence the small body of Pontifical soldiers was easily overwhelmed, and the Garibaldian hordes, although beaten, were always advancing. Rome was filled with consternation. The cutthroats of the revolution spoke of applying gunpowder to

Murder of the Zouave music band.

public edifices. And indeed they set about fulfilling their threat by blowing up the Serratori barracks, which they had undermined, and which buried, one evening, in their ruins, the music band of the Zouaves, whilst they were engaged at a rehearsal. Fortunately the bandsmen were the only victims. The rest of the corps which remained to guard the city was at the moment patrolling at a distance from the barracks. The Garibaldians expected the explosion. They rushed into the streets and endeavored to avail themselves of the terror and confusion which generally prevailed in order to seize the military posts. They managed to assassinate, in the dark, a few soldiers and some gensd'armes ; but they succeeded not even in ringing the alarm-bell at the Capitol, which was intended to be their signal. Their principal leader, a Milanese, whose name was Cairoli, was killed with arms in his hands, together with some twenty of his followers, in a vineyard near the city ; and so failed the enterprise.

The French Cabinet ceased, at length, to persist in the face of the clearest evidence and against the unanimous voice of the national conscience. A small body of soldiers had been sent to the French port of Toulon. It received orders to embark for Civita Vecchia. Catholics were relieved from their anxiety. Meanwhile came new assurances from Florence. A counter-order was given, and the embarkation suspended. Victor Emmanuel and his minister, Ratazzi, thought they understood the secret meaning of this counter-order. They remembered the past, and the troops of Cialdini boldly crossed the Pontifical frontier.

French historians relate that, on receiving this news, all who had any concern for the honor of France believed that it had come to an end, and made up their minds, in sullen silence, to swallow the new disgrace. They who were indifferent, even, became indignant. People who met on the boulevards of Paris asked one another to what extremes those Italian mountebanks (farceurs) would bring them. The enemies of the Pope,

French army order-
ed to Rome.

who were equally hostile to the Emperor, rejoiced, but secretly.
The deputies either protested together with the Catholics, or
dared not show themselves; the ministers were silent.
Finally, the army took its departure from Toulon. It was time
that it should; and this appeared to be well understood.
There was great irresolution in coming to a decision. It was
no less promptly carried into effect. The French army disembarked at Civita Vecchia on the 29th October, under the
command of General de Failly.

Three days earlier, 26th October, the small town of Monte
Rotondo, five leagues from Rome, was attacked by Garibaldi in
person, attended by a band of five thousand four hundred
fighting men. Its garrison consisted of five hundred men of
the legion of Antibes. These few brave soldiers held their
ground for two days and repelled five attacks. They were
compelled at last to yield, having exhausted all their munitions
of war. They retired, but left Garibaldi so much weakened
and disorganized by his inglorious victory that he was unable
for several days to advance. Thus, for the moment, did the
legion of Antibes save Rome.

Monte Rotondo, it is almost superfluous to relate, experienced
the fate of Bagnorea. Nothing comparable
in point of atrocity had occurred since the
invasion of Italy by the barbarians. In
justice to Garibaldi, it must be said that he
rebuked publicly by an order of the day, dated 28th October,
the "shameful excess" of his fellow-adventurers, and proceeded
to expurgate their ranks. But he could not hinder them from
being what they were, a mob of miscreants that the secret
societies of the whole world had discharged on the Pontifical
State. He was not less astonished to meet with so poor a welcome on the part of the people whom it was supposed he came
to deliver. His chief lieutenant, Bertani, bears witness to this
state of things, in the *Riforma* of 18th November, 1867: "It
must be admitted," said this writer, "that the people of the
Roman States have no idea of an Italy one and free. We

*Character of Gari-
baldians—No sympa-
hy with them.*

have not been greeted or encouraged by a single cry of rejoicing; nor have we obtained either any spontaneous assistance, or even a word of consolation, from these brutified people."

General Kanzler, the pro-Minister of War, well understood that it was impossible to defend for any length of time the frontier against bands that were constantly recruited. Accordingly, he ordered all the isolated garrisons to concentrate at Rome. It was more important than anything else to preserve the Papal city from being surprised by the invaders. Garibaldi, when re-inforced, marched in advance of Monte Rotondo. Cialdini followed him at some distance, but without daring as yet openly to join the banditti. The French, however, were *en route*. Kanzler took his departure from Rome on 3rd November, at two o'clock in the morning, followed by 8,000 Pontifical troops and 2,000 French soldiers. "Come," said he, to M. Emilius Keller, Dr. O'Zannam, and some others who had just arrived from Paris, in order to organize the ambulance service of the Pontifical army, "come, and you will see a fine battle." The small army met the enemy at one o'clock in the afternoon, at a short distance from the town of Mentana, the ancient Nomentum from which the Nomentan way (*via Nomentana*) took its name. Garibaldi's command was from 10,000 to 12,000 strong. He placed his men in ambuscade, partly on small hills that were covered with wood, and partly scattered them, as fusileers, along the hedges. His left wing was commanded by Pianciani, who, some time later, was Mayor of Rome. Kanzler's force commenced firing. But what could it avail against an enemy that was invisible and in superior numbers? A veteran of Castelfidardo, Lieutenant-Colonel de Charette, the same who was destined afterwards to immortalize himself at Patay and at Mans, understood that nothing was to be gained by a fusillade. "Forward," he cried, "my Zouaves! charge with the bayonet; and, remember, the French army is looking on." The Zouaves reply: "Live Pius IX!" and spring forward with their leader. The Garibaldians are dislodged from the first hill—from the other hills, and would have

been utterly routed but for the formidable intrenchments presented by the Santucci vineyard, which was laid out in
gardens rising in storeys, one above the other, and intersected
by walls. Garibaldi was posted on the summit, in a villa,
whence he directed his fire without being exposed to personal
danger. His position was, indeed, strong. Charette's troop
was observed to waver. "Forward, Zouaves!" cried their
leader, "or I shall die without you!" As he spoke, his horse
was struck by a ball and fell dead. Meanwhile, the Zouaves
scaled the walls and the ravines, without heeding those who
fell. Garibaldi was disconcerted by this living tornado. He
fell back from his villa to the houses, and thence to the Castle
of Mentana. The Zouaves followed in the face of a murderous
fire, discharged from the walls of the castle; but they always.
advanced, and, finally, repelled, by a bayonet charge, a renewed and general attack of the enemy. Such efforts, however, could not have been sustained for any length of time
unaided, and bravery must, in the end, have given way to
numbers. General de Courten, who directed this attack, sent
to ask assistance from General Polhes, who commanded the
army of France. The French soldiers had been, hitherto,
inactive, although by no means unheeding spectators of the
combat. "Bravo! Zouaves, bravo!" cried they, eagerly
desiring to share in the fight. At a sign from their chief, they
sprang forward in their turn. At their head was Colonel
Saussier, of the 20th regiment of the line, who was afterwards
general and member of the National Assembly at Versailles.
The sudden and hitherto unknown fire of the chassepots carried death and terror within the precincts of the castle. Meanwhile, a detachment of Zouaves managed to place themselves
between Mentana and Monte Rotondo, and so intercepted the
reinforcements which were hastening from the latter place to
join the Garibaldians. At sight of this achievement, the bands,
already much demoralized, were thrown into confusion. Night
came, and, favoring their flight, changed it to a rout. Garibaldi himself, who had so often shouted, *"Rome or death"*—stole

away, under cover of the darkness, like the meanest of the
fugitives. His sons did in like manner. It was expected that
they would renew the battle next day, as Monte Rotondo, which
they still held, presented a convenient position for rallying.
They did nothing of the kind. On the very night which followed the engagement Garibaldi and his sons recrossed the
Italian frontier. "He always runs away" (*si salva sempre*),
said his followers, in the bitterness of their disappointment,
when so shamefully betrayed and abandoned. The French
soldiers, on the other hand, always inclined to raillery and
punning, baptized the action of the preceding day, calling it
the battle of *Montre ton dos*. The Garibaldians, who held the
castle, as well as the rest of the banditti who could not get
away in time, surrendered, unconditionally, to General Polhes.
There was but little bloodshed on the side of the victors, thanks
to the rapidity with which the victory was won. The losses
of the French troops were not more than two killed, two officers and thirty-six privates wounded. Of the Pontifical force ·
there were twenty killed and one hundred and twenty-three
wounded. Several of these died of their wounds.

Among those noble victims who claim the gratitude of the
Catholic world, were names already dear to
De Maistre—Muller.
the church—such as Bernard de Quatre-
barbe, a nephew of the defender of Ancona; Rodolph de Maistre,
grandson of the immortal author of "The Pope;" and John de
Muller, son of the celebrated German controversialist. As if
nothing that is glorious should be wanting to the field of Mentana, it had also its martyrs of charity. The Sisters of St.
Vincent de Paul went and came among the wounded and the
dying, giving their aid alike to all, no matter what their uniform. There was need of water. A Pontifical Zouave, Julius
Watts Russell, ran to find some for a Garibaldian who was at
the point of death. As he was gently raising the head of the
moribund, in order that he might drink, he was himself struck
with a ball and fell dead on the body of him whom he had
endeavored to succour. On his person was found a small note,

in which he thus exhorted himself: "My soul, O, my soul! love God and pursue thy way." What Christian would not be envious of a like death—a death which nobly crowned such a life as these few words necessarily suppose?

The vanquished had been fanaticised by the secret societies as well as by Garibaldi himself, that infuriated enthusiast, who could not write four lines nor utter four words without enshrining therein the treasons of the black race, that pururient sore of Italy; or the *venom* of the Vatican, that nest of vipers; or the lies of Pius IX., that pest, that monster, twice accursed, as priest and as king. So when these people were made prisoners, they expected nothing better than the hardest treatment and the most terrible vengeance. How surprised must they not then have been to find that their wounded were attended to on the field of battle, and the same care and attention extended to them as to the wounded of the Pontifical force, whilst those who were sound met with no other punishment than to be well guarded at first, and afterwards released by degrees, as it became certain that Garibaldi would be in no hurry to renew his game. Finally, a complete amnesty was granted. This extreme clemency of a legitimate government towards an invading banditti presented a noble and happy contrast with the implacable revenge of the usurping King of Piedmont. Victor Emmanuel, in fact, had no hesitation in putting to death the Spanish general Borges and his Neapolitan comrades, who were arrested whilst bearing arms in an endeavor to deliver the kingdom of Naples, and restore its former king, Francis II.

Two men only were excepted from the Pontifical amnesty. These were the authors of that atrocious act, the blowing up of the Serristori barracks. Their crime, indeed, could not be considered as anything connected with the war, but simply as cowardly assassination. Those two wretches, Monti and Tognetti, underwent a regular trial, which lasted more than a year, and at which all the forms required by law were strictly observed. They were convicted, and ended by acknowledging everything. They suffered capital punishment, and, at their execution, begged pardon of God and men. The day after this execution—coming generations will scarcely believe so strange a fact—the Chamber of Deputies at Florence solemnly protested against it, as did also Victor Emmanuel. The secret societies opened a subscription list for the widows of the executed criminals. Victor Emmanuel took part in it. And thus did a king honor parties who commit murder by gunpowder plots. True, this king was the same prince who, in pursuance of a decree issued by Garibaldi, at Naples, in 1861, pensioned the widow of the regicide, Agesilas Milano.

Pius IX. entertained quite a different idea of the duties of royalty. He was persuaded that an example should be made of the foul crime of Monti and Tognetti, and so could not be moved.

Pius IX. visits the wounded rebels.

"A king," said he, "owes justice to all alike, certainly not excepting honest people; and hence assassins must not be allowed to count on impunity." He went kindly to visit the wounded Garibaldians, "those unfortunate people, a great many of whom were only misled, and who, nevertheless, were his children." Two hundred of them had been conveyed to a lower room in the Castle of St. Angelo. He visited them quite alone, and thus addressed them: "Here I am, my friends; you see before you him whom your general calls the Vampire of Italy; you all took up arms against me, and you see that I am only a poor old man! You are in need of shoes, clothes and linen. Well, the Pope on whom you made war will cause you to be supplied with all these things. He will then send you back to your families; only before your departure, you will, from love to me, make a spiritual retreat." The unfortunate rebels could not believe their eyes or their ears. Some turned away from him in sullen wrath, like demons who will not give up hating. Others, in greater numbers, seized hold of the paternal hand which was raised over them to bless them, and bathed it with their tears. The good Pope, marvelled at the designs of God, who brings good out of evil. "*O felix culpa*" ("O happy fault!"), said he, alluding to the prayers of Holy Saturday, "if these children had not borne arms against me, they would not, perhaps, have died so piously."

It was some time before the details of Mentana were known in France. The government, it would appear, feared to acknowledge that the French soldiers took part in the engagement. When, however, the general's report put an end to all doubt on the subject, there were no bounds to the rage of the revolutionary party. The revolution, hitherto, had used Louis Napoleon as a facile and valuable instrument. It could not pardon him Mentana. But France was not all revolutionary. The mass of the nation, honest and loyal, shared not the ideas of the secret societies. Far from regretting what had taken place, the French people dreaded lest there should not have been enough done.

Cialdini, indeed, had been able to withdraw his troops, not with honor but without molestation, within the Italian frontier, whilst no account was required of his violation of the September convention. The ministers continued to discuss Italian unity as freely as they had been in the habit of doing for eight years, and the officious demagogue papers which were devoted to Prince Napoleon began to demand the speedy return of the French troops from Rome, and that by virtue of the famous convention which, according to these politicians, was binding on France, but not on Italy. The legislative body was moved. Not only the deputies who were declared Catholics, and who always divided against the government on the Roman question, but a great number of those also who had never until that time shown any indocility at the moment of voting, resolved to force the government to make a clear and public declaration of its intentions. The debate was opened by M. Thiers in an eloquent speech at the sitting of 4th December. He proved, and the proof was not difficult, that no reliance could be placed on the word of Victor Emmanual or Italian promises. "The

House of Savoy," said he, "goes to a falcon hunt with Garibaldi. If the latter fails he is taken to Caprera. If he succeeds, and takes a kingdom, they say to him, you are the revolution; your prey does not belong to you; it is ours, who are order and legality." Jules Favre, a barrister, shamelessly spoke in a contrary sense, and endeavored to justify Italy. His sophistry met with no response.

The minister, M. Rouher, could not retreat. He made a long speech, in which he defended the policy of Napoleon III. against the two former speakers, and involved himself once more in the inconceivable idea of neither sacrificing Italian unity to the Pope's temporal sovereignty nor that sovereignty to Italian unity. (On the one hand, M. Jules Favre objected that Italy, and chiefly amongst others, Menabrea, the actual head of the Florence Cabinet, whose wisdom and moderation had just been praised by the French minister, ceased not to declare that the possession of Rome was indispensable.) On the other hand, there were loud murmurs which protested against the iniquitous equality which was sought to be established between the victim and his executioner. M. Rouher perceived that the majority which the Imperial government had commanded for sixteen years, was on the point of slipping from him; so, turning to Jules Favre, he declared "that he was not agreed with him on any point—that he absolutely rejected his policy." Then, addressing the Conservatives, he affirmed that they would defend Rome so long as the desired reconciliation did not take place—that France would never, never abandon Rome. He concluded by conjuring the deputies to cling to the government which gave the · battle of Mentana as a pledge of its sincerity. This declaration was greeted with prolonged applause, and it could no longer be doubted that the vote would be almost unanimous. The deputies, however, determined that the head of their church should not be imperfectly protected, required of the minister a distinct explanation of what he meant by defending Rome. They were resolved that the government should not have the power to give up to

Italy the territory around the city which the Pope still possessed, and leave to him only the walls of Rome. This position was maintained by the veteran orator of French parliaments, M. Berryer. A great number of deputies came to his support, so necessary was it understood to be to guard against all subterfuge in transacting with Napoleon III. M. Rouhei was constrained to reascend the tribune. He did so, he said, more fully to express his idea, and declared, whilst the Chamber loudly applauded, that the Emperor guaranteed not only the city of Rome, but also the territory actually possessed by the Holy See, in all its integrity. Such was the memorable sitting of 4th December, 1867, at which the will of France was forced on its despotic ruler. But both for him and the country, French writers assure us, it was too late. If the representatives of the nation, they say, had shown from the beginning the same decision; if the empire had always spoken as on the 4th December, 1867 ; if, above all, it had acted conformably to its words, it would either not have fallen or fallen with honor. But never would we have seen either Italian unity or German unity, and the black flag of Prussia would not wave to-day over Metz, Malhouse and Strasbourg.

Piedmont having withdrawn its threatening force on the approach of the French troops, the Holy See had nothing to dread, for some time at least, from foreign invasion. It remained only to provide against the attacks of banditti such as had been just defeated at Mentana. In this important matter the Holy Father was not left to his own resources. The whole Christian world was in sympathy with him, and anxious for his safety. Volunteers from all Catholic countries hastened to Rome. Even remote Canada, so early as 1868, had sent her three hundred. And these mercenaries, as the enemy called them, served at their own expense. The Bishops of Hungary furnished three squadrons of Hussars, who were all mounted, equipped, and in every way supplied by Hungarian subscriptions. The bishops and nobility of Galicia sent lancers. France, Belgium and Catholic Germany, emulated one another in their efforts to maintain the Pontifical force.

There was nothing warlike in thus providing against possible danger. So long as France held Piedmont bound to treaty stipulations, any army in the service of the Pope could only be employed as a police force in maintaining internal peace, or in repelling such attempts as had recently been made by the irregular bands of Garibaldi against the Pontifical States.

Meanwhile, the arts of peace were not neglected. The Holy Father, as might be supposed, when freed from the fear of invasion and expulsion from his state, applied with renewed zeal to the duties of his sublime office. Nor to these alone did he confine the exercise of his well-directed charity. The agricultural school for children remains a lasting and solid proof of his enlightened benevolence. This establishment is called, in honor of its august founder, the Pio Vigneard (Pia Vigna). It is provided with all the most improved implements, and is confided to the care of the Belgian Brothers of Mercy. It is wholly maintained by the private funds of Pius IX. It may be seen on an eminence to the left of the railway as you approach the city of Rome.

ANNIVERSARY OF THE HOLY FATHER'S ORDINATION.

The anniversary of the elevation of Pius IX. to the Christian priesthood happily occurred during this interval of peace. There was but one feeling throughout the whole Christian world. The warmest expressions of love and devotedness proceeded from every land. All the sovereigns of Europe conveyed by autograph letters their dutiful congratulations, whilst the joy of the people everywhere knew no bounds. At Rome the feast of the golden wedding of Pius IX. lasted three days. Everywhere else, as it fell on the Sunday of the Good Shepherd, it was celebrated in the churches, and often in public places or on the mountains by illuminations or bonfires. Under the name of handsel to Pius IX., the Catholic press opened subscription lists. Notwithstanding the regular payment of Peter's pence, the public generosity was not exhausted.

One journal might be quoted, which alone collected more than one hundred thousand francs. The Archbishop of Cologne, Monsigneur Melchers, observed, in a pastoral instruction which he issued on the occasion, that never before had a Pope been in such intimate and universal relation with the heart of humanity. And indeed it was more consoling to the Supreme Pastor than all other demonstrations to reflect that so many millions on millions of faithful united with him in prayer at the Mass of the 11th of April, all on the occasion participating in the Holy Communion. He felt that the whole universe prayed with him and for him. "O God!" he exclaimed, in presence of some pilgrims who had come to congratulate him in person, "O God! have mercy on me! This is too much happiness! I dread when, ere long, I shall appear before Thy judgment-seat, lest Thou say to me: Thou hast had thy reward on earth! Not to me, but to Thee, O Lord! belongeth the love of Christians." He fully appreciated the numerous offerings and congratulations of the Catholic world. His servants conceived the happy idea of placing in symmetrical order throughout the apartments of the Vatican the rich and numerous gifts which were presented to him on the occasion of his jubilee. Beholding them, he exclaimed: "I also have my universal exposition! It is the fruit not of my industry but of the love of my children." Then, as he turned over the leaves of the gigantic manuscripts which were covered with addresses of devotedness, he added: "This is the true expression of the universal Catholic suffrage."

This auspicious time of peace and rejoicing was not without its sorrows. Among these were the fearful massacres of Christians in China. Nor were these the worst, for they carried with them their consolation. If the Church was cruelly persecuted in China, she won new glory in adding martyrs to the Triumphant army in heaven. The many scandals that occurred throughout Christendom were more truly afflicting. Above all, were truly trying to the paternal heart of the Holy Father those which happened among the Catholic people who protected him in the possession of what remained of his dilapidated patrimony. A court and a political system which were destined soon to disappear were laboring to put an end to Christian education. The prince, cousin of the Emperor, Napoleon III., and the Senator and Academician, Sainte Beuve, held heathenish orgies in the Lenten season, even on Good Friday. To crown the list of evil, apostacy was not wanting. It was of little consequence that one who fell away, although a vehement declaimer, was a shallow theologian ; his loss was, nevertheless, to be deplored. The progress of a low sect in Belgium called Solidaires, the success of a new revolution in Spain, under favor of which the members of religious communities, both of men and of women, were driven from their homes in the name of liberty, together with the opening of revolutionary clubs in Paris, caused Pius IX. to dread catastrophes in the near future. Severe domestic affliction came this year (1869) to aggravate the sorrows of Pius IX. His brother, Count Gabriel Mastai, met with an accident which, at his advanced age, ninety, proved to be serious. The Holy Father, immediately traversing Rome, ascended on his knees the *scala sancta*. A few days later the death of the patient was intimated to him. He shut himself up several hours in his private apartment, in order that none might witness the tears which grief made him shed. Finally, he repaired to the Vatican Basilica, where he prayed for a long time, both before the Holy Sacrament and at the tomb of the apostles.

AN EXERCISE OF SOVEREIGNTY.

Those states which formed the monetary division of Western Europe—France, Belgium, Switzerland and the Holy See, agreed at this time to refound their silver coinage. A model was chosen, which Greece, Portugal, Roumania and some other countries adopted in their turn, and it was understood that the new coinage for each state should be in proportion to its population. Hence it behooved the Pontifical State to issue forty millions of livres or thereby, for a population numbering from three to four millions of souls, including Romagna and Umbria, which the Pope still claimed. The Florence government remonstrated against the issue of forty million livres, on the ground that the Pontiff could not now actually count more than from 600,000 to 700,000 subjects. Napoleon III., always inclined to gratify the revolution, summoned Pius IX. to suspend the issue of his exaggerated coinage, three-fourths of which, it was insisted, should be cast anew with the effigy of Victor Emmanuel. This interference of Napoleon was considered inopportune and unacceptable, the operation of coining being almost completed. Cardinal Antonelli maintained the right of the Holy See. The French and Italian governments agreed to exclude from their circulation, and consequently from that of the whole monetary union, all silver coins which bore the meek and noble likeness of Pius IX. This they did without offering to the public any explanation. The revolutionary party, however, were too honest not to supply this want. They at once gave circulation to the rumor that the coinage of the Pope was of inferior quality. He was pointed out as a money-counterfeiter by the thousand organs of the infidel press. The people, grossly deceived, repelled with indignation, as if it were that of a robber, the likeness of the representative of justice on earth. The Catholics, meanwhile, observed with pain that while this storm of calumny was raging, one of their own number, once a champion of the temporal power, held in the French government the portfolio of finance. The Pontifical treasury subjected itself to considerable sacrifices, in order to diminish the losses and silence the recriminations of those who were compelled to stop its money, which could no longer be circulated. Chemists, in the interest of truth, analyzed the depreciated metal, and declared that it was exactly of the same value as the coinage of Napoleon III. But neither the officious nor the official press took the pains to publish this fact, and the calumny remained. The time was even then at hand, as French writers observe with pain, when France, in her downfallen and exhausted condition, would

have been glad to possess this Pontifical money and dispense
with worthless paper.

THE VATICAN COUNCIL—PURPOSE OF THE POPE IN CONVENING A
GENERAL COUNCIL.

This time of sorrow, mourning and difficulty was succeeded
by a period of unworked activity. It was deemed expedient to
convoke an Œcumenical Council. This important measure
was thought of on occasion of the centenary celebration of the
martyrdom of SS. Peter and Paul. After two years of serious
and mature deliberation and consultation, Pius IX. issued
apostolical letters, convening a council of the whole church at
the Vatican Basilica. The 8th of December, 1869, was appointed as the day for its first assembling. The objects in view
cannot be better described than in the words of the venerable
Pontiff. After a few preliminary paragraphs in his Bull of
Indiction, the Holy Father thus proceeds :

" The Roman Pontiffs, in the discharge of the office divinely
confided to them in the person of Peter of feeding the entire
flock of Christ, have unweariedly taken on themselves the most
arduous labors, and used every possible means in order to have
the various nations and races all over the earth brought to the
light of the Gospel, and by truth and holiness to eternal life.
All men know the zeal and unceasing vigilance with which
these same Roman Pontiffs have kept inviolate the deposit of
faith, discipline among the clergy, purity and science in the
education given to the members of the church, the holiness
and dignity of Christian marriage : how they studied day by
day to promote the Christian education of the youth of both
sexes, to foster among all classes the love of religion, the practice of piety and purity of morals as well as everything that
might conduce to the tranquillity, the good order and the
prosperity of civil society. Whenever great troubles arose, or
serious calamities threatened either the church or social order,
the Roman Pontiffs judged it opportune to convoke general
councils, in order that with the advice and assistance of the

bishops of the Catholic world, whom the Holy Ghost hath established to rule the Church of God, they might, in their united wisdom and forethought, so dispose everything as to define the doctrines of faith, to secure the destruction of the most prevalent errors, defend, illustrate and develop Catholic teaching, restore and promote ecclesiastical discipline and the reformation of morals.

"No one at the present time can be ignorant how terrible is the storm by which the church is assailed, and what an accumulation of evils afflicts civil society. The Catholic Church, her most salutary doctrines, her most revered power, the supreme authority of this Holy See, are all assailed and trampled on by the bitter enemies of God and man. All that is most sacred is held up to contempt; ecclesiastical property is made the prey of the spoiler; the most venerable ministers of the sacraments, men most eminent for their Catholic character, are harassed by unheard of annoyances. The religious orders are suppressed, impious books of every kind and pestilential publications are disseminated, wicked and pernicious societies are everywhere and under every form multiplied. The education of youth is, in almost all countries, withdrawn from the clergy, and, what is far worse, intrusted in many places to teachers of error and evil.

"In consequence of all these facts, to our great grief and that of all good men, and to the irreparable ruin of souls, impiety, corruption of morals, unbridled licentiousness, the contagion of depraved opinions, and of every species of pestilential vice and crime, the violation of all laws, human and divine, prevail everywhere to such an extent, that not only religion but human society itself is thrown into the most deplorable disorder and confusion.

"Wherefore, following in the footsteps of our illustrious predecessors, we have deemed it opportune to call together a General Council, as we had long desired to do.

"This Œcumenical Council will have to examine most diligently, and to determine what it is most seasonable to do, in these calamitous times, for the greatest glory of God, the integrity of faith, the splendor of Divine worship, the eternal salvation of men, the discipline of the regular and secular clergy, and their sound and solid education, the observance of ecclesiastical laws, the reformation of morals, the Christian education of youth, the common peace and universal concord. With the Divine assistance, our labors must also be directed towards remedying the peculiar evils which afflict church and state; towards bringing back into the right road those who have strayed away from truth and righteousness; towards repressing vice and error, in order that our holy religion and her saving doctrines may acquire renewed vigor all over the earth, that its empire may be restored and increased, and that thereby piety, modesty, honor, justice, charity and all Christian virtues may wax strong and flourish for the glory and happiness of our common humanity."

It has been alleged and persistently maintained by the enemies of the Holy See, that Pius IX. sought only to promote his own importance by convening a General Council. Of this calumny the foregoing words, which so plainly and distinctly set forth the purposes of the council, afford an abundant refutation. No man holding a great public office can fulfil faithfully the duties of that office without exalting his own character in the estimation of mankind: Ought he then, because such things exalt him, to leave them undone? This would, indeed, be mistaken humility.

Councils, although not an essential element in the government of the church, are had recourse to in times of difficulty, in order to settle doctrinal disputes, promote morality and establish or restore discipline. With the exception of the Apostolic Council of Jerusalem, no council was held for the first three hundred years of the church's existence. The church, nevertheless, as regarded her spiritual state, was highly prosperous and extended rapidly. Councils came as exigencies arose, and when there was no insuperable impediment to their assembling. They were in their time a source of great and lasting good, whilst their record remains shedding light on the centuries as they pass. There had already been eighteen Œcumenical Councils, that of Trent, held three hundred years ago, having been the last. Causes like to those which occasioned the earlier councils, although in a different state of the world and human society, appeared to call for such action on the part of the church as should powerfully influence the passing age, and cause the light of Divine revelation to penetrate the dark places of the nineteenth century. It was resolved, accordingly, to convoke the Œcumenical Council of the age.

BISHOPS, ETC., BIDDEN TO THE COUNCIL.

It was the duty of the Commission of Direction to decide as to who had a right to be called to, and to sit in, the council. This commission consisted of five cardinals who were presidents, eight bishops and a secretary, the Archbishop of Sardis. There was no difference of opinion. A question, however, arose as to the right of vicars-apostolic to be invited to the council. They were bishops, indeed, but without ordinary jurisdiction. Hence the doubt as to their right to be called. Neither their admissibility, if invited, nor of their decisive vote when admitted was at all questioned. The precedents and practice of the Holy See were in favor of their being called. It was also dreaded lest their exclusion should give rise to questions as to the œcumenicity of the council. All bishops, undoubtedly, were entitled to be invited. It was decided, therefore, that bishops, vicars-apostolic, should be bidden to the council. The Bulls by which former councils had been convoked called together archbishops, bishops, etc. The law, therefore, making no distinction between bishops in ordinary and such as were vicars-apostolic, neither could the commission. *Ubi lex non distinguit nec nos distinguere debemus.*

It was a far more serious matter to invite "the bishops of the Oriental rite who are not in communion with the Apostolic See." An earnest and affectionate letter of invitation was addressed to them. It was presented to the Patriarch of the " Orthodox " Greek Church, who did not consider it worth while to open it. On the same day, it is related, four millions of Bulgarians notified to this patriarch their withdrawal from his jurisdiction. Many bishops of the Greek patriarchate were deeply moved by the most kind and pressing appeal of the Holy Father. He had beseeched and conjured them in the most earnest manner "to come to the general assembly of the bishops of the West and of the whole world, as their fathers had come to the second Council of Lyons and that of Florence, in order that, renewing the charity which existed of old, and restoring the peace which prevailed in the early ages, the fruits of which time has snatched from us, we may behold at last the pure and bright dawn of that union which we so ardently desire." The separated bishops to whom these touching words were addressed, appear to have been profoundly moved. A goodly number, even, actuated by the paternal intentions of the Holy Father, were strongly inclined to meet his advances; but so powerful was the example of the Greek Patriarch of Constantinople, that none of them dared to take the lead. The non-united Patriarch of Armenia replied that he would attend the council. But he failed to do so.

A very considerate letter was also addressed to Protestants and all non-Catholics. Needless to say it was not responded to. At the Council of Trent the same attention was shown, but with an equally unsuccessful result. Julius II. had published the condition on which alone non-Catholics generally could be invited, viz.: that they should recognize the Divine authority of the Church. It was not surely to be expected that, on occasion of the meeting of a General Council, the Catholic Church should abandon, in favor of a comparatively small number of dissenters, her fundamental claim to Divine commission, which was acknowledged throughout all Christendom. The bishops of the Anglican Church were astonished and irritated on finding that they were invited only as other Protestants, and not convoked along with the Fathers of the Council.

Rome thus plainly intimated to them that they have yet to prove their consecration and right to episcopal dignity.

Rev. Dr. Cumming of London, a minister of the Scotch Presbyterian Church, asked, through Archbishop Manning, to be allowed to lay before the council such arguments as could be adduced in support of Protestant opinions. Pius IX. caused the following reply to be sent to the learned minister: "The decisions of former councils could not be shaken by bringing them anew into question, and by discussing what had been already examined, judged and condemned." Two months later, 30th October, 1869, having been informed that his words might have been misunderstood, and that certain Protestants imagined that all access to the Holy See was henceforth closed against them, the Holy Father, in a new Bull which he very considerately issued, declared that: "Far from repelling any one, we, on the contrary, make advances towards all. To those who, led astray by their education, believe in the truth of their opinions, we, by no means, refuse the examination and discussion of their arguments. This cannot be done within the council; but there are not wanting learned theologians whom we shall designate to them, and to whom they can open their minds. May there be many who, in all sincerity, shall avail themselves of this facility! We earnestly pray that the God of mercy may bring about this happy result."

FATHERS WHO ATTENDED THE COUNCIL.

A statement of the number of Fathers who attended the council, at any particular time during its celebration, can hardly convey an accurate idea of the numbers who took part in its proceedings. Some were always arriving and others departing. Some fell sick, and a few died. The number in attendance, however, was always considerable. An official list, published by the Apostolic Chamber, shows the number and quality of such as were entitled to be present, and who could have attended except on account of hindrances arising from sickness, age or impediments thrown in their way by the

W

governments under which they lived. These included 55 cardinals, 11 patriarchs, 7 primates, 159 archbishops, 755 bishops, 6 abbots, 22 mitred abbots-general, 29 generals and vicars-general of orders; in all, 1,044. A later official list of 1st May states the total number at 1,050, new primatial, archiepiscopal and episcopal churches having been erected in the meantime.

On the 8th December there were at Rome : 49 cardinals, 9 patriarchs, 4 primates, 123 archbishops, 481 bishops, 6 abbots, 22 abbots-general, 29 vicars and vicars-general of orders; in all, 723 Fathers. On 20th December there were 743.

The following Bishops of England were in attendance at the council: The Most Rev. Archbishop Manning, of Westminster; the Most Rev. Dr. Errington, Archbishop of Trebizonde; the Right Rev. Dr. Grant, of Southwark; the Right Rev. Dr. Cornthwaite, of Beverly; the Right Rev. Dr. Uullathorne, of Birmingham; the Right Rev. Dr. Clifford, of Clifton; the Right Rev. Dr. Chadwick, of Hexham; the Right Rev. Dr. Amherst, of Northampton; the Right Rev. Dr. Roskell, of Nottingham; the Right Rev. Dr. Vaughan, of Plymouth; the Right Rev. Dr. Turner, of Salford; the Right Rev. Dr. Brown, of Shrewsbury.

There was a somewhat longer list of Irish bishops, viz.: His Eminence Paul, Cardinal-Archbishop of Dublin; the Most Rev. Dr. McGettigan, Primate of all Ireland, Archbishop of Armagh; the Most Rev. Dr. Leahy, Archbishop of Cashel; the Most Rev. Dr. McHale, Archbishop of Tuam; the Right Rev. Dr. Derry, of Clonfert; O'Keane, Fermoy; Kelly, Derry; Moriarty, Kerry; Leahy, Dromore; Gillooly, Elphin; McEvilly, Galway; Furlong, Ferns; O'Hea, Ross; Dorrian, Down and Connor; Butler, Limerick; Conaty, Kilmore; Nulty, Meath; Donnelly, Clogher; Power, Killaloe; McCabe, Ardagh.

The hierarchy had not yet been restored in Scotland; so that country could send only three bishops to the Œcumenical Council. These were the Right Rev. John Strain, Vicar-Apostolic, Edinburgh (afterwards, in the restored hierarchy,

Most Rev. Archbishop of Saint Andrews and Edinburgh); the Most Rev. Dr. Eyre, Archbishop, Glasgow; the Right Rev. Dr. McDonald (in the restored hierarchy, Bishop of Aberdeen), Vicar-Apostolic, Preshome.

All the other civilized nations, with scarcely an exception,* sent their bishops to the general assembly of the Church. France supplied the greatest number, eighty-one. The kingdom of the Two Sicilies came next, being represented by sixty-eight bishops. Next came the States of the Church, sending sixty-two bishops. From Great Britain and Ireland, with the colonies, including Canada, went fifty-five bishops to the great council. Austria and Hungary were nobly represented by forty-three bishops. Spain and the United States of America sent each forty prelates, and the States of South America, thirty; whilst of the Oriental rites there were forty-two bishops. Piedmont, Tuscany, Lombardy and Venetia, together with Modena and Parma, Prussia, Bavaria, Mexico, Belgium, Holland, Portugal, Switzerland, the Isles of Greece, and even the Turkish empire, cheerfully willed that the Catholic prelates of their lands should bear their part in the grand Œcumenical Council which was now about to assemble. All these, with the cardinals, abbots, mitred abbots and generals of religious orders, who were also members of the great assembly, made up the goodly number which has already been adverted to.†

SUBJECTS WHICH IT WAS PROPOSED TO DISCUSS IN THE COUNCIL.

The subjects for discussion were expressed in *schemata*, or draft decrees, which were drawn up by a "congregation," or, as we should say, a committee of one hundred and two ecclesiastics, who were cardinals and others learned in theology and canon law, selected from many nations on account of their superior wisdom and experience. By these alone the *schemata*

---

*If Russia were a little more within the pale of civilization, it would be noted as an exception. Its bishops were not allowed to proceed to Rome.

† The number of prelates at Rome attending the council was never, for any length of time, the same. And writers give the numbers according to the time at which they noted them.

were prepared. They bore not so much as the shadow of the supreme authority. So the council was perfectly at liberty to accept or reject, to change or to modify them, as it should deem fit and proper. Of this we are assured by the words of the Pope, who, in his "Constitution," at the commencement of the council, informed the bishops that he had not given any sanction to the *schemata*, and that consequently in regard to them there was complete freedom.

The *schemata*, six in number, were very comprehensive. It is deeply to be regretted that the council was not allowed time to discuss them all. They concerned:

1. Catholic doctrine in opposition to the manifold errors flowing from rationalism.
2. The Church of Christ.
3. The office of bishops.
4. The vacancy of sees.
5. The life and manners of the clergy.
6. The Little Catechism.

The *schema* on the Church of Christ necessarily involved the question of infallibility. As this question, more than any other subject, appears to have disturbed the equanimity of the outside world, it may not be inappropriate to consider the preliminary labors, as regarded it, of the great theological commission. The *schema* on the Church of Christ extended to fifteen chapters. Having treated, at length, on the body of the church, the commission or committee of 102 theologians could not fail to treat also of the Church's Head. On this point they prepared two chapters. The one spoke of the primacy of the Roman Pontiff, the other of his temporal power. In treating of the primacy, its endowments also necessarily came under discussion. Among these claimed the first place the Divine assistance in matters of faith which was promised to Peter, and in Peter to his successors. This is nothing less than infallibility.

On the 14th and 21st of January, the commission discussed the nature of the primacy. On the 11th of February, it took up the question of infallibility. It was enquired: 1st, whether the infallibility of the Roman Pontiff can be defined as an article of faith; 2nd, whether it ought to be so defined? The first question was answered unanimously in the affirmative. To the second, all, with one exception, replied, expressing concurrence in the judgment that the subject ought not to be proposed to the council unless it were demanded by the bishops. The wording of the judgment is as follows: *Sententia commissionis est, nonnisi ad postulationem episcoporum rei hujus propositionem ab apostolica sede faciendam esse.* ("The judgment of the commission is that this subject ought not to be proposed by the Apostolic See, except at the petition of the bishops.") One member of the commission considered the discussion of the subject inopportune. On account of his dissent, the chapter bearing on infallibility was never completed.

Thus for a second time was the question of infallibility deliberately set aside. As for Pius IX. himself, he had no desire any more than he had need to propose that there should be a dogmatical definition. Even as his predecessors in all preceding ages, he was conscious that his primacy was complete. He had acted on this conviction, exercising his sublime privilege with universal consent, in the face of all Christendom. In 1854, 1862 and 1867, the bishops had abundantly testified in his favor. If an authoritative declaration was called for, it could only be on account of the few who disputed and doubted, and the still smaller number who denied that the Head of the Church on earth can neither err in faith and morals, nor lead into error the church of which he is divinely constituted the Supreme Teacher.

OPENING OF THE COUNCIL.

On the 7th of December, 1869—Vigil of the Immaculate Conception—Pius IX., attended by an imposing suite, repaired to the Church of the Twelve Apostles, in order to inaugurate solemnly a period of nine days' prayer in honor of the Blessed and Immaculate Mary. The following day, at an early hour, the cannon of the Castle of St. Angelo announced to the holy city the great event that had been so long looked forward to. As early as six o'clock a.m. the three naves of St. Peter's were filled with a crowd of the faithful, and all the approaches to the Basilica were thronged with people. At nine o'clock was seen the magnificent procession of mitred abbots, bishops and archbishops, primates, patriarchs and cardinals, that preceded the *sedia gestatoria* which bore the Pope. The sacred cortege required about an hour to traverse the hall (atrium) and the chief nave of St. Peter's, and reach the left* arm of the cross which forms the immense Basilica, and which had been set apart and prepared as a vast chamber for the celebration of the council by that skilful architect, Virginius Vespignani.

1,044 Fathers were invited to be present as members of the council. 808 attended at the opening. Of these there were six archbishops who were also princes, forty-nine cardinals, eleven patriarchs, six hundred and eighty archbishops and bishops, twenty-eight abbots, and twenty-nine generals of religious orders. The entire number surpassed by one hundred and thirty-five the united numbers of all the Fathers of Nice, Constantinople and Ephesus. The day had gone by when the European sovereigns could be bidden to an Œcumenical Council. Several of their representatives, however, attended at the opening. The highest of the Roman nobility were also present. The Colonna and Orsini families enjoyed the honor of being princes attendant at the Papal throne on occasion of all the public ceremonials of the council. Others of the Roman nobility, sovereigns and princes, at the time in the city, were present. Among these were the ex-King of Naples, the Empress of Austria, the ex-Duke and Duchess of Tuscany, the ex-Duke and Duchess of Parma, together with the Doria and Borghese families. Several foreign princes, General Kanzler, commander-in-chief of the Papal forces, and General Dumont, who commanded the French battalions in garrison at Rome, likewise attended.

---

*The *left arm* looking from the door of the Basilica, the *right* looking from the high altar. As was fitting, it was the Gospel side.

The hymn, *Veni Creator*, was sung, and immediately there-after the first session of the Vatican Council was formally opened with the celebration of High Mass. At the conclusion of mass, the secretary of the council placed upon the altar the Book of the Gospels, which always remained open throughout the session. The council then heard a sermon, and the Holy Father intoned the Synodal prayers, which were followed by the Litany of the Saints. Immediately after the chanting of the Gospel, Pius IX. made an allocution to the following effect: " You are met, venerable brethren, in the name of Jesus Christ, to bear witness with us to the word of God ; to declare with us to all men the truth, which is the way that leads to God ; and to condemn with us, under the guidance of the Holy Ghost, the doctrines of false science. God is present in His holy place ; He is with our deliberations and our efforts ; He has chosen us to be His servants and fellow-workers in the great work of His salvation. Therefore, knowing well our own weakness, and filled with mistrust of ourselves, we lift up our eyes and our prayers to Thee, O Holy Ghost, to Thee the source of true light and wisdom."

The *Veni Creator* having been once more sung, the Bishop of Fabriano read from the *Ambo* the decree ordaining the opening of the council. It was in substance as follows : " Is it the pleasure of the Fathers that the Œcumenical Council of the Vatican should be opened, and should be declared open for the glory of the Most Holy Trinity, the custody and declara-tion of the faith and of the Catholic religion ; for the condem-nation of errors which are widely spreading, and the correction of clergy and people ?" The council replied unanimously *placet*. The Pope then declared the council to be opened, and fixed the second public session for the feast of the Epiphany, January 6, 1870. The session closed with the *Te Deum* and the Pontifical benediction. All the public sessions which were afterwards held were opened pretty much in the same man-ner.

DEATH OF TWO DISTINGUISHED MEMBERS OF THE COUNCIL.

At this time the council and the Catholic world had to bewail the death of two very eminent Fathers. Cardinal de Reisach was a man of great and varied learning, of large and refined culture of mind, and was fitted in a special way to understand the diversities of thought which met in the Vatican Council. His loss to the Holy See, great as it would have been at any time, was more seriously felt at the meeting of the council, in preparing for which he had borne a chief part. Cardinal de Reisach was not only one of the foremost members of the Sacred College in the public service of the church, but in private life he was greatly and deservedly loved for his genial and sympathetic character.

The late illustrious Bishop of Southwark, the Right Rev. Thomas Grant, whose zeal induced him to proceed to Rome in the height of a serious illness, was also torn away from the cares of this life and the affection of many friends, when, a little later, he was about to address a luminous discourse to the assembled Fathers. Whilst he stood in the midst of them, there occurred a crisis of his malady from which he never rallied. He was visited on his deathbed, which was that of the faithful servant, by Pius IX., who held him in the highest esteem.

THE SECOND SESSION.

Preparatory to the second session of the council, various commissions were constituted. That of postulates or propositions was appointed by the Pope, and consisted of cardinals who had experience, both as residents of Rome and formerly as nuncios at foreign courts, together with archbishops and bishops selected from each of the chief nations in the council. Its members were twelve cardinals, two patriarchs—Antioch and Jerusalem—ten archbishops, among whom was the Archbishop of Westminster, and two bishops.

It was resolved that the other commissions should be elected by the universal suffrage of the council. The Commission of Faith was elected in the Third General Congregation, on the 20th of December. It was composed of twenty-five members, among whom were remarked the successor of Fenelon in the archiepiscopal see of Cambrai, the Archbishop of Westminster and the Archbishop of Cashel (Ireland), three American bishops, Baltimore, San Francisco, Rio Grande.

The Commission of Discipline consisted of twenty-four members, who represented as many nations—the Bishop of Birmingham, on the part of England.

The Commission on Religious Orders was also chosen; the Bishop of Clifton representing England.

No more being necessary at the earlier sittings of the council, the nomination of all other commissions was postponed.

SECOND PUBLIC SESSION—PROFESSION OF FAITH BY ALL THE MEMBERS OF THE COUNCIL.

The second public session was held on the feast of the Epiphany, January 6th, 1870. It had been always customary at general councils to make a profession of faith. This custom was not departed from at the Vatican Council. As at Constantinople, A. D. 881, and Chalcedon, A. D. 481, was recited the Creed of Nicea, and at subsequent councils was solemnly professed the faith as expressed by those which had preceded them; so at the Council of the Vatican were repeated the articles of Catholic belief, as handed down through Trent and the more ancient councils. First of all, the Holy Father, rising from his seat, read, in a distinct voice, the definitions of the Council of Trent, known as the Creed of Pope Pius IV. The same profession of faith was then read from the *Ambo* by the Bishop of Fabriano. As soon as he had done so, the other Fathers of the Council expressed their adhesion by kissing the Gospel at the throne of the Chief Pastor. Seven hundred bishops of the church, representing more than thirty nations and about* three hundred millions of Christians, thus solemnly professed, with one heart and mind, the same faith in the same

*According to the best statistics that can be found.

form of words. In this wonderful unanimity there is more than nature and philosophy. Through all the changes of nearly nineteen hundred years, this intellectual unity of faith, although minutely defined at Nicea, Constantinople and Trent, has endured unchanged. We cannot but behold in this immutability of Divine faith something far beyond the power of human wisdom. It is surely providential that, in the face of so much unbelief, such witness should have been borne to the unity and universality of the Catholic faith.

And now closed the second public session of the Vatican Council.

THIRD SESSION.

Preparatory to the opening of the third public session of the council, the *schema* " on Catholic faith and on the errors springing from rationalism " was discussed by thirty-five bishops in the general congregations, between the 18th of December and the 10th of January. It contained eighteen chapters, and was sent back to the Commission on Faith in order to be completely remodeled. It was a grand theological document, and was cast in the traditional form of conciliar decrees, taking its shape, as they did, from the errors which it was intended to condemn. It was somewhat archaic, perhaps, in language, but worthy to rank with the decrees of the Councils of Toledo or of Lateran. Having been referred to the Commission on Faith, it was again distributed to the council in its new form on the 14th of March, wholly recast, and was received with general approbation. This new document is quite of a distinct character, and not to be compared with the *schema* by which it was preceded. It contained, instead of eighteen chapters, only an introduction and four chapters, in which every sentence is full of condensed doctrine, the whole having impressed upon it a singular beauty and splendor of Divine truth. The commission was engaged in recasting this *schema* until the end of February. Its subject-matter was what may well be considered the first foundations of natural and revealed religion, viz.: the existence and perfections of

God, the creation of the world, the powers and office of human reason, revelation, faith, the relation of reason to faith and of faith to science. As a consequence of these truths came the condemnation of atheism, materialism, pantheism, naturalism and rationalism.

Whilst the non-Catholic world believed that the Pope and the Fathers of the Council were bestowing all their care on one subject which happened to be more prominently before the public, they were, on the contrary, laboring with the greatest pains to elucidate every subject as it came up for consideration. As has been seen, the most important *schema* on Catholic faith had been already very carefully discussed. On the 18th of March a second discussion took place in the general congregation (or committee of the whole council) on a report being made by the Primate of Hungary. Nine bishops then discoursed on the text of the *schema*, after which, no Father desiring to speak more upon it, the general discussion ended. Each chapter in particular now came to be discussed. In the debate on the first chapter sixteen Fathers took part; on the second, twenty; on the third, twenty-two; on the fourth, twelve; in all, seventy-nine spoke. This discussion occupied nine sittings, and only ended when no one desired to speak any further. The amendments of the bishops were sent with the *schema* to the commission. As soon as they were printed and distributed they were examined by the commission, when a full report was made in the general congregation on the introduction, and the amendments were put to the vote. The text of the introduction was then once more referred. Each of the four chapters was treated in the same manner. To the first there were forty-seven amendments, which, being printed and distributed, the commission reported, and the amendments were put to the vote. Still another revision, and the first chapter was adopted, almost unanimously, on the 1st of April.

The second chapter had sixty-two amendments. Referring to the commission, revising, reporting and voting followed, as in the case of the first chapter, when the second was referred back for final amendment.

The third chapter had one hundred and twenty-two amendments. The same process was followed, in regard to these amendments, as in the case of the first and second chapters. The proceedings lasted two days.

The fourth chapter had fifty amendments, which were subjected to the same process as those of the three first, and sent back to the commission. On the same day, 8th April, the second chapter as amended was passed, and on the 12th of April, the third and fourth, the former unanimously, the latter almost so. When the whole was put to the vote, no *non placet* was given, whilst there were eighty-three *placets juxta modum*. The amendments were all sent, as before, to the commission, and printed in a quarto volume of fifty-one pages. The report was made on the 19th of April, and on the same day the amended text was unanimously accepted. All the time between the 14th of March and the 19th of April was consumed in passing this first *schema*. Sixty-nine members of the council spoke. Three hundred and sixty-four amendments were made, examined and voted upon. Six reports were made by the commission upon the text, which, after its first recasting, had been six times amended. The decree was finally adopted unanimously by the assembled Fathers, all who were present, six hundred and sixty-seven, voting in the third public session, on Low Sunday (Dominica in Abbis), 24th April. This solemn vote of the council was confirmed by the Pope, who, on the occasion, spoke as follows : " The decrees and canons contained in the Constitution just read were accepted by all the Fathers, no one dissenting ; and we, the Sacred Council approving, by our apostolical authority, so define and confirm them." Continuing, he addressed the Fathers of the Council : " You see, beloved brethren, how good and pleasant it is to walk in the House of God in unity and peace. As our Lord gave to His apostles, so I, His unworthy Vicar, in His name, give peace to you. That peace, as you know, casts out fear ; that peace shuts the ear to unwise words. May that peace go with you in all the days of your life ; may that peace be with you in death ; may that peace be your everlasting joy in heaven."

After much deliberation and painstaking, the third public session of the council came to a close.

At less formal sittings was discussed the discipline relating to bishops. On this subject thirty-seven Fathers discoursed in the council. Seven sittings were employed in discussing discipline as concerns the clergy, and thirty-seven Fathers spoke. Forty-one Fathers took part in discussing the *schema* on the Little Catechism. The discussion occupied six sittings. There was no hurrying of matters in the council. None of the discussions were closed until none of the Fathers desired further to be heard. All the *schemata*, it is almost needless to say, having been discussed, were referred to their respective commissions, in order to be revised in accordance with the speeches and the written amendments of the bishops.

Pius IX., meanwhile, was most anxious to aid and promote the labors of the council. Notwithstanding the great increase of ecclesiastical business occasioned by the presence in Rome of so many prelates, the affairs of whose churches, as well as their own more personal matters, required no small degree of attention, he followed, with unabated interest, every stage of its proceedings, and caused a minute account to be given to him every day of what was done in the various committees. These unwonted cares, and the unusual amount of labor and fatigue which they entailed, never induced him to omit any of those devotional offices with which he was accustomed to renew and strengthen his soul. He would not hear of any hurrying in the discussions on the first *schema*—that on faith, but, on the contrary, gave due praise to the pains and labor bestowed by the Fathers on every chapter, word and sentence. It was their object to secure that complete accuracy and perfection of expression which could not fail to prove eminently useful in all time to come. As has been already remarked, the Fathers of the "Congregations" and "Commissions" labored most assiduously in preparing, for the acceptance of the council, the *schema* on faith and doctrine. In the course of the six weeks that it was under review, seventy-nine discourses were delivered, three hundred and sixty-four amendments proposed, examined and voted upon, while six reports were made upon the text of the *schema*, which had been six times amended. The introduction, the four chapters and the eighteen canons, having finally passed the council, were approved by the Holy Father, adopted and promulgated as a Papal "Constitution," which will be known in history as the Constitution *Dei Filius*. It is a master-piece of theological science, and may be compared to priceless gems artistically arranged by skilful hands in the richest settings.

It would be idle, indeed, to recount all the hard and absurd things that have been said by the enemies of the council and the Catholic religion. One of their accusations, if well founded, would be truly crushing. Some scientists, who claim to be very profound, deem it necessary to abjure the Catholic faith, because the Vatican Council has placed an impassable gulf between religion and science, faith and reason. The council anticipated and met this accusation which is so vigorously and persistently urged by the false science of the day. Let us quote from its "Constitution :" "Although faith is above reason, there can never be any real discrepancy between faith and reason, since the same God who reveals mysteries and infuses faith has bestowed the light of reason on the human mind, and cannot deny Himself, nor can truth ever contradict truth. The false appearance of such a contradiction is mainly due, either to the dogmas of faith not having been understood and expounded according to the mind of the church, or to the inventions of opinion having been taken for the verdicts of reason. And not only can faith and reason never be opposed to one another, but they are of mutual aid the one to the other. For right reason demonstrates the foundations of faith, and, enlightened by its light, cultivates the science of things divine ; while faith frees and guards reason from errors, and furnishes it with manifold knowledge.

" So far, therefore, is the church from opposing the cultivation of human arts and sciences, that it, in many ways, helps and promotes it. For the Church neither ignores nor despises the benefits to human life which result from the arts and sciences, but confesses that, as they came from God, the Lord of all science, so, if they be rightly used, they lead to God by the help of His grace. Nor does the Church forbid that each of these sciences, in its sphere, should make use of its own principle and its own method. But while recognizing this just liberty, it stands watchfully on guard, lest the sciences, setting themselves against the Divine teaching, or transgressing their own limits, should invade and disturb the domain of faith."

FOURTH PUBLIC SESSION.

There was only one point in the discussions on the Church of Christ in which the outside world appeared to take an interest, and it is one which the council did not at first contemplate taking into consideration. The Fathers appear to have resolved to limit themselves, in treating of the Church, and consequently of the Head of the Church on earth, to the discussion of the primacy of the Supreme Pastor and of his temporalities. The commission of one hundred and two cardinals, and other learned theologians, had even set aside the question of infallibility when it came before them, one of their number pronouncing a decision on it as inopportune. A great majority of the bishops, however, were strongly of opinion that in view of the outcry which had been raised on this point, the opportunity of an Œcumenical Council being held should not be allowed to pass without defining the belief of the Church in regard to the unerring nature of the decisions, in matters of doctrine and morals, of the successor of St. Peter. At their request, accordingly, it was ordered that the important subject should be introduced in the eleventh chapter of the *schema* on the Church, and prepared in the usual way for the consideration of the council. It could not be laid before the Fathers sooner than the 18th of July, when the fourth solemn session was held. It is proper to remark here that the doctrine in question was never discussed, either in the congregations or committees of the whole council, as to its Divine origin, or as to the fact of its having been revealed; not one of the seven hundred members of the council expressed any doubt as to this. There was no discussion except as to the opportuneness of defining to be of faith what all believed to be so. The *schema* having passed through all the preparatory stages, finally assumed the form of a "dogmatic constitution," which will be known in history as the Constitution, *Pastor æternus*, from the words with which it commences. This Constitution was brought before the council at a solemn session, the fourth and last which it held, the 18th July, 1870. The session was opened with all the usual solemnities. The Pope himself presided in person. The Mass of the Holy Ghost having been celebrated, the Sacred Scriptures were placed upon the lectern on the high altar, and, as was customary, the *Veni Creator* was sung. The Bishop of Fabriano then read the Constitution, or decree *de Romano Pontifice*, from the *Ambo* (pulpit), and the Fathers of the Council were invited to vote. Each Father, accordingly, as his name was called, took off his mitre, rose from his seat and voted. Of the five hundred and thirty-five who were present, five hundred and thirty-three voted *placet* (aye), whilst there were only two nays. The secretary of the council, together with the scrutineers, advanced to the Pontifical throne and declared the result. The Holy Father then confirmed the decision in the usual form. He prayed, at the same time, that they who had considered such a decision inopportune, at a time of unusual agitation, might, in calmer days, unite with the great majority of their brethren, and contend with them for the truth. The insertion here of the allocution which he delivered on the occasion cannot but prove acceptable to all English readers:

"Great is the authority with which the Supreme Pontiff is invested. This authority, however, does not destroy. It builds up. It does not oppress. But, on the contrary, sustains. Very frequently it behooves it to defend the rights of our brethren, the bishops. If some have not been of the same mind with us, let them consider that they have formed their judgment under the influence of agitation. Let them bear in mind that the Lord is not in the storm (2 Kings, xix., 11). Let them remember that, a few years ago, they held the opposite opinion, and abounded in the same belief with us, and in that of this most august assembly, for then they judged in the untroubled air. Can two opposite consciences stand together in the same judgment? By no means. Therefore, we pray God that He who alone can work great things, may Himself enlighten their minds and hearts, that all may come to the bosom of their Father, the unworthy Vicar of Jesus Christ on earth, who loves them and desires to be one with them, and, united in the bond of charity, to fight with them the battle of the Lord. Thus shall our enemies not dare to deride us, but rather be awed, and at length lay down the arms of their warfare in the presence of truth; so that all may say, with St. Augustine: "Thou hast called me unto Thy wonderful light, and behold I see."

Te Deum was now chanted, the Pope intoning the sublime hymn, and with the Pontifical benediction, ended the fourth solemn public session of the Vatican Council. With this council also ended all discussion within the church on those questions in regard to which it pronounced authoritatively. No doubt the enemies of the Catholic faith would have been better pleased if there had been absolute unanimity when the final vote was taken on the widely-discussed question of infallibility. Such a coincidence would have afforded them a pretext, although, indeed, a groundless one, for asserting that there was either collusion or compulsion, whilst in reality there was complete liberty. The two Fathers who voted, nay, constituting a minority of two, acted according to their right, and it was not questioned. These Fathers were Monsignor Louis Riccio, Bishop of Casazzio, in the kingdom of Naples, and the Right Rev. Edward Fitzgerald, Bishop of Petricola (Little Rock, Arkansas), in the United States of America. Immediately after the con-

X

firmation of the "Constitution," these two prelates, advancing
to the Papal chair, solemnly declared their adhesion to the act
of the council. The four dissentient cardinals—Rauscher,
Schwarzenberg, Mathieu and Hohenlohe—who had left the
council when the fourth session was held, also, in their turn,
expressed their assent to the decision of the assembled Fathers.
The opposing bishops did in like manner. All of them, not
excepting Strossmayer, Bishop of Sirmium, who was the most
eloquent orator of the minority in the council, and who
appeared to hesitate longer than the rest, ended by promul-
gating all the decrees of the council in their respective dioceses.
This is more than could be said of Nicea, Chalcedon and Constantinople. For the first time, no bishop persisted in resisting the decisions of an Œcumenical Council. It was now
acknowledged by the whole episcopate that those measures
were timely, wise and salutary, which the Church, ever guided
by the Spirit of God, had deemed it proper to adopt, but which
so many, awed by the spirit of unbelief which was abroad, had
judged were inopportune.

It may have been merely a coincidence. But there can be
no doubt that grandeur was added to a scene, in itself sufficiently imposing, when, as on Sinai of old, lightning flashed
and thunder pealed, as the Fathers of the Council solemnly
rose to give their final vote. "The *placets* of the Fathers,"
writes the correspondent of the London *Times* (Aug. 5, 1870),
" struggled through the storm while the thunder pealed above,
and the lightning flashed in at every window, and down through
the dome and every smaller cupola. '*Placet!*' shouted his
Eminence or his Grace, and a loud clap of thunder followed in
response, and then the lightning darted about the Baldacchino
and every part of the church and council-hall, as if announcing
the response. So it continued for nearly one hour and a half,
during which time the roll was being called, and a more effective scene I never witnessed. Had all the decorators and all
the getters-up of ceremonies in Rome been employed, nothing
approaching to the solemn grandeur of the storm could have

been prepared, and never will those who saw it and felt it forget the promulgation of the first dogma of the church." Less friendly critics beheld, in this magnificent thunder-storm, a distinct voice of Divine anger, condemning the important act of the assembled Fathers. Had they forgotten Sinai and the Ten Commandments? All of a sudden, as the last words were uttered, the tempest ceased; and, at the moment when Pius IX. intoned the *Te Deum*, a sun-ray lighted up his noble and expressive countenance. The voices of the Sixtine choristers, who continued chanting the hymn, could not be heard. They were lost in the united concert of the venerable Fathers and the vast assemblage.

COMPARATIVE IMPORTANCE OF THE VATIACN COUNCIL.

In whatever light we view the Council of the Vatican—the œcumenical of the nineteenth century—it strikes us as being, in ecclesiastical annals, the event of the age. It also marks, in a remarkable manner, the character and progress of the time. The Council of Trent was highly important in its day; and still, after a lapse of three hundred years, its teachings govern the Church. Whilst, as regards the wisdom of its decisions, it cannot be excelled, it was surpassed in many things by the Council of the Vatican.

Trent was attended by comparatively few bishops, who were from Europe, the Eastern Church and the countries bordering on the Mediterranean. The Vatican Council consisted of prelates from at least thirty different nations, from the remotest regions of the habitable globe, from the numerous churches in India which owed their origin to the apostolic zeal of St. Francis Xavier, from North and South America, China, Australia, New Zealand and Oceanica. One-fifth of the churches existed not as yet in the time of Trent which sent their bishops to represent them at the Vatican Council. The countries in which many of these churches flourish had no place, when the Council of Trent was called, on the map of the world. From those vast regions which now constitute the United States of

America, there was not so much as one bishop at Trent. At the Vatican Council there were no fewer than sixty. There were never more than three bishops of Ireland present together at Trent, and four only were members of that council. Twenty Irish prelates attended the Vatican Council. England sent only one bishop to Trent. He is mentioned as Godveus Anglus, Episc. Asaphensis. The Catholics of England were represented by thirteen English bishops at the Council of the Vatican. Scotland had no representation at Trent. The Catholics of that country were most worthily represented at the Vatican by Bishop Strain, now Archbishop of St. Andrews and Edinburgh; Archbishop Eyre, of Glasgow, and Bishop Mc-Donald, of Aberdeen. There was only a very small number of English-speaking bishops at Trent. At the Vatican Council they were particularly numerous, constituting, as nearly as can be calculated, one-fifth of the assembled Catholic hierarchy. At Trent there were not many bishops from countries speaking different languages. Twenty-seven languages, and various dialects besides, were represented by prelates at the Vatican.

The greater facilities for travelling, which this favored age enjoys, no doubt rendered it more easy to attend the Council of the Vatican than it was to journey to Trent, even from the nearest lands. Nevertheless, there was laborious journeying to the Vatican. Prelates from the vast regions of Asia and Africa, America and Australia, knew what they would have to encounter, but they were not deterred. Some, on their way to the Vatican, travelled for whole weeks mounted on camels before they could reach the ports at which it behooved them to embark. Bishop Launy, of Santa Fe, was forty-two days on his land-journey, and travelled on horseback. Such of the laity as visited Trent were comparatively few, and only from places not very distant. One hundred thousand pilgrims, many of them from the most remote regions, repaired to the Vatican. The number of Fathers at any one time in council at Trent was somewhat under three hundred. Seven hundred and eighty-three took part in the Council of the Vatican. The Council of Trent, however, must not be underrated. It was a most important council, and admirably calculated to meet the wants of the time. It marked an era in the history of the Church. It provided remedies for numerous evils, and safety in the midst of danger. It became a power which time has not diminished. For three hundred years it has guided the destinies of Peter's barque, prelates and people wisely accepting its discipline, and meekly obeying its rule. It added, no doubt, to the importance of the Vatican Council that it was held at Rome, in the very centre of Catholicity and of Catholic unity, and near the tombs of the martyred apostles, the founders of the Church. In this it contrasts with Trent, which, although the Fathers assembled at an obscure village in the Tyrol, was not less, on this account, an Œcumenical Council. Papal legates presided at Trent, whilst the Holy Father himself was present at all the solemn sessions of the Vatican Council which have as yet been held.

INFALLIBILITY.

There was no intention at first, as has been shown, of laying the question of infallibility before the council. It happened, however, that a great clamor, in regard to this question, came to prevail both within and without the Church. The enemies of the doctrine railed so strongly against it, and they who did not deny it declaimed so loudly against the opportuneness of pronouncing any decision concerning it, that it was positively forced upon the attention of the assembled Fathers. When, therefore, they came to discuss the primacy and the temporalities of the Sovereign Pontiff in connection with the Church of Christ, they hesitated not to consider, at the same time, his immunity from error when speaking, as Head of the Church and successor of Saint Peter, *ex cathedra* on matters of faith and morals. The learning of theologians and the ability of orators were brought into requisition, and the fact came prominently out that it had been according to the mind of the

Church at all times, that the Pope, the successor of St. Peter, is divinely assisted when pronouncing solemnly *ex cathedra* on questions of faith and morals.   When so pronouncing, the decisions of the Supreme Pastor have always been accepted by the Church, whether dispersed or assembled in council.   It is a received belief among Christians that to every legitimate office is attached a grace of vocation.   Is it not, therefore, in accordance with reason and Christian faith, that such grace should belong, and specially to the highest and most important of all offices ?   Such grace or assistance was promised to St. Peter, and through him to his successors, who are appointed to bear witness throughout all time to the truths of Divine revelation.   For our blessed Lord declared, "I am with you all days."   He could not better have secured the permanence of his religion—the kingdom of God on earth, for the salvation of men in every age of the world.   When the Supreme Pastor speaks in the exercise of his sublime office, the Church also speaks.   The teaching and testimony of the Head of the Church and of the great body of the Church are identical.   They must always be in harmony, as was so admirably shown by the decision of the council on infallibility and the confirmation thereof by the Holy Father—*confirma fratres tuous*—" confirm thy brethren."   Let not the opponents of the Church and her salutary doctrines be carried away by the idea that a subservient council wished only to glorify their spiritual Chief by ascribing to him imaginary personal gifts.   They were incapable of any such thing.   They were an assembly of the most venerable men in Christendom, who felt all the weight of their responsibility to God and men in the exercise of their sacred functions.   Their decision has not altered the position of the Supreme Pastor.   Any writings or discourses which he may produce in his merely personal or more private capacity are received by the Christian world with that degree of consideration to which they are entitled on account of the estimation in which he is held by men as a theologian and a man of learning and ability.   It is only when pronouncing solemnly *ex cathedra*, as the successor of St. Peter and the Head of the Church, on questions of faith and morals, that he is universally believed to be divinely assisted so as to be above the danger of erring, or of leading into error—in other words (and we cannot help who may be offended), that he is infallible.

FRANCO-PRUSSIAN WAR—WITHDRAWAL OF THE FRENCH GARRISON FROM ROME—ADJOURNMENT OF THE COUNCIL.

Events were now at hand which made it impossible for the council to hold another session. The French Emperor had greatly fallen, in the estimation of the people of France, from the time of his shameful abandonment of the chivalrous Maximilian and the popular design of establishing a Latin empire on the continent of America. In order to make amends and regain his *prestige*, he had revived the idea, so dear to the French, of rectifying the Rhine frontier of France by resuming possession of Luxembourg and some other adjacent provinces. He formally intimated his design to Prussia. That Power, however, aware of its rights and conscious of its military superiority, declined all negotiation on the subject. From that moment Prussia held herself in readiness to repel, with the sword, if necessary, any insolence that, in the future, might proceed from her aggressive neighbor, for whose tottering throne war was a necessity. The candidature of Prince Leopold of Hohenzollern for the throne of Spain now afforded a pretext, which Napoleon III. was only too anxious to find, for provoking by a fresh insult his powerful rival. It may be that he dreaded the accession of strength which might eventually accrue to Prussia if the crown of Spain were placed on the head of a Prince of the house of Hohenzollern. Napoleon remonstrated, and threatened war. The youthful German prince generously renounced a candidature which it was not hard to see would lead to a rupture between the two Powers, and cause a destructive war. The King of Prussia, head of the Hohenzollerns, sanctioned, if he did not command, this act of moderation on the part of the prince, his relative. But moderation was of no avail. Napoleon, surrounded by a jacobinical ministry, insisted upon war. The very idea of proposing a German for the throne of Spain appeared to him to be a sufficient cause for issuing a declaration of hostilities. The gauntlet thus thrown down, the Prussian monarch was too chivalrous to decline the challenge. He relied on his great military strength, and could afford to despise the comparatively inferior preparations of the French Empire. With the vast resources of France at his command, the Emperor, one would suppose, might have managed, in the course of three years, to increase and descipline his army, garrison his fortresses and seek alliances. He might have taken more time if necessary. He had no need to precipitate events, as he so recklessly did, by declaring war when there was positively no preparation made for it. We shall presently see whether he were not one of those whom Providence deprives of reason when it has resolved on their destruction. In the absence of more effective preparations, the small garrison at Rome of five thousand men was withdrawn in order to augment the army which all France believed was destined to crush the formidable Teuton and capture Berlin. If, however, this had been Napoleon's only object in recalling the troops, he could have accomplished it as easily by ordering four thousand five hundred of the Roman garrison to join the invading army, leaving the remaining five hundred to guard the city of the Popes. This smaller number would surely have been as able as five thousand to repel a Piedmontese force of sixty thousand men. But there was question of more than mere physical power. So long as it was evident that France protected the Papal city, whether by a greater or smaller number of soldiers, the legions of Piedmont never would have marched against it. Napoleon's minister, M. de Gramont, revealed the pretext: "It is certainly not from strategetical necessity that we evacuate the Roman States, but the political urgency is obvious. We must conciliate the good-will of the Italian Cabinet." Much, indeed, it availed them.

Viterbo was evacuated on the 4th of August. The last remnant of French troops embarked at Civita Vecchia, partly on the 4th and partly on the 6th, the very days on which the French army experienced its first reverses at Weissemberg, Wœrth and Spikeren. Instead of hesitating to perform a most cowardly act, which, viewing it only politically, proclaimed his weakness to all Europe, the Emperor Napoleon made all haste to complete it. He expressed regret. Who will say that he was sincere? Had he not perfected the master-work of his reign—his grand transalpine scheme? The Piedmontese minister, Visconti Venosta, gives a very distinct reply. Writing to the Piedmontese representatives at foreign courts, this minister says that as several governments had desired to know their views in regard to the relation of passing events with the Roman question, his government had no hesitation in making the clearest explanations. The convention of 15th September, 1864, had not sufficed to avert the causes arising abroad which hindered the settlement of the Roman difficulty. He then accuses the Roman Court of having assumed a hostile attitude in the centre of the peninsula, and that the consequences of such a position might be serious for Piedmont on occasion of the Franco-Prussian war and the complications to which it might give rise. Visconti Venosta further states that the basis of a new and definite solution of the Roman question had been confidentially recognized in principle, and was subject only to the condition of opportunity.

It is no pleasure, surely, to convict the late Emperor of a deep-laid conspiracy to revolutionize the Roman State, and rob the Holy Father of his time-honored patrimony. But there is no escaping the conclusion that he had never ceased to plot with the revolutionists. He was not yet vanquished and fallen himself when he left the Sovereign Pontiff to his enemies.

One of the chief calumnies of the time was directed by the revolutionists against Pius IX. They accused the venerable Pontiff of encouraging the Prussian monarch to wage war against France. The falsehood of this accusation can only be equalled by its absurdity. The Holy Father, on the contrary, earnestly endeavored, although in vain, before the commencement of hostilities, to avert the dire calamity of war. So early as 22nd July, 1870, he interposed between the two rival sovereigns. " Sire," he wrote to the King of Prussia, " in the most serious circumstances in which we are placed, it will appear to you unusual to receive a letter from me. But as I hold the office of Vicar of the God of peace in this world, I cannot do less than offer you my mediation. It is my desire that all preparations for war should disappear, and that the evils which inevitably follow should be prevented. My mediation is that of a sovereign who, in his capacity of king, cannot, on account of the smallness of his territory, excite any jealousy, but who, nevertheless, will inspire confidence by the moral and religious influence which he personifies. May God hear my prayers! and may He also accept those which I offer for your Majesty, with whom I desire to be united in the common bond of charity.   Pius PP. IX."

" I have written also to the Emperor of the French."

The King of Prussia replied from Berlin on the 30th July. The kindly monarch expressed himself beautifully and with the finest feeling : " Most blessed Pontiff—I was not surprised but deeply moved when I read the feeling words which you wrote, in order to cause the voice of the God of peace to be heard. How could I be deaf to such a powerful appeal ? God is my witness that neither I nor my people have desired this war. In fulfilment of the sacred duties which God lays on sovereigns and on nations, we have drawn the sword in order to defend the independence and honor of our country, and we are prepared to lay it down as soon as these blessings shall no longer be in danger of being torn from us. If your Holiness could offer me, on the part of him who has so unexpectedly declared war, the assurance of sincerely pacific dispositions and of guarantees against a renewal of such violation of the peace and tranquillity of Europe, I certainly would be far from refusing to accept them at the venerable hands of your Holiness, united as I am with you by the bonds of Christian charity and true friendship. WILLIAM."

The letter of Pius IX. to the French Emperor has not been published, and it is not known whether Napoleon deigned to reply. One thing is certain. He did not either accept the mediation or heed the remonstrances of the Holy Father. He was equally deaf to the warnings of his old allies of Crimean fame. The British government despatched to Paris a member of the cabinet, who, in a prolonged interview with the demented Emperor, argued earnestly on the part of Queen Victoria and her ministry against his purposed violation of the peace of Europe by undertaking an unprovoked, unjust and irrational war.

The war broke out. It was waged disastrously to the French. Pius IX. was deeply grieved. "Poor France!" he exclaimed, as he heard of each new defeat of the nation that he loved so well. He interposed once more. But with the like ill success. Neither could the Germans be checked in their victorious career, nor could the vanquished French be induced to acknowledge their defeat and seek such terms of peace as might possibly have been obtained. On 12th November, 1870, the Holy Father wrote to Mgr. Guibert, Archbishop of Tours, in whose palace was resident a delegation of the French government.

"Neglect nothing," wrote the Pontiff, "we conjure you, in order to prevail on your illustrious guests to put an end to this war. Nevertheless, we are not unaware that it does not depend on them alone, and that we should vainly pursue the great object of peace, if our pacific ministry did not also meet with support on the part of the conqueror. So we have not hesitated to write to this effect to his Majesty the King of Prussia. We cannot, indeed, affirm anything as to the favorable result of the step which we have taken. We have, nevertheless, some ground for hope, as this monarch has in other circumstances shown us much good-will."

Unfortunately, the bold men who had assumed supreme authority in France, and had undertaken the difficult task of saving the country, were incapable of accepting good advice, especially when it came from a Pope. The King of Prussia and his minister, on the other hand, were of the number of those whom victory intoxicates, and whom the power to dare everything deprives of all sense of moderation. Pius IX. did not know them as yet. The representations of Mgr. Guibert to Messrs. Cremieux, Glais Bisoin and Gambetta, were not more successful than those of Mgr. Ledochowski, Archbishop of Posen, who hastened to the presence of King William at Versailles. The earnest endeavors of the archbishop met with less consideration, to all appearance, at least, although it does not appear that, on this occasion, William made any reply to Pius IX.

Notwithstanding these untoward circumstances, the Holy Pontiff never lost confidence in the nation of Charlemagne and St. Louis. France, he said, although sadly exhausted and bathed in blood, would yet show excellent fruits.

The Piedmontese government, which had been for some time established at Florence, now resolved to avail itself of the disasters of France to seize the city of the Popes, and to constitute it the capital of regenerated Italy. The minister, Visconti Venosta, in a circular letter, renewed his calumnies, pretending that a hostile power existed in the centre of Italy, and hypocritically declared that it had become necessary that the government of his master should assume the protection of the Holy See. They would not wait, he said, moreover, till the agitation at Rome should lead to the effusion of blood between the Romans and foreign forces, but would proceed, as soon as they could learn that the opportune time had come, to occupy what remained to the Holy Father of the Roman States. The information which the minister sought came with remarkable rapidity. The day after the circular alluded to was written, another minister, Signor Lanza, declared that the solemn moment had arrived when the government of his king was called upon, in the interest of the Holy See and of Italy, to take measures for the national safety. An envoy was despatched to Rome, with a letter to the Pope, assuring him that the king's government was firmly resolved to give the necessary guarantees for the spiritual independence of the Holy See, and that these guarantees would be hereafter the subject of negotiations with the Powers that were interested in the Papacy. In addition to this mockery of diplomacy, Victor Emmanuel himself wrote to the Pope, expressing his filial devotedness, while at the same time he was preparing, from an excess of affection, to bombard his city and slay his defenders, to rob him from an excessive zeal for justice, to imprison him in order to set him free, and, finally, that he ought to allow all this to be done without complaint, and even thank the good king who took so much care of him.

The Florentine Envoy, Signor Ponza di San Martino, when he came to Rome, made his first visit to Cardinal Antonelli, who received him politely, and did not refuse to ask for him an interview with the Pope. The cardinal, however, declined to have any conversation with him on the object of his mission. "I know already," said he, "all that you could tell me. You are also aware of the reply that I would give. Force, not argument, speaks at present." Pius IX. was more afflicted than surprised when he read King Victor Emmanuel's letter. He was particularly pained by the tone of this document. "How the revolution has abased a Prince of the House of Savoy! It is not satisfied with dethroning kings as often as it can, and with committing their heads to the guillotine. It must also dishonor them." The envoy insisted that the king was sincere; that he was more convinced than any other, that the independence of the Chief of the Church was a necessity; and that he offered real and substantial guarantees to this independence. "And who will guarantee these guarantees?" asked the Pope. "Your king cannot promise anything. He is no longer a king. He depends on his parliament, which, in its turn, depends on the secret societies." The ambassador, more disconcerted than ever, remarked on the difficulties of the time. He claimed, although timidly, that the king ought to be judged according to his intentions, as at the time he was constrained by the aspirations of four-and-twenty millions of Italians. "Your statement is untrue, sir," replied Pius IX. "You calumniate Italy! Of these four-and-twenty millions, twenty-three millions are devoted to me, love and respect me, and only require that the revolution leave them and me in peace. The remaining million you have poisoned with false doctrines and inspired with base passions. These unfortunate people are the friends of your king and the instigators of his ambitious designs. When they have no longer need of him they will cast him aside. My answer will be communicated to you to-morrow. I am too much moved with grief and indignation to be able to write at present." Next day, accordingly, 11th September, the following reply to Victor Emmanuel was conveyed to Signor Ponza:

"SIRE,—Count Ponza di San Martino has handed me a letter which it has pleased your Majesty to address to me. This letter is not worthy of an affectionate son who glories in professing the Catholic faith, and who prides himself on being royally loyal. I dwell not on the details contained in the letter, in order to avoid renewing the pain which a first reading of it gave me. I bless God, who has permitted that your Majesty should overwhelm with bitterness the last years of my life. I cannot admit the demands made in your letter, nor adopt the principles which it contains. I call upon God anew, and commend to Him my cause, which is also wholly His own. I beseech Him to bestow abundant graces on your Majesty, to deliver you from all danger, and to grant you all the mercy which you require." This answer was not waited for. Victor Emmanuel made haste to become the declared enemy of Pius IX. On 11th September, the Pontifical territory was invaded by his orders at three different points—Aquapendente, in the north; Orte and Correse, to the east; and on the south, Ceprano. The invading army amounted to sixty thousand men. After the withdrawal of the French garrison, there remained only at Rome the few soldiers who constituted the army of the Pope. A great portion of these were, to the lasting honor of a remote British dependency, Canadians. They all deserved well of the Holy Father, and had imperilled their lives in his service. On occasion of the great difficulty which had arisen, accordingly, he was pleased to address to them in person special words of comfort and encouragement.

It was evident that, in the adverse circumstances of the time, the Council of the Vatican could not long continue its deliberations. Accordingly, the Holy Father authorized such of the bishops as desired to retire to return to their dioceses until the feast of St. Martin, 11th November following, at which date it was intended to resume the labors of the council. It was not, however, strictly speaking, suspended. Some general congregations (committees) were still held, and the various deputations continued their studies. During this time, the bishops of the minority, one after another, expressed their adhesion. The bishops, on returning to their dioceses, were received with magnificent proofs of the people's fidelity. Some parties pretending that the Constitution, *Pastor æternus*, was not obligatory, because the council was not terminated, Cardinal Antonelli addressed to the Papal Nuncio at Brussels a letter under date of 11th August, which removed all doubt on the subject. The rapid march of events, however, rendered it necessary to interrupt the labors of the assembled Fathers. On 20th October, accordingly, Pius IX. published the Bull, *Postquam Dei Munere*, which suspended them for an indefinite period.

THE WOLF IN THE FOLD.

When all the Pontifical forces had returned from the outposts, on the approach of the formidable Piedmontese invader, and were concentrated at Rome, they numbered not more than some ten thousand men. Such an army was quite inadequate to cope with the superior power of the Florence government.

Pius IX., therefore, in order to prevent an unavailing conflict, placed an order in the hands of his general-in-chief, to the effect that as soon as sufficient resistance was made, in order to show that violence was used against the Holy See, he should surrender the city. This was a trial to the devoted Papal Zouaves, who, during the few moments that fighting was allowed, conducted themselves in the most gallant style, and kept the enemy at bay. Their bravery deserved a better fate than that which befell them and the Roman State. Two lieutenants, Niel and Brondeis, fell, pierced with wounds, exclaiming with their last breath, "Long live Pius IX.!" A brave Alsacian fell by their side. A Canadian Zouave, Hormisdas Sauvet, was also wounded, and declared that he was more fortunate than so many of his fellow-countrymen who had been two years in the Pontifical service without the slightest accident. Another Zouave, whose name was Burel, when wounded in the mouth, and his tongue was destroyed, made a sign that he wished to write. Paper was brought to him, and he thus wrote his will: "I leave to the Holy Father all that I possess." He died the following day. The paper, all covered with blood, was taken to Pius IX., who, in his turn, bedewed it with tears, and desired to keep it as a memorial.

The Italian general Cadorna, an apostate priest, commenced bombarding Rome at five points. At one of these, between the gates Pia and Salara, they speedily effected a breach in an old wall about two feet in thickness, and built of bricks and tufa. It may be conceived with what feelings the brave Papal soldiers beheld the storming column enter the city, whilst they, in obedience to orders, remained inactive spectators. They bore in silence and without moving an arm the insults and even the violence of the fierce soldiery of Piedmont. Finally, after a white flag had been displayed for some time on the Pontifical side, almost in vain, General Kanzler had an interview with Cadorna, at the Villa Albani. It can hardly be said that a convention was resolved on. It would be more true to write that the terms of the conqueror were imposed on the vanquished, and, as a matter of necessity, accepted. The soldiers were better treated than in such circumstances could well be expected. They were allowed to march out of Rome with the honors of war, bearing with them their colors, arms and baggage. When once out of the city, however, they were all obliged to lay down their arms and their colors, with the exception of the officers, who were permitted to retain their swords, their horses and everything that belonged to them. Such soldiers as were foreigners were to be sent to their respective homes by the Italian government. The future position of the Pope's native troops was to be taken into consideration. By the articles of capitulation, it was settled that the Pope should be allowed only the Vatican Palace and that part of Rome which is called the Leonine city. Thus were carried into effect the views of those revolutionists of Paris and Turin who claimed to be moderate. Their programme was that which Prince Napoleon had concocted in 1861.

It is deeply to be regretted that when so little resistance was required, so many of the Pope's brave defenders should have fallen. Some were basely murdered in the streets on the nights of the 20th and 21st September. Without counting these, however, there were sixteen killed, of whom one was an officer, and fifty-eight wounded. Among these last there were two officers, two surgeons and a chaplain. The troops having been so hastily dismissed to their foreign homes, to Civita Vecchia, etc., it is possible that the list may be incomplete. The losses of the Piedmontese were never made known. It is certain, at any rate, that one hundred wounded were received at the hospital " de la Consolation " alone.

Whilst Pius IX. neglected not to warn, remonstrate and use every fair and loyal art of diplomacy, he failed not, at the same time, to have recourse to the spiritual weapon of prayer. As the enemy approached his gates, he repaired to the Lateran Basilica, and there most earnestly addressed his supplications to the God of armies. Notwithstanding his great age, he ascended, on his knees, all the time absorbed in prayer, the twenty-nine steps of the *Scala Santa*, which, at the Palace of Pontius Pilate, was consecrated by the footsteps of our suffering Saviour. On reaching the chapel at the head of the holy stair, he poured forth a prayer by which all who heard it were deeply moved. He beseeched our blessed Lord, whose humble servant and representative he was, to turn aside the wrath of heaven, to prevent the profanation of the holy places, to save his people. He conjured our most loving Saviour, by virtue of His passion, by the pain especially which He suffered when spontaneously ascending that same stair in order to undergo the mockery of judgment by His erring creatures, to have mercy on afflicted Rome, on His people, on His Church—His well-beloved and stainless spouse, to save her temples from desecration and her children from the sword. "Pardon," he concluded, "pardon my people, who are also Thy people. If Thou desirest a victim, O God! take Thy unworthy servant! Have I not lived long enough? Mercy! O God! have mercy, I beseech Thee! But whatever may happen, Thy holy will be done!"

As was always the case when Pius IX. appeared among his people, he was received on this occasion with every demonstration of welcome. As soon as the inhabitants of the locality became aware of his presence, they thronged around his carriage in order to do him honor, and, urged by the circumstances of the time, with that freedom and familiarity of manner peculiar to the Romans, they added to their acclamations and cordial *vivats* words of encouragement and even advice. "Defend yourself, Holy Father! defend us! courage! courage!" A parting benediction, and he left his people of Rome to be with them no more.

All the representatives of foreign States, with the exception of Von Arnim, the Prussian Ambassador, remained with the Holy Father, protesting by their presence against the flagrant violation of a solemn treaty which the Florence government was committing. It is not known that Von Arnim was instructed by his government to act as he did. But none are ignorant that since that time it has dealt severely with him. The diplomatist who rejoiced over the fall of Rome has himself incurred disgrace, and undergoes the punishment of a banished man.

Pius IX., complimenting the ambassadors, called to mind how they had afforded him much comfort on a similar occasion. This was in 1848, and at the Quirinal Palace. He informed them also that he had written to King Victor Emmanuel, but did not know whether he had received his letter. At any rate, he had little hope that it would have any result. His mention of the notorious Bixio, who was with the Italian army, was not without significance. This rabid red republican had threatened that if ever he entered Rome he would throw the Pope and cardinals into the Tiber. "His ideas," the Holy Father observed, "were now probably modified. He was with a king. May it please Heaven to effect a complete transformation and convert this Bixio and so many others."

The students of the American College at Rome, the ambassadors were then told, had offered to take up arms in the service of Pius IX. The Holy Father would not allow them to serve otherwise than by attending to the wounded.

"I wish I could say that I count on you," said the Pope, addressing the ambassadors, "and that one of you will have the honor, as formerly, to extricate the Church and her Chief from difficulty. But the times are changed. The aged Pope, in his misfortunes, cannot rely on any one in this world. But the Church is immortal. Let this never be forgotten."

General Kanzler now brought the intelligence that a breach was made, and the assault on the point of commencing. The Pope having conferred a few moments apart with Cardinal Antonelli, resumed his discourse: "I have just given the order to capitulate. We might still defend ourselves. But to what purpose? Abandoned by everyone, I must yield sooner or later; and I must not allow any useless shedding of blood. You are my witnesses, gentlemen, that the foreigner enters here only by violence, and that if my door is forced, it is by breaking it open. This the world shall know, and history will tell it, one day, to the honor of the Romans, my children. I speak not of myself, gentlemen; I weep not for myself, but for those unfortunate young men who have come to defend me as their Father. You will take care, each of you, of those of your country. There are some from all countries. I recommend them all to you, in order that you may preserve them from such maltreatment as others had to suffer ten years ago. I absolve my soldiers from their oath of fidelity. I pray God to give me strength and courage. Ah! it is not they who suffer injustice that are most to be pitied." Having thus spoken, he took leave of the ambassadors, with tears in his eyes. On the same day, Cardinal Antonelli, by his order, intimated the sad tidings to the governments of all civilized nations. Pius IX. also protested by an allocution to the cardinals. It only remains to chronicle the shameful violation of the treaty, which bound the French nation to protect the Holy Father, by the government temporarily established in France. " The September agreement," wrote a representative of the French republic, under the date of 22nd September, 1870, " virtually ceases to exist by the proclamation of the French republic. I congratulate the King of Italy, in the name of the French government and in my own name, on the deliverance of Rome and the final consecration of Italian unity." Thus was disgrace added to the misfortunes of a great country.

It was some time before order could be restored at Rome. From four thousand to five thousand vagrants and bandits, chiefly Garibaldians, entered the city at the heels of the invading force. The prisons were thrown open, and swelled the ranks of these disorderly bands. During two whole days that these lawless hordes were allowed to commit all kinds of excesses, houses were fired, valuable property destroyed or carried off, some eighty unoffending citizens put to death, and such of the Roman soldiers as were recognized cut down or thrown into the Tiber. Nor was the Italian general in any hurry to repress such proceedings. " *Lasciate il popolo sfogarsi*," coolly said

Cadorna to the parties who entreated him to put an end to such horrors. This general and the men with whom he acted were only robbers on a greater scale. Their commissioners lost not a moment. When tranquillity was somewhat restored, and complaints were made against housebreakers, it was found that everything was already confiscated—libraries, archives, colleges, museums, etc.

Victor Emmanuel had need of the mob which followed his troops. Anxious to give a coloring of right to his brigandage, he resolved, according to the fashion of his Imperial patron and accomplice, to hold a *plebiscitum*. In the city of Rome, with the help of his numerous assemblage of vagrants, he had forty thousand votes, whilst against him there were only forty-six. Something similar was done in the landward part of the Roman State. Better, surely, no right beyond what the sword could give, than such a transparent semblance of right. No wonder that Victor Emmanuel's best friends condemned such an impolitic and ridiculous proceeding. None could be so simple as to believe that there were only forty-six voters against him, when all the numerous officials, both civil and military, protested against his aggression by resigning their offices. It is bad enough when men in authority play fantastic tricks. When the play is badly played, the trickery becomes ridiculous.

It now remained to adhibit the seal of permanency to the *fait accompli*. This was done by the following decree:

Art. 1st. Rome and the Roman Provinces constitute an integral portion of the kingdom of Italy.

Art. 2nd. The Sovereign Pontiff retains the dignity, inviolability, and all the prerogatives of a sovereign.

Art. 3rd. A special law will sanction the conditions calculated to guarantee, even by territorial franchises, the independence of the Sovereign Pontiff and the free exercise of the spiritual authority of the Holy See.

Thus was sacrificed to Italian unity the city of the Popes. Was the sacrifice essential? Florence might have well sufficed.

It was of little avail that the brigands who followed the Piedmontese army were compelled, [by superior power, to moderate their violence. Their robberies were, for the most part, of a private nature, and committed on a small scale. Those of their superiors—the Piedmontese usurpers—were grander and more extensive. They astonished, if they did not terrify, by their magnitude and the daring which achieved them. There were palaces at Rome and soldiers' quarters which had satisfied all the requirements of Papal grandeur. These were nothing to the republican simplicity of the new order of things. No doubt the parliament which had just arrived from Florence required ample space. The costly equipages and hunting studs of a constitutional king were also to be provided for. Could not all this have been done, especially in such a vast city, without expropriating convents, desecrating churches, and even seizing for their purposes the refuges of the sick? It was more than an idea that required such spoliation. But what shall we say when we call to mind that the mere desire to modernize everything threatened the destruction of all those monuments which rendered Rome so dear to travellers from every clime? It had been hitherto the city of the Consuls, of the Emperors, of the Popes. It must now become a commonplace town, with straight lines, rectangles and parallelograms, like Philadelphia, New York, or the *Haussmanized* Paris of Napoleon III. The Royal Palace of the Popes, the Quirinal, was unscrupulously seized, in order to make a city mansion for the King of Italy. It was too magnificent, apparently, for this gentleman prince. He seldom entered it. It may be that he dreaded offending the revolution, to which he owed so much, by too great an affectation of royal style. If the gratitude of such a heartless thing could be relied on, he had no need to fear. Without the sword of Piedmont the revolution never could have entered Rome.

Meanwhile, the Pope was engaged in most anxious deliberation. At last, considering the disturbed state of Europe generally, he concluded that it was better for him to remain at Rome.   A Pontifical ship, which had not been included in the articles of capitulation, awaited his orders in the waters of Civita Vecchia.   This vessel was named the "Immaculate Conception;" and two years later, by order of his Holiness, was laid up at Toulon, under the protection of the flag of France.   A French ship, the "Orenoque," was then placed at the disposal of Pius IX., in case he should wish, at any time, to leave Rome: and later, the "Kleber," which was stationed in the waters of Bastia (Corsica).

The Holy Father had made up his mind so early as the first days of September, 1870, to remain in the city.   His presence, he felt confident, would so far prevent the evils which he feared.   If he were gone, there would be less restraint on the usurping power, when it might wish to confiscate more convents, churches and church property generally.   Almost all the foreign ambassadors remained with him; and this circumstance presented another cause why the new government would be more moderate and circumspect in its attacks on property.

A beautiful legend which the Holy Father recounted, at an interview with Cardinal De Bonnechose, was well calculated to reconcile the Catholic world to the stay of Pius IX. at Rome, even although he was there as a prisoner of the victorious king.   And a prisoner he really was; for he could not have removed to any other country except by a successful stratagem, so closely guarded were all the approaches to the city by the myrmidons of the conqueror.   Taking the cardinal aside, he informed him that he wished to present him with a memorial. "The object in itself is of little value.   The intention with which I give it is all its worth."   It was a small plate of ivory, framed in gold, surmounted by the arms of the Holy See, and representing in the most exquisite manner a moving scene in the life of St. Peter.   "You behold the subject of my frequent meditations for many years.   When the prince of the apostles, fleeing from persecution, quitted Rome, he met, not far from the gate of Saint Sebastian, our Lord Himself, carrying His cross and looking extraordinarily sad : ' *Domine quo vadis?* ' Lord, where are you going?' exclaimed Peter. ' I am going to Rome,' replied our blessed Lord, ' in order to be there crucified anew—to die in your place, as your courage has failed you.' " "Peter understood," continued the Holy Father, " and remained at Rome. I also remain. For if, at this moment, I left the eternal city, it would seem to me as if our Lord addressed to me the same words of reproach. The representation of this scene I am anxious to leave with you as a memorial. It may, in reality, be nothing more than a pious legend. But for me it is a decisive instruction." Pius IX. then delivered the precious medallion to the cardinal.

GUARANTEES WHICH GUARANTEED NOTHING—£120,000 WITH WHICH NOTHING WAS PAID—PETER'S PENCE WHICH PAID EVERYTHING.

In order to give a coloring to his usurpation in the eyes of Christian Europe, and to set at rest any scruples which may have remained in the minds of his adherents, Victor Emmanuel caused a law to be enacted on the 13th March, 1871, which is known as *the law of guarantees*. This law declared the person of the Sovereign Pontiff sacred and inviolable, recognized his title and dignity of sovereign, assured to him an annual endowment of 3,225,000 francs (£120,000), together with the possession of the Vatican and Lateran Palaces, as well as the Pontifical Villa of Castel Gandolfo, and provided for the complete liberty of all future Conclaves and Œcumenical Councils. It requires two parties to every contract or agreement. *The law of guarantees* had no such condition, the Holy Father not being a party to it. He could not accept the honors which the new government pretended to confer, nor the money which it offered. It was not a government by any other law than that of the sword—that of a war not only undertaken against the unoffending, but also in violation of a solemn treaty. Neither was the treasure which it proffered its rightful property. It held it, indeed; but only as the robber holds the purse of his victim, whilst he mocks him by an offer of alms. It was also the merest mockery to pretend to recognize the Pope as a sovereign, whilst, in reality, he was detained as a prisoner, who could not pass beyond the gate of his garden without coming into the custody of the armed police or soldiery of the usurper. By the provisions of this same law of guarantees, full liberty was secured to the Sovereign Pontiff in the exercise of his spiritual office. The persecutions to which the ministers of the Church were frequently subjected, when they dared to obey the orders of the Pope in fulfilling the duties of his and their ministry, show to what extent the framers of the law were sincere. It need only be added, without further comment, that article eighteen confiscated, by anticipation, all ecclesiastical properties, under the pretence that they were to be reorganized, preserved and administered. No wonder that the Pope stigmatized such a law as hypocritical and iniquitous. In the supposition that he could have derived any benefit from accepting it, he would still have been at the mercy of a fickle king and parliament, to whom it was competent, at any moment, to change the law which they had made. The safety of the Holy Father, under Heaven, lay in this, that the newly-erected kingdom of Victor Emmanuel was most ambitious to figure as a State among the States of Europe. To none of these would it have been pleasing to see the venerable Pontiff forcibly driven from the city of the Popes. It was necessary, as far as possible, to blindfold them.

"I have, indeed, great need of money," said Pius IX., when the sum appropriated by the law of guarantees was first presented for his acceptance; "my children, everywhere, impose on themselves the most serious sacrifices in order to supply my wants, at all times so great, but to which you are daily adding. As it is a portion of the property that has been stolen from me, I could only accept it as restitution money. I will never sign a receipt which would appear to express my acquiescence in the robbery." Every succeeding year the form, or rather the farce, of offering the subsidy was renewed and as often rejected. That the offer of so large a sum was hypocritical, and intended only for show, is well proved by the circumstance that the liberal Italian government deprived of their incomes and drove from their places of residence many bishops, whose wants were supplied in their great distress from the resources of the Holy Father.

Love is stronger than hate; and so well-beloved was Pius IX. throughout Catholic Christendom, that contributions of money from every country where there were any Catholics were poured into his treasury, in such abundance as more than compensated for the loss of his Italian revenue. Not only were these contributions, under the name of Peter's pence, sufficient to maintain the venerable Pontiff during the remainder of his days, without its being necessary to accept, as a royal benefaction, any portion of the property that was stolen from him, they also sufficed to enable him to continue their salaries to his former employees, who had almost all remained faithful, as well as to those still required for his service and for transacting the business of the Church. In addition to this, he retained on half or quarter pay a number of the soldiers of his former army, and maintained his establishment of Vigna Pia, together with the hospital of Tata Giovanni, from which the new Roman municipality had meanly withdrawn the subsidy, for no other reason than that in former times it had been a favorite institution of Pius IX. This was not all. The Holy Pontiff maintained, by means of popular schools, a necessary warfare against both Protestant and Atheistic propagandism. The former had been very active ever since the occupation of Rome by the Piedmontese. The various Protestant societies actually spent £100,000 yearly in the vain attempt to Protestantize the Romans. By 1st January, 1875, they had erected three churches and founded twelve missionary residences in the interest of divers denominations—Anglicans, Methodists, American Episcopalians, Vaudois, Baptists, Anabaptists, etc. The Italians have little taste for Protestantism in any of its forms. So there was no danger of discordant and jarring sects coming to prevail. It cannot be denied, however, that the movement increased the number of free-thinkers—a result no less calculated to afflict the Holy Father.

When to these expenses are added those of sustaining the Sacred College, the prelature, the guards, the museums, and bishops that were exiled for the faith, there is shown a monthly expenditure of more than six hundred thousand francs, which is equal to seven millions and a half yearly. These expenses always increased as the elder bishops passed away. Pius IX. appointed successors. But as none of these could, in conscience, ask the royal *exequatur*, which, notwithstanding article sixteen of the notorious guarantees, was still in force, Victor Emmanuel had no hesitation in suppressing the revenues of the bishops. Pius IX. sent to the bishops who were thus deprived of their legitimate incomes five hundred francs monthly, and to archbishops from seven hundred to one thousand francs. He also labored to establish foundations for the education of ecclesiastical students whom a revolutionary and anti-Christian law made subject to military service, thus rendering morally impossible the following out of clerical vocations and the recruiting of the priesthood. From this and such like proceedings, it can easily be seen that the revolutionary *regime*, and the Italian government was nothing less, aimed at the extirpation of Christianity, and that civilization, the only possible civilization which follows in its train.

Misfortune, meanwhile, was not neglected by the Holy Pontiff. He sent vestments to the churches of Paris which had been pillaged by the Commune. He provided, habitually, in like manner, for the churches of poor and remote missions. In July, 1875, he sent twenty thousand francs to the people who had suffered by inundations in the southwest of France, and five thousand francs to such as had similarly suffered at Brescia, in Upper Italy. He bestowed, likewise, large sums for the rebuilding of churches—for instance, eight hundred francs for this pious purpose to the Bishop of Sarsina, and two thousand to the Bishop of Osimo. Charitable institutions were not overlooked, and the Princess Rospigliosi Champigny de Cadore received fifty thousand francs towards the support of the house of St. Mary Magdalen, the object of which was the preservation of young women in the city of Rome.

As regarded works of art or of public utility, the venerable Pontiff was no less munificent. He completed the restoration of the Church of Saint Ange in Peschiera, together with the magnificent contiguous portico called Octavia, and rebuilt the altar with the marbles found by Visconti in the emporium of the Emperors. The tomb of his illustrious predecessor Gregory VII., at Salerno, having become dilapidated, he undertook to restore it at his own cost, and renewed the fine epitaph which Pope Gregory himself had caused to be engraved on the sepulchral stone: *Dilexi justitiam et odivi iniquitatem, et ecce in exilio morior.* (I loved righteousness and hated iniquity, and lo! I die in exile.)

Quite a number of people were employed in the manufacture of mosaics at the Vatican. On this the Romans justly prided themselves. Pius IX. continued to employ these artists, and, as in former times, presented their works to his guests or to the churches of Italy. If he was not still a king, he retained, at least, a truly royal prerogative—that of conferring gifts in every way worthy of royalty. Nothing could exceed the delicacy and graciousness with which he did so. Of this the two Russian Grand Dukes, brothers of the reigning Emperor, were witnesses, when he made a present to them of a splendid table, in mosaic, which they were observed to admire among the more humble furniture of his apartment. The funds must have been, indeed, abundant which could meet so many demands. Although despoiled of his revenues and property, the Holy Father was a richer monarch than the prince who robbed him. So liberally were Peter's pence bestowed and so economically managed, that Pius IX. was able to invest money for the benefit of his successor, although not to such an extent as to render the collection of Peter's pence in the future unnecessary.

It has long been customary, on occasion of the august ceremony of the coronation of the Popes, to address to them, with due solemnity, the words: *Annos Petri tu non videbis.* (Thou wilt not see the years of Peter.) It is related that one of the Popes thus replied to the ominous address: *Non est de fide.* (That is no article of faith.) Pius IX., however, was the first who showed that the words were not strictly prophetic. His Pontificate was prolonged beyond the years of Peter at Rome. Already, on the 16th of June, 1871, when he was enabled to celebrate the twenty-fifth anniversary of his election to the Pontifical chair, he had enjoyed more than the years of Peter. The great apostle, it will be remembered, spent two years after our Lord's ascension in preaching the Gospel at Jerusalem and throughout Judea. After this, Antioch, at the time the capital of the Eastern world, became the scene of his apostolic labors. He was bishop there for seven years when he established the central seat of Christendom at Rome, the metropolis of the known world. The apostle remained there till his martyrdom under Nero, A. D. 67. Thus, Peter was Pope thirty-four years or so, whilst he was Bishop of Rome only twenty-five years and some days. A festival at Rome could not now be held with the wonted circumstance of outward religious pomp. The remarkable anniversary was not, however, less devoutly observed at the Basilicas of St. Peter and St. John Lateran. These immense edifices were crowded with people of all classes and of every age. Nor in this did the Romans stand alone. Prayers and communions were offered up in every diocese of the world, supplicating Heaven for a continuation of the years which had been already so auspiciously granted to the venerable Pontiff. More than a thousand congratulatory messages were flashed along the telegraph lines. All the sovereigns of Europe, with scarcely an exception, paid their dutiful compliments to Pius IX.; the telegram of Queen Victoria being the first that reached him. From the New World as well as from the Old there came numerous deputations. One day, in replying to them, the Holy Father delivered no fewer than twelve discourses in Latin, French, Spanish and Italian. To many of the addresses was appended a singularly great number of signatures. The Bishop of Nevers presented one with two millions of names.

A few days later, 20th September, the Holy Father had to lament the death of his brother, Count Gaetano Mastai. So little, however, was his grief respected by Victor Emmanuel and his government, that their cannon were heard booming joyously in honor of the violent occupation of the city. All Rome was indignant. Patrician and plebeian, all citizens alike, hastened to the Vatican, protesting and presenting addresses of condolence. The *Riforma* (a Roman journal) said, on the occasion : " After two years' sojourn Italy was still as much a stranger as on the first day, so that there was no appearance of friendliness, but rather of a city that still groaned under a military occupation, which it bore with the greatest impatience."

MORE SPOLIATION AND DESECRATION—NO RECONCILIATION.

Robbery, wholesale and sacrilegious, was now the order of the day at Rome. Throughout the city convents were closed and sequestrated, libraries were confiscated, and often dilapidated in transferring them from one place to another. Religious men and religious women were driven from their homes and brutally searched on their thresholds lest they should carry away with them anything that belonged to them. These religious people obtained, every month, as indemnification, twenty-five centimes each daily, and the aged forty centimes ; but they were paid only when the treasury was in a condition to pay them, and this was not the case every month. The poor and the infirm, no longer sustained by Catholic charity, encumbered the hospitals or were associated with the knights of industry, who swarmed from the prisons of Italy. It was in vain that the police were doubled. Robberies increased in the same proportion. The people in such circumstances could not but ask themselves what sacrifices were laid upon himself by the usurping king, who was now the master of the domains of six Italian princes who had never allowed their subjects to go without bread. Before the end of the year 1873, the number of religious houses that were taken, in whole or in part, from their legitimate proprietors, was over one hundred. The intervention of diplomacy saved for a time the Roman College, which was essentially international and not Roman, as formerly no clerks of the city of Rome could attend it, and as it was endowed solely by foreign kings and benefactors. The Italian government consented, not, indeed, to renounce, but only to stay this new spoliation. It claimed all the more credit for its pretended moderation, as it secretly caused the newspapers in its interest to instigate it to listen to no terms. By means of its gensd'armes and its police force, it was master of the secret societies, and allowed them to raise a cry without allowing them to act, whilst it chose its own time for the execution of its wicked purposes.

Pius IX. was deeply grieved when beholding so many evil deeds which he could not prevent. His sorrow found expression in one of his allocutions, that of 1st January, 1873:

"You are come," said he, to parties who had come to compliment him on New Years day, "from divers distant lands in order to offer me your congratulations and wish me a happy new year. The past year, alas! is far from having been a happy one. Society is astray in evil courses. There are people who think that peace prevails at Rome, and that matters are not so bad there as is said. Some strangers, on arriving in the city, even ask for cards of admission to religious ceremonies. I am persuaded that this year also the same request will be made as regards the celebrations of holy week. So long as the present state of things continues, alas! there can be no such celebrations. The Church is in mourning. Rome has lost its character of capital of the Christian world— so many horrible deeds are done, so many blasphemies uttered. Let us beseech the Lord to put an end to such a painful state of things."

Victor Emmanuel, notwithstanding his extraordinary proceedings, appears to have thought that there might be a reconciliation with the Pope. The Emperor of Brazil, a man of science and a celebrated traveller, then at Rome, accepted the office of mediator. One morning, in the year 1872, the Brazilian monarch repaired to the Vatican. The hour of his visit was inopportune, as its object also proved to be. It was seven o'clock in the morning. The Holy Father had not yet finished his Mass when the Emperor was announced. As soon as was possible his Holiness proceeded to receive him. Whether fearing some design, or from dislike only to meet a prince who came from the hostile usurper's court, Pius IX., with an unusual coldness of manner, addressed the Emperor : "What does your Majesty desire ?" "I beg your Holiness will not call me Majesty. Here, I am only the Count of Alcantara." The Holy Father then, without showing the least emotion, said to him : "My dear Count, what do you desire ?" "I am come, your Holiness, in order to ask that you will allow me to introduce to you the King of Italy." At these words the Pontiff rose from his seat, and, looking indignantly at the Emperor, said to him with much firmness : "It is quite useless to hold such language. Let the King of Piedmont abjure his misdeeds and restore to me my States. I will then consent to receive him. But not till then."

CREATION OF CARDINALS—AUDIENCES AND ALLOCUTIONS—THE POPE REALLY A PRISONER—THE PRINCE OF WALES—ENGLAND —IRELAND.

A creation of cardinals was necessary. There were twenty-nine vacant hats. Towards the close of 1873 Pius IX. resolved on twelve new creations. One of these became the occasion of protesting anew against the Italian government. The Society of Jesuits had always been a special object of its hatred. They were the first whom it expelled from Rome, as has been the case in more than one persecution. And now they were robbed, notwithstanding the hopes that the European ambassadors were led to entertain of the Roman College which was their property. The Holy Father met this new brigandage by raising a member of the society to the dignity of cardinal. Tarquini, professor of canon law at the Sapienza (Roman College), was the favored member. Thus did the despoiled Pontiff condemn the ignorance and rebuke the robbery of the new rulers of Rome. "I am aware," said Pius IX. on this occasion, "that the Jesuits do not willingly accept ecclesiastical dignities. I had not, therefore, thought, until now, of conferring the purple on any of their members. But the unjust acts from which your society is suffering at this moment have determined me. It appeared to me to be necessary that I should make known in this way what I think of the ignorant calumnies of which you are the victims, and at the same time give proof to yourself and your brethren of my esteem and friendship."

If, ever since the violent seizure of Rome, it was customary to speak of the Pope as "the prisoner of the Vatican," his enemies, on the other hand, ceased not to insist that he was perfectly free, whilst he obstinately persisted in remaining within the walls of his palace. It has been noticed already that every approach to Rome and the Vatican was strictly guarded by the soldiers of the usurping king. A circumstance which occurred on the evening of the 20th June, 1874, further showed how close the imprisonment was. It was the twenty-eighth anniversary of the coronation of Pius IX. *Te Deum* was celebrated in the Vatican Basilica, and, what rarely happens, the spacious edifice was completely filled. More than one hundred thousand people, as nearly as could be estimated, or two-thirds of all the Romans who were able to leave their houses, were massed as well within the church as on the places St. Peter and Risticucci. When *Te Deum* was over, all eyes instinctively turned towards a window of the second story of the palace. It was the window of the Pope's apartment. Suddenly a white figure appeared at this window, and immediately a cry arose from below. It was the voice of the Roman citi-

z

zens; a voice so grand that it might be said to express the mind of a whole people, as they saluted their king, who was a prisoner. It continued for some time, and, although the window was at once closed, the prolonged acclamation of the faithful Romans rose louder and louder, until the Piedmontese troops came on the ground and swept away the crowd. The people departed without making any resistance. The police, nevertheless, arrested some twelve persons, of whom six were ladies of the best society of Rome. These ladies were at once set at liberty. But four young men of the number of those arrested were detained and afterwards condemned, one of them to two years, and the rest to several months' imprisonment, for having cried, "Long live the Pontiff-King." This crime they pretended not to deny. Could it be doubted any longer that the Pope was a prisoner? It was not only on moral grounds that he could not leave the Vatican. There were also bayonets and fire-arms between him and the nearest streets of Rome. It was only in the beginning of the year 1875 that Pius IX. could no longer refrain from visiting the Basilica of St. Peter. He had not been within it for four years and a half. Every necessary precaution was observed on occasion of his visit. The gates of the temple were kept shut, and none were present but members of the chapter and some other persons required for the service of the Church. The Holy Father entered by the stair which forms direct communication between his palace and the holy place. As may well be understood, he prayed for some time with his accustomed earnestness, that it would please God to put an end to the evils by which the Church was so sorely afflicted.

Pius IX. was indefatigable in giving audiences and receiving deputations from every country where there were members of the Catholic Church. On such occasions he never failed to speak words of edification and encouragement. It was even said that he spoke too much. They were not, however, of the number of his friends who call him il Papa verboso. He was endowed with a wonderful gift of speech, and he always used it effectively. His discourses were invariably to the purpose, the subject of them being suggested by the most recent events, by the nationality of his visitors, or by the expressed pious intentions which brought them to his presence. He made allusion very often to the Gospel of the preceding Sunday, or to the festival of the day, and concluded by imparting his benediction, which his hearers always received kneeling, and seldom without tears. The addresses of Pius IX. delivered at the Vatican have been preserved by the stenographic art, and fill many volumes. His ideas sometimes found expression in conversations with distinguished visitors. Such was the case on occasion of the visit, in 1872, of the Prince of Wales, the heir apparent of the British Crown. His Royal Highness showed his good taste by declining the use of Victor Em-. manuel's equipages in coming to the Vatican. The Princess also made manifest her respect for the well-known sentiments of Pius IX. in regard to showy toilettes by appearing in a plain dress. There was a striking contrast between the placid old man, so near the close of his career, and the handsome young couple, in the flower of their age. The Prince and the Pope appeared delighted at meeting; and the eyes of the Princess, who looked alternately at the animated figure of her husband and the benevolent countenance of the venerable Pontiff, were suffused with tears. The Pope began the conversation by expressing his great admiration for the character, both public and private, of the Queen of Great Britain; and smiling expressively, and not without a slight degree of Italian irony, he thanked the British ministers who, more than once, had offered him, in the name of the Queen, an asylum on British territory. "You see, Prince, I have not left Rome quite as soon as some of your statesmen supposed I would." The Holy Father then alluded to the existing state of things, adding: "In my present condition I am assuredly more happy than those who consider themselves more the masters of Rome than myself. I have no fear for my dynasty. It is powerfully protected. God Himself is its guardian. He also looks to my

succession and my family. You are not unaware that these
are no other than the Church. I can speak without offence to
the Prince of Wales of the instability of Royal Houses, that
which he represents being firmly anchored in the affections of
a wise people." "I am delighted," replied the Prince, smiling
expressively, "to find that your Holiness has so good an opinion of our people." "Yes, indeed, I respect the English
people," continued the Holy Father, "because they are more
truly religious, both as regards feeling and conduct, than many
who call themselves Catholics. When, one day, they shall
return to the fold, with what joy will we not welcome that
flock which is astray, but not lost!" The Prince and Princess,
being rather incredulous, received this benevolent aspiration
with a good-natured smile. "Oh! my children," resumed the
Pontiff, "the future has in store for mankind the most strange
surprises. Who could have imagined, two years ago, that we
should see a Prussian army in France? I hesitate not to say
that your ablest statesmen expected sooner to see the Pope at
Malta than Napoleon III. in England. As regards myself,
you will observe I am, indeed, robbed of my States, but God,
who, at any moment, withdraws the possessions of this world,
can also restore them a hundred-fold. Is the dynasty of the
Head of the Church, on this account, less secure? I may, for
a time, be driven from Rome. But when your children and
grandchildren shall come to visit the holy city, they will see,
as you see to-day—let the temporal power be more or less considerable—an old man, clothed in white, pointing the way to
heaven for the good of hundreds of millions of human consciences. To compensate for the absence of subjects immediately around him, he will have devoted adherents at all
times and everywhere." The conversation turning on Ireland,
the Holy Father spoke in the warmest terms of the fidelity of
the Catholics of that country. "You know, Prince, the
results of persecution. It does not make us any more Catholics. Your Royal Mother follows a policy quite different from
that of her predecessors, in regard to Ireland, and you are,

like her, aware that good Catholics are always good subjects." That country, the Pope continued to observe, had need of the vigilant and energetic superintendence of its devoted prelates, whom he praised in the highest terms. "For," said he, "the wolf—I do not mean Protestantism—but the wolf of anarchy and infidelity is abroad, I fear, in the regions of the West." He referred to the organization called "the International," and expressed his astonishment that "any princes should be still so blind as to take pleasure in making war on the Church, at a period when the foundations of civil society were threatened on every side."

The chief cause of the Holy Father's grief and poignant sorrow, under his calamities, was the loss of souls. "Ah!" said he, in a conversation with Mgr. Langenieux, Archbishop of Rheims, "I could bear my misfortunes courageously, and God would give me strength to withstand the evils which afflict the Church. But there is one thing I cannot forgive those who persecute us. They eradicate the faith of my people—they kill the souls of the children of unfortunate Italy." The Pontiff, as he uttered these words, moved his hand towards his breast, and as his fingers ruffled his white robe, he exclaimed, in a tone that was truly heartrending: "They tear away my heart!"

"It was sublime," adds the archbishop, "the great soul of the Pope subdued us, and, at the same time, inspired us with light and fortitude."

RELATIONS OF PIUS IX. WITH FOREIGN STATES—SWITZERLAND—
GERMANY.

The party in Europe who desired the suppression of the Pope's temporal rule professed to be actuated by zeal for promoting a more free and useful exercise of his spiritual authority. It soon became manifest that this was the merest sham. Switzerland, guided by that narrow kind of Protestantism which has so often asserted its power, pretended to see only in the Pope the Chief of the small Roman State; when deprived of that State, he was no longer a prince or dignitary, with whom diplomatic relations could be held. His legate at Berne, accordingly, was informed that he must take his departure from the territory of the Swiss Confederation. It is well understood that this ungracious measure was secretly advised and promoted by Germany. That Power speedily followed the example, although not at first in a very direct or open way. The German ministry appointed to the Embassy of the Vatican Cardinal Hohenlohe, the only one of the cardinals who proved unfaithful to Pius IX. in the hour of his great distress. The Pope remonstrated against the appointment. The inflexible Prussian minister, Bismarck, replied that he would send no other, suspended and finally abolished diplomatic relations between the new Empire and the Holy See. It is by no means matter for surprise that a man of Prince Bismarck's views and character should have so acted, or even that he should have become the promoter of the greatest and most unwarrantable persecution by which any nation has been disgraced, or to which any portion of the Church has been subjected in modern times. This minister, who may be truly described as the political scourge of Germany, is as fanatical in religion as he is coarse and sceptical in politics. He abandoned his party, and became, or feigned to become, a liberal in order to gratify his hatred of the Catholic Church. He belongs to that branch of Protestantism which is called " orthodox " (*lucus a non lucendo*). On occasion of the debate, 14th April, 1874, on the law which withdrew the salaries of the Catholic clergy, a Protestant conservative member of the representative body, Count de Malrahn, declared that he would vote for this law, because it would affect only the Catholics, without interfering with the rights of the Evangelical denomination. Bismarck, by his reply, not only showed an utter absence of all political faith, but at the same time a degree of political hypocrisy with which all true history will never cease to stigmatize him. " I must express the great joy which I experience on hearing the declaration of the preceding speaker.

If, at the commencement of the religious conflict, the conservatives had taken this ground, and sustained the government in the name of the Evangelical religion, I never would have been under the necessity of separating from the Conservative party."

From Chancellor Bismarck's own words, therefore, it may be concluded that it was excessive sectarian fanaticism which made him an infidel and hypocrite in politics, a traitor to his party, and a savage persecutor of the Church. When there was question in December, 1874, of obtaining an act for the suppression of the Prussian legation to the Holy See, the deep-rooted hatred of Prince Bismarck and his absolute want of conscience became still more apparent. He audaciously accused the Court of Rome of having been the ally of France, and even of the revolution in the war against Prussia in 1870. He pretended that if the Œcumenical Council was closed abruptly, it was in order to leave complete liberty of action to Napoleon III.; and, as facts were necessary in order to support this extraordinary and false assertion, he ascribed to Monsignor Meglia, at the time nuncio at Munich, the words, " Our only hope is in the revolution." As the chancellor uttered this odious calumny, he suddenly took ill. He became pale, stammered, and had recourse, four or five times, to a glass of water, which was beside him, in order to recover his spirits and find the words which he should use. The whole parliament was struck with this incident. The Abbe Majunke, editor of the Catholic journal *Germania*, was, however, the only one who spoke of it publicly. Such an offence against the omnipotent chancellor could not, of course, be overlooked. M. Majunke was summoned to the police office, and thence consigned to prison, notwithstanding his inviolability as deputy, and the protestations of the *Reichstag* (parliament). What a grand conception Chancellor Bismarck must have had of constitutional government !

The great success of William I. in the Franco-Prussian war appears to have so elated that monarch that he considered there was nothing which he might not successfully undertake. He had annexed to Prussia some of the lesser States of Germany, and made a German Empire. The Church in Germany enjoyed many privileges and immunities under his predecessors, who, for the most part, were, like himself, Protestants. Whether it was that he desired to show himself a better Protestant than his ancestors, or that he could not emancipate himself from the control of the minister who had so long guided, with singular success, the destinies of the empire, as well as his own career, or that he believed it to be a political necessity to act according to the views and carry out the principles of the German and European "Liberals"—the party of revolution and unbelief—he resolved to oppose no impediment to his chancellor and the liberal majority of parliament in their endeavors to destroy the Catholic Church in Germany, unless it chose to become as a mere department of the State, acting and speaking in the name of the State, receiving its appointments from the State, as well as the funds requisite for the support of its ministers, accepting all its orders and instructions, even in the most spiritual things, from the State; in fine, looking to the State as the sole source of all its authority, honor, power and influence. There was nothing like the German Empire. It had conquered in gigantic wars with two Powers that were considered the greatest in continental Europe. It had attained a degree of power and greatness, scarcely if at all inferior to that of the first Napoleon, and, like Napoleon, it aimed at more. It sought, like him, to have the Church, no less than the police courts, in every respect, in all circumstances and on all occasions, completely at its orders. This ill-judged ambition accounts for the long list of oppressive laws which were enacted at Berlin for the enslavement of the Catholic Church. They are known as the "May Laws," all of them having been passed, although not in the same year, in the month of May. Dollinger, Hohenlohe and the rest of the anti-Catholic Bavarian *coterie*, deluded the Emperor and his minister with the idea of an independent German *alt*, or Old

Catholic Church. They sold their country to the new empire, politically. But they could not sell its church. One of these *alt-Catholics*, Dr. Schulte, recommended persecution as the surest means of eradicating the ancient church. "Let his twenty thousand florins be withdrawn from such a one, his twelve thousand thalers from such another; let the salaries of the bishops and chapters be suppressed, and the result will soon be manifest. The humbler clergy will rejoice. Since 18th July, 1870, there has been neither belief in Christ nor religious conviction among the bearers of mitres and tonsures." Thus was the Prussian minister led to imagine that he had only to transfer the benefices of the Catholic dignitaries to the *alt-Catholics* in order to constitute an independent German Church, which would unite the whole of Germany religiously, as he had already united it politically. All Catholics, of course, would be members of this new Church. The State Protestantism of Prussia would, in due time, join this State Church, and there would be, if not one Faith and one Baptism, one Church and one State.

The calculations of Chancellor Bismarck were, however, at fault. He soon discovered that the clergy were grossly calumniated, and that the *alt-Catholic* Church in which he trusted never counted more than thirty priests; that this number increased not, and that the hundreds of thousands of adherents of whom the pseudo bishop, Reinkens, boasted, were only some twenty thousand to thirty thousand, scattered over all Germany. These had no principle of cohesion. They could not agree as to any fundamental point of religious doctrine or discipline. According to a census made in 1876, they numbered only one hundred and thirty-six, in a population of twenty-five thousand Catholics, at the city of Bonn, which M. Reinkens had selected as the seat and centre of his episcopal ministrations. Meanwhile, there was a considerable reaction in prevaricating Bavaria. The Catholic minority was changed into a majority, and the Prussian Catholic representation, which was called the fraction of the centre, was strengthened at the elections of 1874 by an increase from twenty-five to forty votes. The chancellor, although enlightened, was not corrected. Nothing could divert him from his evil purpose. By a strange confusion of ideas, he called *Kulturcampf* (struggle for civilization) the open war which he waged against the Church, the source of all civilization and of liberty of conscience. The persecuting laws which, with the aid of the so-called "liberal" party, or party of unbelief, he succeeded in causing to be enacted were to the following effect. As was to be expected of the blind political fanaticism of the party, the Jesuits were the first objects of hostility, and the first victims of persecution. The May laws required that these unoffending individuals should be expelled without any form of trial, and deprived of their rights of citizens. At the same time, certain religious orders which, it was pretended, were affiliated with the Jesuits, were subjected to the like treatment:

All ecclesiastical seminaries were suppressed, the solons of legislation pretending that it was necessary to oblige the candidates for the priesthood to imbue their minds in lay schools, with the ideas and wants of modern society.

The new laws abolished articles fifteen, sixteen and eighteen of the Prussian Constitution, which guaranteed the autonomy of the different forms of worship; they bestowed on the State the nomination to ecclesiastical functions, and went so far as to forbid bishops the use of their right to declare apostates excluded from the Catholic communion.

They suppressed the subsidies and allowances which the State, until that time, paid to the diocesan establishments and the clergy generally, notwithstanding that such subsidies were not gratuitously bestowed by the government, but were nothing else than, as in France and Belgium, the restitution, in part, of the debt due by the State to the Church. It was provided, however, that such members of the clergy as should make their submission should at once have their salaries restored. By a refinement of cruelty, all collections and subscriptions, whether public or private, for the requirements of public worship and the support of the clergy were forbidden, and elective lay commissions were charged with the management of all ecclesiastical property. Finally, all religious orders, as well of men as of women, were suppressed, with the exception, and that provisionally only, of such as were devoted to the care of the sick.

If Chancellor Bismarck really believed, at any time, that the Catholic clergy were without faith and conscience, ready to submit to any terms the State might impose, in order to save their incomes and the institutions of the Church, he must have been greatly surprised when he found them all, without exception, prepared to welcome poverty, imprisonment and exile, rather than abandon the inalienable rights of conscience. On the 26th May, 1873, the Bishops of Prussia signed a collective declaration, in which they stated, with regret, that it was impossible for them to obey. " The Church," said they, " cannot acknowledge the heathen state principle, according to which the laws of the State are the source of all right, and the Church possesses only such rights as it pleases the State to grant. By so doing, it would deny its own Divine origin, and would make Christianity wholly dependent on the arbitrary will of men." In regard to temporal matters connected with the Church they could afford to be less strict; and so they authorized their people to take part in the election of the new lay managers of the properties of the churches. This wise policy was attended with the most happy results. The chancellor's plans were everywhere completely marred. He had reckoned that the Catholics would abstain from voting, and so allow a "liberal" (infidel) minority, however small, to dispose of the churches and presbyteries.

In reviewing the news of the day, we have been accustomed to think of only one or two more eminent prelates suffering under the lash of persecution. The truth is, that the whole Church suffered. The persecution was as cruel as an age which does not permit the shedding of blood would tolerate. The bishops were crushed with fines on account of each act which they performed of their spiritual office. Such fines they refused to pay, lest they should acknowledge the justice of their condemnation. Their movable property, accordingly, was seized and sold at auction, and they themselves were immured in the prisons, where they were mixed up with felons condemned to the same labors, and designated, like them, by numbers. It was all in vain. Nothing could shake their constancy. At Berlin was erected a sort of ecclesiastical tribunal, which arrogated to itself the power of deposing from sees, and which actually pretended to depose the Archbishop of Posen, the Bishop of Paderborn, the Prince-Bishop of Breslau, and several other prelates. The fortresses of Germany were filled with priests, whose only crime was that they *obeyed God rather than men.* The public ways were crowded with priests who had been deprived, afterwards *interned,* and finally banished. Numerous religious people, both men and women, were in the like sad position, thronging the road of exile. The people, in tears, escorted these victims of heathenish rage. They chanted, as they went, the psalm, "*Miserere,*" and the canticle, "*Wir sind im waren Christenthum*" ("we are in true Christianity"), until they reached the railway depots. The Prussian gensd'armes, who were often no more than two or three in number, were astonished to find that they could so easily conduct their prisoners, whom thousands and tens of thousands of other men, the greater number of whom were veteran soldiers, accompanied, as they passed, expressing their regrets and good wishes.

Persecution is impolitic no less than it is cruel and immoral. The German people, to say the least, were shocked by the tyranny of their government. Nothing could prevent them from showing what they felt and thought, on occasion of the release of the prisoners at the end of their two years' term of imprisonment. They took every possible means of expressing their satisfaction. Thus, at Munster, when Bishop Warendorf returned, the inhabitants paid no attention to the prohibition of the burgomaster, who, by order of the government, intimated that he would repress, by force, every external and public demonstration. The whole city rushed to the gate, St. Mauritius, by which the released prisoner was to enter. Count Droste-Erhdroste proceeded to receive him in a magnificent carriage, drawn by four horses, which was followed by four more carriages in charge of his servants, who were in complete gala dress. An immense crowd strewed flowers along the route as the bishop advanced, and ceased not to hail him with joyous acclamations until he reached his residence, where the first families of the country were in attendance to receive him. In the evening, the whole town, with the exception of the public buildings, was illuminated. The citizens of Posen were preparing a like triumphal reception for their archbishop, Cardinal Ledochowski, on occasion of his release in February, 1876, from the fortress of Ostrowo, where he had been incarcerated for two years, when he was carried off in the night-time and transported beyond the limits of his diocese, in which he is forbidden ever again to set foot. Two suffragan bishops were left behind. They also were imprisoned at Gnesten, one for having administered the Sacrament of Confirmation without special leave from the government, the other for having consecrated the holy oils on Maunday Thursday, 1875. By such acts, which evidently belonged to the spiritual order, they were held to be guilty of sedition and a violation of the rights of the State.

The whole Catholic world was deeply moved by this modern and unprovoked persecution. All could not speak, indeed; but all were in sympathy with the clergy and faithful people of Germany. The bishops of France would have brought war upon their country by uttering a word of disapproval. The irascible chancellor actually sought to raise a quarrel with that country on account of a slight and inoffensive allusion which fell from the lips of two of the bishops. Could he not see that he will be branded throughout the ages as a persecutor and a short-sighted politician? Great Britain and America could speak without fear or hindrance. And they were not slow to send their words of consolation and encouragement to their suffering brethren of Germany. The Cardinal-Archbishop of Westminster wrote in a strain which may be described as apostolical, to the Archbishop of Cologne, the Primate of Germany, greeting "with the greatest affection both himself and his brethren, the other bishops who are in prison for having defended the authority and liberty of the Church." This letter was reproduced by all the newspapers, and could not have escaped the notice of the Prussian minister. Nevertheless, he was silent. Although sensitive in the extreme, as regarded France and Belgium, his knowledge of geography and naval statistics, no doubt, enabled him to possess his soul in patience.

Pius IX. could not but feel for his afflicted children of Germany. He was moved, accordingly, to address a very earnest remonstrance to the Emperor, William I. This was done so early as August, 1873. He could not believe that such cruel measures proceeded from a prince who had so often given proof of his Christian sentiments. He had even been informed that his Majesty did not approve of the conduct of his government, and condemned the laws which were enacted against the Catholic religion. "But, if it be true that your Majesty does not approve of these measures (and the letters which you formerly addressed to me appear to me to prove sufficiently that you do not think well of what is actually taking place),—if, I say, it is not with your sanction that your government continues to extend more and more those repressive measures against the Christian religion which so grievously injure that religion, must you not come to the conclusion that such measures can have no other effect than to undermine your throne?" He may possibly have thought so, when, a little later, his life was attempted by parties who are known to seek the destruction of religion and civil government at the same time. Be this as it may, his reply to Pius IX. was not in his usual kindly style. It was scarcely polite, and appeared to be the work of the savage chancellor rather than of the good-natured monarch.

The appeal of Pius IX. produced no result. The Emperor's government added to the harshness of his refusal by advising him to address a letter of congratulation to the new bishop of the *alt-Catholics*. This was done, as was expressed, "on account of his complete deference to the State and his acknowledgment of its rights." In another letter, which was also made public, William I. recalled to mind those ancient Emperors of Germany who were the irreconcilable enemies of the spiritual supremacy of the Popes, and intimated that he was resuming the work of Frederick Barbarossa and Henry IV. The association was unfortunate. The chancellor's commentary was more so. "We shall never," he boasted, "go to Canossa!" These words, spoken before the assembled parliament, were a defiance of Divine Providence. Was it forgotten that there were other snows than those of Canossa, in which Emperors could perish? The first Napoleon pursued, in regard to the Church, the same policy that Germany was now pursuing. He defied the religious power, and contemptuously asked *whether the arms could be made to fall from the hands of his soldiers?* They did so fall, nevertheless, when the demented Emperor led his legions into the snows of Russia.

Pius IX. could not behold without concern the deep distress of his brethren in Germany. He addressed an Encyclical letter, under date of 5th February, 1875, to the Bishops of Prussia, lamenting the persecution which tried them so severely, dwelling at great length on the evils of the *May laws*, praising the constancy of the clergy, and exhorting them to continued patience and perseverance. The whole doctrine of the Encyclical may be said to be expressed in the following words:

"Let those who are your enemies know that you do no injury to the royal authority, and that you have no prejudice against it when you refuse to give to Cæsar what belongs to God; for it is written, '*We must obey God rather than men.*'"

This eloquent letter, like everything else that was done in order to mitigate the most trying persecution of modern times, remained without any other result than to afford some comfort to the clergy of the afflicted Church of Germany.

Pius IX., in order to show still further his appreciation of the constancy under persecution of the German clergy, conferred the dignity of Cardinal on Archbishop Ledochowski, who courageously accepted the proffered honor. The persecuting government prevented him from ever enjoying it in his diocese, by condemning him to perpetual banishment. This was, at least, an approach to the cruelty practised on Fisher, the illustrious English Confessor, who was consigned to the Tower of London because he would not sanction the divorce of Henry VIII., and acknowledge the Royal Supremacy in questions of religion. The Pope of the time sent him a cardinal's hat. But the enraged king took care that he should never wear it by cutting off his head. The time was past when blood could be shed in hatred of the truth, even by so hard a tyrant as the Prussian minister. In the nineteenth century, however, as well as in the sixteenth, there would not be wanting those who would resist unto blood for religion's sake.

It was comparatively an easy matter to deprive and banish the legitimate pastors, but not quite so easy to find priests so unprincipled as to become their successors. The politic chancellor, apparently, had not thought of this beforehand. In the course of five years he could find only two ecclesiastics who would consent to accept benefices at his hands. All those on whom he might have counted for establishing a schism in the Church had already joined, with all the encouragement which the minister could bestow, the *alt-Catholic* sect, which, as has been shown, was destined to prove a failure. It is almost superfluous to say that the parishioners studiously avoided all communication in things spiritual with the nominees of the State. Meanwhile, the faithful people were not left destitute. Zealous young priests from the seminaries visited them privately at their houses, and ministered to their religious wants. Such as so acted were arrested and conducted to the frontier. They returned by the next railway train. They were then cast into prison. As soon as they were free they returned to the post of duty. There was in Germany a revival of the Primitive Church—of the zeal and self-sacrifice of the apostolic age. All this was met by the closing of the seminaries, the severest blow that had, as yet, been struck against the cause of religion. The chancellor, nevertheless, was not successful. The newspapers in his interest, which he designated as the *reptile press*, laughed at his short-sightedness. He had counted on accomplishing his purpose by some six months of persecution. Generations would not suffice. The endurance of the Church is unconquerable. It is as an anvil which wears out many hammers. That which Chancellor Bismarck applied, so vigorously, will prove to be no exception.* Southern Germany, it is a pleasure to record, abhors the ridiculous *Kulturkampf* of Chancellor Bismarck. Louis II., of Bavaria, would fain follow in his wake. But, as is shown by the large Catholic majorities at the elections, he is not seconded, even passively, as in Prussia, by the Bavarian people. The persecution, attended by its essential results, is rendering all Germany more Catholic than ever. When its work shall have been accomplished, what will remain ? The Church or the *Kulturkampf* ?

In the meantime many innocent persons must suffer; many time-honored institutions will have been swept away; in the pursuit of an ideal civilization, and by means of cruelties unworthy of an enlightened age, many monuments which owed their origin to the superior civilizing power of Christianity will have disappeared forever. In addition to all this, feelings hostile to the Church, and prejudices hurtful as they are groundless, are everywhere created. Pius IX. complained of this unfortunate state of things, when he said (10th January, 1875): "The revolution, not satisfied with persecuting

*There appeared at Munich, in 1874, an ingenious caricature. It represented the Prussian chancellor, endeavoring, with a Krupp gun, which he used as a lever, to overthrow a church emblem of Catholicism. Satan comes on the scene, and says: "What are you doing, my friend ?" Bismarck, "This church embarrasses me; I want to upset it." Satan, "It embarrasses me, too. I have been laboring 1800 years to demolish it. If your Excellency succeeds, I pledge myself to resign my office in your favor."

Catholics in Prussia, excites, on both sides of the Alps, those governments which profess to be Catholic, but which have only too plainly led the way, in the shameful career of religious oppression. It excites them to persist, more boldly than ever, in the work of persecution, and these governments execute its behests. God will arise, some day, and, addressing the Protestant oppressor, he will say to him : Thou hast sinned—grievously sinned ; but the Catholic governments, on all hands, have still more grievously sinned. *Majus peccatum habent.*"

ITALY—EDUCATION.

At the time of the Piedmontese invasion, there were in the city of Rome, one hundred and sixty-eight colleges or public schools.

The number of schools was twenty thousand, whilst the whole population of the city was two hundred and twenty thousand. The pupils are classed as follows, according to the statistics of his Eminence the Cardinal-Vicar, in 1870 :

Students, boarding in seminaries and colleges	703
Students, day scholars, gratuitously taught in the schools	5,555
Students, day scholars, who paid a small fee	1,603
Total	7,941
Girls, boarding in *refuges*	2,986
" day scholars, gratuitously taught	6,523
" " who paid a small fee	2,871
Total	11,380
General total	19,321

Thus, including the orphans of both sexes, at *St. Michael de Termini* and other asylums, pupils are in the proportion of one to ten inhabitants. This is not inferior to Paris, and surpasses Berlin, so much spoken of as a seat of education. This

Prussian (now German capital) reckoned, in 1875, only eighty-five thousand scholars for a population of nine hundred and seventy-four thousand souls, or ten scholars to one hundred and fourteen citizens. The Godless schools, established by the new rulers, have impeded, only to a certain extent, the development given to education by the Government of Pius IX. In the poorer quarters of the city some parties have been either intimidated by the threats of the *Department of Charity*, or gained by the offer of bounties to themselves and a gratuitous breakfast to their children. But, generally, the people of Rome still resist, and several Christian schools have considerably increased since 1870, the number of their pupils. This is all the more remarkable, as the ruling faction showed a strong determination to put an end entirely to Christian education. By the end of 1873, the usurping government had confiscated more than one hundred monasteries, convents, and other establishments of public education. A Lyceum was set up in place of the celebrated Roman College, from which its proprietors, the Rev. Fathers of the Society of Jesuits, were finally expelled in 1874. The better to show their *animus* on the occasion, the new Rulers tore down a magnificent piece of sculpture, in marble, which adorned the gate, and on which was engraved the blessed name of the Saviour, replacing it by the escutcheon in wood of Victor Emmanuél.

As if to give zest to robbery, the Godless tyrants proposed that the professors of the Roman College should continue their lessons, as functionaries of the Italian government, and after having qualified by accepting diplomas from a lay university It would, indeed, have been comical to see such men as Secchi, Franzelin, Tarquini, and many, besides, the first professors in the world, seated on scholars' benches, to be examined by the semi-barbarous officials, whether civil or military, of the Piedmontese King. Pius IX., although pressed by many wants, provided an asylum for science. He called together the Jesuit Fathers who had been dispersed, in the halls of the American and German Colleges. There, although somewhat pinched for room, they continued their international courses, the most extensive that ever were known.

The new Rulers, however, it is only proper to observe, never dared to drive Father Secchi from his observatory.

There ought never to have been any difficulty in Italy as regards education. The Italians were, and are still, of one mind, and not divided, like us, into numerous denominations, all of which have to be considered without prejudice to their religious views. The usurping Italian government allotted one million of francs (£40,000) per annum, for elementary education at Rome. Not one half of the children for whom this bounty is intended, avail themselves of it—a fact which shows that the popular want has not been met. The outlay only burdens the ratepayers without advancing the end for which it is designed—elementary education. Private persons supply the need according to the popular desire, by means of regionary schools, supported entirely at their own expense, and with a laudable degree of self-sacrifice. The same state of things prevails, generally, throughout Italy, as is shown by a circular of the minister of public instruction. The new government aims at nothing less than the subversion of religious principle. This the Italians resist, and will continue to resist. The government schools for secular and irreligious education, among the upper classes, are like those for elementary teaching, very thinly attended, parents preferring to send their children abroad, and, when this cannot be afforded, to such ecclesiastical colleges and seminaries as are still in existence. The State schools have already a monopoly in the conferring of degrees and the consequent civil advantages. It is proposed to go still further, and, actually, to close by force, all the higher schools in which religion is recognized, even as the school established by the Pope in the city of Rome, was recently put down. It is thus that these emancipators of mankind understand liberty !

As regards female education, especially, the people will never, willingly, give up the schools that are conducted by

"Sisters" or "Nuns." The education which such schools afford is universally appreciated—among ourselves who are divided, but more particularly among the Italians, who are all Catholics. It is in vain *to kick against the goad*, and this the Italian government will learn, some day, when it is cast forth as a rotten institution by the people, whose dearest wishes it ignores. It is of no use to suppose that Italy is advanced to a state of irreligion, and so requires a system of Godless education. The contrary is well known. State systems, based, not on statistical facts, but, on idle suppositions, must needs come to nought.

ITALY—RELIGION.

"A free Church in a free State"—the great idea of such Italian liberals as had any conception of a church at all, was surely to be realized when the fellow-countrymen of Count de Cavour came to rule at Rome. What was the case? There was neither a free church nor a free State? That State is not free, wherein the people are not fairly represented. The new Italian State could not claim any such representation. It was held in such contempt that the great majority of the Italian people, unwisely, indeed, we who are accustomed to constitutional government would say, declined to take part in the elections. Thus the entire control of the country was left in the hands of two comparatively small factions—the *moderate* and the *extreme* radicals. It is of little importance to the mass of the Italian people which of these factions holds sway for the moment. They both legislate and execute the laws in opposition to the will of the nation, and in the sense and for the benefit of the prevailing faction. They are both alike characterized by hatred of the Christian faith and all religious institutions. This feeling impels them to war against everything connected with Christianity, and to substitue what the Germans of the same school call *Kulturkampf*, or, *a struggle for culture*, on principles the very opposite of those on which is founded the high civilization of the nineteenth century. No doubt these apostles of *Kulturkampf* have a much higher civilization in store for mankind. But it must be admitted that they follow a strange way of bringing about the much-desired consummation. Robbery and sacrilege they believe, or profess to believe, will promote the great object of their ambition, and so they practice, to their heart's content, robbery and sacrilege. Have they forgotten that, according to their code, it is a *Jesuitical* teaching, that evil may be done in order to produce good. These legislators and administrators of laws claim to be superior to the *effete* errors of the age. Why then should they still cling to those of the despised *Jesuits?* Because, no doubt, it serves the purpose of the moment, and affords some relief to, if it does not satisfy, an insatiable passion. On approaching Rome they affected much reverence for the Holy Father and the institutions of religion. They could do nothing less, accordingly, than enact their now famous *law of guarantees*, which assured complete protection to the Pope and the institutions over which he presided. Let us enquire for a moment how this law was enforced. It surpassed, in generosity to the church, the legislation of the most chivalrous monarchs. It gave up the royal rights of former kings in regard to nominating and proposing to ecclesiastical offices. It dispensed with the oath of bishops to the king, and formally abolished (see articles fifteen and sixteen) the *exequatur*, as it is called, authorizing the publication and execution of all notable acts of ecclesiastical authority. Such clear and apparently solemn regulations appeared to be inviolable. Nevertheless, whilst one hundred and fifty bishops were named by Pius IX., from the commencement of the Piedmontese invasions till the month of August, 1875, no fewer than one hundred and thirty-seven of this number were not acknowledged by the civil power, because they did not apply for and obtain the *exequatur*. The ministry was not satisfied with this. It pushed its tyranny to such an extreme as to refuse in future, to grant the *exequatur* and to expel from their residences all bishops who should not possess it. Not only did the government withhold the incomes of the bishops, and confiscate the revenues which the piety of the people had devoted for their support, it also employed its gensd'armes and police agents in seizing the prelates at their homes and casting them into the streets. The new rulers went further still, and displayed their financial genius in a way peculiar to themselves. They actually subjected to the tax on moveable property, the alms which the bishops received from the Sovereign Pontiff, who, like themselves, was robbed of his proper income. Thus did the beggarly government make money out of the small resources of those who, when the exchequer failed to fulfil its duties, endeavored themselves, as best they could, to make up for this dereliction.

Military conscription is essentially tyrannical. It is particularly so when used as an arm of offence against the church. It was applied to ecclesiastical students, and even to such as were in holy orders, expressly for the purpose of depriving the church of recruits from the seminaries. None could now be found to renew the ranks of the clergy, except such as were invalids or of weak constitutions, or who, by miracle, persevered in their vocation, after four years' service in military barracks.

The public robbers, notwithstanding their professions and guarantees, audaciously laid sacrilegious hands on the properties of the Basilicas of St. Peter and St. John Lateran, which they themselves had expressly reserved for the use of the Holy See. They hesitated not even to seize the funds of the celebrated missionary college—Propoganda. These properties they did not simply annex, as they did so many, besides, that belonged to the Church. They created a liquidating junta or commission, as they called it, which should change all immovable ecclesiastical properties that were not already confiscated into national rent. Such national rent, as is well known, had only an ephemeral value. It was, at best, variable; and Italy, which was partially bankrupt when it reduced the interest due to its creditors, will, sooner or later, according to the opinion of the ablest writers, land in complete bankruptcy.

The rents substituted by force, instead of real property, will then possess the value of the *assignats* of the first French revolution.

The endowments of Propaganda, appointed by Christian generosity, at different epochs, were not designed for the use of Rome or Italy, or any Catholic country whatever. Their object was the support of remote missions. This was well understood. The very name of the institution shows that it was. In vain did Cardinal Franchi apply to the tribunals. The properties of the great universal institution, as well as those of the Chapters, were sold at public auction, and the confiscation, although not immediate, was in course of being accomplished. The state of things did not improve on the advent to power of Messrs. Nicotera and Depretis, the former a radical of the most extreme views, and the latter, very little, if at all, better. These revolutionists having gained the object of their ambition, might have been inclined to halt in their mad career; but, their party driving them onward, they proceeded to still more rigid and cruel measures. It is not too much to say that such men are digging a grave for the House of Savoy and Italian unity.

The measures aiming at the destruction of religion may be summarized as follows:

1st. They have introduced civil registration of births, as an equivalent and alternative to Christian baptism.

2nd. They have permitted and encouraged civil interment instead of Christian burial.

3rd. They have abolished oaths in courts of law.

4th. They have systematically encouraged the profanation of the Sunday and the great festivals of Christmas, Easter, etc., by ordering the prosecution of the government buildings and other public works on Sundays; by ostentatiously holding their sessions on those days; by ordering public lectures in the universities and higher schools on Sundays as on week days, etc.

5th. They have established civil marriage as an equivalent before the law for Christian marriage, and as necessary, in all cases, besides the religious ceremony.

6th. They have established a recognized system of public immorality by indemnities, and deriving from this shameful source a revenue which is applied to augment the secret service funds.

It is easily observed that in every detail of this enumeration, religion and morals are directly attacked. The Pope, who is the chief of religion and the great preacher of morality, cannot give any countenance to such things. Far less can he identify himself with such anti-Christian legislation. This is the insuperable impediment to his reconciliation with the present Rulers of "United Italy." He can resist evil, and resist unto blood, as so many of his sainted predecessors have done. But when there is question of accepting it, his only word must be, as it has always been, *non possumus*. What would men say, if He, who is the Head of the Church, and the chief guardian of the truth confided to Her keeping, could be brought by the threats or caresses of ephemeral worldly Powers, *to call good evil, and evil good ?*

ITALY—CRIME.

Religion, when persecuted in any country, fails not to wreak vengeance on the persecuting power. In such countries, virtue, generally, respect for law, order and authority, as well as public security, rapidly diminish, and the State discovers, although too late, that, in aiming at the Church, it has struck against itself a deadly blow.

Since the inauguration of the much vaunted *Kulturkampf*, socialism has increased to such a degree in Germany as to appal even Chancellor Bismarck, whilst Italy, at the same time that it closed its convents and Catholic colleges, was obliged to multiply not only its military barracks, but also its prisons. In no part of Italian territory have these preventives of crime, if, indeed, they may be so-called, proved sufficient. So rapid has been the increase of crime, that, according to official statistics, in the Province of Rome alone, seven thousand two hundred and ninety-three cases were ascertained and brought before the tribunals, in 1874. This is just double what appeared in the criminal courts under the Pontifical government. In the whole kingdom there were eighty-four thousand prisoners, or criminals under restraint. This is thirty-five thousand more than in France, the general population of which is greater by one-third, and four times more than in Great Britain, the population of which is about the same as that of united Italy. This state of crime is not surprising when it is considered that the rulers themselves have never ceased to set the example of the most unscrupulous and merciless theft and robbery. The new civil code, besides, appears to have had no other object in view than to obliterate all idea of right, and to legitimatize all robberies, past, present and future, in the unfortunate kingdom of Italy. Article seven hundred and ten of this code declares, plainly, *that property is acquired by possession.*

At Rome, barristers, judges, and even the most revolutionary journalists are assassinated by private vengeance, in broad day, in the street, or in their offices, and no one dare molest the murderers. In Romagna it was found necessary to bring to justice an association of assassins, who were, for the most part, persons of good education and men of property. In Sicily matters were still worse. There, a society of Brigands, called *Maffia*, holds the island in a state of perpetual terror. Numerous Garibaldians who have been without employment since 1870, and were long tolerated, on account of former complicity, added to the ranks of this fraternity. The *Maffia* rid themselves of another society, the *Kamorra*, by the successive assassination at Palermo alone, of twenty-three of its chiefs. All these crimes remain unpunished, none daring to bear witness against the guilty.

In the departments of government there is not less moral disorder. The finances are mismanaged and dilapidated. Notwithstanding the enormous and oppressive increase of taxation, together with the forcible appropriation of ecclesiastical property, deficits are the order of the day, and the nation has been, more than once, and probably is still, on the verge of bankruptcy. Truly, may the Italians, who are twenty-three to one, exclaim, in their distress: *Quo usque tandem abuteris patientia nostra?* "How long, O disastrous revolution! wilt thou abuse our patience?"

Nor are the better thinking Italians without blame. Why did they not take part—why do they not still take part in the elections, and return, as they well may, a majority to the would-be constitutional parliament? Their numbers would, undoubtedly, be imposing and influential. So much so, indeed, that they must finally obtain admission, without burdening their conscience with an obnoxious oath. What did not Daniel O'Connell, Ireland's liberator, accomplish, by causing himself alone to be elected for an Irish constituency, and by proceeding to demand the seat to which he was elected in the British parliament, without uttering an oath which shocked his conscience?

RUSSIA AND THE EAST.

The cruel and sanguinary persecution of Catholics in the Russian Empire was a cause of intense sorrow to Pius IX. He could do nothing towards alleviating the sufferings of those unfortunate people. The Tsar, Alexander II., shows in his treatment of his Ruthenian subjects of the united Greek Church, that he is wholly unworthy of the reputation for enlightenment and benevolence with which he has been credited. The Empress, indeed, is blamed, together with her fanatical favorite, Melle. Bludow, the Minister of Public Instruction, Tolstoy, and Gromeka, Governor of Siedlce, for having urged him to use the power of the empire in forcing conversions to Russo-Greek *orthodoxy*. That the heads of a semi-barbarous nation should so advise is not surprising. The Tsar, who is an absolute monarch, cannot be excused. There is every reason, besides, for holding him personally responsible. When he was at Warsaw, a peasant woman, bearing a petition, succeeded in obtaining admission to his presence. As soon as he learned that the petition begged toleration for the united Greek Church, he replied by inserting in all the newspapers a confirmation of the orders formerly given for the extinction of that church. Count Alexandrowicz de Constantinovo was repeatedly warned by the Russian authorities that he had no right to attend the Latin churches, which, being less persecuted, were a refuge for the united Greeks, when, indeed, as was rarely the case, they were allowed to enjoy it. The Count, hoping to be more liberally dealt with by the enlightened Tsar, who was said to surpass in all that was great and noble, his tolerant predecessor, Alexander I., proceeded to St. Petersburgh. The Tsar made a reply to his representation, which, in the case of an ordinary mortal, would be taken for a proof of stupidity, or of impenetrable ignorance. " The Orthodox religion is pleasing to me. Why should it not please you also ?" It remained only for the Count to sell his properties and abandon his country. More humble members of the obnoxious church could not so easily escape. The savage treatment to which they were subjected can only be briefly alluded to here. A persecution which has lasted more than a hundred years, and is not yet at an end, is more a subject for the general history of the church than for the life of Pius IX. A few facts, therefore, must suffice.

In the important diocese of Chelm, particularly, the most ingenious devices were had recourse to, in order to delude the Catholic people, and induce them to comply with the requirements of the Russo-Greek Church. All these failing, force was had recourse to, and it was used, assuredly, without stint or measure. Seizure of property, imprisonment, the lash and exile to Siberia, proved equally unavailing, as persecution, in every form, must always be. Greater excesses were then had recourse to.

They who dared to perform a pilgrimage, take part in a religious procession, or enter a Catholic Church, were shot down like the wild game of the forests, by the fanatical myrmidons of the Tsar. In January, 1874, the people of Rudno were forced to abandon their dwellings and take refuge in the woods. At Chmalowski, several united Greeks, of whom three were women, were flogged to death by Cossack troops. At Pratulin, in the district of Janow, when a number of people assembled in a cemetery, were guarding the door of the church against apostate priests, a German colonel, who commanded three companies of Cossacks, ordered his troops to fire. Nine of the people fell dead on the spot. A great many more were mortally wounded. Of these four died within the day. "Thus does the Tsar punish rebels," said the savage colonel to the mayors of the neighboring villages, whom he had forced to witness the execution. At Drylow, five men were slain on the same day, and in the same cruel way as at Pratulin. So recently as August, 1876, a body of peasants, returning from a pilgrimage, were attacked by Russian soldiers. They defended themselves bravely, as best they could, with no better weapons than their walking canes. Six of the troops fell, and thirty, one of whom was an officer, were wounded. Reinforcements coming to the aid of the military, the peasants were defeated, and a great number of them killed and wounded. Among the latter were many women, and seven children. Two hundred arrests were made, the next and following days. The prisoners were at first immured in the Citadel of Warsaw. It is not probable that they will ever be allowed to visit their kindred or their native villages.

Pius IX., being partially informed of such cruelties, which it was utterly beyond his power to prevent, wrote to the United Greek Archbishop of Lemberg, Sembratovicz, conjuring him to send to the sorely persecuted people all the help in his power, both spiritual and material. He declared, at the same time, by the Bull, "*omnem sollicitudinem*," dated 13th May, 1874, that the Liturgies proper to the Eastern Churches, and parti. cularly that of the United Greeks, which was settled by the Council of Tamosc, in 1720, were always held in high esteem by the Holy See, and ought to be carefully preserved. Hearing that a Bull which concerned them had arrived from Rome, the Ruthenian peasants sent secretly to Lemberg, in order to procure it. Their envoys entering Galicia without passports, incurred the risk of being sent to Siberia. When the Bull was once obtained, the people assembled in groups, in remote places, and any one who could read, read it to the rest of the company. It was held in honor as a relic. When the Russians discovered that the Bull was known to the people, they did their best to cause it to be misunderstood, both among the clergy and the laity. They insisted, even, that the Pope had discarded the Greek rite; that henceforth, they who adhered to Rome, could not celebrate either the Mass of St. John Chrysostom or that of St. Basil, and that the marriage of secular priests, together with the Sclavonic language, would cease to be tolerated.

It has been attempted to conceal from the civilized world the more atrocious circumstances of the Russian persecution. But the darkest deeds of the darkest despotism cannot be always done in the dark. The press of continental Europe has informed the public mind. If anything were wanting to satisfy English readers, generally, it would be found in the despatch of Mr. Marshall Jewell, Minister of the United States, at St. Petersburgh, to Mr. Secretary Fish. This document is dated at the United States Legation at St. Petersburgh, 23rd February, 1874. The minister begins by stating that he took great pains to be correctly informed, regarding the state of matters, before writing his report. This, he adds, was not done without difficulty, as the affair was kept very quiet at St. Petersburgh. Certain repressive measures for the conversion of the Ruthenian Catholics having proved inadequate, "new and more stringent orders were given a few weeks later. In consequence of these orders, several priests (thirty-four, I have been told) who persisted in performing the former services, were arrested. In some localities the peasants refused to go to the churches when the Orthodox priests officiated, until they were forced to go by the troops. In other localities they assembled in crowds, shut the churches, and prevented the priests from performing the offices. In one case, it is said, a priest was stoned to death. Conflicts arose between the peasants and the armed force. On such occasions many persons were maltreated, and in the case of the village of Drelow—28th February—thirty peasants were slain, and many more wounded. It is said, even, that several soldiers were killed. It is reported that the prisons at Lublin and Kielce are crammed with prisoners. The peasants have also been flogged, men receiving fifty, women twenty-five, and children ten lashes each. Some women, more determined and outspoken than the rest, were punished with a hundred lashes. Like troubles, it is said, have occurred at Pratulin and other localities, with loss of life. . . . Last summer, the peasants of divers villages, in the Government of Lublin, were constantly obliged to submit to examination, and to appear before the courts. It was, in consequence, impossible for them to cultivate their fields; and, hence, they have been reduced almost to a state of famine.   (Signed.)   MARSHALL JEWELL."

THE EAST—CHURCH IN THE TURKISH EMPIRE.

It is comparatively an easy undertaking to create trouble and disturbance in the church. It is not so easy, however, to establish a schism. The Prussian chancellor learned this fact when he beheld the failure of his *alt-Catholic* scheme in Germany. Having tried the same game in Turkey, his projects, notwithstanding the aid and countenance of the Mussulman Power, proved abortive. The government of the sublime Porte had been very tolerant hitherto, as regarded its Catholic subjects. In the early days of Pius IX. it had concurred with the Holy See in establishing a Catholic bishop at Jerusalem; it protected pilgrimages and processions; it favored colleges and institutions for ecclesiastical education; and to such a degree that, under its auspices and through its care, there are several flourishing seminaries which renew the intellectual life of the people who follow the Latin rite. A united Bulgarian church

has been founded and is daily gaining strength. The Maronites
are almost completely restored after the disaster of 1860. The
number of Greek Catholics or Melchites, has been almost
doubled, so great is the number of conversions. The same
may be said of the Chaldean or Armenian Catholics. These
last are probably the best informed and the most influential of
the Christian populations under the Sultan's rule. Prussian
intrigue, and a momentary renewal of Mussulman fanaticism,
have done much to check, if not wholly to destroy this happy
state of things. One Kupelian, aspiring to be patriarch of
Armenia, was put forward by rich and influential parties as
the administrator of their nation, and they succeeded in obtaining from the Porte his investiture, as the only true Head of
the Armenian Catholics. The legitimate chief, Hassoum,
Patriarch of Cilicia, protested. In vain, however, as France
was no longer able to maintain his right. The last ambassador of that country representing Napoleon III., had even supported the pretensions and favored the machinations of the
Kupelianites. The Porte was induced to treat Hassoum as a
seditious person, and banished him from the country. The
exile found his way to Rome, where he was kindly received by
Pius IX. He did not return to Constantinople till 1876.
Meanwhile, persecution was cruelly carried on. Bishops were
expelled from their sees, rectors from their parishes, churches,
monasteries and hospitals were seized by force of arms. At
Damascus, Broussa, Sinope, Mardyn, Mossoul, all the principal towns of the Ottoman Empire, Armenian Catholics were
forcibly driven from their churches, in order to make room for
mere handfuls of Kupelianists. The persecution extended as
far as Cairo. At Augora, twelve thousand Armenian Catholics
were dispossessed in favor of twelve dissenters, one of these
twelve being an apostate monk, the delegate of Kupelian. At
Adana, the church, the school, and the residence of the Catholic Armenian bishop, with all the revenues attached thereto,
became the prey of two individuals, a priest and a lay person.
At Trebizonde, the bishop was expelled by Russian bayonettes.

and died of grief.   The value of property taken from Catholics is estimated at one hundred millions of livres.   For what, it may be asked, was the power of an empire exercised, and so much robbery perpetrated ?   In favor, at least, one would say, of some important sect ?   No such thing.   It was all for the would-be Kupelian schism, seven hundred strong.   It is needless here to say how soon the degenerate Sultan, Abdul Aziz, and his prevaricating empire met their reward, whilst the legitimate Armenian patriarch, Hassoum, so long the victim of persecution, has been restored, is honored by the government of his country and held in the highest esteem by the Chief Pastor of the Christian fold.   All this was foretold by Pius IX., although, indeed, the Holy Pontiff pretended not to utter a prophecy.   In a letter intended for the consolation of the banished Archbishop of Mardyn, in Mesopotamia, and the Armenian Catholics, he says : "It behooves us not to lose courage, nor to believe that the triumph of iniquity will be of long continuance.   For, does not the Scripture say : 'The wicked man is caught in his own perversity ; he is bound by the chains of his crimes, and he who digs a pit for others will fall into it himself ; he who casts a stone into the path of his neighbor, will strike against it and stumble ; finally, he who lays a snare for another will be caught therein himself.'   This war, venerable brother, is waged, not so much against men as against God.   It is because of hatred to his name that his ministers and faithful people are persecuted.   Persecution constitutes their merit and their glory.   God will at length arise and vindicate his cause.   Whilst I applaud your firmness, I most earnestly exhort you never to let it fail you, but to possess your soul in patience, to wait confidently, and, at the same time, courageously, for, you rely not on your own strength, but on the power of God, whose cause you maintain.   Your constancy will confirm that of your brethren of the clergy and of the flock confided to your care.   It will lead to a moral victory, assuredly more brilliant and more solid than the ephemeral success of violence."

It was not long till the news of the day bore that many distinguished persons were returning to the one fold. A moral victory for the Armenian Catholics was following fast in the wake of successful force. The number of Kupelianists was diminishing. The churches and church properties of Adana and Diabekir, were abandoned by them in 1876, and the schism was in course of being extinguished.

The Chaldean patriarch, Audon, rashly undertook to establish a schism. Towards the end of February, 1873, he was reconciled to Pius IX., and relieved from the censures which he had incurred. The Chaldean Catholics gave a great deal of trouble. However anxiously Pius IX. labored for their salvation, they are insignificant in point of numbers, scarcely as many as would constitute a parish in any of our cities. Any further historical notice of them may, therefore, be very properly dispensed with.

CHINA—INDIA—JAPAN—WONDERFUL CHANGE.

China, where the light of Christianity has sought so long to penetrate and dispel the dismal gloom of heathen darkness, may now, at length, be said to enjoy the greatest possible degree of religious liberty. The European Powers, Great Britain and France, whilst securing the freedom of trade, and generally that intercourse which is customary between civilized nations, neglected not, at the same time, to establish such relations as render safe and available the labors of Christian missionaries. If, in Tonquin, there occurred a fearful massacre of Christians, it was due to the indiscretion of a French officer who exceeded his orders, and excited against his fellow-countrymen and the Christian populations, generally, the anger of the pagan Mandarins. The vengeance of these chiefs was prompt, sweeping and cruel. In the localities inhabited by Christians only some women and little children were spared. Not a house was left. The French government probably, from unwillingness to recognize, in any way, the action of its officer, refrained from punishing these atrocities. A treaty, placing the whole country of Tonquin under the protection of France,. was concluded with the Emperor of Annam, who is the Liege Lord of Tonquin, and thus liberty to preach the Gospel secured for the future.

In India and Western China, liberty of conscience has long prevailed. Pius IX. was, in consequence, enabled to increase the number of vicariâtes-apostolic in those countries, as well as in China proper, in proportion to the growth of the faithful people, however inconsiderable it was, as yet, in the midst of countless numbers of heathens and Mahometans.

The Pontificate of Pius IX. would be for ever memorable, if only on account of the new era which appears, at length, to have dawned for the long benighted empire of Japan. That empire was as a sealed book to all Christian nations. As is well known, no traveller or merchant from any Christian land could set foot on its territory without first performing the revolting ceremony of trampling on the chief emblem of the Christian faith. At one time, nevertheless, there were many Christians in Japan, and, as will be seen, heathen prejudice and persecution had not been able to extinguish the Divine light. It may be conceived how searching and cruel the persecution was when it is remembered that, in the early part of the seventeenth century, there were two millions of Christians, and, about the same time, almost as many martyrs. All missionaries who, since 1630, landed on the inhospitable shores of Japan, were immediately seized, tortured, and put to death. It was generally believed that the Christian people were totally exterminated. Pius IX., notwithstanding, as if actuated by some secret inspiration, the very first year of his Pontificate, created a vicariate-apostolic of Japan. Several endeavors to enter into communication with the Japanese were made ; but, for a long time, to no purpose. The sealed-up empire, at length, opened its ports to Great Britain and the United States of America. Such was the power of trade. The other civilized nations could no longer be excluded. Japan concluded a treaty with France by virtue of which the subjects of the latter State were secured in the free exercise of their religion among the Japanese. Mgr. Petitjean, who was, at the time, the vicar-apostolic, availed himself of such favorable relations to erect a church at Yokohama, and establish his residence at Nagasaki. All this was happily accomplished under the encouraging auspices of Pius IX. One day, as the vicar-apostolic had concluded the celebration of Mass, some inhabitants of a large village named Ourakami, near the city, came to him with countenances, expressive, at the same time, of joy and fear. Addressing him, they said: "Have you and your priests renounced marriage, and do you honor in your prayers the Mother of Christ?" The missionary replying in the affirmative, the Japanese fell on their knees and exclaimed: "You are, indeed, the disciples of Saint Francis Xavier, our first apostle. You are the true brethren of our former Jesuit Fathers. At last, after a lapse of two hundred years, we behold, once more, the priests of the true faith!" They gave thanks to God, shedding abundance of tears, with which mingled those of the good missionary; "religion," they added, "is free only to strangers. The law has not ceased to punish us Japanese Catholics with death. No matter; receive us, nevertheless, and instruct us. The lapse of time and the want of books have, perhaps, disfigured in our memories the teachings of truth. There will happen to us whatever it shall please God to appoint."

Four thousand families, comprising fourteen thousand individuals, had secretly persevered, clinging to the Catholic faith since the days of the Apostolic Xavier. Notwithstanding all the prudence of the missionaries, the secret of their relations with the natives became known to the local police, and more than four thousand inhabitants of Ourakami were arrested, bastinadoed, imprisoned or transported to the North. Their punishment lasted four years. One-third of their number died of want, but few of them gave way. The survivors of these persecuted people were finally restored to their country, and through the representations of the European consuls, religious liberty was granted, at least, provisionally, to natives as well as strangers. Thus did Pius IX., at length, enjoy the consolation to behold, established in peace, the church which St. Francis Xavier had planted in the Empire of Japan, and which was so celebrated in the annals of Christian heroism.

PERSECUTION IN BRAZIL.

Gonsalvez de Oliveira, Bishop of Olinda, had found it necessary to warn his diocesans against the machinations of certain secret societies, which were alike hostile to the Church and to the State. They had obtained so much influence with the latter as to be able to attack, with impunity, the Sisters of Charity, and the priests of the Lazarist congregation, as well as all other zealous priests who sought to restore the discipline of the church. Whilst, on the one hand, the bishop was sustained by the congratulations and encouragement of the Holy See, and by the deference to ecclesiastical authority of many Catholics who had been accustomed to consider the secret societies as most inoffensive associations, he was urged, on the other hand, by the fury of the chiefs of those societies, who, alone, know all that they aim at and hold secret.

The Emperor, Don Pedro II., influenced by his free-thinking *entourage*, judged that the pastoral letter should be denounced to the Council of State. The councillors declared that it was an illegal document, not having received the Imperial *placet* "required by the Constitution of the Empire." Now commenced the most heartless, and, as is always the case, unavailing persecution. By order of the ministry, the procurator-general summoned the Bishop of Olinda before the Supreme Court of Rio Janeiro. The intrepid prelate replied by a letter, in which he declared that he could not, in conscience, appear before the Supreme Court, because it was impossible to do so, without acknowledging the competence of a civil court in matters purely religious. On 3rd January, 1874, the bishop was ordered to go to prison. He intimated that he would yield only to force. The chief of police, accordingly, accompanied

by two army officers, repaired to the Episcopal palace, and
conducted Mgr. de Oliveira to the port where a ship of war was
in attendance, to transport him to the maritime arsenal of
Rio Janeiro, one of the most unwholesome stations in Brazil.
There the illustrious prisoner was visited by Mgr. Lacerda,
Bishop of Rio Janeiro, who took off his pectoral cross, which
was a family keep-sake,·and placing it around the neck of
Mgr. Oliveira, said: "My Lord, you have full jurisdiction
throughout this land to which you are brought as a captive.
My clergy, the chapter of my cathedral, all will be most happy
to obey your orders. Have the goodness to bless us all. The
blessing of those who suffer persecution in the cause of Christ
is a pledge of salvation." Bishop Lacerda, before retiring,
handed to the prisoner a large sum of money, in order that he
should want for nothing, and promised to renew his visit as
often as the gaolers would permit. Almost all the bishops of
Brazil sent congratulatory telegrams to the imprisoned bishop.
One of them went so far as to identify himself with the action
of the Bishop of Olinda, by doing in like manner. It was the
Bishop of Para, who was speedily transferred from his Episcopal palace to prison. The administrator who filled his place,
having refused to remove the interdict which had been pronounced against certain confraternities which admitted members of the secret societies, was condemned on 25th April, 1875,
to six years of forced penal labor. Four years of the like
torture were decreed against the administrator of Olinda for a
similar offence. So much for the humanitarian Emperor of
Brazil and his enlightened advisers.

It was not long till new elections raised to power, men who
had more respect for the Episcopal office, and the wretched
Brazilian persecution came to an end.

The Bishop of Olinda was no sooner set at liberty than he
repaired to Rome, in order to give an account of his conduct to
Pius IX. The Holy Father gave him every proof of the warmest affection.

The lesser States of South America, which, on being emancipated from the yoke of Spain, had chosen the republican form of government, became a source of intense anxiety to the Holy Father. Venezuela, Chili, the Argentine Republic, and, even Hayti, appear to have been seized with the spirit of the time. They had become too great, one would say, to accept humbly the teachings of religion. Even Chili, where comparative moderation prevailed, made an attempt to subordinate in all things, spiritual as well as temporal, the Church to the State. The bishops, as in duty bound, protested; and, being unanimously supported by the people, the attack of Chilian free-thinkers, on public peace and liberty, was abandoned. The trouble in Hayti arose more from a desire, on the part of the negross, to have native priests than any real hostility to religion. The government ignorantly assumed the right to appoint the chief administrators of the Church. The people were painfully affected by this unwarrantable encroachment on the spiritual power. It was hardly to be supposed that Peru should be out of the fashion. Pius IX. appears, however, to have settled the difficulties of the Peruvians, by granting to their presidents the same right of patronage which was formerly enjoyed by the Kings of Spain. The religious troubles of Mexico were not so easily composed. The civil authorities of that sadly unsettled republic, urged, it is believed, by the secret societies, aimed at nothing less than the total suppression of religion. On 24th November, 1874, they decreed that no public functionary or body of officials, whether civil or military, should attend any religious office whatsoever. "The Sunday or Sabbath day," they impiously ruled, "shall henceforth be tolerated only in as far as it affords rest to public employees." Religious instruction, together with all practices of religion, was prohibited in all the establishments of the federation of the States and the municipalities. No religious act could be done except in the churches, and there, only, under the superintendence of the police. No religious institution was authorized to acquire real estate or any capital accruing from such property. Article nineteen of this detestable legislation, and which was carried by one hundred and thirteen to fifty-seven votes, interdicted the Sisters of Charity from living in community and wearing publicly their costume. Thus were expelled from Mexico four hundred sisters, who performed their charitable offices in the hospitals, schools and asylums of the country. Public opinion was roused, but to no purpose. The good sisters were allowed to embark for France, bearing with them the fate of thousands of the unfortunate. They may, perhaps, be replaced by the Prussian chancellor's deaconesses: of this sisterhood, the best suited for the Mexican climate, would, no doubt, be that portion which fled from Smyrna on the approach of an epidemic.

ECUADOR.

In the midst of so many discontented, turbulent, persecuting, semi-barbarous States, there was one where there was neither discontent, nor turbulence, nor persecution. This favored Republic of Ecuador was in close communion with Pius IX., and its president discarding all the fine-spun views and chimerical theories of the time, ruled, as became the chief of a free State, according to the wishes and the generally accepted principles of his people. A republic, so governed, provided it remain uncorrupt, cannot fail to enjoy the highest degree of prosperity compatible with its position and material resources. Not only did Ecuador itself enjoy the fruits of its truly free and rationally republican government, it was able also to extend the blessings of its Christian and liberal civilization to neighboring tribes. Moved by the example and the representations of the good people of Ecuador, nine thousand savages of the Province of Oriente were induced to adopt the habits of Christian civilization. The government of the enlightened president, Garcia Moreno, was so abundantly blessed that, in twelve years, the trade of Ecuador was doubled, as were also the number of its schools and the sum of its public revenues.

So bright an illustration of the good-working of sound principles was not to be tolerated. The love of a grateful and prosperous people could not protect their great and successful fellow-citizens against the weapons of secret conspirators. Political fanatics, who were strangers in Ecuador, and who, according to their own declaration, bore no personal ill-will to the president, struck the fatal blow. "I die," said the illustrious victim, as he expired, "but God dieth not!" The assassins were they who hold that God has no business in this world. "*Dixit insipiens; non est Deus.*"

Pius IX. lamented the death of Garcia Moreno, as he had lamented some seven-and-twenty years before, the untimely fate of his own minister, Count Rossi. He extolled the President of Ecuador in several allocutions, as the champion of true civilization and its martyr. He caused his obsequies to be solemnized in one of the Basilicas of Rome, over which he still held authority, and ordered that his bust should be placed in one of the galeries of the Vatican.

In the estimation of a certain class of politicians, Moreno was behind the age. In reality he was far in advance of it. The mania for Godless government, Godless education, Godless manners, and generally a Godless state of society, is only a passing phase on the face of the world. If, indeed, it be anything more, woe to mankind! Despair only can harbor the idea of its long continuance. The social and political chaos which darkens the age, must, surely, a litile sooner or a little later, give way to that order which is heaven's first law. Moreno beheld, through the storms that raged around his infant State, the early dawn of this better day. This light led him onwards. History will place him, not only among heroes and sages, but also among the most renowned initiators of great movements. His death is a glorious protest against the Godless, reckless, revolutionary sects. His high career will be as a monument throughout the centuries, constantly reminding mankind that, in this age, which may well be called the age of chaos and confusion—confusion in politics, confusion in the social State, confusion of ideas—there was, at least, one favored spot, where truth, order and justice reigned, and there was a contented and happy people.

The Protestant and free-thinking majority in Switzerland were jealous of the prosperity of the Catholic Church. They must, therefore, if possible, divide, and by dividing, weaken, if not destroy, the Catholic body. The most efficient means they could think of was the establishment of an old or *alt-Catholic* Church on the model of that of Germany. The idea was at hand, and the elements were not far to seek. Among the Swiss Catholic clergy there were none so weak as to betray their church. In the coterminous country—France, where there are fifty thousand parochial priests, some thirty were found already in disgrace among their brethren, who were ready to form the nucleus of the proposed schismatical church. The pretext was the pretended novelties introduced by the Œcumenical Council of the Vatican, which, they insisted, changed the character of the ancient Catholic Church. The schism once on foot, the majority in the State affected to treat the real Catholics as dissenters, and the handful of schismatics as the Catholic Church of Switzerland. Founding on this idea, persecution was speedily inaugurated. First came the secularization of several abbeys, which the revolution of the sixteenth century had respected, in the northern cantons, and the confiscation of the Church of Zurich, which was handed over to the *alt-Catholics*. Their next measure was the expulsion of Mgr. Mermillod, Bishop of Hebron and Coadjutor of Geneva. Mgr. Lachat, Bishop of Bale, was then deprived, and, on a purely theological pretext, his public adhesion to the Council of the Vatican. The sixty-nine parish priests of Bernese Jura, having declared in writing that they remained faithful to the Bishop of Bale, were, in their turn, suspended from their offices and driven, at first, from their parishes, and afterwards from the country. As there was not a sufficient number of foreign priests to replace the dispossessed clergy, the number of parishes was arbitrarily reduced from seventy-six to twenty-eight. It was regulated that nominations should, henceforth, be made by the government alone, and by a single stroke of the pen were suppressed, both the Concordat concluded with Rome, in 1828, and the act of re-union of 1815, by which, when Bernese Jura, formerly French, was incorporated with Switzerland, an engagement was made with France to respect, in every way, the liberty of Catholic worship. France was not in a position, at the time, to enforce the terms of the treaty. They who dared to call it to mind, accordingly, were sent to prison or heavily fined.

Almost all the Bernese clergy, when banished from their churches and presbyteries, sought shelter and protection on the hospitable soil of France. From that country they returned often, under cover of night, to their forsaken parishes, in order to administer the sacraments and perform other religious offices for the consolation of their flocks, hastening back to the land of liberty and safety before the approach of day. The persecution was carried to such extremes that the Catholics were not only deprived of their churches, but forbidden, under severe penalties, to assemble for Divine worship, even in barns or such-like places. "As an official of the State of Bearn," wrote a school inspector to a school mistress, "you are bound to strive, with all your might, that the purposes of the said State, as regards attendance at public worship, be carried out. If your conscience does not admit of your attending the Church which is recognized and approved by the government, I leave you at liberty to refrain from attending any worship, but I forbid you to go to the barn, where the deprived parish priest officiates, because I would not have you set a bad example to your children."

No encouragement or word of consolation that Pius IX. could bestow, was wanting to his persecuted children of Switzerland. In addressing Bishop Lachat, whom he received with every mark of friendship, when he came to represent the sad

condition to which he was reduced, the Holy Father said:
" To you also it is now given to experience the greatest happiness that can fall to the lot of an apostolic man. This happiness is thus expressed in the New Testament: *Ibant gaudentes,
quoniam digni habiti sunt pro nomine Jesu contumeliam pati.*
They went away rejoicing, because they were thought worthy
to suffer reproach for the name of Jesus."

The Prussian chancellor, as devoid of humanity as he was
short-sighted in statesmanship, forbad the exiled clergy of
Switzerland to set foot in the annexed Province of Alsace.
The brutal conduct of the chancellor could, however, only
injure himself. It stigmatizes him as a persecutor throughout
the ages, as long as history shall be read, whilst the sufferers
to whom he refused shelter and bread, found abundant compensation in the generous hospitality of the French nation.

Mentita est iniquitas sibi. The persecution brought little
benefit to either the Protestant or infidel party in the Bernese
Legislature, by whom it was inaugurated, whilst the moral
power of the Catholics was greatly increased. Travellers
relate that " the Catholics of Jura treat with a degree of contempt, as immense as is their faith, the apostate priests who
banished the true ministers of God. They assembled in barns
and all sorts of out-buildings, all remaining faithful to God,
the Holy Church and their parish priests. Faith which slept
in some souls is reawakened and endowed with new life.
Bernese Jura is more Catholic than ever."

The Central Council of the Swiss Confederation, at length,
became ashamed of the inglorious name which the Canton of
Bearn was making for the common country—the country of
William Tell—so highly famed for its love of liberty and its
noble hospitality. Perhaps, also, they were not unconcerned
to find that travellers from other lands protested, in their way,
against the barbarous persecution, and left their money in
more favored lands.

The Bernese government was advised, either to proceed
legally and regularly against the parish priests, or to recall

them.   There being nothing on which to found legal proceedings, the exiles returned to their country at the end of 1875.
The persecution was not, however, at an end. Neither churches,
nor presbyteries, nor liberty, were restored. The faithful clergy,
rich in the fidelity of their devoted flocks, fulfilled the duties of
their ministry in the darkness of night, using every precaution
in order to escape the snares of the police, and to avoid fines
and imprisonment, which were now the punishment instead of
exile.

GREAT BRITAIN AND THE BRITISH COLONIES.

Taking leave of the dark and dreary pages which bear the
melancholy record of persecution, we turn, with a feeling of
relief, to the more cheering picture presented by those countries where the great principle of religious liberty has come, at
length, to be fully understood.   It was a great day for the
united kingdom of Great Britain and Ireland, when the legal
disabilities which weighed so long on the Catholic people, were
removed.   It was the noble and powerful protest of a mighty
empire against the narrow and irrational spirit of persecution,
which still disgraces so many of the European nations.   If
ever the Catholics, by superiority of numbers, which is far
from being an impossible state of things, should come to sway
the destinies of that empire, the glorious fact will be remembered and bear its fruit.   England, Ireland and Scotland,
already enjoy an abundant measure of their reward, in the
increase of piety and of that righteousness which exalteth a
nation.   This is manifest in many ways.   It is particularly
shown forth by the more friendly feeling towards the Catholics
of the empire which now universally prevails.   We may not be
supposed to know much, here in Canada, about the state of
sentiment or opinion in England.   But when we appeal to the
testimony of so eminent an Englishman as Cardinal Newman,
what we affirm cannot be easily gainsaid.   In a discourse
recently delivered at Birmingham, on the growth of the Catholic Church in England, the very learned cardinal noted the

striking contrast between the feeling towards Catholics in
Cardinal Wiseman's time and that of the present day, and
accounted for the improvement by showing that there is now a
much better knowledge of the Catholic religion among Protestants. "What I wish to show," said his Eminence, "and
what I believe to be the remarkable fact is, that whereas there
have been many conversions to the Catholic Church during the
last thirty years, and a great deal of ill-will felt towards us, in
consequence, nevertheless, that ill-will has been overcome, and
a feeling of positive good-will has been created instead in the
minds of our very enemies, by means of those conversions
which they feared from their hatred of us. How this was, let
me now say: The Catholics in England, fifty years ago, were
an unknown sect amongst us. Now there is hardly a family
but has brothers or sisters, or cousins or connections, or friends
and acquaintances, or associates in business or work, of that
religion, not to mention the large influx of population from the
sister island; and such an interpenetration of Catholics with
Protestants, especially in our great cities, could not take place
without there being a gradual accumulation of experience,
slow, indeed, but therefore the more sure about individual
Catholics, and what they really are in character, and, whether
or not, they can be trusted in the concerns and intercourse of
life; and I fancy that Protestants, spontaneously, and before
setting about to form a judgment, have found them to be men
whom they could be drawn to like and to love quite as much
as their fellow-Protestants—to be human beings in whom they
could be interested and sympathize with, and interchange good
offices with, before the question of religion came into consideration."

The increase in the number of Catholics and of Catholic
institutions in Great Britain, has kept pace with the growth of
friendly sentiments in their regard. That island, "the mother
of nations," appears to be destined to unite by means of her
ever spreading language, the immense family of mankind.
For what end and purpose none can tell. The hidden ways of

Divine Providence are known to God alone. We may, nevertheless, in view of certain well-known facts, presume to draw the veil of mystery aside, and discover so far the secret of God's mercy. In Pius the Ninth's time the number of Catholics has been doubled in Great Britain, as well as in the United States of America, Canada, Australia, remote India and the Cape of Good Hope.

At the time of the election of Pius IX., there were in England and Scotland eight hundred and twenty Catholic priests. There are now two thousand and eighty-eight.* The number of churches and chapels had grown from six hundred and twenty-six to one thousand three hundred and fifteen. Within the last twenty years religious houses for men had increased from twenty-one to seventy-three, and convents for religious sisters, from ninety-seven to two hundred and thirty-nine. Catholic schools and colleges had more than doubled their number, being now one thousand three hundred, whilst a little over twenty years ago it was five hundred.

In the British colonies, generally, including British America, Australia, India, and the West Indies, there were, in 1855, no more than forty-four Episcopal Sees, several of which owed their erection to Pius IX. By the year 1876, the solicitude of the same venerable Pontiff had raised to eighty-eight, the number of archbishops and bishops who exercised the duties of their sacred office, throughout the Colonial Empire of Great Britain. In the whole empire there cannot be fewer than one hundred and twenty-five prelates, whether vicars-apostolic, archbishops, bishops, or prefects-apostolic.

In no country have the benefits of religious liberty been more abundantly enjoyed than in

---

*A later estimate than at page 120.

In 1869, the two Provinces of Ontario and Quebec, formerly Canada West and Canada East, counted ten dioceses and seven hundred and seventy-nine churches. Including Sherbrooke, Chicoutimi, and the vicariate-apostolic of Northern Canada, there are now thirteen dioceses in the two provinces, whilst, during the seven years anterior to 1876, there was an increase of one hundred and seventy-three churches, making, in all, one thousand one hundred and seventy-one. In the same period religious houses had increased from seventy-three to one hundred and ninety-six. Education of a religious character is, at the same time, amply provided for. There are, in the Province of Quebec, three thousand one hundred and thirty-nine parochial, and altogether three thousand six hundred and thirty elementary schools, for a population of one million eight hundred and eighty-two thousand souls. These schools, without including educational institutions of a more private kind, which are very numerous in Lower Canada (Quebec), allow one school to every six hundred people. It may be doubted whether Prussia, even, which possesses greater facilities for education than any other European country, comes up to this standard. The increase of Catholic people everywhere, throughout the country, keeps pace with the building of churches and the establishing of Catholic schools and other religious institutions. This increase is particularly noticeable in the towns and cities, where the growth of the Catholic population is remarkably rapid.

In all the British dependencies, liberty, as understood by the British people, prevails; and, wherever it is held in honor and exercises its legitimate influence, religion flourishes. Contrast, for instance, Australia, when a penal colony, and when liberty was unknown with Australia, as it is to-day. In 1804 two priests were permitted, by the civil power, to perform the duties of their sacred office. Their labors sufficed for the very limited spiritual wants of the colony. By 1827 these wants had so slightly increased that two priests were still able to meet them all. One of these was Dr. Ullathorne, now

Bishop of Birmingham, assisted by another priest and a lay teacher. So late as 1842, matters were little better, Hobart-town having one priest, but no church. Australia, meanwhile, was growing in importance, and it came to possess, as became an important British colony, constitutional government. This was a new era for the cause of religion. Australia has now, 1880, two archbishoprics and ten other episcopal 'sees. In three of the dioceses, Melbourne, Sandhurst and Perth, there are no fewer than one hundred and thirty-five priests.

THE UNITED STATES OF AMERICA.

At the epoch of Independence, 1776, the number of Catho-lics in the new republic was estimated at twenty-five thousand. The spiritual wants of this comparatively small body were ministered to by nineteen priests, who were under the jurisdic-tion of the bishop Vicar-Apostolic of London, England. By 1790, the number of priests was doubled, and a bishop was appointed. In 1840, there were in the United States one million five hundred thousand Catholics. By 1855, they had grown to two millions. In the twenty-one years from 1855 to 1876 the increase was from two millions to six million five hundred thousand. This extraordinary growth, though rapid, was, nevertheless, vigorous and healthy. There was a corres-ponding increase in the numbers of the clergy, as well as of religious and educational institutions. For the instruction and spiritual comfort of so great a flock, there were, in 1879, no fewer than five thousand three hundred and fifty-eight priests, with fifty-six bishops and archbishops, five thousand and forty-six churches, three thousand seven hundred and eleven oratories and missionary stations. Religious houses have also increased in due proportion. In 1855, there were only fifteen religious houses for men in all the United States. There are now ninety-five. Communities of religious sisters, who chiefly devote themselves to works of charity and instruc-tion, also flourish. In 1855 'there were only fifty such com-munities. There are now two hundred and twenty-five. Edu-

cational institutions of a religious character also abound. In
1800, there was only one Catholic academy for girls in all the
United States. At the present day they number more than
four hundred. Catholic colleges have increased from two to
sixty-four.

The number of parochial schools is not so great, in proportion to the population, as in the Province of Quebec. This is
accounted for by the still defective state of religious liberty in
the United States. There is a sort of State fanaticism there
in favor of common or national schools. Whilst Catholics cannot avail themselves of such institutions, which provide only a
Godless education, they are, nevertheless, heavily taxed for
their support. Being so burdened, it is surely much to the
credit of the Catholics of the United States that they, in addition, support two thousand two hundred and forty-four parochial schools, besides six hundred and sixty-three colleges or
academies, and twenty-four seminaries, for higher and ecclesiastical education. Notwithstanding the drawback alluded to,
Pius IX. entertained a high idea of the North American
Republic, and he showed that he did so when he declared that
it was almost the only country wherein he could exercise, without hindrance, the duties of his sublime office. He further
evinced his appreciation by raising several American bishops
to the dignity of archbishop, and one to that of cardinal. The
Archbishop of New York is the first American who has enjoyed
the high position of cardinal. He was formally thanked for
this well-merited honor by the President of the United States,
and all America concurred in extolling the wisdom of the choice
which gave the dignity to the Most Rev. Archbishop McCloskey,
of New York.

HIERARCHY OF SCOTLAND.

One of the latest labors of Pius IX. was that which he undertook, on the urgent request of the Catholics of Scotland, in connection with the restoration of the ancient Scottish hierarchy.
The venerable Pontiff, now so far advanced in years, did not

live to complete this important work. The late reverend and learned Dr. Grant, President of the Scotch College at Rome, ceased not, meanwhile, to promote, as representing the Catholics of Scotland, the institution of the hierarchy. His knowledge of the country and historical research eminently qualified him for the task. The work, so happily commenced under the auspices of Pius IX., was brought to a conclusion soon after the accession of his successor, Leo XIII. The Most Rev. John Strain, well known as a sound theologian and eminently practical preacher, was appointed Archbishop of St. Andrews and Edinburgh. The learned prelate thus became the successor of the ancient Archbishops of St. Andrews and Primate of Scotland. The other Episcopal Sees erected were Glasgow, Aberdeen, Dunkeld, Galloway, Argyll and the Isles. Glasgow, in consideration of its former honors, was made an archbishopric, but without suffragans. The archbishop is a member of the Synod of St. Andrews and Edinburgh. To the undying honor of the people of Scotland, there is nothing more to record. There were no commotions, no eloquent appeals for the purpose of allaying groundless fears and calming the popular mind, to burden the tale of the historian. An unsuccessful attempt at riot, by some rowdies, in a city of six hundred thousand souls, confirms rather than derogates from the absolute truth of this statement.

There are already in the Archdiocese of St. Andrews and Edinburgh several important religious institutions. Among these may be mentioned four communities of religious sisters. The sisters, called "Ursulines of Jesus," have two establishments in the city of Edinburgh, and devote themselves entirely to education and charity. There are fifty-four churches, chapels and stations. The missions, properly so-called, are twenty-eight in number, and forty-three priests, of whom thirteen are members of religious societies, perform all the missionary duty and minister to the spiritual wants of the congregations. It cannot be said that education is neglected, and such education as recognizes religious principle; there being, in addition to the convent schools, thirty-six congregational or parochial schools.

In the Archdiocese of Glasgow, one hundred and twenty-one priests, of whom twenty-four are members of religious societies, attend to the spiritual wants of the missions and congregations. The Glasgow missions count fifty-nine, with seventy-eight churches, chapels and stations. The congregational or parochial schools number one hundred and eighty-six, in addition to religious educational institutions.

Aberdeen has forty-seven priests, of whom seven are members of the Benedictine Order. It has thirty-two missions, with fifty-one churches, chapels and stations. Colleges, convents, and congregational schools, are in proportion to the Catholic population.

Dunkeld contains within its borders the important seaport town of Dundee, and the ancient city of Perth, where may still be seen the Church of St. John, against which the Knox Iconoclasts cast the first stone—the sad prelude to their furious onslaught on all the sacred edifices of the land. At Dundee there is a numerous Catholic population. In the whole diocese there are thirty-three priests, of whom twelve are members of the religious Society of Redemptorists. There are religious communities of Sisters of Mercy, Little Sisters of the Poor, and Ursulines of Jesus. The Marist Brothers and Redemptorists have their monasteries, and there is a creditable number of congregational schools.

The ancient See of Whithorn (Candidacasa) is now known as the diocese of Galloway. It dates from St. Ninian, the apostle of the Southern Picts, by whom it was founded in 397. It was destroyed in the time of the Scandinavian invasions, and remained extinct from 803 till 1180. It fell again at the epoch of the Reformation, and had no bishop from the death of Andrew Durie, in 1558, till the appointment of Bishop McLachlan by Leo XIII. The residence of the bishop is at Dumfries, where there is a numerous congregation and an elegant church.

Argyll and the Isles is a diocese full of promise. The traditions of its piety in ancient days are a rich inheritance. It has already thirty-eight churches, chapels and stations, to-gether with some numerous congregations.

INCREASE AND NUMBER OF CATHOLICS THROUGHOUT THE WORLD IN THE TIME OF PIUS IX.

About the time of the accession of Pius IX., the Catholic population of the world was estimated by scientific men at two hundred and fifty-four million six hundred and fifty-five thousand (see the *Scientific Miscellany* of the time). Since that time there has been a very considerable increase. How great it has been we may judge from the statistics with which we are most familiar, those of Great Britain and the British Colonies, as well as those of the United States of America. The eminent statisticians, Drs. Behm and Wagner, hold that the number of Protestants has more than doubled in the same period. Some thirty-five years ago, according to the *Scientific Miscellany*, the Protestant population of the world was forty-eight million nine hundred and eighty-nine thousand. Without saying that the learned men alluded to are wrong in estimating them now at one hundred and one million, it may be claimed that Catholics have enjoyed at least as great an increase. The tendency of the latter, in the present age, is to spread and to spread rapidly, whilst among Protestants, according to their own ablest writers, there exists no such expansive power. An opinion prevails among those who are not friendly to the Catholic Church, that such an institution can only take root and grow in an age of ignorance, or among ignorant people. This opinion enjoys not the sanction of the most distinguished Protestant authors and preachers. Baron Macaulay writes: "We often hear it said that the world is constantly becoming more and more enlightened, and that the enlightenment must be favorable to Protestantism and unfavorable to Catholicism. We wish that we could think so. But we see great reason to doubt whether this is a well-founded expectation. We see that during the last two hundred and fifty years the human mind has been in the highest degree active; that it has made great advances in every branch of natural philosophy; that it has produced innumerable inventions, tending to promote the convenience of life; that medicine, surgery, chemistry, engineering, have been very greatly improved; that government, police and law, have been improved, though not to so great an extent as the physical sciences. Yet we see that during these two hundred and fifty years Protestantism has made no conquests worth speaking of. Nay, we believe that as far as there has been change, that change has been in favor of the Church of Rome. We cannot, therefore, feel confident that the progress of knowledge will necessarily be fatal to a system which has, to say the least, stood its ground in spite of the immense progress made by the human race in knowledge since the time of Queen Elizabeth." If, then, Protestantism, as regards increase and development, has been at a stand-still for the last two hundred and fifty years, whilst it is admitted on all hands that Catholicism has been growing rapidly, it is not, surely, unreasonable to claim that the increase of Catholics keeps pace with that of Protestants. The claim, however, must be waived, as it would give a greater expansion to the Catholic Church than Catholics can suppose it is entitled to. If the number of Catholics had doubled within the last five-and-thirty or forty years, as that of Protestants is alleged by the learned statisticians to have done, they would now count five hundred and nine million three hundred thousand. Behm and Wagner estimate them at two hundred and seventy million.

---

* The late celebrated preacher, Dr. Cumming, also admitted the expansive power which is characteristic of the Catholic Church. And in doing so, he bore witness to its actual growth in his time. In a lecture delivered at Brentford, England, in 1860, he said: " He would do the priests of the Church of Rome the justice to say that a more earnest, energetic, a more industrious body he did not know in any portion of our church; they were laboring incessantly for what they believed to be the truth, and he would that he could say without success, but he was sorry to say *with great success.* He saw going over to the Church of Rome a section of the nobility and many ministers of our church. These were well instructed, and ought to have known better. In England, account for it as they could, it had made progress to such an extent, during the last twenty years, that it had doubled its churches and doubled its priests."—Lecture at Brentford, England, 1860.

Judging by the facts alluded to, this estimate is certainly below the mark, and we shall still be considered as determining for a low figure when we reckon the Catholic population of the whole world at three hundred million.

The heathen masses are still the most numerous. But, if the statement recently made by the Secretary of the Chinese Legation, at Washington, may be relied on, they are not overwhelmingly so. This statement reduces the population of China from the fabulous number of four hundred million to one hundred million. It is not, surely, reasonable to suppose, as the world has so long supposed, that one nation, China, has a population double that of all the nations of India. The whole heathen world, therefore, cannot count more than six hundred and fifty million souls—too many to be still in darkness and the shadow of death. But let each believer labor to convert a heathen, and there will be light at last. The believing portion of mankind is not so far behind, in point of numbers, at least. It consists of:

300,000,000 Catholics.

90,000,000 members of the Greek Church ⎫ According to
101,000,000 Protestants   ⎬ Drs. Behm and
7,000,000 Jews   ⎭ Wagner.

ANNIVERSARY OF THE EPISCOPAL CONSECRATION OF PIUS IX.

The 3rd of June, 1877, was a great day for Rome and the Catholic world. Of all the *fetes* which Pius IX. was favored to celebrate, there was none more honored than the anniversary of his episcopal consecration. One would say that the faithful Catholic people everywhere had resolved to make it an occasion of protesting against the treatment to which the venerable Pontiff was subjected, and the false principles which governed the Italian faction, by which he was so cruelly persecuted. Pilgrims came from all lands and crowded the streets of the Papal city; for such it still was. Notwithstanding all the efforts of the usurping government, the Roman people acknowledged no other ruler at Rome than the Holy Father. During six months of the year 1877, the devoted Catholics of every nation ceased not to throng the streets, the approaches to and from the halls of the Vatican Palace. Nor did they come empty-handed. They were literally laden with gold and silver, together with an endless variety of other rich and appropriate gifts. A month before the anniversary day, there were already five hundred chalices, as well as other church plate, jewellery, vestments, altar linens, etc., deposited in the Vatican. An eye-witness beheld these precious offerings suitably laid out in one of the largest galleries, forming an immense treasury, from which the benevolent Pontiff supplied the poorer missions throughout the world. Congratulatory addresses were constantly presented, and Pius IX. was indefatigable in receiving these proofs of the faith and love of his spiritual children. Day after day he made replies to deputations, and often, four times a day without appearing fatigued or giving any sign that his bodily strength or vigor of mind was failing him. Day after day, throughout the whole summer of 1877, the faithful people ceased not to astonish the new masters of Rome, who flattered themselves with the belief that faith was dead in the world, and would no longer be an impediment to their domination. They beheld pilgrims from every clime in vast numbers, of which they could form no estimate. They also heard their voice, and wondered at their admirable unanimity. "All of us, whoever we are, Christians of every nation and of every tongue," said the Bishop of Poitiers, speaking in the name of his fellow-Catholics, "we have all been brought here by the desire, the necessity we are under, to offer our tribute of regret and love to the venerated Pontiff, whom the whole world honors with all the veneration of filial duty. After having placed at his feet our presents and our respectful homage, we come to offer, in this sanctuary, our thanksgiving and our prayers—our thanksgiving, for Pius IX. has been preserved to us beyond the term of all preceding Pontificates—our prayers for his remaining in this life is, at present, our only pledge of safety."*

* Discourse delivered in the Church of St. Peter *ad vincula*, 1st June, 1877, by the Bishop of Poitiers.

On occasion of the memorable anniversary, Pius IX. proclaimed a jubilee, and thus afforded to all his children throughout the universe an opportunity of uniting with those of Rome in one common prayer and act of thanksgiving. Numberless communions, in every Catholic land, on the very day of the anniversary—3rd June—bore witness to the lively faith which universally prevailed, and made it plain as noon-day to the unbelieving that the body of the Church is united by the bond of charity, even as is the family by the ties of blood. The power of such a celebration was widely felt. And the revolutionists of Italy believed that something must be done in order to counteract its influence. They could not propose, as they had done six years before on occasion of the anniversary of Pius the Ninth's exaltation to the Popedom, to display on all the public edifices of Rome the flag of revolutionized Italy in fraternal union with that of the Pontiff and the Church. It must, therefore, be unfurled in direct opposition to the cause of the Holy Father. A festive commemoration of the " constitutional statute " was ordered to be held on the 3rd June, the day of the Papal celebration. The scheme proved to be more than a failure. It was intended as an insult to the Pope and protest against the Christian faith. In reality it became a testimony which redounded to the honor of the Holy Father and the glory of religion. What cared the Romans, or the people of the Roman territory, for the "constitutional statute" of Charles Albert ? Their *vivats* were all for Pius IX. and his more constitutional constitution.

"Long live Pius IX.!—Pius IX., our only King!" No other cry was heard in the streets of Rome, or in the wide campagna. The populations of the country as well as of the city were alike devoted to Pius IX., and would have no other to rule over them. The usurping revolutionists must needs retaliate. In doing so, they still more degraded their *fete* of the " constitutional statute."

On occasion of royal *fetes*, favors are liberally dispensed. This order of things was now reversed. Parties convicted of illuminating their houses, of displaying white and yellow colors, or of expressing in words their loyalty to Pius IX., were sentenced to imprisonment.

DEATH OF ANTONELLI AND PATRIZI.

Shortly before the anniversary celebration, Pius IX. had to lament the death of his faithful Secretary of State, Cardinal Antonelli. This intrepid statesman had done battle courageously during six-and-twenty years for the Church, the Holy See and the temporal sovereignty of the Roman Pontiff, who had been threatened in his life, his priestly honor and his character for integrity. The devoted cardinal defied both the poniard and the tongue of the calumniator. Although able to unmask the most secret intrigues of the revolutionists, he could not avert the blow which it was permitted that they should strike against the time-honored institutions of his country. They appear to have been destined to reign for a time. Their success did not appal Antonelli nor shake his fidelity. In evil report and good report he stood by his sovereign, and shared his exile as well as the honor which he enjoyed in the more auspicious days of his glorious Pontificate.

Three weeks later, Cardinal Patrizi, who was Vicar of Rome and chief counsellor of Pius IX. in all matters connected with the government of the church, was called from this earthly scene. Thus was the aged Pontiff destined to be tried by new afflictions. The success of his enemies and of the enemies of the Church, the privation and humiliation to which he was subjected, were rendered more severe by the death of his dearest friends who were also his ablest supporters. He was grieved, but could not be crushed by so many calamities. He remained until his health utterly failed equal to his high position.

An additional cause of sorrow to the Holy Father was the enactment of the Italian Legislature, known as the *Mancini law*. This law was in downright opposition to the *law of guarantees*. It made it a crime to preach the Gospel. On pretence of repressing the abuses of the clergy, their offences against the laws and institutions of the State, it forbade all apostolic preaching. It was too late. Nero, even, was not in time, and all the fury of persecution could not uproot the belief in virtue which prevailed. The clergy shall no longer say that fraud, robbery, lying, violence and assassination are sins. But *cui bono?* The world has already its convictions—prejudices, the philosophy of *Kulturkampf* may call them—in regard to all such things, and no law that an infidel parliament can enact will suffice to eradicate them. It could only sadden the heart of the Chief Pastor to see the power which ruled in his country and in his stead laboring so strenuously but ineffectually to demolish the edifice of the church, which, for so many ages, had been assailed in vain. It was the height of presumption, surely, when a few modern Italians, a miserable minority of their own nation, undertook a task which defied all the power of Imperial Rome. In a country where liberty is better understood, a powerful voice was raised in condemnation of the *Mancini law*. The British *Catholic Union* protested against the cruel enactment as an attack not only on the liberty of the Church but also on the very existence of the Christian faith in Italy. This purpose was, indeed, avowed by many of its supporters in the Italian parliament.

Pius IX. could not fail to protest against such an attack on that liberty which is the birthright of every Christian. In a Consistorial Allocution of 12th March, 1877, he exposed the plot which the revolutionists had prepared in order to prevent the Holy Father from accomplishing his appointed mission—that of instructing and edifying the whole flock of Christ. That his protest was fully justified and demanded by the circumstances of the case was abundantly shown by the rage which it excited among the ruling faction. Their press did its best to dissemble, and affected to treat with contempt the Pope's address. It contained only "lame and doubtful reasonings—such arguments as are termed paralogisms or involuntary sophisms, which escape the notice of their authors." The government, in unison with the press, sought to stifle the importunate voice of the Pontiff. The council of ministers went so far as to resolve on prosecuting any journals that should dare to publish the Papal allocution. But they found it was too late. The obnoxious document was already printed in France, and, consequently, open to the civilized world. So the wrath of the ministry was allowed to cool. It sought, nevertheless, to be revenged. The minister of justice, accordingly, addressed a circular to the procurators-general, in which he denounced the language of Pius IX. as "excessive and violent." The Pope himself he railed as a factious person, as a fomenter of sedition and revolt. He also charged him with ingratitude. For what was he ungrateful? Had they not robbed him of his sovereignty and his property? Did they not now hold him closely guarded in the Vatican? They spared his life, indeed, but made him understand that he was their prisoner, as, in reality, he was. To have gone farther would have been to outrage all Italy, which they were so anxious to conciliate, and the great Powers, whose forbearance they so much needed. Cardinal Simeoni, who had succeeded Antonelli as Secretary of State, in a circular addressed to the Papal nuncios, pointed out the weakness and gross injustice of Mancini's letter. The secret societies, on the other hand, congratulated their most dear and most active *brother*, and expressed the hope *that he would not stop until he reached the end to which he so nobly tended.* The minister of justice fully acceded to the wishes of the *brethren*, and they could rely upon it that he would persevere until he compassed the destruction of the Papacy. Such good resolutions deserved a reward. They awarded him, accordingly, what they called a *diploma of honor.*

The *Mancini law*, notwithstanding all the efforts of its supporters, never became law. There is not much in this history to be placed to the credit of Victor Emmanuel. Nevertheless, he, all of a sudden, opposed the enactment ·of the odious law which he had allowed to be prepared and presented in his name to the representative chamber. By expressing his repugnance to it, he caused it to fail in the Senate. It is related that it was on the representation of his daughter, the Princess Clotilde, that he so acted.

PLAN FOR ELECTING A POPE.

One of the most daring enterprises of the Italian ministry was their scheme, in conjunction with the Prussian chancellor, for the election of a Pope on the demise of Pius IX. Hitherto, when the Popes enjoyed their temporal sovereignty, the Cardinal Camerlingo, or high chamberlain, directed everything from the time of the Pope's decease until the election of a successor. It was the purpose of the ministry to arrogate to themselves the attributes of this high dignitary, who acted, temporarily, as the Sovereign of Rome. For the attainment of their end, fraud, lying and forgery were freely had recourse to. It being understood that there existed a Bull relating to the election of Pius the Ninth's successor, and that it was in the custody of Mgr. Mercurelli, the Secretary of Pontifical briefs, a high price was offered to any one who should treacherously deliver it into the hands of the revolutionists. Such a temptation was not to be resisted. A cunning scribe, who could imitate the handwriting of Mercurelli, made a copy of an ancient Bull of Pius VI., adapting it to the circumstances of the time. To the great confusion of the astute chancellor and his associates, the Italian ministers, the forgery was discovered, and the sage statesmen befooled in the sight of all Europe by a common felon. Nothing, however, was to be left undone that was calculated, as the conspirators conceived, to secure the election of a Pope who would reject the decisions of the Vatican Council. For this end it was proposed to take military possession of the

Vatican Palace, and appoint a commissioner to superintend the election and carry out the views of the faction. This iniquitous plot appears to have been overthrown by a vigorous article which was published in the *Osservatore Romano*. It is said to have been inspired by Pius IX. It stated, among other things, that "the Vatican changes not with the changes of the times, and the Lord, who has protected it in the past, and given visible proofs of His continued protection, will protect it in the future, and defend it against all, whatever artifices, whether secret or open, its enemies may employ, in order to conquer and overthrow it." The revolutionary journals, whose constant cry was "war to the knife" on the Church and the Papacy, could not refrain from expressing their astonishment, it ought to be said their admiration, of this masterly document. "It is impossible," said the *Republique Francaise* of 28th July, 1877, "not to be struck by the tone of authority, the vehemence and the menaces, the ardent and deep-rooted faith which prevail from beginning to end of this extraordinary production."

ILLNESS OF THE POPE—VICTOR EMMANUEL AT THE VATICAN.

In the autumn of 1877, the health of Pius IX. began to fail. He caught cold and had a renewal of rheumatic attacks. He was obliged, in consequence, to discontinue giving audiences. Finally, by the advice of his physicians, he kept his bed continuously for three weeks, from 20th November. The Pope's indisposition appears to have been quite a God-send to the ever-busy press of the hostile faction. There were, of course, spasms, fainting fits, mortification of the extremities, etc. The Pope is dying—the Pope is dead!—and the enemy rejoiced, as over a hard-won victory. But the end was not yet. The Holy Father recovered, and was able to hold a Consistory and deliver an allocution on the 28th of December.

There was one at Rome who felt differently from the party with whom he acted in regard to the illness and possible death of the Pope. This was no other than King Victor Emmanuel. The dethroned Pontiff was still a power that helped to stem the tide of red republican revolution which rolled so angrily against the tottering throne of united Italy. The barrier was in danger. Only the slender thread of an exhausted life saved it from giving way. The king was awe-struck, and sought comfort in the Palace of the Vatican.*

What passed at the extraordinary interview none will ever know. All that can be found on record is that the King of Italy retired with a lightened heart from the mansion of the Sovereign Pontiff. Pardon, benediction, renewal of promises —what may there not have been? That the meeting was not without result, an event which was not at that time far distant clearly shows.

The restoration of Pius IX. to comparative health was matter for thanksgiving and congratulation. A consistory was held, accordingly, on the 28th of December, 1877. The cardinals having assembled, the Holy Father thus addressed them : "We rejoice in the Lord at having experienced how faithfully you sustain the burden of the apostolic ministry : and, at the same time, for having enjoyed the sweet consolation to find the sorrows of our soul alleviated by your virtue and the constant affection of your charity." The venerable Pontiff concluded this address, which was destined to be his last in solemn consistory, by inviting the members of the Sacred College "to offer up their prayers assiduously to the throne of Divine mercy for himself and for the Church," representing that the strength of Christians is in prayer, in the power of God, which the prayer of His creature, made in his image, causes to be exerted. And who is stronger than God? *Quis ut Deus?*

The aged Pontiff, whom the revolutionists of Italy and other countries cried out against with such vehemence of hatred and malediction, asked no other favor for himself of the Supreme Giver than the pleasure to impart once more his benediction from the Vatican to the city and the whole world. On occasion of some foreign ladies resident at Rome coming to present him with a rich canopy for decorating the Vatican

* *La Captivite de Pie IX. par Alexander de St. Albin. Paris, 1878. Pages 513 and 514.*

lodge, at the benediction he gave utterance to the following prayer: "Lend new strength, O Lord, to Thy Vicar on earth; give new vigor to his voice and to his arm, in order that, in the present crisis, it may be permitted him, as a sign of reconciliation and peace to bless once more solemnly the whole Catholic people, and that thus, through Thy assistance, society may be restored to a state of tranquillity and the practice of all the Christian virtues." He adored, without knowing it, the Divine will, which was not that he should ever again impart his apostolic benediction from the Vatican. This he knew not, and could not pretend to know. But he was comforted in the firm belief that the benediction would never cease to be dispensed. On the same day, he said, addressing the Roman ladies who presented a carpet for the solemn benediction: "At this time of darkness and tribulation, when we are in the power of our enemies, you may say to me: 'We have exerted ourselves so much, we have offered up so many prayers, shed so many tears, and, notwithstanding, all to no purpose.' The time will come when this present will be made use of. *Tota nocte laborantes.* . . The Romans have, indeed, prayed. They have given signal proof of their fidelity and their piety, amid the gloom and trouble of our national catastrophes, and why have they, as yet, obtained nothing? But what do I say? Are those evidences of affection which every day reach the Holy See to be reputed as nothing? Is that earnestness of prayer which prevails at Rome and throughout the Catholic world to no purpose? In the most desert regions and remotest countries vows and prayers are offered up for our deliverance. Your prayers and communions are so many petitions, laid at the foot of the altar, which cannot fail to be heard. As our Lord, who was pleased to show Peter where to cast his nets, in order to have an abundant draught of fish, teaches us also how we shall escape from the abyss of calamity into which our sins, perhaps, have thrown us. . . Although I, who, at present, am the Vicar of Christ, may not, one of my successors will, see Rome, which is our city, restored to its pristine state, tranquil and flourishing as it was some months ago. He will also behold all the rights of this Holy See completely recovered."

By one of two things only, as far as man can see, is it possible that Italy should be emancipated from its present bondage, and governed according to the wishes of its people. A constitutional monarchy, such as Pius IX. sought so long to establish, would be the most secure and permanent guarantee for peace and liberty in the south of Europe. A remedy for present evils may also be found in a thoroughly representative system of government, which the system that prevails for the moment in Italy has no claim to be. There cannot, however, be representative government so long as the Italian people allow a reckless faction, which is only a small minority of the nation, to control the elections, manopolize the votes, and constitute themselves the legislature of the country. Patience is a virtue. But it may be abused. It certainly has been so in the case of Italy, and by a base conspiracy. When will the people arise in their might, and, by their immense superiority in numbers as well as intelligence, cast off the yoke of the conspirators—the incubus which crushes and degrades them in the eyes of mankind?

KING VICTOR EMMANUEL SANCTIONS ARRANGEMENTS FOR THE FUNERAL OF PIUS IX.—DEATH OF VICTOR EMMANUEL.

On the 29th December, 1877, King Victor Emmanuel came to Rome on business of the State, as if the city of the Popes were *de jure* as well as *de facto* his capital. On the 31st of the same month, his ministers induced him to affix his royal signature to some new acts of brigandage and usurpation, which they had prepared, but which could not be accomplished until the death of Pius IX. At the same time, a decree regulating the funeral of the Pope was drawn up and signed by the king. Royal honors were to be restored, but only when they could not be enjoyed. The Holy Father, although stripped of his sovereignty in life, was to be honored when dead as a sovereign prince. It was appointed that mourning should be worn throughout all the Kingdom of Italy. Court liveries, even, were got ready, and also the minutest details of mourning apparel. Nothing was wanting but death—and death came—but not the death that was so ardently desired. Scarcely had Victor Emmanuel signed the funeral decree, which was intended to be, at the same time, the death-warrant of the Papacy and the Church, when he was taken suddenly ill. He was anxious to leave Rome, where his stay was always as short as possible, but was detained by the receptions of New Year's day, and in order to attend a diplomatic dinner on the 6th of January. On that very day, a three-fold malady laid him on his deathbed. He became at once the victim of pleuro-pneumonia, together with the fatal malaria and miliary fevers. There was no hope of his recovery. To leave Rome was impossible. "Carry me hence, at any rate," cried the dying king, in an agony of horror; "I must not die at the Quirinal." It was too late. The physicians would not allow him to be moved. Unhallowed force placed him in the sacred palace of the Conclave. Greater force held him there. The prince who said, "We are at Rome, and at Rome we shall remain," was doomed to die at Rome. After death, too, he must remain at Rome, notwithstanding the wishes of all his kindred and of his son and successor. The new king expressed to a deputation of the municipality of Turin with what pain he made the sacrifice which policy required. The policy of the revolutionary faction would not allow Victor Emmanuel to have his last resting-place with his ancestors at the Superga. Policy forbade that death even should liberate him who was called the liberator of Italy. Policy hoped to perpetuate usurpation, by holding the usurper in the usurped capital. The dead king remained in death, as he had ever been in life, the captive of the faction.

As soon as Pius IX. became aware of the critical state of King Victor Emmanuel, he sent to him his own chaplain, Bishop Marinelli, with full authority to reconcile the dying monarch to the church on his expressing repentance and retracting. This dignitary went thrice to the palace, and was as often repelled by the watchful ministers, who strictly guarded the person of the king. They dreaded lest so public a retractation as he was, at the time, able to make, and as would have been required, should prove injurious to their schemes.

Later, when there was no hope of recovery, anxious that the king should have the credit of being at peace with the Church, they allowed his own chaplain, the Rev. Signor Azenio, to approach his bed-side. This worthy priest, being fully authorized, heard the confession of King Victor Emmanuel, and administered to him the Sacraménts of the Church. As the most Holy Sacrament was borne to the monarch's death-bed, Prince Humbert, Princess Margaret, and, together with them, ten ministers and dignitaries of the Court, bearing lighted torches, accompanied the priest; and as Victor Emmanuel received the Viaticum and Extreme Unction, they all fell upon their knees. (9th January, 1878.) This conclusion, so consoling to the departing soul, was gall and wormwood to the worldly ministers. The founder of United Italy, before he could have the benefit of the last sacred rites, prayed to be pardoned all his crimes against the Sovereign Pontiff and the Church. By acknowledging and condemning his faults, he also condemned the unhallowed work which was forwarded by so much usurpation and sacrilege. The Christian-like end of Victor Emmanuel did not meet the views of the ministers. (*Osservatore Romano* of 10th January.) Accordingly, they endeavored immediately to lessen its effect on the public mind. Their journals, unable to deny the truth, even acknowledging the benefit they had by the king's confession and communion, cunningly labored to counteract the same by the grossest misrepresentation. They related that the king, at the moment of his death, had spoken both as a Christian and an infidel revolutionist. They made him thus retract his retractation. "In all that I have done, I am conscious of having always fulfilled my duties as a citizen and a prince, and of having done nothing against the religion of my ancestors." As his conscience was thus at ease, for what did he beg pardon of the Sovereign Pontiff and the Church? Of what could he repent who acknowledged no sin?

L'Osservatore Romano, in reply, reiterated all that it had already stated on the highest authority. "Let there be an end, once for all," said this excellent journal, "to the profane language which dares rashly to intervene between the dying man and his God, of whom the priest is the representative.

The Church, appealed to on so short a notice, and in the awful
hour of the death agony, mercifully extends her hand to him
who is about to approach the presence of the Sovereign Judge,
and opens to him, as far as possible, the way of salvation ; but
she strictly sees to it that her holy laws be fully observed."
Policy makes laws which it violates as easily as it makes them.
The Church can never break her laws, which are of Divine
origin.   Victor Emmanuel, accordingly, must have submitted
to the laws of the Church, in order to be reconciled to the
Church, to Pius IX. and to God.

At the death of the king the revolutionists were struck with
consternation.   "Victor Emmanuel is no more!" said the
Liberta, "and Italy is like a warrior without his sword." They
all felt as if the edifice which they had raised were falling to
pieces.   They took no blame to themselves, however.   They
ascribed not to their folly or their wickedness the danger
which threatened them. "God is unjust," said one of the party,
as he announced to the Romans the king's death.   Considering the term of human life, it was no doubt unjust, to remove
from this world a man at the advanced age of eight-and-fifty
years !   Another, as the remains of the "father of his country"
were borne to the Pantheon, blasphemously exclaimed : "That
everlasting Pantheon ! so long the altar of inanimate gods
—now the temple of a hostile *Deity !*"

Although Pius IX., with his usual goodness and consistency,
authorized the clergy to take part in the funeral of the deceased king, thus according what was due to the honor of a
Christian who had been reconciled to God and the Church, the
ceremony which, otherwise, would have been so solemn, was
sadly marred by processions of secret societies, Grand Orients
and Garibaldians, which followed the funeral car to the Church
of St. Mary of the Martyrs.

The Pantheon was not too grand for so great a king.   It
was only fitting that he who had lent himself to the baleful
work of paganizing modern Rome should have his final resting-place in the temple that was so long sacred to Rome's
heathen *deities.*

---

* That *was* the Pantheon, or temple of all the Gods.   It is now the Church
called *St. Mary of the Martyrs* (*Sæ Mariæ ad Martyres*).

The Holy Father had so well recovered from his illness, and his health was so good during the months of December and January, 1877–78, that he was able to transact business daily with the cardinals, heads of congregations and other prelates. It was for him the revival—the lucid interval—which so often precedes the final scene. Notwithstanding the pompous obsequies which the late king had prepared for Pius IX., the venerable Pontiff still lived, and was able to protest against the pretensions of the successor of that king, and to defend against his usurpation the Church and her inalienable rights. The proclamation of King Humbert was met by a protest addressed to all the Powers from the Cardinal-Secretary of State, and Pius IX. himself raised his voice in order to vindicate publicly those writers who had spoken the truth concerning the deceased prince. The whole world was moved by the solicitude of the Holy Father in laboring so as that Victor Emmanuel should die as became a Christian, and in providing that his funeral should be conducted according to the consoling ceremonial of the Church. It now became his duty to take care lest the irreconcilable enemies of religion should succeed in availing themselves of these circumstances in order to deceive and induce mankind to believe that the Godless revolution was in sympathy with Pius IX. and the Church. The venerable Pontiff was still able to take to task the indiscreet writers who, from mistaken zeal, maintained that such an incongruous coalition had taken place or was possible.

A very great number of people of all ranks conceived the happy idea of celebrating the seventy-fifth anniversary of Pius the Ninth's first communion. This afforded another great occasion for uniting in prayer all over the wide extent of the Catholic Church. The *fete* occurred on the 2nd of February, "Candlemas day," or the purification of the Blessed Virgin. The Holy Father was able, all exhausted as he was, to leave his couch, celebrate Mass, and even repair to the throne-room of the Vatican, where he performed the ceremony of distributing blessed tapers to the cardinals, bishops and heads of religious orders. He spoke also with his accustomed eloquence to those whom it gave him so much pleasure to see gathered around him. He addressed himself particularly to the parish priests of Rome, recommending above all things to their pastoral solicitude, the children of the city who bore so important a part in the celebration of the anniversary. He expatiated on the value of Christian education, and exhorted the pastors to stir up the zeal of parents. His apostolate had begun with children in the happy days of *Tata Giovanni*. It was only fitting that his last exhortation should be all in their interest and for their happiness.

All, in expressing his gratitude for the prayers that were offered in his behalf, he asked was that they should be continued, hoping always "that He who had commenced a good work would not fail to bring it to a successful termination." But it is not given to man to complete or perfect anything in this life; and that pontificate of thirty-two years, which was still more astonishing by its acts and labors than by its long duration, was destined to leave its good work incomplete. It will be continued, nevertheless, and men will be made to understand that it is not alone Mastai's work, or any man's work, but the cause of Him who guides, with irresistible power, the destinies of mankind.

Pius IX., however, had accomplished his appointed task. He had celebrated, and with a wonderful renewal of health, his last festival and his last anniversary. Four days later, in the evening of the 6th February, he was seized with a slight attack of fever, which caused no alarm. It was the prelude, however, to more serious attacks, which shortly succeeded one another in rapid succession till the moment of his death. At four o'clock in the morning a potion was administered, in order to soothe the feverish agitation of the patient. Its good effect was only of short duration. As his physician entered, "this time," said he, "my dear doctor, all is over." He did not share the hopes of those who attended the celebration of Candlemas day. He understood that his last hour on earth was near at hand, and he requested that the Holy Viaticum and Extreme Unction should be administered.

As soon as the doleful tidings reached the city, the people were bid to prayer by a general ringing of the bells. Great numbers of the faithful sought the approaches to the Vatican. Many entered and crowded the halls and ante-chambers of the

palace, offering up their prayers, with abundance of tears, as
Bishop Marinelli, whom, only one month before, Pius IX. had
sent to assist King Victor Emmanuel, conveyed the Viaticum
to the chamber of death and administered the Sacraments.
As the malady increased it attacked the lungs (not the brain,
as the infidel newspapers falsely represented), rendering difficult and painful the breathing of the patient. Nevertheless,
Pius IX. calmly and distinctly repeated the prayers for the
dying, which Cardinal Bilio had begun to recite. At the end
of the Act of Contrition, he said, with great humility and confidence, " *Col vostro adjuto*,"† and expressed his Christian
hope, saying, " *In Domum Domini ibimus.*"‡ As the cardinal,
bathed in tears, hesitated to pronounce the words of final adieu
—"*Proficiscere anima Christiana*"§—the Holy Father inspired
the courage so necessary at the hour of separation, he,
himself uttering the words, " *Si Proficiscere.*" He must bless,
once more, the Sacred College, the members of which were all
kneeling around him. Cardinal Bilio, in their name, asked
him to impart his blessing. Extending his right hand, he
blessed them for the last time. Scarcely had the hand that
had been so often raised in blessing mankind fallen on the
couch when the eyes became dim. A little before four o'clock
the death agony commenced. A few moments before six Pius
IX. ceased to live.

"Eternal rest give to him, O Lord," devoutly said the cardinal, "and may perpetual light shine upon him." These
words conveyed the mournful fact that Pius IX. lived no more.
They were, at the same time, the occasion of an outburst of
love and devotedness, which showed that this wonderful Pope
still commanded in death that affection which, in his lifetime, had been often so gloriously manifested.

Cardinals, prelates, nobles, people of Rome, guards and
servants, struggled and crowded on each other, in order to
press, once more, forehead and lips on those sacred hands

* Their purpose is sufficiently manifest. But the calumny did not avail
them. Pius the Ninth's last illness was of such a character as to render impos-
sible congestion of the brain. He possessed to the end his mental faculties.
And when the power of speech failed, he was still able to express his thoughts,
which were clear and distinct, by looks and gestures.
† " With the aid of Thy grace."
‡ " We shall enter into the House of the Lord."
§ "Depart, Christian soul."

which could never more be raised to bless them. It was a singularly affecting scene. The wail of sorrow and the unfeigned expression of esteem and love arose also as the tidings spread throughout the wide extent of the Catholic world.

The deceased Pontiff needs no eulogium. His memory will be as green throughout the centuries to come as on the day of his decease. It is impossible, however, to avoid calling to mind the words of Saint Cyprian, spoken in praise of Pope Cornelius, and most appropriately applied by the pious and learned Bishop of Poitiers to Pius IX: "After a promotion which he had neither desired nor sought, but which was due to him alone who makes Pontiffs, what activity from the first moment he was in office! what boldness of initiative! And, what we must chiefly consider and praise, what strength of faith and what courage in having perseveringly and intrepidly held the sacerdotal chair at Rome, at a time when, through opposition to the priesthood, were uttered such fearful threats, and when the Powers of the world were more inclined to undergo any kind of reverse rather than that the Priest of God should occupy at Rome a throne which was the rival of their earthly throne. If, in the midst of so much agitation, the power of the Lord evidently protected the priest whom he had chosen, that priest, nevertheless, in resisting, suffered all that it was possible to suffer, and overcame, by his priestly energy, those for whom were in store other and ulterior defeats."

ST. CYPRIAN, Epist. LII., *ad Antonianum.*

The death of Pius IX., long so ardently desired by the Italian ministry, came upon them unawares at last. They had no scheme or plot in readiness, to thwart the action of the cardinals in the election of a successor to the Pontificate.[*] The Conclave, accordingly, assembled in due course, and, on the third day of its meeting, elected to the Chair of Peter Cardinal-Archbishop Pecci, Bishop of Perugia, who will be known in history as LEO XIII.

[*] The crisis in the Eastern question, the attitude of the Holy Father on the occasion of Victor Emmanuel's sudden demise, the consequent devolution of the crown to a n w overeign, the scandal of the Prime Minister's (Crispi's) notorious criminality before the law necessitating his unwilling resignation and the fall of the ministry, the suddenness of the Holy Father's decease; all these events and conditions, in their several degrees and kinds, made the moment at which it had to meet astonishingly propitious for the holding of the Conclave in the Vatican itself.

—FINIS.—